The Collected Supernatural and Weird Fiction of Mrs Oliphant Volume 1

The Collected Supernatural and Weird Fiction of Mrs Oliphant Volume 1

Including One Novel "The Complete Little Pilgrim Series", Four Novelettes "The Secret Chamber", "The Land of Suspense", "A Visitor and His Opinions", "Earthbound" and Two Short Stories of the Strange and Unusual

Mrs Oliphant

LEONAUR

*The Collected
Supernatural and Weird
Fiction of
Mrs Oliphant
Volume 1*
*Including One Novel "The Complete Little Pilgrim Series", Four Novelettes "The Se-
cret Chamber", "The Land of Suspense", "A Visitor and His Opinions", "Earthbound"
and Two Short Stories of the Strange and Unusual*
by Mrs Oliphant

FIRST EDITION

Leonaur is an imprint
of Oakpast Ltd

Copyright in this form © 2014 Oakpast Ltd

ISBN: 978-1-78282-369-8 (hardcover)
ISBN: 978-1-78282-370-4 (softcover)

http://www.leonaur.com

Publisher's Notes

Contents

The Secret Chamber   7

The Land of Suspense   40

The Complete Little Pilgrim Series   83

A Christmas Tale   252

"Dies Iræ" The Story of a Spirit in Prison   276

A Visitor and His Opinions   303

Earthbound   351

The Secret Chamber

1

Castle Gowrie is one of the most famous and interesting in all Scotland. It is a beautiful old house, to start with,—perfect in old feudal grandeur, with its clustered turrets and walls that could withstand an army,—its labyrinths, its hidden stairs, its long mysterious passages—passages that seem in many cases to lead to nothing, but of which no one can be too sure what they lead to. The front, with its fine gateway and flanking towers, is approached now by velvet lawns, and a peaceful, beautiful old avenue, with double rows of trees, like a cathedral; and the woods out of which these grey towers rise, look as soft and rich in foliage, if not so lofty in growth, as the groves of the South.

But this softness of aspect is all new to the place,—that is, new within the century or two which count for but little in the history of a dwelling-place, some part of which, at least, has been standing since the days when the Saxon Athelings brought such share of the arts as belonged to them to solidify and regulate the original Celtic art which reared incised stones upon rude burial-places, and twined mystic knots on its crosses, before historic days.

Even of this primitive decoration there are relics at Gowrie, where the twistings and twinings of Runic cords appear still on *some* bits of ancient wall, solid as rocks, and almost as everlasting. From these to the graceful French turrets, which recall many a grey *château*, what a long interval of years! But these are filled with stirring chronicles enough, besides the dim, not always decipherable records, which different developments of architecture have left on the old house. The Earls of Gowrie had been in the heat of every commotion that took place on or about the Highland line for more generations than any but a Celtic pen could record. Rebellions, revenges, insurrections, conspiracies, nothing in which blood was shed and lands lost, took place in Scotland, in which they had not had a share; and the annals of the house are very full, and not without many a stain. They had been a bold and vigorous race—with much evil in them, and some good; never insignificant, whatever else they might be. It could not be said, however, that they are remarkable nowadays.

Since the first Stuart rising, known in Scotland as "the Fifteen," they have not done much that has been worth recording; but yet their family history has always been of an unusual kind. The Randolphs could not be called eccentric in themselves: on the contrary, when you knew them, they were at bottom a respectable race, full of all the country-gentleman virtues; and yet their public career, such as it was, had been marked by the strange leaps and jerks of vicissitude.

You would have said an impulsive, fanciful family—now making a grasp at some visionary advantage, now rushing into some wild speculation, now making a sudden sally into public life—but soon falling back into mediocrity, not able apparently, even when the impulse was purely selfish and mercenary, to keep it up. But this would not have been at all a true conception of the family character; their actual virtues were not of the imaginative order, and their freaks were a mystery to their friends. Nevertheless these freaks were what the general world was most aware of in the Randolph race. The late earl had been a representative peer of Scotland (they had no English title), and had made quite a wonderful start, and for a year or two had seemed about to attain a very eminent place in Scotch affairs; but his ambition was found to have made use of some very equivocal modes of gaining influence, and he dropped accordingly at once and for ever from the political firmament.

This was quite a common circumstance in the family. An

apparently brilliant beginning, a discovery of evil means adopted for ambitious ends, a sudden subsidence, and the curious conclusion at the end of everything that this schemer, this unscrupulous speculator or politician, was a dull, good man after all—unambitious, contented, full of domestic kindness and benevolence. This family peculiarity made the history of the Randolphs a very strange one, broken by the oddest interruptions, and with no consistency in it. There was another circumstance, however, which attracted still more the wonder and observation of the public. For one who can appreciate such a recondite matter as family character, there are hundreds who are interested in a family secret, and this the house of Randolph possessed in perfection.

It was a mystery which piqued the imagination and excited the interest of the entire country. The story went, that somewhere hid amid the massive walls and tortuous passages there was a secret chamber in Gowrie Castle. Everybody knew of its existence; but save the earl, his heir, and one other person, not of the family, but filling a confidential post in their service, no mortal knew where this mysterious hiding-place was. There had been countless guesses made at it, and expedients of all kinds invented to find it out. Every visitor who ever entered the old gateway, nay, even passing travellers who saw the turrets from the road, searched keenly for some trace of this mysterious chamber. But all guesses and researches were equally in vain.

I was about to say that no ghost-story I ever heard of has been so steadily and long believed. But this would be a mistake, for nobody knew even with any certainty that there was a ghost connected with it. A secret chamber was nothing wonderful in so old a house. No doubt they exist in many such old houses, and are always curious and interesting—strange relics, more moving than any history, of the time when a man was not safe in his own house, and when it might be necessary to secure a refuge beyond the reach of spies or traitors at a moment's notice. Such a refuge was a necessity of life to a great medieval noble. The peculiarity about this secret chamber, however, was that some secret connected with the very existence of the family was always understood to be involved in it. It was not only the secret hiding-place for an emergency, a kind of historical possession presupposing the importance of his race, of which a man might be honestly proud; but there was something hidden in it of which assuredly the race could not be proud. It is wonderful how easily a family learns to pique itself upon any distinctive possession.

A ghost is a sign of importance not to be despised; a haunted room is worth as much as a small farm to the complacency of the family that owns it. And no doubt the younger branches of the Gowrie family—the light-minded portion of the race—felt this, and were proud of their unfathomable secret, and felt a thrill of agreeable awe and piquant suggestion go through them, when they remembered the mysterious something which they did not know in their familiar home. That thrill ran through the entire circle of visitors, and children, and servants, when the earl peremptorily forbade a projected improvement, or stopped a reckless exploration. They looked at each other with a pleasurable shiver. "Did you hear?" they said. "He will not let Lady Gowrie have that closet she wants so much in that bit of wall.

He sent the workmen about their business before they could touch it, though the wall is twenty feet thick if it is an inch; "ah!" said the visitors, looking at each other; and this lively suggestion sent tinglings of excitement to their very finger-points; but even to his wife, mourning the commodious closet she had intended, the earl made no explanations. For anything she knew, it might be there, next to her room, this mysterious lurking-place; and it may be supposed that this suggestion conveyed to Lady Gowrie's veins a thrill more keen and strange, perhaps too vivid to be pleasant. But she was not in the favoured or unfortunate number of those to whom the truth could be revealed.

I need not say what the different theories on the subject were. Some thought there had been a treacherous massacre there, and that the secret chamber was blocked by the skeletons of murdered guests,—a treachery no doubt covering the family with shame in its day, but so condoned by long softening of years as to have all the shame taken out of it. The Randolphs could not have felt their character affected by any such interesting historical record. They were not so morbidly sensitive. Some said, on the other hand, that Earl Robert, the wicked earl, was shut up there in everlasting penance, playing cards with the devil for his soul. But it would have been too great a feather in the family cap to have thus got the devil, or even one of his angels, bottled up, as it were, and safely in hand, to make it possible that any lasting stigma could be connected with such a fact as this. What a thing it would be to know where to lay one's hand upon the Prince of Darkness, and prove him once for all, cloven foot and everything else, to the confusion of gainsayers!

So this was not to be received as a satisfactory solution, nor could any other be suggested which was more to the purpose. The popular mind gave it up, and yet never gave it up; and still everybody who visits Gowrie, be it as a guest, be it as a tourist, be it only as a gazer from a passing carriage, or from the flying railway train which just glimpses its turrets in the distance, daily and yearly spends a certain amount of curiosity, wonderment, and conjecture about the Secret Chamber—the most piquant and undiscoverable wonder which has endured unguessed and undeciphered to modern times.

This was how the matter stood when young John Randolph, Lord Lindores, came of age. He was a young man of great character and energy, not like the usual Randolph strain—for, as we have said, the type of character common in this romantically-situated family, notwithstanding the erratic incidents common to them, was that of dullness and honesty, especially in their early days. But young Lindores was not so. He was honest and honourable, but not dull. He had gone through almost a remarkable course at school and at the university—not perhaps in quite the ordinary way of scholarship, but enough to attract men's eyes to him. He had made more than one great speech at the Union. He was full of ambition, and force, and life, intending all sorts of great things, and meaning to make his position a stepping-stone to all that was excellent in public life. Not for him the country-gentleman existence which was congenial to his father. The idea of succeeding to the family honours and becoming a Scotch peer, either represented or representative, filled him with horror; and filial piety in his case was made warm by all the energy of personal hopes when he prayed that his father might live, if not for ever, yet longer than any Lord Gowrie had lived for the last century or two.

He was as sure of his election for the county the next time there was a chance, as anybody can be certain of anything; and in the meantime he meant to travel, to go to America, to go no one could tell where, seeking for instruction and experience, as is the manner of high-spirited young men with parliamentary tendencies in the present day. In former times he would have gone "to the wars in the Hie Germanie," or on a crusade to the Holy Land; but the days of the crusaders and of the soldiers of fortune being over, Lindores followed the fashion of his time. He had made all his arrangements for his tour, which his father did not oppose. On the contrary, Lord Gowrie encouraged all those plans, though with an air of melancholy indulgence which his son could not understand. "It will do you good," he said, with a sigh. "Yes, yes, my boy; the best thing for you." This, no doubt, was true enough; but there was an implied feeling that the young man would require something to do him good—that he would want the soothing of change and the gratification of his wishes, as one might speak of a convalescent or the victim of some calamity.

This tone puzzled Lindores, who, though he thought it a fine thing to travel and acquire information, was as scornful of the idea of being done good to as is natural to any fine young fellow fresh from Oxford and the triumphs of the Union. But he reflected that the old school had its own way of treating things, and was satisfied. All was settled accordingly for this journey, before he came home to go through the ceremonial performances of the coming of age, the dinner of the tenantry, the speeches, the congratulations, his father's banquet, his mother's ball. It was in summer, and the country was as gay as all the entertainments that were to be given in his honour.

His friend who was going to accompany him on his tour, as he had accompanied him through a considerable portion of his life—Almeric Ffarrington, a young man of the same aspirations—came up to Scotland with him for these festivities. And as they rushed through the night on the Great Northern Railway, in the intervals of two naps, they had a scrap of conversation as to these birthday glories. "It will be a bore, but it will not last long," said Lindores. They were both of the opinion that anything that did not produce information or promote culture was a bore.

"But is there not a revelation to be made to you, among all the other things you have to go through?" said Ffarrington. "Have not you to be introduced to the secret chamber, and all that sort of thing? I should like to be of the party there, Lindores."

"Ah," said the heir, "I had forgotten that part of it," which, however, was not the case. "Indeed I don't know if I am to be told. Even family dogmas are shaken nowadays."

"Oh, I should insist on that," said Ffarrington, lightly. "It is not many who have the chance of paying such a visit—better than Home and all the mediums. I should insist upon that."

"I have no reason to suppose that it has any connection with Home or the mediums," said Lindores, slightly nettled. He was himself an *esprit fort*; but a mystery in one's own family is not like vulgar mysteries. He liked it to be respected.

"Oh, no offence," said his companion. "I have always thought that a railway train would be a great chance for the spirits. If one was to show suddenly in that vacant seat beside you, what a triumphant proof of their existence that would be! but they don't take advantage of their opportunities."

Lindores could not tell what it was that made him think at that moment of a portrait he had seen in a back room at the castle of old Earl Robert, the wicked earl. It was a bad portrait—a daub—a copy made by an amateur of the genuine portrait, which, out of horror of Earl Robert and his wicked ways, had been removed by some intermediate lord from its place in the gallery. Lindores had never seen the original—nothing but this daub of a copy. Yet somehow this face occurred to him by some strange link of association—seemed to come into his eyes as his friend spoke. A slight shiver ran over him. It was strange. He made no reply to Ffarrington, but he set himself to think how it could be that the latent presence in his mind of some anticipation of this approaching disclosure, touched into life by his friend's suggestion, should have called out of his memory a momentary realisation of the acknowledged magician of the family.

This sentence is full of long words; but unfortunately long words are required in such a case. And the process was very simple when you traced it out. It was the clearest case of unconscious cerebration. He shut his eyes by way of securing privacy while he thought it out; and being tired, and not at all alarmed by his unconscious cerebration, before he opened them again fell fast asleep.

And his birthday, which was the day following his arrival at Glenlyon, was a very busy day. He had not time to think of anything but the immediate occupations of the moment. Public and private greetings, congratulations, offerings, poured upon him. The Gowries were popular in this generation, which was far from being usual in the family. Lady Gowrie was kind and generous, with that kindness which comes from the heart, and which is the only kindness likely to impress the keen-sighted popular judgment; and Lord Gowrie had but little of the equivocal reputation of his predecessors. They could be splendid now and then on great occasions, though in general they were homely enough; all which the public likes.

It was a bore, Lindores said; but yet the young man did not dislike the honours, and the adulation, and all the hearty speeches and good wishes. It is sweet to a young man to feel himself the centre of all hopes. It seemed very reasonable to him—very natural—that he should be so, and that the farmers should feel a pride of anticipation in thinking of his future speeches in Parliament.

He promised to them with the sincerest good faith that he would not disappoint their expectations—that he would feel their interest in him an additional spur. What so natural as that interest and these expectations? He was almost solemnised by his own position—so young, looked up to by so many people—so many hopes depending on him; and yet it was quite natural. His father, however, was still more solemnised than Lindores—and this was strange, to say the least. His face grew graver and graver as the day went on, till it almost seemed as if he were dissatisfied with his son's popularity, or had some painful thought weighing on his mind. He was restless and eager for the termination of the dinner, and to get rid of his guests; and as soon as they were gone, showed an equal anxiety that his son should retire too.

"Go to bed at once, as a favour to me," Lord Gowrie said. "You will have a great deal of fatigue—tomorrow."

"You need not be afraid for me, sir," said Lindores, half affronted; but he obeyed, being tired. He had not once thought of the secret to be disclosed to him, through all that long day. But when he woke suddenly with a start in the middle of the night, to find the candles all lighted in his room, and his father standing by his bedside, Lindores instantly thought of it, and in a moment felt that the leading event—the chief incident of all that had happened—was going to take place now.

2

Lord Gowrie was very grave, and very pale. He was standing with his hand on his son's shoulder to wake him; his dress was unchanged from the moment they had parted. And the sight of this formal costume was very bewildering to the young man as he started up in his bed. But next moment he seemed to know exactly how it was, and, more than that, to have known it all his life. Explanation seemed unnecessary. At any other moment, in any other place, a man would be startled to be suddenly woke up in the middle of the night. But Lindores had no such feeling;

he did not even ask a question, but sprang up, and fixed his eyes, taking in all the strange circumstances, on his father's face.

"Get up, my boy," said Lord Gowrie, "and dress as quickly as you can; it is full time. I have lighted your candles, and your things are all ready. You have had a good long sleep."

Even now he did not ask, What is it? as under any other circumstances he would have done. He got up without a word, with an impulse of nervous speed and rapidity of movement such as only excitement can give, and dressed himself, his father helping him silently. It was a curious scene: the room gleaming with lights, the silence, the hurried toilet, the stillness of deep night all around. The house, though so full, and with the echoes of festivity but just over, was quiet as if there was not a creature within it—more quiet, indeed, for the stillness of vacancy is not half so impressive as the stillness of hushed and slumbering life.

Lord Gowrie went to the table when this first step was over, and poured out a glass of wine from a bottle which stood there,—a rich, golden-coloured, perfumy wine, which sent its scent through the room. "You will want all your strength," he said; "take this before you go. It is the famous Imperial Tokay; there is only a little left, and you will want all your strength."

Lindores took the wine; he had never drunk any like it before, and the peculiar fragrance remained in his mind, as perfumes so often do, with a whole world of association in them. His father's eyes dwelt upon him with a melancholy sympathy. "You are going to encounter the greatest trial of your life," he said; and taking the young man's hand into his, felt his pulse. "It is quick, but it is quite firm, and you have had a good long sleep." Then he did what it needs a great deal of pressure to induce an Englishman to do,—he kissed his son on the cheek. "God bless you!" he said, faltering. "Come, now, everything is ready, Lindores."

He took up in his hand a small lamp, which he had apparently brought with him, and led the way. By this time Lindores began to feel himself again, and to wake to the consciousness of all his own superiorities and enlightenments. The simple sense that he was one of the members of a family with a mystery, and

16

that the moment of his personal encounter with this special power of darkness had come, had been the first thrilling, overwhelming thought. But now as he followed his father, Lindores began to remember that he himself was not altogether like other men; that there was that in him which would make it natural that he should throw some light, hitherto unthought of, upon this carefully-preserved darkness. What secret even there might be in it—secret of hereditary tendency, of psychic force, of mental conformation, or of some curious combination of circumstances at once more and less potent than these—it was for him to find out.

He gathered all his forces about him, reminded himself of modern enlightenment, and bade his nerves be steel to all vulgar horrors. He, too, felt his own pulse as he followed his father. To spend the night perhaps amongst the skeletons of that old-world massacre, and to repent the sins of his ancestors—to be brought within the range of some optical illusion believed in hitherto by all the generations, and which, no doubt, was of a startling kind, or his father would not look so serious,—any of these he felt himself quite strong to encounter. His heart and spirit rose. A young man has but seldom the opportunity of distinguishing himself so early in his career; and his was such a chance as occurs to very few. No doubt it was something that would be extremely trying to the nerves and imagination. He called up all his powers to vanquish both.

And along with this call upon himself to exertion, there was the less serious impulse of curiosity: he would see at last what the Secret Chamber was, where it was, how it fitted into the labyrinths of the old house. This he tried to put in its due place as a most interesting object. He said to himself that he would willingly have gone a long journey at any time to be present at such an exploration; and there is no doubt that in other circumstances a secret chamber, with probably some unthought-of historical interest in it, would have been a very fascinating discovery. He tried very hard to excite himself about this; but it was curious how fictitious he felt the interest, and how conscious he was that it was an effort to feel any curiosity at all on the subject. The fact was, that the Secret Chamber was entirely secondary—thrown back, as all accessories are, by a more pressing interest. The overpowering thought of what was in it drove aside all healthy, natural curiosity about itself.

It must not be supposed, however, that the father and son had a long way to go to have time for all these thoughts. Thoughts travel at lightning speed, and there was abundant leisure for this between the time they had left the door of Lindores' room and gone down the corridor, no further off than to Lord Gowrie's own chamber, naturally one of the chief rooms of the house. Nearly opposite this, a few steps further on, was a little neglected room devoted to lumber, with which Lindores had been familiar all his life. Why this nest of old rubbish, dust, and cob-webs should be so near the bedroom of the head of the house had been a matter of surprise to many people—to the guests who saw it while exploring, and to each new servant in succession who planned an attack upon its ancient stores, scandalised by finding it to have been neglected by their predecessors.

All their attempts to clear it out had, however, been resisted, nobody could tell how, or indeed thought it worth while to inquire. As for Lindores, he had been used to the place from his childhood, and therefore accepted it as the most natural thing in the world. He had been in and out a hundred times in his play. And it was here, he remembered suddenly, that he had seen the bad picture of Earl Robert which had so curiously come into his eyes on his journeying here, by a mental movement which he had identified at once as unconscious cerebration.

The first feeling in his mind, as his father went to the open door of this lumber-room, was a mixture of amusement and surprise. What was he going to pick up there? some old pentacle, some amulet or scrap of antiquated magic to act as armour against the evil one? But Lord Gowrie, going on and setting down the lamp on the table, turned round upon his son with a face of agitation and pain which barred all further amusement: he grasped him by the hand, crushing it between his own. "Now my boy, my dear son," he said, in tones that were scarcely audible. His countenance was full of the dreary pain of a looker-on— one who has no share in the excitement of personal danger, but has the more terrible part of watching those who are in deadliest peril.

He was a powerful man, and his large form shook with emotion; great beads of moisture stood upon his forehead. An old sword with a cross handle lay upon a dusty chair among other dusty and battered relics. "Take this with you," he said, in the same inaudible, breathless way—whether as a weapon, whether as a religious symbol, Lindores could not guess. The young man took it mechanically. His father pushed open a door which it seemed to him he had never seen before, and led him into another vaulted chamber. Here even the limited powers of speech Lord Gowrie had retained seemed to forsake him, and his voice became a mere hoarse murmur in his throat. For want of speech he pointed to another door in the further corner of this small vacant room, gave him to understand by a gesture that he was to knock there, and then went back into the lumber-room. The door into this was left open, and a faint glimmer of the lamp shed light into this little intermediate place—this debatable land between the seen and the unseen. In spite of himself, Lindores' heart began to beat. He made a breathless pause, feeling his head go round. He held the old sword in his hand, not knowing what it was.

Then, summoning all his courage, he went forward and knocked at the closed door. His knock was not loud, but it seemed to echo all over the silent house. Would everybody hear and wake, and rush to see what had happened? This caprice of imagination seized upon him, ousting all the firmer thoughts, the steadfast calm of mind with which he ought to have encountered the mystery. Would they all rush in, in wild *déshabille*, in terror and dismay, before the door opened? How long it was of opening! He touched the panel with his hand again.—This time there was no delay. In a moment, as if thrown suddenly open by someone within, the door moved.

It opened just wide enough to let him enter, stopping half-way as if someone invisible held it, wide enough for welcome, but no more. Lindores stepped across the threshold with a beating heart. What was he about to see? the skeletons of the murdered victims? a ghostly charnel-house full of bloody traces of crime? He seemed to be hurried and pushed in as he made that step. What was this world of mystery into which he was plunged—what was it he saw?

IIe saw—nothing—except what was agreeable enough to behold,—an antiquated room hung with tapestry, very old tapestry of rude design, its colours faded into softness and harmony; between its folds here and there a panel of carved wood, rude too in design, with traces of half-worn gilding; a table covered with strange instruments, parchments, chemical tubes, and curious machinery, all with a quaintness of form and dimness of material that spoke of age. A heavy old velvet cover, thick with embroidery faded almost out of all colour, was on the table; on the wall above it, something that looked like a very old Venetian mirror, the glass so dim and crusted that it scarcely reflected at all, on the floor an old soft Persian carpet, worn into a vague blending of all colours.

This was all that he thought he saw. His heart, which had been thumping so loud as almost to choke him, stopped that tremendous upward and downward motion like a steam piston; and he grew calm. Perfectly still, dim, unoccupied: yet not so dim either; there was no apparent source of light, no windows, curtains of tapestry drawn everywhere—no lamp visible, no fire—and yet a kind of strange light which made everything quite clear. He looked round, trying to smile at his terrors, trying to say to himself that it was the most curious place he had ever seen—that he must show Ffarrington some of that tapestry—that he must really bring away a panel of that carving,—when he suddenly saw that the door was shut by which he had entered—nay, more than shut, indiscernible, covered like all the rest of the walls by that strange tapestry. At this his heart began to beat again in spite of him. He looked round once more, and woke up to more vivid being with a sudden start. Had his eyes been incapable of vision on his first entrance? Unoccupied? Who was that in the great chair?

It seemed to Lindores that he had seen neither the chair nor the man when he came in. There they were, however, solid and unmistakable; the chair carved like the panels, the man seated in front of the table. He looked at Lindores with a calm and open gaze, inspecting him. The young man's heart seemed in his throat fluttering like a bird, but he was brave, and his mind made one final effort to break this spell. He tried to speak, labouring with a voice that would not sound, and with lips too parched to form a word. "I see how it is," was what he wanted to say. It was Earl Robert's face that was looking at him; and startled as he was, he dragged forth his philosophy to support him. What could it be but optical delusions, unconscious cerebration, occult seizure by the impressed and struggling mind of this one countenance? But he could not hear himself speak any word as he stood convulsed, struggling with dry lips and choking voice.

The Appearance smiled, as if knowing his thoughts—not un-kindly, not malignly—with a certain amusement mingled with scorn. Then he spoke, and the sound seemed to breathe through the room not like any voice that Lindores had ever heard, a kind of utterance of the place, like the rustle of the air or the ripple of the sea. "You will learn better tonight: this is no phantom of your brain; it is I."

"In God's name," cried the young man in his soul; he did not know whether the words ever got into the air or not, if there was any air;—"in God's name, who are you?"

The figure rose as if coming to him to reply; and Lindores, overcome by the apparent approach, struggled into utterance. A cry came from him—he heard it this time—and even in his extremity felt a pang the more to hear the terror in his own voice. But he did not flinch, he stood desperate, all his strength concentrated in the act; he neither turned nor recoiled. Vaguely gleaming through his mind came the thought that to be thus brought in contact with the unseen was the experiment to be most desired on earth, the final settlement of a hundred questions; but his faculties were not sufficiently under command to entertain it. He only stood firm, that was all.

And the figure did not approach him; after a moment it subsided back again into the chair—subsided, for no sound, not the faintest, accompanied its movements. It was the form of a man of middle age, the hair white, but the beard only crisped with grey, the features those of the picture—a familiar face, more or less like all the Randolphs, but with an air of domination and power altogether unlike that of the race. He was dressed in a long robe of dark colour, embroidered with strange lines and angles. There was nothing repellent or terrible in his air—nothing except the noiselessness, the calm, the absolute stillness, which was as much in the place as in him, to keep up the involuntary trembling of the beholder. His expression was full of dignity and thoughtfulness, and not malignant or unkind. He might have been the kindly patriarch of the house, watching over its fortunes in a seclusion that he had chosen. The pulses that had been beating in Lindores were stilled. What was his panic for? A gleam even of self-ridicule took possession of him, to be standing there like an absurd hero of antiquated romance with the rusty, dusty sword—good for nothing, surely not adapted for use against this noble old magician—in his hand —

"You are right," said the voice, once more answering his thoughts; "what could you do with that sword against me, young Lindores? Put it by. Why should my children meet me like an enemy? You are my flesh and blood. Give me your hand."

A shiver ran through the young man's frame. The hand that was held out to him was large and shapely and white, with a straight line across the palm—a family token upon which the Randolphs prided themselves—a friendly hand; and the face smiled upon him, fixing him with those calm, profound, blue eyes. "Come," said the voice. The word seemed to fill the place, melting upon him from every corner, whispering round him with softest persuasion. He was lulled and calmed in spite of himself. Spirit or no spirit, why should not he accept this proffered courtesy? What harm could come of it? The chief thing that retained him was the dragging of the old sword, heavy and useless, which he held mechanically, but which some internal feeling—he could not tell what—prevented him from putting down. Superstition, was it?

"Yes, that is superstition," said his ancestor, serenely; "put it down and come."

"You know my thoughts," said Lindores; "I did not speak."

"Your mind spoke, and spoke justly. Put down that emblem of brute force and superstition together. Here it is the intelligence that is supreme. Come."

Lindores stood doubtful. He was calm; the power of thought was restored to him. If this benevolent venerable patriarch was all he seemed, why his father's terror? why the secrecy in which his being was involved? His own mind, though calm, did not seem to act in the usual way. Thoughts seemed to be driven across it as by a wind. One of these came to him suddenly now —

How there looked him in the face,
An angel beautiful and bright,
And how he knew it was a fiend.

The words were not ended, when Earl Robert replied suddenly with impatience in his voice, "Fiends are of the fancy of men; like angels and other follies. I am your father. You know me; and you are mine, Lindores. I have power beyond what you can understand; but I want flesh and blood to reign and to enjoy. Come, Lindores!"

He put out his other hand. The action, the look, were those of kindness, almost of longing, and the face was familiar, the voice was that of the race. Supernatural! was it supernatural that this man should live here shut up for ages? and why? and how? Was there any explanation of it? The young man's brain began to reel. He could not tell which was real—the life he had left half an hour ago, or this. He tried to look round him, but could not; his eyes were caught by those other kindred eyes, which seemed to dilate and deepen as he looked at them, and drew him with a strange compulsion. He felt himself yielding, swaying towards the strange being who thus invited him. What might happen if he yielded? And he could not turn away, he could not tear himself from the fascination of those eyes. With a sudden strange impulse which was half despair and half a bewildering half-conscious desire to try one potency against another, he thrust forward the cross of the old sword between him and those appealing hands. "In the name of God!" he said.

Lindores never could tell whether it was that he himself grew faint, and that the dimness of swooning came into his eyes after this violence and strain of emotion, or if it was his spell that worked. But there was an instantaneous change. Everything swam around him for the moment, a giddiness and blindness seized him, and he saw nothing but the vague outlines of the room, empty as when he entered it. But gradually his consciousness came back, and he found himself standing on the same spot as before, clutching the old sword, and gradually, as though a dream, recognised the same figure emerging out of the mist which—was it solely in his own eyes?—had enveloped everything. But it was no longer in the same attitude.

The hands which had been stretched out to him were busy now with some of the strange instruments on the table, moving about, now in the action of writing, now as if managing the keys of a telegraph. Lindores felt that his brain was all a twist and set wrong; but he was still a human being of his century. He thought of the telegraph with a keen thrill of curiosity in the midst of his reviving sensations. What communication was this which was going on before his eyes?

The magician worked on. He had his face turned towards his victim, but his hands moved with unceasing activity. And Lindores, as he grew accustomed to the position, began to weary—to feel like a neglected suitor waiting for an audience. To be wound up to such a strain of feeling, then left to wait, was intolerable; impatience seized upon him. What circumstances can exist, however horrible, in which a human being will not feel impatience? He made a great many efforts to speak before he could succeed. It seemed to him that his body felt more fear than he did—that his muscles were contracted, his throat parched, his tongue refusing its office, although his mind was unaffected and undismayed. At last he found an utterance in spite of all resistance of his flesh and blood.

"Who are you?" he said hoarsely. "You that live here and oppress this house?"

The vision raised its eyes full upon him, with again that strange shadow of a smile, mocking yet not unkind. "Do you remember me," he said, "on your journey here?"

"That was—a delusion." The young man gasped for breath.

"More like that you are a delusion. You have lasted but one-and-twenty years, and I—for centuries."

"How? For centuries—and why? Answer me—are you man or demon?" cried Lindores, tearing the words as he felt out of his own throat. "Are you living or dead?"

The magician looked at him with the same intense gaze as before. "Be on my side, and you shall know everything, Lindores. I want one of my own race. Others I could have in plenty; but I want *you*. A Randolph, a Randolph! And *you*. Dead! do I seem dead? You shall have everything—more than dreams can give—if you will be on my side."

Can he give what he has not? was the thought that ran through the mind of Lindores. But he could not speak it. Something that choked and stifled him was in his throat.

"Can I give what I have not? I have everything—power, the one thing worth having; and you shall have more than power, for you are young—my son! Lindores!"

To argue was natural, and gave the young man strength. "Is this life," he said, "here? What is all your power worth—here? To sit for ages, and make a race unhappy?"

A momentary convulsion came across the still face. "You scorn me", he cried, with an appearance of emotion, "because you do not understand how I move the world. Power! 'Tis more than fancy can grasp. And you shall have it!" said the wizard, with what looked like a show of enthusiasm. He seemed to

25

come nearer, to grow larger. He put forth his hand again, this time so close that it seemed impossible to escape. And a crowd of wishes seemed to rush upon the mind of Lindores. What harm to try if this might be true? To try what it meant—perhaps nothing, delusions, vain show, and then there could be no harm; or perhaps there was knowledge to be had, which was power. Try, try, try! the air buzzed about him. The room seemed full of voices urging him. His bodily frame rose into a tremendous whirl of excitement, his veins seemed to swell to bursting, his lips seemed to force a yes, in spite of him, quivering as they came apart. The hiss of the *s* seemed in his ears. He changed it into the name which was a spell too, and cried, "Help me, God!" not knowing why.

Then there came another pause—he felt as if he had been dropped from something that had held him, and had fallen, and was faint. The excitement had been more than he could bear. Once more everything swam around him, and he did not know where he was. Had he escaped altogether? was the first waking wonder of consciousness in his mind. But when he could think and see again, he was still in the same spot, surrounded by the old curtains and the carved panels—but alone. He felt, too, that he was able to move, but the strangest dual consciousness was in him throughout all the rest of his trial. His body felt to him as a frightened horse feels to a traveller at night—a thing separate from him, more frightened than he was—starting aside at every step, seeing more than its master.

His limbs shook with fear and weakness, almost refusing to obey the action of his will, trembling under him with jerks aside when he compelled himself to move. The hair stood upright on his head—every finger trembled as with palsy—his lips, his eyelids, quivered with nervous agitation. But his mind was strong, stimulated to a desperate calm. He dragged himself round the room, he crossed the very spot where the magician had been—all was vacant, silent, clear. Had he vanquished the enemy? This thought came into his mind with an involuntary triumph. The old strain of feeling came back. Such efforts might be produced, perhaps, only by imagination, by excitement, by delusion ——

Lindores looked up, by a sudden attraction he could not tell what: and the blood suddenly froze in his veins that had been so boiling and fermenting. Someone was looking at him from the old mirror on the wall. A face not human and life-like, like that of the inhabitant of this place, but ghostly and terrible, like one of the dead; and while he looked, a crowd of other faces came behind, all looking at him, some mournfully, some with a menace in their terrible eyes.

The mirror did not change, but within its small dim space seemed to contain an innumerable company, crowded above and below, all with one gaze at him. His lips dropped apart with a gasp of horror. More and more and more! He was standing close by the table when this crowd came. Then all at once there was laid upon him a cold hand. He turned; close to his side, brushing him with his robe, holding him fast by the arm, sat Earl Robert in his great chair. A shriek came from the young man's lips. He seemed to hear it echoing away into unfathomable distance. The cold touch penetrated to his very soul.

"Do you try spells upon me, Lindores? That is a tool of the past. You shall have something better to work with. And are you so sure of whom you call upon? If there is such a one, why should He help you who never called on Him before?"

Lindores could not tell if these words were spoken; it was a communication rapid as the thoughts in the mind. And he felt as if something answered that was not all himself. He seemed to stand passive and hear the argument. "Does God reckon with a man in trouble, whether he has ever called to Him before? I call now" (now he felt it was himself that said): "go, evil spirit!—go, dead and cursed!—go, in the name of God!"

He felt himself flung violently against the wall. A faint laugh, stifled in the throat, and followed by a groan, rolled round the room; the old curtains seemed to open here and there, and flutter, as if with comings and goings. Lindores leaned with his back against the wall, and all his senses restored to him. He felt blood trickle down his neck; and in this contact once more with the physical, his body, in its madness of fright, grew manageable. For the first time he felt wholly master of himself. Though the magician was standing in his place, a great, majestic, appalling figure, he did not shrink. "Liar!" he cried, in a voice that rang and echoed as in natural air—"clinging to miserable life like a worm—like a reptile; promising all things, having nothing, but this den, unvisited by the light of day. Is this your power—your superiority to men who die? is it for this that you oppress a race, and make a house unhappy? I vow, in God's name, your reign is over! You and your secret shall last no more."

There was no reply. But Lindores felt his terrible ancestor's eyes getting once more that mesmeric mastery over him which had already almost overcome his powers. He must withdraw his own, or perish. He had a human horror of turning his back upon that watchful adversary: to face him seemed the only safety; but to face him was to be conquered. Slowly, with a pang indescribable, he tore himself from that gaze: it seemed to drag his eyes out of their sockets, his heart out of his bosom. Resolutely, with the daring of desperation, he turned round to the spot where he entered—the spot where no door was,—hearing already in anticipation the step after him—feeling the grip that would crush and smother his exhausted life—but too desperate to care.

3

How wonderful is the blue dawning of the new day before the sun! not rosy-fingered, like that Aurora of the Greeks who comes later with all her wealth; but still, dreamy, wonderful, stealing out of the unseen, abashed by the solemnity of the new birth. When anxious watchers see that first brightness come stealing upon the waiting skies, what mingled relief and renewal of misery is in it! another long day to toil through—yet another sad night over! Lord Gowrie sat among the dust and cobwebs, his lamp flaring idly into the blue morning. He had heard his son's human voice, though nothing more; and he expected to have him brought out by invisible hands, as had happened to himself, and left lying in long deathly swoon outside that mystic door. This was how it had happened to heir after heir, as told from father to son, one after another, as the secret came down.

One or two bearers of the name Lindores had never recovered; most of them had been saddened and subdued for life. He remembered sadly the freshness of existence which had never come back to himself; the hopes that had never blossomed again; the assurance with which never more he had been able to go about the world. And now his son would be as himself—the glory gone out of his living—his ambitions, his aspirations wrecked. He had not been endowed as his boy was—he had been a plain, honest man, and nothing more; but experience and life had given him wisdom enough to smile by times at the coquetries of mind in which Lindores indulged.

Were they all over now, those freaks of young intelligence, those enthusiasms of the soul? The curse of the house had come upon him—the magnetism of that strange presence, ever living, ever watchful, present in all the family history. His heart was sore for his son; and yet along with this there was a certain consolation to him in having henceforward a partner in the secret—some one to whom he could talk of it as he had not been able to talk since his own father died. Almost all the mental struggles which Gowrie had known had been connected with this mystery; and he had been obliged to hide them in his bosom—to conceal them even when they rent him in two. Now he had a partner in his trouble. This was what he was thinking as he sat through the night. How slowly the moments passed! He was not aware of the daylight coming in.

After a while even thought got suspended in listening. Was not the time nearly over? He rose and began to pace about the encumbered space, which was but a step or two in extent. There was an old cupboard in the wall, in which there were restoratives—pungent essences and cordials, and fresh water which he had himself brought—everything was ready; presently the ghastly body of his boy, half dead, would be thrust forth into his care.

But this was not how it happened. While he waited, so intent that his whole frame seemed to be capable of hearing, he heard the closing of the door, boldly shut with a sound that rose in muffled echoes through the house, and Lindores himself appeared, ghastly indeed as a dead man, but walking upright and firmly, the lines of his face drawn, and his eyes staring. Lord Gowrie uttered a cry. He was more alarmed by this unexpected return than by the helpless prostration of the swoon which he had expected. He recoiled from his son as if he too had been a spirit. "Lindores!" he cried; was it Lindores, or someone else in his place? The boy seemed as if he did not see him. He went straight forward to where the water stood on the dusty table, and took a great draught, then turned to the door. "Lindores!" said his father, in miserable anxiety; "don't you know me?" Even then the young man only half looked at him, and put out a hand almost as cold as the hand that had clutched himself in the Secret Chamber; a faint smile came upon his face. "Don't stay here," he whispered; "come! come!"

Lord Gowrie drew his son's arm within his own, and felt the thrill through and through him of nerves strained beyond mortal strength. He could scarcely keep up with him as he stalked along the corridor to his room, stumbling as if he could not see, yet swift as an arrow. When they reached his room he turned and closed and locked the door, then laughed as he staggered to the bed. "That will not keep him out, will it?" he said.

"Lindores," said his father, "I expected to find you unconscious. I am almost more frightened to find you like this. I need not ask if you have seen him ——"

"Oh, I have seen him. The old liar! Father, promise to expose him, to turn him out—promise to clear out that accursed old nest! It is our own fault. Why have we left such a place shut out from the eye of day? Isn't there something in the Bible about those who do evil hating the light?"

"Lindores! you don't often quote the Bible."

"No, I suppose not; but there is more truth in—many things than we thought."

"Lie down," said the anxious father. "Take some of this

wine—try to sleep."

"Take it away; give me no more of that devil's drink. Talk to me—that's better. Did you go through it all the same, poor papa?—and hold me fast. You are warm—you are honest!" he cried. He put forth his hands over his father's, warming them with the contact. He put his cheek like a child against his father's arm. He gave a faint laugh, with the tears in his eyes. "Warm and honest," he repeated. "Kind flesh and blood! and did you go through it all the same?"

"My boy!" cried the father, feeling his heart glow and swell over the son who had been parted from him for years by that development of young manhood and ripening intellect which so often severs and loosens the ties of home. Lord Gowrie had felt that Lindores half despised his simple mind and duller imagination; but this childlike clinging overcame him, and tears stood in his eyes. "I fainted, I suppose. I never knew how it ended. They made what they liked of me. But you, my brave boy, you came out of your own will."

Lindores shivered. "I fled!" he said. "No honour in that. I had not courage to face him longer. I will tell you by-and-by. But I want to know about you."

What an ease it was to the father to speak! For years and years this had been shut up in his breast. It had made him lonely in the midst of his friends.

"Thank God," he said, "that I can speak to you, Lindores. Often and often I have been tempted to tell your mother. But why should I make her miserable? She knows there is something; she knows when I see him, but she knows no more."

"When you see him?" Lindores raised himself, with a return of his first ghastly look, in his bed. Then he raised his clenched fist wildly, and shook it in the air. "Vile devil, coward, deceiver!"

"Oh hush, hush, hush, Lindores! God help us! what troubles you may bring!"

"And God help me, whatever troubles I bring," said the young man. "I defy him, father. An accursed being like that must be less, not more powerful, than we are—with God to back us. Only stand by me: stand by me ——"

"Hush, Lindores! You don't feel it yet—never to get out of hearing of him all your life! He will make you pay for it—if not now, after; when you remember he is there; whatever happens, knowing everything! But I hope it will not be so bad with you as with me, my poor boy. God help you indeed if it is, for you have more imagination and more mind. I am able to forget him sometimes when I am occupied—when in the hunting-field, going across country. But you are not a hunting man, my poor boy," said Lord Gowrie, with a curious mixture of a regret, which was less serious than the other. Then he lowered his voice. "Lindores, this is what has happened to me since the moment I gave him my hand."

"I did not give him my hand."

"You did not give him your hand? God bless you, my boy! You stood out?" he cried, with tears again rushing to his eyes; "and they say—they say—but I don't know if there is any truth in it." Lord Gowrie got up from his son's side, and walked up and down with excited steps. "If there should be truth in it! Many people think the whole thing is a fancy. If there should be truth in it, Lindores!"

"In what, father?"

"They say, if he is once resisted his power is broken—once refused. *You* could stand against him—you! Forgive me, my boy, as I hope God will forgive me, to have thought so little of His best gifts," cried Lord Gowrie, coming back with wet eyes; and stooping, he kissed his son's hand. "I thought you would be more shaken by being more mind than body," he said, humbly. "I thought if I could but have saved you from the trial; and *you* are the conqueror!"

"Am I the conqueror? I think all my bones are broken, father—out of their sockets," said the young man, in a low voice. "I think I shall go to sleep."

"Yes, rest, my boy. It is the best thing for you," said the father, though with a pang of momentary disappointment.

Lindores fell back upon the pillow. He was so pale that there were moments when the anxious watcher thought him not sleeping but dead. He put his hand out feebly, and grasped his father's hand. "Warm—honest," he said, with a feeble smile about his lips, and fell asleep.

The daylight was full in the room, breaking through shutters and curtains and mocking at the lamp that still flared on the table. It seemed an emblem of the disorders, mental and material, of this strange night; and, as such, it affected the plain imagination of Lord Gowrie, who would have fain got up to extinguish it, and whose mind returned again and again, in spite of him, to this symptom of disturbance. By-and-by, when Lindores' grasp relaxed, and he got his hand free, he got up from his son's bedside, and put out the lamp, putting it carefully out of the way. With equal care he put away the wine from the table, and gave the room its ordinary aspect, softly opening a window to let in the fresh air of the morning. The park lay fresh in the early sunshine, still, except for the twittering of the birds, refreshed with dews, and shining in that soft radiance of the morning which is over before mortal cares are stirring.

Never, perhaps, had Gowrie looked out upon the beautiful world around his house without a thought of the weird existence which was going on so near to him, which had gone on for centuries, shut up out of sight of the sunshine. The Secret Chamber had been present with him since ever he saw it. He had never been able to get free of the spell of it. He had felt himself watched, surrounded, spied upon, day after day, since he was of the age of Lindores, and that was thirty years ago. He turned it all over in his mind, as he stood there and his son slept. It had been on his lips to tell it all to his boy, who had now come to inherit the enlightenment of his race. And it was a disappointment to him to have it all forced back again, and silence imposed upon him once more. Would he care to hear it when he woke? would he not rather, as Lord Gowrie remembered to have done himself, thrust the thought as far as he could away from him, and endeavour to forget for the moment—until the time came when he would not be permitted to forget?

He had been like that himself, he recollected now. He had not wished to hear his own father's tale. "I remember," he said to himself; "I remember"—turning over everything in his mind—if Lindores might only be willing to hear the story when he woke! But then he himself had not been willing when he was Lindores, and he could understand his son, and could not blame him; but it would be a disappointment. He was thinking this when he heard Lindores' voice calling him. He went back hastily to his bedside. It was strange to see him in his evening dress with his worn face, in the fresh light of the morning, which poured in at every crevice. "Does my mother know?" said Lindores; "what will she think?"

"She knows something; she knows you have some trial to go through. Most likely she will be praying for us both; that's the way of women," said Lord Gowrie, with the tremulous tenderness which comes into a man's voice sometimes when he speaks of a good wife. "I'll go and ease her mind, and tell her all is well over ——"

"Not yet. Tell me first," said the young man, putting his hand upon his father's arm.

What an ease it was! "I was not so good to my father," he thought to himself, with sudden penitence for the long-past, long-forgotten fault, which, indeed, he had never realised as a fault before. And then he told his son what had been the story of his life—how he had scarcely ever sat alone without feeling, from some corner of the room, from behind some curtain, those eyes upon him; and how, in the difficulties of his life, that secret inhabitant of the house had been present, sitting by him and advising him. "Whenever there has been anything to do: when there has been a question between two ways, all in a moment I have seen him by me: I feel when he is coming. It does not matter where I am—here or anywhere—as soon as ever there is a question of family business; and always he persuades me to the wrong way, Lindores. Sometimes I yield to him, how can I help it? He makes everything so clear; he makes wrong seem right. If

34

I have done unjust things in my day——"

"You have not, father."

"I have: there were these Highland people I turned out. I did not mean to do it, Lindores; but he showed me that it would be better for the family. And my poor sister that married Tweedside and was wretched all her life. It was his doing, that marriage; he said she would be rich, and so she was, poor thing, poor thing! and died of it. And old Macalister's lease —— Lindores, Lindores! when there is any business it makes my heart sick. I know he will come, and advise wrong, and tell me—something I will repent after."

"The thing to do is to decide beforehand, that, good or bad, you will not take his advice."

Lord Gowrie shivered. "I am not strong like you, or clever; I cannot resist. Sometimes I repent in time and don't do it; and then! But for your mother and you children, there is many a day I would not have given a farthing for my life."

"Father," said Lindores, springing from his bed. "two of us together can do many things. Give me your word to clear out this cursed den of darkness this very day."

"Lindores, hush, hush, for the sake of heaven!"

"I will not, for the sake of heaven! Throw it open—let everybody who likes see it—make an end of the secret—pull down everything, curtains, walls. What do you say?—sprinkle holy water? Are you laughing at me?"

"I did not speak," said Earl Gowrie, growing very pale, and grasping his son's arm with both his hands. "Hush, boy; do you think he does not hear?"

And then there was a low laugh close to them—so close that both shrank; a laugh no louder than a breath.

"Did you laugh—father?"

"No, Lindores." Lord Gowrie had his eyes fixed. He was as pale as the dead. He held his son tight for a moment; then his gaze and his grasp relaxed, and he fell back feebly in a chair.

"You see!" he said; "whatever we do it will be the same; we are under his power."

And then there ensued the blank pause with which baffled men confront a hopeless situation. But at that moment the first faint stirrings of the house—a window being opened, a bar undone, a movement of feet, and subdued voices—became audible in the stillness of the morning. Lord Gowrie roused himself at once. "We must not be found like this," he said; "we must not show how we have spent the night. It is over, thank God! and oh, my boy, forgive me! I am thankful there are two of us to bear it; it makes the burden lighter—though I ask your pardon humbly for saying so. I would have saved you if I could, Lindores."

"I don't wish to have been saved; but I will not bear it. I will end it," the young man said, with an oath out of which his emotion took all profanity. His father said, "Hush, hush." With a look of terror and pain, he left him; and yet there was a thrill of tender pride in his mind. How brave the boy was! even after he had been there. Could it be that this would all come to nothing, as every other attempt to resist had done before?

"I suppose you know all about it now, Lindores," said his friend Ffarrington, after breakfast; "luckily for us who are going over the house. What a glorious old place it is!"

"I don't think that Lindores enjoys the glorious old place today," said another of the guests under his breath. "How pale he is! He doesn't look as if he had slept."

"I will take you over every nook where I have ever been," said Lindores. He looked at his father with almost command in his eyes. "Come with me, all of you. We shall have no more secrets here."

"Are you mad?" said his father in his ear.

"Never mind," cried the young man. "Oh, trust me; I will do it with judgment. Is everybody ready?" There was an excitement about him that half frightened, half roused the party. They all rose, eager, yet doubtful. His mother came to him and took his arm.

"Lindores! you will do nothing to vex your father; don't make him unhappy. I don't know your secrets, you two; but look, he has enough to bear."

"I want you to know our secrets, mother. Why should we have secrets from you?"

"Why, indeed?" she said, with tears in her eyes. "But, Lindores, my dearest boy, don't make it worse for *him*."

"I give you my word, I will be wary," he said; and she left him to go to his father, who followed the party, with an anxious look upon his face.

"Are you coming, too?" he asked.

"I? No; I will not go: but trust him—trust the boy, John."

"He can do nothing; he will not be able to do anything," he said.

And thus the guests set out on their round—the son in advance, excited and tremulous, the father anxious and watchful behind. They began in the usual way, with the old state-rooms and picture-gallery; and in a short time the party had half forgotten that there was anything unusual in the inspection. When, however, they were halfway down the gallery, Lindores stopped short with an air of wonder. "You have had it put back then?" he said. He was standing in front of the vacant space where Earl Robert's portrait ought to have been. "What is it?" they all cried, crowding upon him, ready for any marvel. But as there was nothing to be seen, the strangers smiled among themselves. "Yes, to be sure, there is nothing so suggestive as a vacant place," said a lady who was of the party. "Whose portrait ought to be there, Lord Lindores?"

He looked at his father, who made a slight assenting gesture, then shook his head drearily.

"Who put it there?" Lindores said, in a whisper.

"It is not there; but you and I see it," said Lord Gowrie, with a sigh.

Then the strangers perceived that something had moved the father and the son, and, notwithstanding their eager curiosity, obeyed the dictates of politeness, and dispersed into groups looking at the other pictures. Lindores set his teeth and clenched his hands. Fury was growing upon him—not the awe that filled his father's mind. "We will leave the rest of this to another time,"

37

he cried, turning to the others, almost fiercely. "Come, I will show you something more striking now." He made no further pretence of going systematically over the house. He turned and went straight upstairs, and along the corridor. "Are we going over the bedrooms?" someone said. Lindores led the way straight to the old lumber-room, a strange place for such a gay party. The ladies drew their dresses about them. There was not room for half of them. Those who could get in began to handle the strange things that lay about, touching them with dainty fingers, exclaiming how dusty they were. The window was half blocked up by old armour and rusty weapons; but this did not hinder the full summer daylight from penetrating in a flood of light. Lindores went in with fiery determination on his face. He went straight to the wall, as if he would go through, then paused with a blank gaze. "Where is the door?" he said.

"You are forgetting yourself," said Lord Gowrie, speaking over the heads of the others. "Lindores! you know very well there never was any door there; the wall is very thick; you can see by the depth of the window. There is no door there."

The young man felt it over with his hand. The wall was smooth, and covered with the dust of ages. With a groan he turned away. At this moment a suppressed laugh, low, yet distinct, sounded close by him. "You laughed?" he said, fiercely, to Ffarrington, striking his hand upon his shoulder.

"I—laughed! Nothing was farther from my thoughts," said his friend, who was curiously examining something that lay upon an old carved chair. "Look here! what a wonderful sword, cross-hilted! Is it an Andrea? What's the matter, Lindores?"

Lindores had seized it from his hands; he dashed it against the wall with a suppressed oath. The two or three people in the room stood aghast.

"Lindores!" his father said, in a tone of warning. The young man dropped the useless weapon with a groan. "Then God help us!" he said; "but I will find another way."

"There is a very interesting room close by," said Lord Gowrie, hastily—"this way! Lindores has been put out by—some changes that have been made without his knowledge," he said, calmly. "You must not mind him. He is disappointed. He is perhaps too much accustomed to have his own way."

But Lord Gowrie knew that no one believed him. He took them to the adjoining room, and told them some easy story of an apparition that was supposed to haunt it. "Have you ever seen it?" the guests said, pretending interest. "Not I; but we don't mind ghosts in this house," he answered, with a smile. And then they resumed their round of the old noble mystic house.

I cannot tell the reader what young Lindores has done to carry out his pledged word and redeem his family. It may not be known, perhaps, for another generation, and it will not be for me to write that concluding chapter: but when, in the ripeness of time, it can be narrated, no one will say that the mystery of Gowrie Castle has been a vulgar horror, though there are some who are disposed to think so now

The Land of Suspense

1

The young man set out upon his walk at the entrance of a broad valley, through which there was visible here and there the glimmer of a great river. It was broken in outline by many little hills, such as one sees in the loveliest part of Italy, each crowned by its little groups of habitations, in varied and delightful inequalities of height and form, which seemed to throw a radiance of life and living over the beautiful green slopes, fields, and trees in which these points of light and peace were set. Lines of blue hills receding towards the distant peaks, which were great enough to be called mountains, stretched in noble ridges on either side; and the landscape was one which filled the traveller with a sense of beauty and satisfaction, while drawing his mind and his steps on by a hundred suggestions of fairer things still unrevealed.

And the morning was fresh and sweet, beyond even that "*innocent brightness of the newborn day*," of which few can resist the charm. The sky was flooded with the early sunshine. The valley glowed under it with the dew still undried upon the grass, much of which was half buried in flowers, and soft with the whiteness of the daisies rejoicing in the light. The young man had come over a pass between the hills when this prospect bursting upon him for a moment took away his breath—but it was only for a moment. He paused to gaze upon the road before him, and then with a delightful consciousness that his walk would bring him into fuller possession of this new world unknown to him, he set out upon his way.

The curious thing was, that he did not know where he was going, nor what place this was, nor the direction in which it would lead him, though all the while he walked quickly on with the sure and certain steps of a man familiar with every turn of the path. For some time he went on, unconscious of this, or at least without thinking of it in the ease of his being. He had always been fond of walking, and there was a pleasure in the mere sense of movement, after some recent absence from that delight—absence and confinement which he was aware of, though he could not render to himself any reason for it. He was in full career, feeling as if his foot just touched and no more the path which was not then a highroad but a winding path across the slopes, upon which the flowery fields encroached—when it first occurred to him hazily with a happy sense of amusement that he did not in the least know where he was going. No matter—he was going as if he very well knew where: and there came into his mind a scrap of lovely verse, about "*a spirit in my feet,*" and he began to sing it to himself as he went on. Certainly there was a spirit in his feet that knew better where he was going than he.

Thus he went, without pause or weariness, for a long way,—so long, that at last he began to wonder how it was that the daylight did not change, that there was no difference in the skies to correspond with the hours which he must have been walking. In himself he was like the day, unchanged, without the faintest suggestion of fatigue; and it was only by the long vista behind him, and the distance of the hills from which he had come, that he felt how long a time he had been afoot. When this thought occurred to him he sat down upon the low embankment which marked the line of the wood, for he had by this time reached the highway—to rest, as he said to himself, though he felt no need of rest—really to measure with his eyes the length of the valley before him, which went widening away into the blue recesses of distant hills, so that you could trace no end to it.

The highroad led along the side of the river at this point,

through groups of beautiful trees; and at some distance on the other side there was planted a great town spreading far back into the valley, which seemed, from the inequalities of its buildings, to be built on innumerable little hills, and shone white under the sunshine with many towers and spires, in great stateliness and beauty. It was here for the first time that the traveller saw any concourse of people. Upon the slopes he had met but few, mostly solitary individuals, with here and there a group of friends. They were a people of genial countenance, smiling, and with friendly looks; but it surprised and a little wounded him that they took no notice of him, did not give him so much as a good morning—nay, even pushed him off the path, though without the least appearance of any unkindly feeling.

As he sat upon the roadside and watched the people of this unknown land coming and going across the bridge from the town, his heart was moved within him by the sight of so many fellow-creatures, all, as it seemed, so gay, so kind, so friendly, but without a sign or look as if they recognised his existence at all. It seemed to him a long time since he had exchanged a word with any one, and a great sense of loneliness took possession of him. He had not felt this upon the little-frequented paths from which he had come; but here, among so many, to receive not even a look from any passer-by seemed to him an injury and a disappointment which it was hard to bear.

He reflected, however, that in the country from which he came such a thing might easily have happened with a wandering foreigner resting upon the roadside, whom nobody knew: yet he was scarcely comforted by this thought, for he felt sure that at least such a stranger would have been looked at, if no more—would have met the questioning of many eyes, some with perhaps a smile in them, and all curious to know what he did there. Even curiosity would have been something: it would have been kinder than to ignore him completely as these people were doing: yet there was nothing in their look to make him believe that they were unfeeling or discourteous.

After a while he felt that he could bear this estrangement

from his kind no longer, and getting up on his feet, he said "Good morning" to a group that were passing, feeling in himself that there was a wistfulness, almost an entreaty in his tone. He saw that they were startled by his address, and looked round first, as if to see where his voice came from—yet in a moment answered, with what seemed almost an outcry of response and greeting, saying "Good morning," and "God bless you!" eagerly.

Then one made himself the spokesman of a group, and advanced a step towards him, yet still with an uncertainty, and eyes that did not exactly meet his, but wavered as if unable to fix his face. "Are you going to our town?" he said; "can any of us be of use to you?" and there was a murmur among all as of assent, "any of us," as if to press help upon him if he needed it: but he required no help—it was only recognition that he wanted, a kind word.

"No," he said; "I am going there" and he pointed towards the farther end of the valley. A number had gathered round him, all looking at him with great kindness, but with the same uncertainty of gaze, all eagerly bending toward him to hear what he said. Their looks warmed his heart, yet a little repelled him too, as if there was something between him and them which made it better to go on, and try no further communication. "I am going there" he repeated, moving a step onward: and immediately they all spoke together in a wonderful accord of voices, saying, "God be with you! God save you! God bless you!" some of them so much in earnest that there seemed to him to be tears in their eyes. There was something in these words which seemed to urge him on, and he resumed his journey, passing through, and looking back upon them, and waving his hand to them in sign of farewell.

And they all stood looking after him, calling after him "God bless you!" and "God save you!" until the sense of distance from them melted away, and his whole being seemed warmed with their kind looks and good wishes. He could hear them, too, all talking together and saying, "It is one of the travellers," to which the others answered again, "God save him!" as if it was the greeting of that country to all that went through.

Thus he went on again, always keeping his course towards the western end of the valley, and pleased with this encounter, even though there was that something in it which startled him, as he seemed to have startled them. Looking across the river at the city, with all its white terraces shining in the sun, and its high towers and pinnacles against the sky, and the river at its feet reflecting every point and shining height, as if it were another city at the feet of the true town, he thought he had never seen so beautiful a place; but what town it was or who the people were who dwelt there he knew not. All he knew was that they were his fellows, that they had bidden God bless him, that they wished him well: and this gave him great refreshment as he went on, feeling no fatigue, but now more than ever wondering that though he did not know where he was going, he was yet going on straight and swift as if he were sure of the way.

For a little time the road ran by the river, but then parted from its winding course, and presently broke into several ways, where a stranger in that place might so easily have lost himself, not knowing which to take. But he found no difficulty, nor even paused to choose his way, going lightly on without any hesitation, as one who knew exactly how the bearings lay.

By this time the sun was lower in the heavens, and a sweet look of evening had come over the sky—the look which suggests home-going, and that labours of all kinds and travel should be drawing to some end of rest and ease. And since the pause he had made on his journey, short as it was, and his second setting forth, there had stolen into his mind a wonderful sense that he was going, not upon an excursion into an unknown world, but home. The sensation was one that he did not know how to explain to himself, for he knew that it was not the home from which he had come, nor any accustomed place. And he did not know where it was, nor what he might find there; but the impression grew upon him more and more strongly as he went on. And many thoughts came with this thought.

He did not think of the home from which he had come. It

appeared to him as something far, far away, and different from all that he saw or that surrounded him now. But the thought that he was going home, though not there, brought a seriousness into his thoughts which he had not been conscious of when he set forth first in the morning, in all the enthusiasm of the beautiful unknown place into which he marched forward so confident and full of cheer.

He became more serious now. Vaguely there came into his mind a recollection that his former goings home had not been always happy. There had been certain things in which he was to blame. He could not have said what things, nor how this was, his consciousness and memory being a little blurred, as if something had come between him and the former things which had moved his life; but yet he was vaguely aware that he had been to blame. And his mind filled with all manner of resolutions and thoughts of a goodness to come, which should be perfect as the face of nature, and the purity of the air and the sky. He said to himself that never again—never again! though his recollection failed him when he tried to make clear to himself what it was which should never again be.

It was vague to him, leaving only a sense that all had not been as this was about to be; but yet the fervour of his conviction of the better things to come was as intense as if he had perfectly conceived what there was to be done, and what there had been. Never again, never again!—no more as of old: but all perfect and spotless in the new. These resolutions distilled into his mind like dew, they shed themselves through his being like some delightful balm, refreshing him as though his heart had grown dry, but now was filled with calm and a quiet happiness of hoping and anticipation, though he did not know what he anticipated any more than what it was which had made a shadow in the past

In this mood he began again to ascend a little upon a path which broke off from the highway towards one of the little towns or villages raised above the level of the valley, with towers and trees mingling on the little height, which made him think of an old Tuscan picture. He went towards it, with an eagerness rising within him and a confidence that it was here that his destination was. All the day long he knew that he had been travelling to this spot, and recognised it though he knew it not. He went on unhesitating, gradually making out the ranges of building, which were of beautiful architecture, though in a style unknown to him, with graceful pinnacles rising as light as foam against the sky, and open arcades and halls, cool and bright, where every door stood open, and he could see sheer above him as he mounted the winding way the groups of men and women in the houses, and many faces at the windows looking out, as if on the watch for some one who was coming. Were any of them looking out for him he wondered to himself? without any sense that it was unlikely there should be watchers looking for him in a place where he had never been before, in an unknown country which was strange to all his previous knowledge.

But no restraining consciousness like this was on him as he hastened up the steep way, and suddenly turning round the corner of the wall, which was wreathed with blossoming plants in a glow of colour and fragrance, came in sight of the wide and noble gateway all open, with its pillars glowing in the westering light, and no sign of bolt or bar or other hindrance to shut out any wayfarer. In front of it stood a group of figures, which seemed to be on the watch for someone. Did they expect some prince or lordly visitor? were they the warders of the gate? They stood two and two, beautiful in the first glow of youth, their fair, tall, elastic forms clothed in white, with the faint difference which at that lovely age is all that seems to exist between the maiden and the youth. They were like each other as brothers might be, and the traveller felt suddenly with a strange bound of his heart that he knew these faces, though not whom they belonged to, nor who they were. They were as the faces of others whom he had known in the land that was so far off behind him: and all at once he knew that they were looking for no prince or potentate but for himself, all strange as he was, unacquainted with this place, and with all that was here.

They stood looking far along the valley from that height,

and asking each other, "Do you see him? do you see him?" but they did not seem to be aware that he was there, standing close to them, looking at them with eager eyes. He stood silent for a moment, thinking they must perceive him, yet wondering how they would know him, having never seen him before: but soon became impatient and troubled by that pause, and, vexed to be overlooked, said suddenly, "I am here—if perhaps you are looking for me."

They were startled, and turned their faces towards him, but with that strange wistful look as if they him not which he had remarked in the people whom he met by the bridge—and then they came hastily forward and surrounded him as if with an angelic guard, and he saw with a strange tremor that tears had come into their eyes. "Oh our brother!" said one, in a voice so full of pity that it seemed to him that he pitied himself, though he knew not why, in sympathy. And "Speak," said the others, "Speak, that we may know you." While, "Oh my brother," cried the first again, "it is not thus we hoped to see you." This voice seemed to pierce into his inmost heart, and sadness came over him as if his hope had fallen away from him, and this after all was not his home.

"This is who I am," he said; and he told them his name, and that he had come from afar off, and had come straight here without a pause, thinking that this was his home.

They surrounded him closely, as closely as if they would embrace him, and said to him, but with tears, one speaking with another, "It is your home: and we are your brothers and your sisters, and we have known you were coming, but hoped that you would come otherwise. But we love you not the less, oh our brother, our brother! we love you none the less—God save you! God bless you! There is no one here that does not love you and bless you and pray for you. Dear brother, son of our mother! would to God you had but come to us in other wise."

"I cannot tell what you mean," he said, with a trembling coming over him. "If I am your brother, why do you not take me in? I have travelled far today, from the very opening of the

47

valley, and never paused—always thinking that there was home at the end—and now you stand between me and the door, and weep, and will not let me in."

"Brother," they said all together, "brother!" It seemed as if in that word lay all sweetness and consolation and pity and love. The circle seemed to open round him, leaving the great wide doorway full of the low sunshine from the west clear before him, and someone came out and stood upon the threshold and stretched out his hands, calling to him, "My son, my son!"

It seemed to the young man that it wanted but a few steps to carry him to the arms of this man who called to him, and to whom his heart went out as if it would burst from his breast. But he that had walked so lightly all day long and felt no weariness, found himself now as one paralysed, incapable of another step. He stood and gazed piteously at the wide open gate, and him who stood there, and knew that this was the place to which he had been travelling, and the home he desired, and the father that he loved. But he could not make another step. His feet seemed rooted to the ground. There came from him a great outburst of tears and anguish, and he cried to them, "Tell me, tell me!—why is it I cannot go?"

The white figures gathered all round him again, as if they would have taken him in their arms, and the first of them spoke, weeping, putting out her hands: "Brother," she said, "those that come here, those that come home, must first be clothed with the building of God, the house not made with hands; those who are unclothed, as you are, alas! they cannot come in. Brother, we have no power, and you have no power. The doors are open, and the hearts are open, and would to God you could come in; but oh, my brother! what can I say? It is not for us to speak; you know—"

"I know," he said, and stood still among them silent, his heart hushed in his bosom, his head bowed down with trouble, hearing them weeping round him, and well aware that he could not go up, not had he the strength of a giant. He stood awhile, and then he said, "My home was never closed to me before; never have I failed of entrance there and welcome, and my mother's light always burning to guide me. She would have torn me from these stones, and brought me in had she been here. Never, never, was there a question———! And yet," he cried, wildly, "you called that earth, and this you call heaven!" This he cried, not knowing what he said: for never before had there been any thought in his mind what the name of this country was.

Then his sister called him by his name, and the sound of his name half consoled him, and half made the contrast more bitter, reminding him of that place from whence he came, where his was the innermost seat and the best welcome, while here he was kept outside. "Do not be so sore discouraged," she said, "for one day you will come and enter at the gate with joy, and nothing will be withheld from you; and we will go to the Great Father and plead with Him, that it may be soon, and then your spirit will be no longer unclothed, and all will be well."

"Unclothed!" he cried; "I know not what you mean," and he turned from them, pushing them from him, and hurried down the winding way which he had ascended with so light a heart. There were still the faces at the windows looking out; but though he would not look at them, he saw that they were troubled, and many voices sounded out upon the sweet air, calling to him, "God save you! God bless you!" over and over again, till the whole world seemed full of the sound. But he took no heed of it as he fled along the way in indignation and bitter disappointment, saying to himself, "*And that was called earth, and this they say is heaven.*"

2

At the foot of the hill was a wood encircling its base, with many winding paths going through, and yet here and there masses of shadow from the trees, in which a man might hide himself from every eye, and even from the shining of the daylight, which seemed to the young man in all the glory of the sunset to mock him as he fled away from the place which was his home. It was the dimness and the shadow that attracted him now, and not the glory of the western sky or the dazzling of the light. In the very heart of the wood, kept by a circle of great trees standing all around like a bodyguard, there was a little opening—a grassy bank like velvet, all soft with mosses, with little woodland blossoms creeping over the soil, and all the woodland scents and fragrance and sound and silence, far from any sound or sight of men.

The young man pushed through the copses and between the great boles of the trees, and flung himself upon the cool and soft and fragrant bank; he flung himself upon his face and hid it there, with a longing to be rid even of himself and his consciousness in that soft and sheltering shade; but all the while knowing, as he had often discovered before, that however you might cover your eyes, and even burrow in the earth, you could not escape from that most intimate companion, nor shut your ears to his reasonings or his upbraidings. Elsewhere, when one of those moments came, and himself confronted and seized himself, there had always been those at hand who helped him out of this encounter. The crowd, or the tumult and conflict of living, or pleasure, or pain, or some other creature, had stolen in and stopped that conflict. But now was the hour in which there was nothing to intervene.

And at first what was in his mind was nothing but bitter disappointment and rage and shame. He, whose coming back had always been with joy, even when it came with tears, before whom every door had been thrown open, and whom all about him had thanked with wistful looks for coming home: but now he was shut out. This was too great an event, too unlooked for, to permit any other thought beside it He remembered himself of all the dear stories of his youth, of him whom his father saw afar off and rushed to meet him, not waiting for the confession that was on his lips. And that was how hitherto it had happened to him: and here, where he now was, was not this the most mercifullest place of all, where everything was love and forgiveness? He said this to himself, not realising what place it was, not knowing anything, though he had seized upon the name of heaven in his first horror of wonder and upbraiding, to point the bewailing and reproach.

For a long time he lay with his hot brow pressed against those soft couches of moss, closing out with his hands the light from his eyes, in a despair and anguish unspeakable—asking himself why he had come here at all, to be rejected and shut out? Why, why had he not taken another path he wot of, and plunged, and gone—— Where? where? He caught his sobbing breath, that burst from his bosom like a child's, in Leavings and sore reiterations of distress. Where? where? There would have been welcome in that place; and bands of jovial companions, and noise, and shoutings. Where? he did not know where.

But at last this convulsion and passion softened away, and he raised his head and looked himself in the face. Ah, was not this what I said, I said! Was not this what we thought upon many a morning, to forget it ere the night? Was not this what we knew, you and I? but you would not listen or hear. When we saw the mother's light in the window, when the door was thrown open, wide open, did not we know that the time would come——? This was what his other self said in his ear. He leaned his head upon his hands and looked out in the sweetness of the darkening shade, with fixed eyes that saw nothing except the past, which gripped his heart and stayed his breath and came back upon him in dreadful waves of recollection and consciousness.

He saw scenes which he had scorned when he was in them, and loathed, and gone back to, and wallowed, foaming—always with rage and shame of himself. And they had cost him already his other life, and pangs innumerable; the price which he had paid for nought, hard blood-money for that which was no bread— which he had known to be no bread even while he consumed it—the husks which the swine did eat That was how the other man had named it, the man whom his father ran to meet and fell on his neck—but not here. There had been to himself also those who fell upon his neck and forgave him before he said a word—but not here.

This was not how he had felt when he set out this morning

upon the beautiful way in the sunshine. He had been sure then that all was well: every evil thought had departed out of his mind; his heart was tender and soft, loving God and man, and the thought of a life in which there should be no reproach, no shadow, no evil, had been sweet to him as is the exquisite relief that comes after pain.

He remembered how he had sung songs as he walked, in the ease of his heart. And now! Shut out, a homeless wanderer, unclothed: what was that she said? unclothed: he did not know what she meant; but the rest which he did know was enough—enough and more than enough: he was abandoned, forsaken, the door shut upon him—worse than that, open, but he unable to enter: left to himself to spend the night in the wood—or anywhere, who cared?—though he himself was blameless now, having done nothing to deserve this doom, having felt his heart so soft and a tenderness which was more than innocence, a longing for every good in his heart. Oh the other life which he had left! the homely house, the quiet room, the face all smiling weeping, at the door!

"*And that they called earth; and this they say is heaven.*"

He said this aloud, unawares—and suddenly he was answered by another voice, which seemed to be near him, the voice of another man standing somewhere close by, which said, "No, you are mistaken; this is not heaven."

The young man raised his head and looked round him; and the hair rose up upon his head, and a thrill of shrinking and terror went over him, for he saw no one. He looked round him, drawing back against the tree which crowned the bank, and clutching at it in his alarm: he was no coward, but where is the man who can be suddenly accosted by a voice while seeing no one, and not be afraid? "I must have dreamed I heard it," he said to himself: but rose up with an impulse of agitation to leave the place in which such delusions could be.

Then he heard the voice again, but this time lower down, and now close to him, as if a man had suddenly sat down beside him upon the bank. "Are you so new?" it said, with a half laugh. "Have you not discovered that you too are invisible, like me?"

"Invisible!" The young man's voice shook with fear and wonder, wavering as if blown out by the wind, though there was no wind.

"Be consoled," said the other; "it is no bad life: there is no fire nor brimstone here: and there is hope for those who love hope. Let us talk: it wiles the hours away."

While the other spoke, the young man, with a trembling in every limb, held up his hands into the air, and gazed with his eyes, first at one and then at the other—at the places where he felt them, where they ought to be. He felt every nerve thrill and every finger tremble and shake, but he saw nothing. Awe and terror seized upon him. He rushed from the bank, which sloped under his feet and made him look to his footing, and flung himself against the trunk of one of the great trees. He felt the touch of it, the roughness of the bark, the projection of the twigs here and there: but at the same time he saw it clear, standing with its feet deep in the fern and undergrowth, and no human body against it—this while he felt still the thrill and shock with which he came in contact with that great substantial thing. And he uttered a great cry, "I am then no more a man!" in a voice which rang shrill with horror and misery and dismay.

"Yes," said the other, "you are still a man. And be consoled. In some things it is better than the old life. You have no wants and no weariness, likewise no work, no responsibility. Be consoled. The discovery is painful for a moment, but you will find companions enough. What has happened to you is no more than has happened to many other men: and we have great freedom, and society at our pleasure. There is a future before us, though it may be thousands of years away.

"A future!" cried the young man; "nay, let me die and be done with it What manner of man are you that can look calmly on a future like this? My God, to live and live and be nothing, as I am now!"

"I am," said the other, "just such a manner of man as you will be tomorrow. It is a shock when you discover it first—but what then? Life is but thought. There is a great prejudice in favour of a visible body, at all events in the race from which we come. But you will perceive how little in reality it matters when you realise how many things you can do and enjoy, even with that deprivation. You might never have found it out, or not for a long time, but for my friendly aid—for it is friendly, I assure you. It breaks the illusion. You will no longer expect from those others that which they have not to give. Sit down by me, and cease measuring yourself against that tree. The tree is solid, but not you—yet there are many consolations. Sit down again, and let us talk."

The young man stood pressing himself against the tree, his forehead against the roughness of the bark which dinted the soft flesh, his arms stretched round it, not long enough to span its girth, but pricked by the little growths which incrusted it. He clung to the great trunk as if it gave him a hold upon something tangible, the only thing that remained to him. They had not seen him, then, these fair creatures, at the gate. That which they heard, that which they addressed, was only a voice. Nobody had seen him along the way. Those who said "God save you" had meant something which he did not yet understand. There was reason for the pity in their eyes and the tears which he had seen them shed. He had seen them, but not they him.

He was no man, but only a voice. The horror grew into an awe which quenched the cries with which his heart was bursting. He without a faculty impaired, hearing everything, seeing everything, feeling with such intensity as he had never felt before! Yet he was now no man, but a voice. The calamity was so great and so unlocked for, that his very voice, the thing he now was, seemed to die in his throat, and his heart in his breast: though all the time he felt his heart beating, bounding, as never in moments of the greatest emotion it had done before, and the blood coursing like a great flood through the veins that were not, and from head to foot of that human frame which existed no longer. Oh terrible doom! oh awful day!

"Come and sit by me, and let us talk," said the other voice.

And then there came a melting and a softening over this forlorn soul. If he was thus for ever banished from common sight—if he was, indeed, exiled from home and every tender fellowship, a thing that no man or woman could ever take by the hand again—still to hear another voice was something in this awful mystery of anguish. He loosed himself from his tree, but kissed its rough bark with a kind of passion as he drew himself away. His finger had caught a sharp twig, and it hurt him; his brow was marked, he could feel it, with the scales of the bark. This gave him a little comfort in his desolation. And then there was still the Voice. He came back and threw himself upon the flowery bank, which sent forth its wild fragrance suddenly as he pressed it, as it might have done if——This also gave him a little consolation, as if it were a verification of the being which he felt in every pulse and every limb.

"You were saying," said the other, "that this was called heaven."

"Ah, no!" said the young man with a voice of despair. "I see my mistake. It is rather——"

"Do not make any more mistakes," said the other, quickly. "It is neither one nor the other. It is the land of Suspense, where we all are until a day which no one knows—a visionary day which, perhaps, may never come, seeing it has been threatened and delayed for all the ages. Ah! you cannot imagine the worlds-full there are of us! and some of the great Romans tell you that the tradition was in their time as now,"

"The Day of Judgment!" said the young man, very low.

"Well! that is what they say. But in the meantime, not to discourage you, it is better here than life was before. There are few pleasures—those things that one despised one's self for enjoying, when time was. But the mind is free—and there are a thousand things to learn. And there is society everywhere. We are here in multitudes. There are almost more of us, I believe, than of—those others."

"Those others!" repeated the young man—he looked up where through the thick foliage there was a glimpse of the tow-

55

ers and roof-trees of that home which he could not enter. His companion spoke as if they were enemies: but his own spirit rebelled against that thought.

"The good people," said the voice, as with a sneer. "What made them to differ, do you ask? Oh, they made their preparations. While we led *joyeuse vie* and had no thought for tomorrow, they took their measures. I am not sure that those who have passed by the Temple in the wood have the best of it even now; but at least we have not much to complain of. There is no suffering: we are left to ourselves: we go where we will, and have great facilities: and, as I tell you, the best of company. Only make up your mind to the one loss, and we have really much to congratulate ourselves upon."

The young man made no reply: he began to hate this voice, with its evenness of speech, the calm and the encouragement of its tone. He had known men who spoke so, who were content to live, though life had no hope, with a sneer at those who were other than they. And though a moment ago he had been almost glad to turn to another being deprived and naked like himself, he felt now that if he were but alone, it would be more easy to bear. The Voice went on talking to him with the pleasure of one who has found a new hearer. And sometimes he listened, and sometimes heard it as though he heard it not. Sometimes even it caught him with an ingenious word and made him laugh; but then his mind would stiffen into silence, and the horror and gloom swept over him again like the dark waves over a wreck at sea.

3

All the night long he sat there leaning his head upon his hands, sometimes leaning against the great trunk of the tree behind him, which gave him a sensation of forlorn comfort, the only thing that recognised him as still tangible, a thing of flesh and blood. He sat there amid all the fragrant breathing of the night as in the lap of a mother who cooled his forehead with dewy touches, and subdued his soul into the calm of inanimate things. And yet there was nothing inanimate in this great realm of nature where the air was fresh and free, like the air upon a mountain-top where there is no wind but only a sense of being far above all hindrance or soil, and near to heaven.

The sky above was alive with stars, stars that were something more than stars, that had rounded and expanded into orbs of light and seemed almost within reach, as if there might be means of entering them and knowing their secrets. The light that came from them was enough to make everything visible in a tender and soft radiance where every variety of shade had its own transparency and sweetness of lovely meaning—such a light as never was on sea or shore. Through the openings of the trees he could see far off the whole course of the valley clear in that mystic glow which was without colour, where all was clear as in a vision, unlike the brightness of the day.

The towers and pinnacles rose up on his right hand over the trees as if made of silver: the little floating vapours in the sky, the great pulsing and movement of the worlds of light above, the air which was as a rapture of purity and freedom,—all conveyed to the young man's bosom the sensation of boundless space, and a lofty height beyond the thoughts of men. And there was a subdued glow along the edge of the horizon, as if there it passed into pure light as the stars did round their boundaries, hiding the life within.

Sometimes this young man had felt even upon the homely earth something of that movement that is in the spheres, the swaying of the great planet as it ran its course in the heavens; but here it seemed like a faint stir of life in everything, a subtle and all-pervading current, a movement majestic, almost visible, in rhythm and measure, like God Himself proceeding onward always in His supernal way. After a time, when the beating of the river of life in his own ears, the throbbing of his heart and current of his blood, were calmed by this greater movement and mystery, he gazed abroad upon the majestic night with a hush of reverence and of awe in which there was adoration. He was silent while God passed by, and felt the sweep of the great stars following in His train, and the air upon his face, the breath of their going, and the thrill of that vast procession through illimitable skies. He, a spirit, though not blessed, yet as a spirit recognised the great course of innumerable worlds and circles of being, following the mighty footsteps of their King.

Thus one moment of amazed and trembling revelation gave him rest in the glory of the night, and stilled the lesser voices and murmurs that filled his ears: but as a man is after all the centre of all systems to himself, the tide of thought and feeling rolled back, and with it the despair which the knowledge of his own condition had brought upon him. When his eyes came back to his immediate surroundings, the sudden sight of the green mound on which he sat, with all its undergrowth of moss and starry decoration of minute flowers, vacant under the faint light, as if there was no one there, drove his soul almost to madness in the sudden rediscovery.

He felt the soft knots of the grass and cushion of the moss under him, yet when he looked there was nothing there. He grasped it with his hands and found it empty, though the moss seemed to yield and the blades of grass to bend under his weight. It was like madness rising up into his brain, and he felt with a mingling of ideas distraught that he must spring to his feet and rush forth after God upon His awful way, crying to Him, entreating, blaspheming, forcing His attention, though it was through that incomprehensible whirl of space, and threading the unseen path from star to star.

But that wild impulse, like others, died away. A man, be he ever so rebellious, learns to know that the impossible hedges all his steps: and he sank back upon his tree, suppressing himself, binding himself into the submission which he knew at the bottom of his heart was his only hope. He felt no fatigue, notwithstanding his long journey and the dreadful disappointment at the end. None of those imperious needs of the flesh which fill up bo much of the time and distract so many of the thoughts of earth, moved him at all. He was free from everything, weariness and pain, and food and sleep and shelter. No thought of these things filled his mind. He did not even remark his exemption, so natural it seemed. He knew only the impossibility that girded him round and round.

He could not change the condition he had come to. No one could change it. Such as it was he had to endure it, to find the reason for it, to discover the compensation. To go mad, and dash his head against the confines of the world, and force a reversal from God of his sentence was impossible. Ah! he fell low again, with his face hidden in the softly rustling grass. The impossible girt him round with its circle of iron. Rebel, submit, content himself, go mad—these were all things that could be done. But reverse God's sentence, no! not if he had the strength of giants, not if he had the power of the whole world, upon a little sod of whose surface his wounded spirit lay.

Presently he had controlled himself, and was sitting again with his back against his tree and his head leaning on his hands, gazing out upon the night yet seeing nothing. And as he sat there all his life rolled out before him like a long panorama—his little life with all its broken scenes, of which he had never known the meaning. Often he had thought they had no meaning, as certainly they had no intention, no plan, but only a foolish impulse, a touch from some one here and there, who had pushed him unthinking to one side or another—not the straight way. "What a succession of accidents it was to end in this! no purpose in it— no meaning: all a foolish rush here or there haphazard, the affair of a moment, although fate had taken up the changeful threads and woven it into certainty for ever.

He saw himself a boy, hesitating with one foot on the upper slope, drawn back by errant fancy, by curiosity, by accident— always by accident!—then, finding the lower road the easier, the higher hard to begin, putting off till tomorrow and tomorrow— but no meaning in it, oh, no purpose, no settled plan of rebellion, no intention to offend. He went over this again and again, till he felt himself a deeply injured man.

Never had he meant any harm: he had even tried not to hurt any one else while he took his own pleasure, and he remembered the words that had been in the air following him wherever he went—nobody's enemy but his own. That was true, that was true! He had not tempted anyone, nor ever defied God, whom he never doubted, for whose name, had there been need for that, he felt that he could have died rather than have been apostate to it. The tears came into his eyes with this thought.

He had been wrong, very wrong: he had always known that, and hated it—yet done the same again: but never with any blasphemous meaning, never defying God, always knowing that the other way was the best, and hoping one day when his hour of pleasure was over——And what had he not paid already for his folly!—of all that he might have done in the other life, he had done nothing; of all that he might have attained, nothing. He had wrought no deliverance in the earth. It was all loss, loss, miserable failure: and hearts breaking, his own as well as the rest. But no purpose in it. He had never intended any day of his disobedience, from first to last, to deny his Maker or insult Him. Never, never! It was the one thing he was certain of amid all the doubts and changes, all the confusions in his life.

And, perhaps, this was how it happened, that when he had set out on his journey that morning—was it still the same morning, not twenty-four hours off, the morning of yesterday?—his heart had been so light. He had anticipated nothing but good. He had made sure that all the links of his old habits would be broken, that he would be lifted without effort of his to a better sphere. He had not said this to himself in words, nor, indeed, was he clear in his mind that he expected anything definite, or what it was he; expected—but only something good, happiness that would bring back all that he had missed in the time that was past.

Of one thing he had been very sure, that he would not err again: he had thought of the ways of men, so vain and melancholy, with a great relief in being done with them. And too glad and thankful he would have been to be done with them! to take his place in the home where he believed he was going, and his share of all the duty there, whatever it might be. But now—no home, no duty, no life for him. He was nothing—no man, a Voice, and no more.

How many times, in what an infinity of time and leisure, did he go over these thoughts? The night stole on, all glorious in quiet and repose—some of the wondrous lights above gliding out of sight as the world in which he was ascended and descended, going down into the night, and then with a half-sensible turn and thrill turning round to the day—and some came up into sight in the great round of the firmament that had been unseen before. Then a thrill ran through the wood, and voices began to awaken in the trees—little tongues of birds twittering, wakest thou, sleepest thou?—among the branches, before all their little world was roused and the great hymn began. The young man had not been prepared for that hymn, and it took him strangely in a surprise and passion of sympathy: he said to himself that he had not known there were birds here, and the moisture came to his eyes.

Then he tried to join with a note of his man's voice and startled them all, till he saw his mistake and tried instead a low and soft whistle, which they took for the note of a new comrade and burst forth again. The young man felt his spirit all subdued by that morning hymn, and tried to say his prayers in a great confusion, stammering, not knowing what words to use. The old prayers seemed so out of place. And then he remembered what all the people had said to him—God save you!—and repeated it with a faltering and a trembling—God save me! God save me! Not *give me this day my daily bread"* Was that old-fashioned? out of date? He trembled, and all his strength seemed to melt like water, and he said only, God save me! God save me! not knowing what he said.

All these strange emotions filled the time and the world about him, yet was his mind free to note the growth of the morning, coming fresh as it seemed out of the hand of God: the great valley came slowly to life and to the light, and the silence filled with sound as water wells up in a fountain. As for himself, he did not stir, but watched, not now despairing, nor even questioning, but still: a spectator wondering and looking on, hushed to the bottom of his heart, to see what all things did, having for himself no duty, no work; and feeling, so far as he felt at all, a nothingness, as if he were part of the mound on which he lay, where he fancied vaguely the grasses had begun already to grow over him.

What would they do, they who were other than he, they to whom everything belonged, though to him nothing belonged? He watched what they would do, what the morning would bring to them, with much eagerness in his heart; but the thickness of the trees and the brushwood, which was very close in that direction, shut out his view. And perhaps his curiosity was not so great as he thought, for his mind filled with many thoughts which revolved about himself, and presently he forgot all that was around him, and became, still a spectator indeed, but a spectator of his own being, and of those things which were going on in it.

And it seemed now that the thing most natural to him, who now possessed nothing of his own, was to go back upon the time when he possessed so much, love and companionship, and hope and the power of doing, and pleasure of every kind. His heart had grown sick of that life before he left it, and he had often felt it empty of everything, and that all was vanity. But now his heart returned to it, longing and wondering how he should ever have been so weary. Then he had been a man, but now was nothing, a Voice only, no more. And when he remembered how, in the smallest thing as in the greatest, he had chosen and taken his own way, and had pleasure in his will and independence, and had done this and that because he pleased, with no other reason for it, and that now there was nothing for him to choose, nothing to do—himself nothing, and all his ways nothing, a straw blown upon the wind!

In the other life there had been threatenings of punishment and torture, but never of this—and he thought to himself, though with a shiver, that the fire and the burning would have been more easy to bear, and perhaps a fierce encounter with the devils who tormented lost souls—a rising up against them, and call for justice out of the pit. To fight, to struggle, to resist, these fierce joys seemed to attract him, to revive his heart. But here there was nothing—neither good nor evil, neither use nor destruction. The Power which he had offended despised him, would not lay a finger on him, left him to rot and perish. No! worse by far than that, to go on in nothingness for ever and ever, to be and not to be, at one and the same time——

As these thoughts began to quicken and whirl through his brain—for though he began in quiet they gradually gained velocity and strength, till the rush was like the blazing of fire or the sweep of water in a flood, consuming and carrying him away—he became aware of an external sound which drove them away at once like a flight of birds careering out of sight. And looking up whence the sound came, he saw a movement as of someone searching amid the brushwood, and presently the thick branches were pushed aside and a face suddenly appeared, looking in to the opening in which the young man sat. It was a face which awakened in him at first a great throb of loving and kindness, being a countenance he had longed for for many a day, thinking that had it shone upon him on earth it might have saved him from all his follies: but along with this there came a rush of resentment into his mind which checked the cry of "Father!" which had come to his lips.

And he sat unmoving, allowing those eyes to search through the shade, though he knew that till he spoke he could never be found. It gave him a kind of angry pleasure to see the curves of anxiety round them, the eagerness of the look. Ah, he was sorry! but what was that when he had shut his door, when he had made no effort to bring the wanderer in. "My mother," said the young man, "would have been different: never would she have rested and left me outside;" but then there struck him like an arrow the thought of many moments in the past when he had said to himself, "If my father had been here!"

The other figure stood wistfully under the shadow of the tree—a man not old, full of the dignity and strength of life—

like one who knew much and had seen much, and whose hands were full of serious affairs. You might have been sure that he had left for a moment many things that called for his care to come here on this quest. His eyes were clear, shining with truth and justice and honour. Such eyes shine like stars even in the earth, and the eyes of the helpless understand and the poor cry to them. Nothing could disturb the heavenly quiet in them, the look of a soul at peace; but the curves of the eyelids were troubled, and the strain of anxious love was in his face. After a moment he said, the softness of his voice seeming to search through the silence as his eyes searched through the void, "My son! are you here, my son?"

The young man still paused a little, unwilling to relieve the other, yet not willing to lose the pleasure of revealing like a reproach his own abandoned state. "I am here," at last he said.

The father pushed through the trees and came to him quickly, and once more there came into the young man's mind the story of him who saw his son a long way off, and ran and fell upon his neck. Had he himself been as of old, this was what his father would have done—but how can a man embrace a voice? Yet the movement melted him, and made him rise to his feet to meet the other, though still with that unreasoning resentment in his mind, as though the door had been shut upon him, which was not shut, though he was unable to cross the threshold. There was authority and command, as of one used to rule, in the face of this man who was his father: but everything else was veiled with the great pity and love that was in his voice. "It was not thus we hoped to welcome you, my son, my son! "he cried, coming near, with his arms stretched out.

"How is it," cried the young man, "that I feel all my members from head to foot, and every faculty, and yet you see me not, touch me not? It makes a man mad to be, and yet not to be."

"God save you!" said the father, with tears. "God aid you! We know not how it is—nor can we do anything to help. It is for your purification, and because that which is must have its natural accomplishment. The sins of the flesh destroy the flesh, as is just. But you, you are still able to love, to think, to adore your God in His works. My son, accept and submit—and the better day will come."

"Submit! to be nothing!" said the young man. And then he cried bitterly, "Have I any choice? It is stronger than I am. I must submit, since you will not help, nor anyone. If my mother—" and here his voice broke. It was not that his mind felt all the bitterness with which he a poke: and he knew that no one could help him: yet having in him still all the humanness of a child, it gave him pleasure to wound one who might have helped him had things been otherwise, and to prove that he was abandoned and forsaken, he who hitherto had always been helped and forgiven. He looked for reproof, but none came.

His father, standing so near him, looking at him with such tender pity, said nothing but "My son!" and as these two words, whether from the Most High God or from the faltering lips of a man, enclose all of love that words can carry, what was there more that could be said?

"My son," he said, "it is not permitted here that we should discuss or that we should justify the ways of our God. Though you cry out against them, you know that they are just and very merciful, punishing not, but permitting that this which must be, should be accomplished in you. Yet not without hope. All that is of the spirit is yours as before. You can judge, you can understand, you can know. And above all you can love. What is greater than the mind and the heart! You are but naked of this frame, this body which is beloved and blessed because it is as the body of the Lord. But even for this not without hope. My child, the day will come when you will not think only of yourself. You will begin to think of Him who for us lived and died and lived again, and is for ever and ever. You will not consent to wipe out His name, but stand for Him among your fellows. And other things that are not you will fill your heart——"

"That are not me!—but who is so miserable as I?" cried the young man, covering his face with his hands.

The father paused for pity, looking at him with eyes that were full of tears. "It has not been given to you, oh my son," he said, "to pass by the Temple in the wood: yet still it may be. Heretofore you have done what you would, but not here: for here the will of God reigns alone, and man can contradict it no more. Yet from time to time," he said, "from time to time there is in this great Land of Suspense, as in all the worlds where the myriads of our brethren dwell, a day of grace, when the Lord Himself passes through. As he goes to visit the spheres of His dominions there is no place where He does not pass through, and hears every cry and heals every soul that comes to Him. Beloved be His name! Blessing and love breathe round about Him, and no one whom it touches can withstand that holy breath."

The young man looked up, and for a moment it seemed that the eyes of the heavenly man and of the spirit met, and that he who was in the body, that house of God not made with hands, saw him who was out of the body: for the eyes of the son were full of tears like those of the father, and he said with a broken voice, "So I have always been taught to think of Him. I am no stranger, my father, my father! I have sinned but yet I am of His house."

"God bless thee, my son," the father said.

4

After this there came weary mornings and evenings, or what he felt to be such, taking no account of them, yet rousing ever from his thoughts to feel the glory of the day and the sweetness of the night; for neither tempest nor trouble was there, and the other great worlds that are visible in the dark, rolling along their course in the world of space, became as the houses of friends opening their doors, showing ever another and another world of men, some like those others, white men and shining, some in hosts of vague faces like the shadow of crowds which he knew to be as himself: and the sensation of all those multitudes about who peopled what we call the sky, multitudes more than could be numbered, being all those who had lived and died on the earth since its wonderful story began, silenced and soothed him as we are soothed to know that others are as we are, treading the same path.

Many things were there which he could not understand. Sometimes it appeared to him that he could see the signs of great commotion in one of those neighbouring worlds, and shouting afar off, which came but as a murmur to his ears; and once it seemed to him that he saw a great procession coming forth, as if the King were making a visitation from one star to another, and a great shining bridge of light was thrown from planet to planet, by which He went and came.

It was a long time, however, before he saw that passing through of which his father had told him. Yet one day, in the rising of the morning, a note as of a silver bugle suddenly penetrated the spheres, and everything stirred with expectation, the very air and the birds in the trees, and everything that had life. He himself, drawn he could not tell how, almost against his will, by something that overmastered him, that made his breath come quick and his heart beat, hastened to the hill behind the wood, and placed himself on the highest point, where he could see all that went on below.

Fain would his feet have gone farther, fain would they have carried him to the level of the valley which he could see stretching far to the east and to the west: for already he saw the first of the great procession appearing, and all the inhabitants of the town which should have been his home pouring forth in bands, in glistening garments, with flowers and palms to strew upon the path of Him that was coming. The young man knew who it was that was coming, and his heart seemed to go forth out of his breast towards that great Traveller; but there was something in him that held back, and that made him cover his face in an anguish of shame.

For who was he that he should dare to look upon the Lord as He passed, blessing all men upon His way? Something came floating up to him upon the air like a waft of blessing: was it a call to him—the sound of his name? He knew not, but dug his hands into the roots of the grass, and dared not to lift up his eyes.

And in the meantime the great procession went on, while his heart, as it were, contended with him and cried, moaning and foaming and struggling, that he should go, while still he kept back ashamed, asking himself how he dared to look the Lord in the face, or hear Him blessing the people, and find there was no word for him? There he lay, feeling every member of his frame contend with him to get to the feet of the Lord, yet he holding back: until all the wonderful marching of the train had passed along and become bat an indistinct radiance upon the way, when he lifted his eyes and looked after them, and broke into a great weeping, thinking that still he saw One in the midst like none whom he had ever seen before, One to whom his heart went out, and whom he would have given heaven and earth to follow. But the moment was over, and he could now follow no more.

This happened but once, and it may not be supposed that he spent all the endless time he had at his disposal in so agitating a way. By moments these thoughts came upon him and possessed him: yet seldom, for he was seldom alone, his fellow-inhabitants, both of one side and the other, coming to him continually and occupying him with other plans and ideas. Many visitors he had from the town upon the hill, the dwelling of his kindred: but time fails us to tell of these, and all the tender words they said, and their pity and their love. Sometimes he would speak with them—sometimes, if other things were in his mind, would make no response nor let them know where to find him, preferring the society of those who were as himself, and were with him always, sometimes one, sometimes many, talking and making expeditions here and there.

They led him to many wonderful places, and showed him great sights, and many mysteries of the spheres became visible to him, and knowledge not permitted to earth, so that he could now solve many questions and find them simple, which, in the days of his former life, he could remember to have thought upon with awe as things that it was impossible to fathom. Thus he became wise, and more learned than the sages of the former world, and found a certain pleasure in these things which he learned and saw.

And it soon became apparent to him that many of his new companions held the belief that it was they who were the fortunate ones, being disencumbered of all hindrances and cares, with no duty or responsibility, but free to follow their pleasure, to go where they pleased, to enjoy knowledge and science and all the pleasures of the mind. There were some indeed who were like himself, and would not be comforted because of being no longer men but only voices, without identity, without substance, and incapable of uniting themselves to each other save with the loosest ties. They were not brethren for joy and for sorrow, for neither was there: they could not stand by each other, or pledge themselves to be true friends for death and life, for of that there was no need. They were but acquaintances, each lost in the invisible when they parted, walking and talking together as long as each pleased the other, with no fellowship of mutual labour, or the sharing of work trouble. Wherever one voice accosted another there was acquaintance, but nothing that went further; for they had no mutual hopes or fears or anything to link them more closely together.

And many of those who had been long in this condition had made a belief for themselves, and tried to teach it to the newcomers, that this was the perfect life; for was not all freedom among them, no bondage, not even that of staying in one place, or confining yourself to one kind of associates, no pain, no limitations, but each free to learn all he could, to perfect his genius, to increase his knowledge? Was not this enough for any soul? And some of them scoffed at the idea of any reckoning yet to come, pointing oat the unreasonableness of it, the impossibility of even recollecting, far less answering for, the events which had happened perhaps hundreds of years before, during the short time when one inhabited that foolish body, by some thought a disgusting thing, "a collection of sewers."

And if there was no great day to come, which the very oldest spirits said had been threatened thousands of years since in their recollection and had never come to anything, what came of the equally old and foolish traditions of a divine personage ruling over all? As for the men who lived in all those villages and towns, who thought they were better than their neighbours, whom with their restricted faculties they could not see, what were they but labourers still, with work and responsibilities upon them,— how much less happy than they who went free!

There were many, however, who were very uneasy when such conversation as this prevailed, and of these was the young man, whose thoughts were very fluctuating in respect to himself, but never on this point. "If you had seen, as I did," he would say, "the procession pass; and felt the heart tear out of you to go and fling itself at His feet." The elders laughed at such words, and bade him wait till he had seen it a hundred times, and without any feeling at all: but the others made a pause which betrayed some uneasy thoughts, and secretly were glad that they could not see each other's faces or betray the strange response in their own minds to what he said. One voice, a little tremulous, spoke, and said that these things which he called body and heart were an illusion, a distorted recollection of the chrysalis state in which their consciousness began; and another, that the body which had been mentioned was like a dog, and faithful, in its brutal way, to what it had been taught.

They were all together, that company of wandering souls, in a great tower which stood upon the extreme edge of the world in which they dwelt, and which was built upon the rock, standing out into the illimitable world of space as into the sea, with precipices immeasurable sinking down below, lower than thought could reach, while the great tower rose higher than thought, swung upon that giddy edge, and, though built of indestructible rock, quivering in the great sweep of the atmosphere more tremendous than on the highest mountain-top. There were all the secrets of the celestial world revealed, and all the movements of the stars, and the workings of the planetary system, and all the wonderful apparatus by which they were observed and noted. And many men of the other kind were in that place, were at work and busy, whose duty it was to watch over the balance and the trim of all these blazing worlds, and to see that each kept in its orbit, and all its attendant stars in their places, that there might be no wavering in the march of the heavens.

The wanderers went and came, through all these wonderful sights, and no one noted their coming and their going: for all the others were busy with their work and occupation, never slackening in their watch. And the young man, and some of his younger companions with him, looked upon them with envy, longing, but in vain, for some part or lot in the matter, and not to be thus unseen and without use in the great universe which seemed to go on without them though enclosing them in its great and mystic round. And as they gazed out from that watchtower one of the others pointed to a little darkling planet hanging upon the skirts of space, half seen amid the glory of the greater stars. "That speck," he said, "is what we called the Earth, and bragged of as something great and wonderful in our time. Look at it, contemptible! dim with smokes and fogs, and the breath of toiling men."

"Yet it was our mother," said the young man, "and there we lived, and there we died."

"If you call that, the throes of the birth-hour, living: and the journey hither dying—trifling incidents of our career." It was the same voice which had first accosted him when he arrived in that world which now spoke, and there were many with him, the elder spirits: while with the young man were many of the newcomers, still sore and wounded to feel themselves dropped out of everything, and humbled to feel that they were but voices, and no longer men and women as of old. And they turned with the young man as he stretched out his arms, leaning on the parapet, unto the wide and whirling world of space.

"Oh little earth!" he said, "full of vapour and smoke and the thoughts of men, rising up to heaven. At least we were something then, not nothing: and dear Love was there, and all the hopes of God."

"Why not now also—why not now?" said something, that was but a tremble and a quiver by his side. "Because," said the

71

elder spirit, "we need not these ancient visions. Free souls are we in the world of thought, despising all that is below, knowing nothing that is above. What do ye murmur at, ye crew? What would ye have, insatiate souls! The universe is ours to admire and to enjoy. We go where we will, we live as we will. You want these phalansteries, these houses on the hills! prisons and bondage. What need ye, beyond what we have?"

The young man leaned over, the great wind playing with him, as if it subdued its force not to carry away this light and petty scrap of being. And stretching out his hands, he said, "What we want—it is God and Love."

This he said, not so much out of his own heart, as because there was something of that in him which poets have. And being so, he knew that it was true. And the spirits round him murmured and sobbed and repeated, "God and Love." And the others were silent and said no word.

He went back afterwards to his living place in the wood, which he had come to love because it was near the home of those who were his; and a number of those wanderers went with him, talking of what he had said and of what was in their hearts. "We thought it was here we should have found Him," they said; "we thought that to come hither was all that was wanted. Tell us, thou! has He failed! We were never His servants, yet we believed that He would save us at the end."

"This is not the end—it is but the beginning," the young man said.

"And will He save us, will He save us—at the end?" The voices all together were like a blast of weeping wind.

Then the young man turned upon them and cried, "What are we? what are we? Let us perish if He will, but He be all in all"

This he said because of something that had come into him he knew not how: he felt it and obeyed its impulse, but knew not why. For still the first thing in his own heart, as in theirs, was to be saved—to be once more a man in His image, and no longer a wandering ghost unclothed. To be and to be seen of his fellows, and to speak with other men—even if it should bring pain and sorrow; for sorrow and pain are higher things than to be nothing, though at your ease and free as the wind.

He sat all that night through on his favourite mound, thinking and pondering within himself; and as he thought of all he had seen and the great Universe that had opened upon him at the height of that watch-tower, the wondrous circle of the stars, and all the mysteries of being which hung upon His breath who made them, he began to understand what he himself had said, and his eyes grew wet as when he had seen the Lord pass and his heart had fought with him to get free to fling itself in the Master's path. He had held it back then, but not now. He looked up to the skies above him, and saw those glorious worlds for ever moving in that sublime circle around the unseen throne; and this world in which he was swaying softly turning toward the highest Light.

And he said to himself what one had said thousands of years ago—a shepherd-boy under the starry heavens—"What is man that Thou art mindful of him?" And it seemed to him that he himself, about whom he had been spending so many thoughts, murmuring because of his losses, and convulsing all the quiet wood with longings after another state—he himself, who had been the centre of the world to him, was indeed nothing, no more than a drop of dew or a blade of grass in the great Universe of God. And he cried out, but softly, to the One that hears all things, "Be Thou! for ever and ever! and let me be nothing, for nothing I am. But Thou, be Thou supreme and all in all!"

5

In the glory of the morning the young man awoke, for even in the solemnity of his act, giving up everything, even hope if the Lord so willed, he had been surprised by that human sweetness of sleep which was not necessary to his state of being, yet delightful as the dew when it came, refreshing the soul. There was never anything but fair weather in that world, yet it seemed to him when he opened his eyes that no day had ever been so fair as this; and he asked himself, Was it perhaps Easter or some great holiday, of which he had lost count in the passing of the years and the days? Everything shone and glistened and sent forth breathings of delight under the shining of the sun, and the whole world was gay, and every drop of dew was like another perfect world of joy and blessing. He could not rest where he was on so happy a morning, but went forth and visited all the wood, as one visits one's friends when there is a great rejoicing to see that they are rejoicing too.

At last he found himself upon that pleasant knoll from which he could see the whole valley lying in a rapture under the joyful light; and he saw that there was much movement in the town near him, and once more faces at all the windows, and white figures looking over the parapet of the ascent where he had gone up, but had not been admitted. They were looking then for someone, someone who would be of his kindred; and it would be an event for him as well as for them, and perhaps even he would gain something—a companion, a friend. But he stopped these thoughts while they were in his mind, and tried to think what it would be to him if the newcomer was received where he had not been received, and came as a man in the body which God gave—to be among the others, not banished into nothingness.

For a long time he was in doubt, for no one came up the ascending path except those whom he knew, whose business it was, and he looked in vain for a stranger; and there began to rise in his heart a half hope half fear that he for whom they were all looking should come as he himself had done—invisible: a voice only, and no man. But lo! while he watched there came forth from the silver line of the great highway a single figure, of one who sang as he came—not in haste, but almost slowly, standing still and looking round him from time to time, as if the beauty of the world was so sweet to him that he could not go on, then turning his face towards the town and proceeding upon his way.

The young man put out his hands, and suddenly clasped them

together, and gazed in a suspense upon which his whole being seemed to hang. It was he, it was he! He had known the outline against the light while it was still but a shadow; he had recognised every footstep, and the turn of the head, and every line and every movement. Oh, how easy to know those who are one's own, however far off!—the familiar gesture, the little movement that is nothing, that a stranger would never see. He sprang up to rush down the hill and meet him, calling his name, and reflecting that even those at the gate, though they were there to welcome him, could not know him as he did. But his feet were as rooted to the soil, and he sank down again with a sob in his bosom, and a strong pang that seemed to rend him in twain. Not for him, not for him, was this delight, to meet his brother and fall upon his neck, and ask a thousand things of home!

To look on was all that was permitted to him. Why should he go, who was nothing, who could not take his hand, or show his face where those were who were the people of the Lord? He sank down upon his knoll, and covered his face with his hands, and heard the tumult of glad voices, and the welcomes and shouts of joy with which the wayfarer was taken in. He listened to every word, while the voices streamed up the steep ascent and the stranger was brought with rejoicing to his father's house. Was he glad too? Was there a pang in his heart, thinking that these welcomes had been prepared for him too, till it was discovered what he was? His voice, which was all he had, seemed choked in his throat. He could not speak, he could not cry. Vanity of vanities, nothing of nothingness! even his voice went from him, and he was no more than a thought.

Thus it was that he did not see, because he could not look: but heard every sound and the footsteps on the stones, and the shouts from above and the songs below. When they died away he felt in the bitterness of his heart as if he had been again shut out, as if it had been the day of his first refusal; but, more bitter still, shut out, and for ever shut out, and never again to bold converse with his kin and rejoice with them. For what should he rejoice? That he was shut out, and that the open gates were barred against him, and only him? But at least they might have let him share the joy that his brother had come and was more happy than he.

He sprang up and turned away, still covering his face, that he might not see those walls and towers into the heart of which the joy of welcome had swept, and were now but faintly heard—and went quickly away and hid himself in the heart of the wood: not in his accustomed place,—partly because his heart was sick of all that lived and breathed about him, and partly in perversity, that they might not find him when they came to search for him, as he knew they were sure to do. Ah! why was this? why was this, that an event which was so joyful should throw him back, back into the abyss from which his soul had escaped? He had escaped from himself; he had consented to be nothing, and to know that he was nothing—that it was not for him that heaven and earth should be disturbed, as if an atom was to make so much commotion for its own wellbeing; but now this atom once again blotted out both God and Heaven.

He struggled manfully in his heart to come to an end "I know," he said to himself, "that it was not fit that I who had sinned should be rewarded. I have come to little harm. I suffer nothing. I have the whole world left, more beautiful than heart had conceived. And once in a thousand years the Lord will pass by, and I shall see Him, even if it be no more. And they will all come to comfort me and talk to me, and not forget me—and my brother——" But he did not say my brother. He said a name; and at the sound of that name a great sobbing seized him, and the recollection of so many things that were past, and the home that never had been closed against him, and the love that had been his all his life. And then there came upon him suddenly another thought, at the coming of which his heart stood still, and strained upon all its chords as if it would sink away from him: and he fell upon his knees and lifted up his head and cried with an awful cry, "God! the mother, the mother!"

And the far distant earth seemed to roll up under his vision and open, and show a house desolate and a woman who sat within. And he who was himself desolate, yet within sight of the joy, forgot himself and everything that was his, to think of her. The mother, the mother! he flung himself on his face, he rose again to his feet, he stood and held out his hands to God, calling to him and repeating His name, "God! God!" and then "Father!" if, perhaps, that might reach him better. "For now she is alone," he cried. And then in his trouble he reproached the Most High God, and cried out, "Thou are not alone; Thou hast Thy Son."

And he forgot all his trouble and complaining, and became all one prayer, one cry for another, for one who was desolate and had now no child. Then straight like an arrow from a bow he went away, leaving his wood and the home of his kindred, and the valley, hastening he knew not where. For in his heart he felt that there must be some way, some place in which he could reach the footstool of the great Father, and pray to be forgotten and blotted out forever, rather than that she should be left to weep alone.

6

It was close to one of those great bridges by which the Lord passed to the other worlds around,—a bridge that rose light as the sea-foam, built of white marble and of alabaster, and every line marked with fine gold, which sometimes shone as if with jewels, and sometimes seemed to melt away in the clouds as if it had not been; bat whether it was built of the stones of the earth, or whether of vapours and cloud, flung itself boldly across the abyss, and bore the army and the attendants of the Lord whenever He came. And near to this place, where the broad highway seemed itself to march and continue along the bridge, there was a cathedral in the wood. The young man had heard of it from many. It was by this great temple that those others passed who preserved their being as men: and those who were but Voices moaned and lamented often, saying that they had missed the way.

But it was not for this, nor indeed knowingly at all, that the young man made his way here: but only in the height of his anguish, that he might find some holy place where God might listen to his cry.

The day had come towards its end, and the glory of the sunset lit up the white and glorious bridge which spanned the air and clouds, and disappeared into a mystery of the unseen such as no eyes of man could penetrate or trace, to the other side. The young man did not pause to look at this wonder of the world, but turned aside to the temple in the wood. His footsteps were drawn towards it, he scarcely knew how: but until he saw it he knew not that this was that Temple of which he had heard.

But of that great cathedral what tongue can tell? for it was not built by hands, nor were its arches created and its pillars put into their place by any workman, whether mortal or immortal; for where it stood it grew with its feet in the living soil, and every column a living tree straight and noble, and the vault above woven of foliage, which changed and moved with every breath, and let in the changings of the light, living too, and moving ceaselessly from east to west through all the brilliant hours of the day; and during the night a great vision of stars was in the place where the lights should be, like silver lamps upon the altar, and in the lofty fragrant roof, where the leaves trembled and glistened: and its floor was made of living flowers throwing up their fragrance, which was sweeter than incense: and day by day it lived and grew, pushing higher and higher towards the skies, straight and tall and strong, reaching upward like the living thing it was.

The sunset was still upon the western front, and streaming upon the great doorway, which was ever open, and wreathed in every climbing thing that blows, the long branches clinging one to another to find a place, and the flowers thickening and clustering upon the holy arch in an eagerness to be there: and there was a sound within of noble music and choirs unseen, which sang their hymns of praise to God both through the night and in the day.

The young man went in without a pause, thinking neither of the beautiful place nor of the strangeness of it, but only that it was the temple not made with hands, where the Lord loved to pause on his journey, and where the great Father came to commune with His Son, and which the ever-living Spirit had chosen for a place to dwell in: although not in this place or any other was that great Presence bound, but might be called upon by every path, and even in the common highroad where all men went to and fro. The young man did not remember except in a confusion what it was he had heard of the cathedral in the wood, nor knew he why he came, except with a thought that it was the holiest place; and now there was no thought in his mind but only one, to call upon every Holy name,—that of the Father, who surely knew if there was any knowledge, what love was in the heart of a mother: and of the Son, who knew what sorrow was, and to be forsaken, above all men that ever lived: and of Him whose name was the Comforter.

He flung himself upon the floor, and in the great silence—for the music rolled away and was heard no more when he came in—called and called upon these Holy names. "You who are together," he cried, "leave not her alone!" And in the anguish of his prayer he was bold, and reminded the Lord that this was the image He had chosen of a love that never failed. "Can a woman forget her child, that she should not have compassion on the son of her womb." And should He above, who knows best, He who loves most, leave the woman to be alone, alone!

Presently words failed him, and he only knew that he held her as it seemed up in his arms to God. And slowly the living day died out of the cathedral in the wood, and the living night came in and shone through the tracery of the vault above, and the stars in their places lit up the living walls, and everything breathed a silent worship up to the heavens, the flowers with their odours and the leaves with their greenness: and every noble tree stood up and called upon the name of the Lord. And the swallow and the sparrow, God's little children, and many a singing bird weary with the joy and the song of day, nestled among the branches and went to sleep in His care. And over the young man there came a great calm instead of the anguish of that prayer, and as the soft hours stole on to midnight, and the great stillness wrapt him round and round, fatigue and peace stole over him, and he fell asleep in the middle of his prayer among the flowers.

There were those about who were coming and going for ever, faint with longing and desire to enter the Temple of the wood. But as in that world there are no bolts and bars, but only an unseen bond upon the feet and upon the heart of a man, so that he cannot go where he would until it is his hour—all that these longing souls could do was to linger and gaze and await the moment when they might enter. And many were always gathered about the door, gazing in where they so fain would be. And they saw the young man lying upon the flowers, and wondered at him that he should sleep in so blessed a place.

And some said, "God forbid that I should sleep if I were there"; and some, "God save him though he sleeps!" And one who stood almost upon the threshold, and knew that he should be one of the first to pass, hushed these voices and said low, "It is the beginning of the mystery and of the new birth." And a murmur arose very softly, and a faint crying, "What did he do to attain the heavenly gift?" But the soul upon the threshold hushed them all: "Sleep came upon him while he prayed. Be still and see the goodness of the Lord: he prayed not for himself but for another."

The night had gone while these voices went and came: and he that spoke last caught with his words the little morning breeze which at that moment sprang up with the first glimmer of the sun; and all around the living walls of that house not made with hands it breathed back the words, "not for himself but another," like a song: and blowing in at the wide door—for nothing can stop the winds of God, which make all the world pure—breathed over the young man where he lay.

And in his sleep he felt the soft touch upon his forehead like the hand of his mother, and waking, having prayed for her till he slept, prayed again when he was roused, with a soft cry of "God save her!" while still he was but half awake. And in the waking he lay a long time forgetting where he was. And he saw something white and wonderful stretched upon the flowers where he lay, and knew not what it was. Then slowly as he came to himself he remembered everything, and saw from the east the first arrow of gold that told of the sunrise, and in the great peace of his heart he prayed no more, for it seemed to him that his prayer was heard. So sweet was that calm that he lay and did not move, recollecting himself, and saying to himself that it was good to be here, and listening to the birds, which were all awake and already singing the morning song which he had learned to know so well. And some descended swift through the air, and perched close to him upon the steps of the altar and on the lower pinnacles, and sang as if to burst their throats in a tumult and outcry of joy. Blessed creatures, little children of God! he followed with a smile one that came almost within reach of his hand.

And then his eyes were drawn again to something white and wonderful which lay as he lay upon the floor. Someone, he said to himself, had laid an angel's mantle over him as he slept; and there came a rush of soft tears to his eyes, and his heart melted with gratitude and kindness. But when he moved it moved with him, and putting out an astonished hand, he suddenly touched and knew that this was he—no mantle even of an angel, but the body of a man. Oh, Holy House not made with hands! oh, Temple of the Lord!—for this was he.

And a voice said:

"He hath accepted that which was allotted to him, and acknowledged that it was just; therefore there is now given to him the higher state.

"He hath acknowledged his Lord; wherefore his Lord doth not forget to acknowledge him.

"And here he hath come to seek the face of God, not for himself but for another; wherefore he goes hence blessed, with the blessing he has not sought."

The young man had not gone back half the way to the city of his fathers when he was met by a shining company, all radiant in their best apparel, with music and with song; and in front of all was his brother, whose arrival he had beheld before he set forth. And lo! while all men looked and held their breath, they stood together, two fair young men—fairer than they had been on earth, or than any man is to whom has not been given the House not made with hands. And together they went back to their father's house to do the work which God might give them, whether it was humble or whether it was great, until the day should come when the books shall be opened and all the worlds stand together in their armies and battalions before the face of the Lord. But of that day knoweth no man, not even the Son, but the Father—as was told us by our Lord.

As for the prayer which he made, and which was answered in a way he asked not, it is still unfulfilled: yet they know it is not forgotten, for nothing is forgotten before God.

The Complete Little Pilgrim Series

1: A LITTLE PILGRIM IN THE UNSEEN

She had been talking of dying only the evening before, with a friend, and had described her own sensations after a long illness when she had been at the point of death. "I suppose," she said, "that I was as nearly gone as anyone ever was to come back again. There was no pain in it, only a sense of sinking down, down—through the bed as if nothing could hold me or give me support enough—but no pain." And then they had spoken of another friend in the same circumstances, who also had come back from the very verge, and who described her sensations as those of one floating upon a summer sea without pain or suffering, in a lovely nook of the Mediterranean, blue as the sky.

These soft and soothing images of the passage which all men dread had been talked over with low voices, yet with smiles and a grateful sense that "the warm precincts of the cheerful day" were once more familiar to both. And very cheerfully she went to rest that night, talking of what was to be done on the morrow, and fell asleep sweetly in her little room, with its shaded light and curtained window, and little pictures on the dim walls. All was quiet in the house: soft breathing of the sleepers, soft murmuring of the spring wind outside, a wintry moon very clear and full in the skies, a little town all hushed and quiet, everything lying defenceless, unconscious, in the safe keeping of God.

How soon she woke no one can tell. She woke and lay quite still, half roused, half hushed, in that soft languor that attends a happy waking. She was happy always, in the peace of a heart that was humble and faithful and pure, but yet had been used to wake to a consciousness of little pains and troubles, such as even to her meekness were sometimes hard to bear. But on this morning there were none of these. She lay in a kind of hush of happiness and ease, not caring to make any further movement, lingering over the sweet sensation of that waking. She had no desire to move nor to break the spell of the silence and peace. It was still very early, she supposed, and probably it might be hours yet before anyone came to call her. It might even be that she should sleep again. She had no wish to move, she lay at such luxurious ease and calm.

But by and by, as she came to full possession of her waking senses, it appeared to her that there was some change in the atmosphere, in the scene. There began to steal into the air about her, the soft dawn as of a summer morning, the lovely blueness of the first opening of daylight before the sun. It could not be the light of the moon, which she had seen before she went to bed; and all was so still, that it could not be the bustling, wintry day which comes at that time of the year late, to find the world awake before it. This was different; it was like the summer dawn, a soft suffusion of light growing every moment.

And by and by it occurred to her that she was not in the little room where she had lain down. There were no dim walls or roof, her little pictures were all gone, the curtains at her window. The discovery gave her no uneasiness in that delightful calm. She lay still to think of it all, to wonder, yet undisturbed. It half amused her that these things should be changed, but did not rouse her yet with any shock of alteration. The light grew fuller and fuller round, growing into day, clearing her eyes from the sweet mist of the first waking. Then she raised herself upon her arm. She was not in her room, she was in no scene she knew. Indeed it was scarcely a scene at all, nothing but light, so soft and lovely, that it soothed and caressed her eyes.

She thought all at once of a summer morning when she was a child, when she had woke in the deep night which yet was day, early, so early that the birds were scarcely astir, and had risen up with a delicious sense of daring and of being all alone in the mystery of the sunrise, in the unawakened world which lay at her feet to be explored, as if she were Eve just entering upon Eden. It was curious how all those childish sensations, long forgotten, came back to her as she found herself so unexpectedly out of her sleep in the open air and light. In the recollection of that lovely hour, with a smile at herself, so different as she now knew herself to be, she was moved to rise and look a little more closely about her, and see where she was.

When I call her a little Pilgrim, I do not mean that she was a child; on the contrary, she was not even young. She was little by nature, with as little flesh and blood as was consistent with mortal life; and she was one of those who are always little for love. The tongue found diminutives for her, the heart kept her in a perpetual youth. She was so modest and so gentle, that she always came last, so long as there was anyone whom she could put before her. But this little body, and the soul which was not little, and the heart which was big and great, had known all the round of sorrows that fill a woman's life, without knowing any of its warmer blessings. She had nursed the sick, she had entertained the weary, she had consoled the dying. She had gone about the world, which had no prize or recompense for her, with a smile. Her little presence had been always bright. She was not clever; you might have said she had no mind at all; but so wise and right and tender a heart, that it was as good as genius. This is to let you know what this little Pilgrim had been.

She rose up, and it was strange how like she felt to the child she remembered in that still summer morning so many years ago. Her little body, which had been worn and racked with pain, felt as light and unconscious of itself as then. She took her first step forward with the same sense of pleasure, yet of awe, suppressed delight and daring and wild adventure, yet perfect safety. But then the recollection of the little room in which she had fallen asleep came quickly, strangely over her, confusing her mind. "I must be dreaming, I suppose," she said to herself, regretfully; for it was all so sweet that she wished it to be true.

Her movement called her attention to herself, and she found that she was dressed, not in her nightdress, as she had lain down, but in a dress she did not know. She paused for a moment to look at it, and wonder. She had never seen it before; she did not make out how it was made, or what stuff it was, but it fell so pleasantly about her, it was so soft and light, that in her confused state she abandoned that subject with only an additional sense of pleasure. And now the atmosphere became more distinct to her. She saw that under her feet was a greenness as of close velvet turf, both cool and warm, cool and soft to touch, but with no damp in it, as might have been at that early hour, and with flowers showing here and there. She stood looking round her, not able to identify the landscape because she was still confused a little, and then walked softly on, all the time afraid lest she should awake and lose the sweetness of it all, and the sense of rest and happiness. She felt so light, so airy, as if she could skim across the field like any child. It was bliss enough to breathe and move, with every organ so free.

After more than fifty years of hard service in the world, to feel like this, even in a dream! She smiled to herself at her own pleasure; and then once more, yet more potently, there came back upon her the appearance of her room in which she had fallen asleep. How had she got from there to here? Had she been carried away in her sleep, or was it only a dream, and would she by and by find herself between the four dim walls again? Then this shadow of recollection faded away once more, and she moved forward, walking in a soft rapture over the delicious turf. Presently she came to a little mound, upon which she paused to look about her. Every moment she saw a little farther: blue hills far away, extending in long, sweet distance, an indefinite landscape, but fair and vast, so that there could be seen no end to it, not even the line of the horizon,—save at one side, where there seemed to be a great shadowy gateway, and something dim beyond.

She turned from the brightness to look at this, and when she had looked for some time, she saw, what pleased her still more, though she had been so happy before, people coming in. They were too far off for her to see clearly, but many came each apart, one figure only at a time. To watch them amused her in the delightful leisure of her mind. Who were they? she wondered; but no doubt soon some of them would come this way, and she would see. Then suddenly she seemed to hear, as if in answer to her question, someone say, "Those who are coming in are the people who have died on earth."

"Died!" she said to herself aloud, with a wondering sense of the inappropriateness of the word which almost came the length of laughter. In this sweet air, with such a sense of life about, to suggest such an idea was almost ludicrous. She was so occupied with this, that she did not look round to see who the speaker might be. She thought it over, amused, but with some new confusion of the mind. Then she said, "Perhaps I have died too," with a laugh to herself at the absurdity of the thought.

"Yes," said the other voice, echoing that gentle laugh of hers, "you have died too."

She turned round, and saw another standing by her, a woman, younger and fairer, and more stately than herself, but of so sweet a countenance that our little Pilgrim felt no shyness, but recognised a friend at once. She was more occupied looking at this new face, and feeling herself at once so much happier (though she had been so happy before) in finding a companion who would tell her what everything was, than in considering what these words might mean. But just then once more the recollection of the four walls, with their little pictures hanging, and the window with its curtains drawn, seemed to come round her for a moment, so that her whole soul was in a confusion. And as this vision slowly faded away (though she could not tell which was the vision, the darkened room or this lovely light), her attention came back to the words at which she had laughed, and at which the other had laughed as she repeated them. Died?—was it possible that this could be the meaning of it all? "Died?" she said, looking with wonder in her companion's face, which smiled back to her.

"But do you mean—You cannot mean—I have never been so well: I am so strong: I have no trouble—anywhere: I am full of life."

The other nodded her beautiful head with a more beautiful smile, and the little Pilgrim burst out in a great cry of joy, and said,—"Is this all? Is it over?—Is it all over? Is it possible that this can be all?"

"Were you afraid of it?" the other said. There was a little agitation for the moment in her heart. She was so glad, so relieved and thankful, that it took away her breath. She could not get over the wonder of it.

"To think one should look forward to it so long, and wonder, and be even unhappy trying to divine what it will be—and this all!"

"Ah, but the angel was very gentle with you," said the young woman; "you were so tender and worn, that he only smiled and took you sleeping. There are other ways. But it is always wonderful to think it is over, as you say."

The little Pilgrim could do nothing but talk of it, as one does after a very great event. "Are you sure, quite sure, it is so?" she said. "It would be dreadful to find it only a dream, to go to sleep again, and wake up—there—" This thought troubled her for a moment. The vision of the bedchamber came back; but this time she felt it was only a vision. "Were you afraid too?" she said, in a low voice.

"I never thought of it at all," the beautiful stranger said; "I did not think it would come to me. But I was very sorry for the others to whom it came, and grudged that they should lose the beautiful earth, and life, and all that was so sweet."

"My dear!" cried the Pilgrim, as if she had never died, "oh, but this is far sweeter! And the heart is so light, and it is, happiness only to breathe. Is it heaven here? It must be heaven."

"I do not know if it is heaven. We have so many things to learn. They cannot tell you everything at once," said the beautiful lady. "I have seen some of the people I was sorry for, and when I told them, we laughed—as you and I laughed just now—for pleasure."

"That makes me think" said the little Pilgrim; "if I have died, as you say—which is so strange, and me so living—if I have died, they will have found it out. The house will be all dark, and they will be breaking their hearts. Oh, how could I forget them in my selfishness, and be happy! I so light-hearted, while they—"

She sat down hastily, and covered her face with her hands and wept. The other looked at her for a moment, then kissed her for comfort, and cried too. The two happy creatures sat there weeping together, thinking of those they had left behind, with an exquisite grief which was not unhappiness, which was sweet with love and pity. "And oh," said the little Pilgrim, "what can we do to tell them not to grieve? Cannot you send? cannot you speak? cannot one go to tell them?"

The heavenly stranger shook her head.

"It is not well, they all say. Sometimes one has been permitted; but they do not know you," she said, with a pitiful look in her sweet eyes. "My mother told me that her heart was so sick for me, she was allowed to go; and she went and stood by me, and spoke to me, and I did not know her. She came back so sad and sorry, that they took her at once to our Father; and there, you know, she found that it was all well. All is well when you are there."

"Ah," said the little Pilgrim, "I have been thinking of other things. Of how happy I was, and of *them*; but never of the Father,—just as if I had not died."

The other smiled upon her with a wonderful smile.

"Do you think he will be offended—our Father—as if he were one of us?" she said.

And then the little Pilgrim, in her sudden grief to have forgotten him, became conscious of a new rapture unexplainable in words. She felt his understanding to envelop her little spirit with a soft and clear penetration, and that nothing she did or said could ever be misconceived more. "Will you take me to him?" she said, trembling yet glad, clasping her hands. And once again the other shook her head.

89

"They will take us both when it is time," she said: "we do not go at our own will. But I have seen our Brother—"

"Oh, take me to him!" the little Pilgrim cried. "Let me see his face! I have so many things to say to him. I want to ask him—Oh, take me to where I can see his face!"

And then once again the heavenly lady smiled.

"I have seen him," she said. "He is always about—now here, now there. He will come and see you, perhaps when you are not thinking. But when he pleases. We do not think here of what we will—"

The little Pilgrim sat very still, wondering at all this. She had thought when a soul left the earth that it went at once to God, and thought of nothing more, except worship and singing of praises. But this was different from her thoughts. She sat and pondered and wondered. She was baffled at many points. She was not changed, as she expected, but so much like herself; still—still perplexed, and feeling herself foolish; not understanding: toiling after a something which she could not grasp. The only difference was that it was no trouble to her now. She smiled at herself and at her dullness, feeling sure that by and by she would understand.

"And don't you wonder too?" she said to her companion, which was a speech such as she used to make upon the earth, when people thought her little remarks disjointed, and did not always see the connection of them. But her friend of heaven knew what she meant.

"I do nothing but wonder," she said, "for it is all so natural, not what we thought."

"Is it long since you have been here?" the Pilgrim said.

"I came before you; but how long or how short I cannot tell, for that is not how we count. We count only by what happens to us. And nothing yet has happened to me, except that I have seen our Brother. My mother sees him always. That means she has lived here a long time, and well—"

"Is it possible to live ill—in heaven?" The little Pilgrim's eyes grew large, as if they were going to have tears in them, and a little shadow seemed to come over her. But the other laughed softly, and restored all her confidence.

"I have told you I do not know if it is heaven or not. No one does ill, but some do little, and some do much, just as it used to be. Do you remember in Dante there was a lazy spirit that stayed about the gates and never got farther? But perhaps you never read that."

"I was not clever," said the little Pilgrim, wistfully; "no, I never read it. I wish I had known more."

Upon which the beautiful lady kissed her again to give her courage, and said,—

"It does not matter at all. It all comes to you, whether you have known it or not."

"Then your mother came here long ago?" said the Pilgrim. "Ah, then I shall see my mother too."

"Oh, very soon, as soon as she can come; but there are so many things to do. Sometimes we can go and meet those who are coming; but it is not always so. I remember that she had a message. She could not leave her business, you may be sure, or she would have been here."

"Then you know my mother? Oh, and my dearest father too?"

"We all know each other," the lady said with a smile.

"And you? did you come to meet me—only out of kindness, though I do not know you?" the little Pilgrim said.

"I am nothing but an idler," said the beautiful lady, "making acquaintance. I am of little use as yet. I was very hard worked before I came here, and they think it well that we should sit in the sun and take a little rest, and find things out."

Then the little Pilgrim sat still and mused, and felt in her heart that she had found many things out. What she had heard had been wonderful, and it was more wonderful still to be sitting here all alone, save for this lady, yet so happy and at ease. She wanted to sing, she was so happy; but remembered that she was old; and had lost her voice; and then remembered again that she was no longer old, and perhaps had found it again. And then it occurred to her to remember how she had learned to sing, and how beautiful her sister's voice was, and how heavenly to hear her,—which made her remember that this dear sister would be weeping, not singing, down where she had come from; and immediately the tears stood in her eyes.

"Oh," she said, "I never thought we should cry when we came here. I thought there were no tears in heaven."

"Did you think, then, that we were all turned into stone?" cried the beautiful lady. "It says God shall wipe away all tears from our faces, which is not like saying there are to be no tears."

Upon which the little Pilgrim, glad that it was permitted to be sorry, though she was so happy, allowed herself to think upon the place she had so lately left. And she seemed to see her little room again, with all the pictures hanging as she had left them, and the house darkened, and the dear faces she knew all sad and troubled, and to hear them saying over to each other all the little careless words she had said as if they were out of the Scriptures, and crying if anyone but mentioned her name, and putting on crape and black dresses, and lamenting as if that which had happened was something very terrible. She cried at this, and yet felt half inclined to laugh, but would not, because it would be disrespectful to those she loved. One thing did not occur to her, and that was, that they would be carrying her body, which she had left behind her, away to the grave. She did not think of this, because she was not aware of the loss, and felt far too much herself to think that there was another part of her being buried in the ground. From this she was aroused by her companion asking her a question.

"Have you left many there?" she said.

"No one," said the little Pilgrim, "to whom I was the first on earth; but they loved me all the same; and if I could only, only let them know—"

"But I left one to whom I was the first on earth," said the other, with tears in her beautiful eyes; "and oh, how glad I should be to be less happy if he might be less sad!"

"And you cannot go? you cannot go to him and tell him?

Oh, I wish," cried the little Pilgrim; but then she paused, for the wish died all away in her heart into a tender love for this poor, sorrowful man whom she did not know. This gave her the sweetest pang she had ever felt, for she knew that all was well, and yet was so sorry, and would have willingly given up her happiness for his. All this the lady read in her eyes or her heart, and loved her for it; and they took hands and were silent together, thinking of those they had left, as we upon earth think of those who have gone from us, but only with far more understanding and far greater love. "And have you never been able to do anything for him?" our Pilgrim said.

Then the beautiful lady's face flushed all over with the most heavenly warmth and light. Her smile ran over like the bursting out of the sun.

"Oh, I will tell you," she said. "There was a moment when he was very sad and perplexed, not knowing what to think; there was something he could not understand. Nor could I understand, nor did I know what it was, until it was said to me, 'You may go and tell him.' And I went in the early morning before he was awake, and kissed him, and said it in his ear. He woke up in a moment, and understood, and everything was clear to him. Afterward I heard him say, 'It is true that the night brings counsel. I had been troubled and distressed all day long, but in the morning it was quite clear to me.' And the other answered, 'Your brain was refreshed, and that made your judgment clear.' But they never knew it was I! That was a great delight. The dear souls, they are so foolish," she cried, with the sweetest laughter, that ran into tears. "One cries because one is so happy; it is just a silly old habit," she said.

"And you were not grieved—it did not hurt you—that he did not know—"

"Oh, not then, not then! I did not go to him for that. When you have been here a little longer, you will see the difference. When you go for yourself, out of impatience, because it still seems to you that you must know best, and they don't know you, then it strikes to your heart; but when you go to help them,—ah," she cried, "when he comes, how much I shall have to tell him! 'You thought it was sleep, when it was I; when you woke so fresh and clear, it was I that kissed you; you thought it your duty to me to be sad afterward, and were angry with yourself because you had wronged me of the first thoughts of your waking—when it was all me, all through!'"

"I begin to understand," said the little Pilgrim. "But why should they not see us, and why should not we tell them? It would seem so natural. If they saw us, it would make them so happy and so sure."

Upon this the lady shook her head.

"The worst of it is not that they are not sure, it is the parting. If this makes us sorry here, how can they escape the sorrow of it, even if they saw us?—for we must be parted. We cannot go back to live with them, or why should we have died? And then we must all live our lives, they in their way, we in ours. We must not weigh them down, but only help them when it is seen that there is need for it. All this we shall know better by and by."

"You make it so clear, and your face is so bright," said our little Pilgrim gratefully, "you must have known a great deal, and understood even when you were in the world."

"I was as foolish as I could be," said the other, with her laugh that was as sweet as music; "yet thought I knew, and they thought I knew. But all that does not matter now."

"I think it matters, for look how much you have showed me. But tell me one thing more: how was it said to you that you must go and tell him? Was it someone who spoke? Was it—"

Her face grew so bright that all the past brightness was as a dull sky to this. It gave out such a light of happiness, that the little Pilgrim was dazzled.

"I was wandering about," she said, "to see this new place. My mother had come back between two errands she had, and had come to see me and tell me everything; and I was straying about, wondering what I was to do, when suddenly I saw someone coming along, as it might be now—"

She paused and looked up, and the little Pilgrim looked up

too, with her heart beating, but there was no one. Then she gave a little sigh, and turned and listened again.

"I had not been looking for him, or thinking. You know my mind is too light; I am pleased with whatever is before me. And I was so curious, for my mother had told me many things; when suddenly I caught sight of him passing by. He was going on, and when I saw this a panic seized me, lest he should pass and say nothing. I do not know what I did. I flung myself upon his robe, and got hold of it,—or at least I think so. I was in such an agony lest he should pass and never notice me. But that was my folly. He pass! As if that could be!"

"And what did he say to you?" cried the little Pilgrim, her heart almost aching, it beat so high with sympathy and expectation.

The lady looked at her for a little without saying anything.

"I cannot tell you," she said, "any more than I can tell if this is heaven. It is a mystery. When you see him you will know. It will be all you have ever hoped for, and more besides, for he understands everything. He knows what is in our hearts about those we have left, and why he sent for us before them. There is no need to tell him anything, he knows. He will come when it is time; and after you have seen him you will know what to do."

Then the beautiful lady turned her eyes toward the gate, and while the little Pilgrim was still gazing, disappeared from her, and went to comfort some other stranger. They were dear friends always, and met often, but not again in the same way.

When she was thus left alone again, the little Pilgrim sat still upon the grassy mound, quite tranquil and happy, without wishing to move. There was such a sense of well-being in her, that she liked to sit there and look about her, and breathe the delightful air, like the air of a summer morning, without wishing for anything.

"How idle I am!" she said to herself, in the very words she had often used before she died; but then she was idle from weakness, and now from happiness. She wanted for nothing. To be alive was so sweet. There was a great deal to think about in what she had heard, but she did not even think about that, only resigned herself to the delight of sitting there in the sweet air and being happy. Many people were coming and going, and they all knew her, and smiled upon her, and those who were at a distance would wave their hands. This did not surprise her at all, for though she was a stranger, she too felt that she knew them all; but that they should be so kind was a delight to her which words could not tell. She sat and mused very sweetly about all that had been told her, and wondered whether she too might go sometimes, and with a kiss and a whisper clear up something that was dark in the mind of someone who loved her. "I that never was clever!" she said to herself, with a smile. And chiefly she thought of a friend whom she loved, who was often in great perplexity, and did not know how to guide herself amid the difficulties of the world.

The little Pilgrim half laughed with delight, and then half cried with longing to go, as the beautiful lady had done, and make something clear that had been dark before, to this friend. As she was thinking what a pleasure it would be, someone came up to her, crossing over the flowery greenness, leaving the path on purpose. This was a being younger than the lady who had spoken to her before, with flowing hair all crisped with touches of sunshine, and a dress all white and soft, like the feathers of a white dove. There was something in her face different from that of the other, by which the little Pilgrim knew somehow, without knowing how, that she had come here as a child, and grown up in this celestial place. She was tall and fair, and came along with so musical a motion, as if her foot scarcely touched the ground, that she might have had wings: and the little Pilgrim indeed was not sure as she watched, whether it might not perhaps be an angel; for she knew that there were angels among the blessed people who were coming and going about, but had not been able yet to find one out. She knew that this newcomer was coming to her, and turned towards her with a smile and a throb at her heart of expectation. But when the heavenly maiden drew nearer, her face, though it was so fair, looked to the Pilgrim like another face, which she had known very well,—indeed, like the homely and troubled face of the friend of whom she had been thinking. And so she smiled all the more, and held out her hands and said, "I am sure I know you;" upon which the other kissed her and said, "We all know each other; but I have seen you often before you came here," and knelt down by her, among the flowers that were growing, just in front of some tall lilies that grew over her, and made a lovely canopy over her head. There was something in her face that was like a child: her mouth so soft, as if it had never spoken anything but heavenly words, her eyes brown and golden, as if they were filled with light. She took the little Pilgrim's hands in hers, and held them and smoothed them between her own. These hands had been very thin and worn before, but now, when the Pilgrim looked at them, she saw that they became softer and whiter every moment with the touch of this immortal youth.

"I knew you were coming," said the maiden; "when my mother has wanted me I have seen you there. And you were thinking of her now that was how I found you."

"Do you know, then, what one thinks?" said the little Pilgrim, with wondering eyes.

"It is in the air; and when it concerns us it comes to us like the breeze. But we who are the children here, we feel it more quickly than you."

"Are you a child?" said the little Pilgrim, "or are you an angel? Sometimes you are like a child; but then your face shines, and you are like—You must have some name for it here; there is nothing among the words I know." And then she paused a little, still looking at her, and cried, "Oh, if she could but see you, little Margaret! That would do her most good of all."

Then the maiden Margaret shook her lovely head. "What does her most good is the will of the Father," she said.

At this the little Pilgrim felt once more that thrill of expectation and awe. "Oh, child, you have seen him?" she cried.

And the other smiled. "Have you forgotten who they are that always behold his face? We have never had any fear or trembling.

97

We are not angels, and there is no other name; we are the children. There is something given to us beyond the others. We have had no other home."

"Oh, tell me, tell me!" the little Pilgrim cried.

Upon this Margaret kissed her, putting her soft cheek against hers, and said; "It is a mystery; it cannot be put into words; in your time you will know."

"When you touch me you change me, and I grow like you," the Pilgrim said. "Ah, if she could see us together, you and me! And will you go to her soon again? And do you see them always, what they are doing? and take care of them?"

"It is our Father who takes cares of them, and our Lord who is our Brother. I do his errands when I am able. Sometimes he will let me go, sometimes another, according as it is best. Who am I that I should take care of them? I serve them when I may."

"But you do not forget them?" the Pilgrim said, with wistful eyes.

"We love them always," said Margaret. She was more still than the lady who had first spoken with the Pilgrim. Her countenance was full of a heavenly calm. It had never known passion nor anguish. Sometimes there was in it a far-seeing look of vision, sometimes the simplicity of a child. "But what are we in comparison? For he loves them more than we do. When he keeps us from them, it is for love. We must each live our own life."

"But it is hard for them sometimes," said the little Pilgrim, who could not withdraw her thoughts from those she had left.

"They are never forsaken," said the angel maiden.

"But oh! there are worse things than sorrow," the little Pilgrim said; "there is wrong, there is evil, Margaret. Will not he send you to step in before them, to save them from wrong?"

"It is not for us to judge," said the young Margaret, with eyes full of heavenly wisdom; "our Brother has it all in his hand. We do not read their hearts, like him. Sometimes you are permitted to see the battle—"

The little Pilgrim covered her eyes with her hands. "I could not—I could not; unless I knew they were to win the day!"

"They will win the day in the end. But sometimes, when it was being lost, I have seen in his face a something—I cannot tell—more love than before. Something that seemed to say, 'My child, my child, would that I could do it for thee, my child!'"

"Oh! that is what I have always felt," cried the Pilgrim, clasping her hands; her eyes were dim, her heart for a moment almost forgot its blessedness. "But he could; oh, little Margaret, he could! You have forgotten, 'Lord; if thou wilt thou canst—'"

The child of heaven looked at her mutely, with sweet, grave eyes, in which there was much that confused her who was a stranger here, and once more softly shook her head.

"Is it that he will not then?" said the other with a low voice of awe "Our Lord, who died—he—"

"Listen!" said the other; "I hear his step on the way."

The little Pilgrim rose up from the mound on which she was sitting. Her soul was confused with wonder and fear. She had thought that an angel might step between a soul on earth and sin, and that if one but prayed and prayed, the dear Lord would stand between and deliver the tempted. She had meant when she saw his face to ask him to save. Was not he born, did not he live and die, to save? The angel maiden looked at her all the while with eyes that understood all her perplexity and her doubt, but spoke not. Thus it was that before the Lord came to her, the sweetness of her first blessedness was obscured, and she found that here too, even here, though in a moment she should see him, there was need for faith.

Young Margaret, who had been kneeling by her, rose up too and stood among the lilies, waiting, her soft countenance shining, her eyes turned towards him who was coming. Upon her there was no cloud nor doubt. She was one of the children of that land familiar with his presence. And in the air there was a sound such as those who hear it alone can describe,—a sound as of help coming and safety, like the sound of a deliverer when one is in deadly danger, like the sound of a conqueror, like the step of the dearest beloved coming home. As it came nearer, the fear melted away out of the beating heart of the Pilgrim. Who could fear so near him? Her breath went away from her, her heart out of her bosom to meet his coming. Oh, never fear could live where he was! Her soul was all confused, but it was with hope and joy. She held out her hands in that amaze, and dropped upon her knees, not knowing what she did.

He was going about his Father's business, not lingering, yet neither making haste; and the calm and peace which the little Pilgrim had seen in the faces of the blessed were but reflections from the majestic gentleness of the countenance to which, all quivering with happiness and wonder, she lifted up her eyes. Many things there had been in her mind to say to him. She wanted to ask for those she loved some things which perhaps he had overlooked. She wanted to say, "Send me." It seemed to her that here was the occasion she had longed for all her life. Oh, how many times had she wished to be able to go to him, to fall at his feet, to show him something which had been left undone, something which perhaps for her asking he would remember to do.

But when this dream of her life was fulfilled, and the little Pilgrim, kneeling, and all shaken and trembling with devotion and joy, was at his feet, lifting her face to him, seeing him, hearing him—then she said nothing to him at all. She no longer wanted to say anything, or wanted anything except what he chose, or had power to think of anything except that all was well, and everything—everything as it should be in his hand. It seemed to her that all that she had ever hoped for was fulfilled when she met the look in his eyes. At first it seemed too bright for her to meet; but next moment she knew it was all that was needed to light up the world, and in it everything was clear. Her trembling ceased, her little frame grew inspired; though she still knelt, her head rose erect, drawn to him like the flower to the sun. She could not tell how long it was, nor what was said, nor if it was in words.

All that she knew was that she told him all that ever she had thought, or wished, or intended in all her life, although she said nothing at all; and that he opened all things to her, and showed her that everything was well, and no one forgotten; and that the things she would have told him of were more near his heart than hers, and those to whom she wanted to be sent were in his own hand. But whether this passed with words or without words, she could not tell. Her soul expanded under his eyes like a flower. It opened out, it comprehended and felt and knew. She smote her hands together in her wonder that she could have missed seeing what was so clear, and laughed with a sweet scorn at her folly, as two people who love each other laugh at the little misunderstanding that has parted them.

She was bold with him, though she was so timid by nature, and ventured to laugh at herself, not to reproach herself; for his divine eyes spoke no blame, but smiled upon her folly too. And then he laid a hand upon her head, which seemed to fill her with currents of strength and joy running through all her veins. And then she seemed to come to herself, saying loud out, "And that I will! and that I will!" and lo, she was kneeling on the warm, soft sod alone, and hearing the sound of his footsteps as he went about his Father's business, filling all the air with echoes of blessing. And all the people who were coming and going smiled upon her, and she knew they were all glad for her that she had seen him, and got the desire of her heart. Some of them waved their hands as they passed, and some paused a moment and spoke to her with tender congratulations. They seemed to have the tears in their eyes for joy, remembering every one the first time they had themselves seen him, and the joy of it; so that all about there sounded a concord of happy thoughts all echoing to each other, "She has seen the Lord!"

Why did she say, "And that I will! and that I will!" with such fervour and delight? She could not have told, but yet she knew. The first thing was that she had yet to wait and believe until all things should be accomplished, neither doubting nor fearing, but knowing that all should be well; and the second was that she must delay no longer, but rise up and serve the Father according to what was given her as her reward. When she had recovered a little of her rapture, she rose from her knees, and stood still for a little, to be sure which way she was to go. And she was not aware what guided her, but yet turned her face in the appointed way without any doubt. For doubt was now gone away forever, and that fear that once gave her so much trouble lest she might not be doing what was best. As she moved along she wondered at herself more and more. She felt no longer, as at first, like the child she remembered to have been, venturing out in the awful lovely stillness of the morning before anyone was awake; but she felt that to move along was a delight, and that her foot scarcely touched the grass.

And her whole being was instinct with such lightness of strength and life, that it did not matter to her how far she went, nor what she carried, nor if the way was easy or hard. The way she chose was one of those which led to the great gate, and many met her coming from thence, with looks that were somewhat bewildered, as if they did not yet know whither they were going or what had happened to them,—upon whom she smiled as she passed them with soft looks of tenderness and sympathy, knowing what they were feeling, but did not stop to explain to them, because she had something else that had been given her to do. For this is what always follows in that country when you meet the Lord, that you instantly know what it is that he would have you do.

The little Pilgrim thus went on and on toward the gate, which she had not seen when she herself came through it, having been lifted in his arms by the great Death Angel, and set down softly inside, so that she did not know it, or even the shadow of it. As she drew nearer, the light became less bright, though very sweet, like a lovely dawn, and she wondered to herself to think that she had been here but a moment ago, and yet so much had passed since then. And still she was not aware what was her errand, but wondered if she was to go back by these same gates, and perhaps return where she had been. She went up to them very closely, for she was curious to see the place through which she had come in her sleep,—as a traveller goes back to see the city gate, with its bridge and portcullis, through which he has passed by night.

The gate was very great, of a wonderful, curious architecture, having strange, delicate arches and canopies above. Some parts of them seemed cut very clean and clear; but the outlines were all softened with a sort of mist and shadow, so that it looked greater and higher than it was. The lower part was not one great doorway, as the Pilgrim had supposed, but had innumerable doors, all separate and very narrow, so that but one could pass at a time, though the arch enclosed all, and seemed filled with great folding gates, in which the smaller doors were set, so that if need arose a vast opening might be made for many to enter.

Of the little doors many were shut as the Pilgrim approached; but from moment to moment one after another would be pushed softly open from without, and someone would come in. The little Pilgrim looked at it all with great interest, wondering which of the doors she herself had come by; but while she stood absorbed by this, a door was suddenly pushed open close by her, and someone flung forward into the blessed country, falling upon the ground, and stretched out wild arms as though to clutch the very soil. This sight gave the Pilgrim a great surprise; for it was the first time she had heard any sound of pain, or seen any sight of trouble, since she entered here. In that moment she knew what it was that the dear Lord had given her to do. She had no need to pause to think, for her heart told her; and she did not hesitate, as she might have done in the other life, not knowing what to say.

She went forward and gathered this poor creature into her arms, as if it had been a child, and drew her quite within the land of peace; for she had fallen across the threshold, so as to hinder any one entering who might be coming after her. It was a woman, and she had flung herself upon her face, so that it was difficult for the little Pilgrim to see what manner of person it was; for though she felt herself strong enough to take up this newcomer in her arms and carry her away, yet she forbore, seeing the will of the stranger was not so. For some time this woman lay moaning, with now and then a great sob shaking her as she lay. The little Pilgrim had taken her by both her arms, and drawn her head to rest upon her own lap, and was still holding the hands, which the poor creature had thrown out as if to clutch the ground. Thus she lay for a little while, as the little Pilgrim remembered she herself had lain, not wishing to move, wondering what had happened to her; then she clutched the hands which grasped her, and said, muttering,—

"You are someone new. Have you come to save me? Oh, save me! Oh, save me! Don't let me die!"

This was very strange to the little Pilgrim, and went to her heart. She soothed the stranger, holding her hands warm and light, and stooping over her.

"Dear," she said, "you must try and not be afraid."

"You say so," said the woman, "because you are well and strong. You don't know what it is to be seized in the middle of your life, and told that you've got to die. Oh, I have been a sinful creature! I am not fit to die. Can't you give me something that will cure me? What is the good of doctors and nurses if they cannot save a poor soul that is not fit to die?"

At this the little Pilgrim smiled upon her, always holding her fast, and said,—

"Why are you so afraid to die?"

The woman raised her head to see who it was who put such a strange question to her.

"You are someone new," she said. "I have never seen you before. Is there anyone that is not afraid to die? Would *you* like to have to give your account all in a moment, without any time to prepare?"

"But you have had time to prepare," said the Pilgrim.

"Oh, only a very, very little time. And I never thought it was true. I am not an old woman, and I am not fit to die; and I'm poor. Oh, if I were rich, I would bribe you to give me something to keep me alive. Won't you do it for pity?—won't you do it for pity? When you are as bad as I am, oh, you will perhaps call for someone to help you, and find nobody, like me."

"I will help you for love," said the little Pilgrim; "someone who loves you has sent me."

The woman lifted herself up a little and shook her head. "There is nobody that loves me." Then she cast her eyes round her and began to tremble again (for the touch of the little Pilgrim had stilled her). "Oh, where am I?" she said. "They have taken me away; they have brought me to a strange place; and you are new. Oh, where have they taken me?—where am I?—where am I?" she cried. "Have they brought me here to die?"

Then the little Pilgrim bent over her and soothed her. "You must not be so much afraid of dying; that is all over. You need not fear that any more," she said softly; "for here where you now are we have all died."

The woman started up out of her arms, and then she gave a great shriek that made the air ring, and cried out, "Dead! am I dead?" with a shudder and convulsion, throwing herself again wildly with outstretched hands upon the ground.

This was a great and terrible work for the little Pilgrim—the first she had ever had to do—and her heart failed her for a moment; but afterward she remembered our Brother who sent her, and knew what was best. She drew closer to the newcomer, and took her hand again.

"Try," she said, in a soft voice, "and think a little. Do you feel now so ill as you were? Do not be frightened, but think a little. I will hold your hand. And look at me; you are not afraid of me?"

The poor creature shuddered again, and then she turned her face and looked doubtfully, with great dark eyes dilated, and the brow and cheek so curved and puckered round them that they seemed to glow out of deep caverns. Her face was full of anguish and fear. But as she looked at the little Pilgrim, her troubled gaze softened. Of her own accord she clasped her other hand upon the one that held hers, and then she said with a gasp,—

"I am not afraid of you; that was not true that you said! You are one of the sisters, and you want to frighten me and make me repent!"

"You do repent," the Pilgrim said.

"Oh," cried the poor woman, "what has the like of you to do with me? Now I look at you, I never saw anyone that was like you before. Don't you hate me?—don't you loathe me? I do myself. It's so ugly to go wrong. I think now I would almost rather die and be done with it. You will say that is because I am going to get better. I feel a great deal better now. Do you think I am going to get over it? Oh, I am better! I could get up out of bed and walk about. Yes, but I am not in bed,—where have you brought me? Never mind, it is a fine air; I shall soon get well here."

The Pilgrim was silent for a little, holding her hands. And then she said,—

"Tell me how you feel now," in her soft voice.

The woman had sat up and was gazing round her. "It is very strange," she said; "it is all confused. I think upon my mother and the old prayers I used to say. For a long, long time I always said my prayers; but now I've got hardened, they say. Oh, I was once as fresh as any one. It all comes over me now. I feel as if I were young again—just come out of the country. I am sure that I could walk."

The little Pilgrim raised her up, holding her by her hands; and she stood and gazed round about her, making one or two doubtful steps. She was very pale, and the light was dim; her eyes peered into it with a scared yet eager look. She made another step, then stopped again.

"I am quite well," she said. "I could walk a mile. I could walk any distance. What was that you said? Oh, I tell you I am better! I am not going to die."

"You will never, never die," said the little Pilgrim; "are you not glad it is all over? Oh, I was so glad! And all the more you should be glad if you were so much afraid."

But this woman was not glad. She shrank away from her companion, then came close to her again, and gripped her with her hands.

"It is your—fun," she said, "or just to frighten me. Perhaps you think it will do me no harm as I am getting so well; you want to frighten me to make me good. But I mean to be good without that—I do!—I do! When one is so near dying as I have been and yet gets better,—for I am going to get better! Yes! you know it as well as I."

The little Pilgrim made no reply, but stood by, looking at her charge, not feeling that anything was given her to say,—and she was so new to this work, that there was a little trembling in her, lest she should not do everything as she ought. And the woman looked round with those anxious eyes gazing all about. The light did not brighten as it had done when the Pilgrim herself first came to this place. For one thing, they had remained quite close to the gate, which no doubt threw a shadow. The woman looked at that, and then turned and looked into the dim morning, and did not know where she was, and her heart was confused and troubled.

"Where are we?" she said. "I do not know where it is; they must have brought me here in my sleep,—where are we? How strange to bring a sick woman away out of her room in her sleep! I suppose it was the new doctor," she went on, looking very closely in the little Pilgrim's face; then paused, and drawing a long breath, said softly, "It has done me good. It is better air—it is—a new kind of cure!"

But though she spoke like this, she did not convince herself; her eyes were wild with wondering and fear. She gripped the Pilgrim's arm more and more closely, and trembled, leaning upon her.

"Why don't you speak to me?" she said; "why don't you tell me? Oh, I don't know how to live in this place! What do you do?—how do you speak? I am not fit for it. And what are you? I never saw you before, nor any one like you. What do you want with me? Why are you so kind to me? Why—why—"

And here she went off into a murmur of questions. Why? why? always holding fast by the little Pilgrim, always gazing round her, groping as it were in the dimness with her great eyes.

"I have come because our dear Lord who is our Brother sent me to meet you, and because I love you," the little Pilgrim said.

"Love me!" the woman cried, throwing up her hands. "But no one loves me; I have not deserved it." Here she grasped her close again with a sudden clutch, and cried out, "If this is what you say, where is God?"

"Are you afraid of him?" the little Pilgrim said. Upon which the woman trembled so, that the Pilgrim trembled too with the quivering of her frame; then loosed her hold, and fell upon her face, and cried,—

"Hide me! hide me! I have been a great sinner. Hide me, that he may not see me;" and with one hand she tried to draw the Pilgrim's dress as a veil between her and something she feared.

"How should I hide you from him who is everywhere? and why should I hide you from your Father?" the little Pilgrim said. This she said almost with indignation, wondering that anyone could put more trust in her, who was no better than a child, than in the Father of all. But then she said, "Look into your heart, and you will see you are not so much afraid as you think. This is how you have been accustomed to frighten yourself. But now look into your heart. You thought you were very ill at first, but not now and you think you are afraid; but look into your heart—"

There was a silence; and then the woman raised her head with a wonderful look, in which there was amazement and doubt, as if she had heard some joyful thing, but dared not yet believe that it was true. Once more she hid her face in her hands, and once more raised it again. Her eyes softened; a long sigh or gasp, like one taking breath after drowning, shook her breast. Then she said, "I think—that is true. But if I am not afraid, it is because I am—bad. It is because I am hardened. Oh, should not I fear him who can send me away into—the lake that burns—into the pit—" And here she gave a great cry, but held the little Pilgrim all the while with her eyes, which seemed to plead and ask for better news.

Then there came into the Pilgrim's heart what to say, and

she took the woman's hand again and held it between her own. "That is the change," she said, "that comes when we come here. We are not afraid any more of our Father. We are not all happy. Perhaps you will not be happy at first. But if he says to you, 'Go!'—even to that place you speak of—you will know that it is well, and you will not be afraid. You are not afraid now,—oh, I can see it in your eyes. You are not happy, but you are not afraid. You know it is the Father. Do not say God,—that is far off,—Father!" said the little Pilgrim, holding up the woman's hand clasped in her own. And there came into her soul an ecstasy, and tears that were tears of blessedness fell from her eyes, and all about her there seemed to shine a light.

When she came to herself, the woman who was her charge had come quite close to her, and had added her other hand to that the Pilgrim held, and was weeping and saying, "I am not afraid," with now and then a gasp and sob, like a child who after a passion of tears has been consoled, yet goes on sobbing and cannot quite forget, and is afraid to own that all is well again. Then the Pilgrim kissed her, and bade her rest a little; for even she herself felt shaken, and longed for a little quiet, and to feel the true sense of the peace that was in her heart. She sat down beside her upon the ground, and made her lean her head against her shoulder, and thus they remained very still for a little time, saying no more.

It seemed to the little Pilgrim that her companion had fallen asleep, and perhaps it was so, after so much agitation. All this time there had been people passing, entering by the many doors. And most of them paused a little to see where they were, and looked round them, then went on; and it seemed to the little Pilgrim that according to the doors by which they entered each took a different way. While she watched, another came in by the same door as that at which the woman who was her charge had come in. And he too stumbled and looked about him with an air of great wonder and doubt. When he saw her seated on the ground, he came up to her hesitating, as one in a strange place who does not want to betray that he is bewildered and has lost his way. He came with a little pretence of smiling, though his countenance was pale and scared, and said, drawing his breath quick, "I ought to know where I am, but I have lost my head, I think. Will you tell me which is—the way?"

"What way?" cried the little Pilgrim; for her strength was gone from her, and she had no word to say to him. He looked at her with that bewilderment on his face, and said, "I find myself strange, strange. I ought to know where I am; but it is scarcely daylight yet. It is perhaps foolish to come out so early in the morning." This he said in his confusion, not knowing where he was, nor what he said.

"I think all the ways lead to our Father," said the little Pilgrim (though she had not known this till now). "And the dear Lord walks about them all. Here you never go astray."

Upon this the stranger looked at her, and asked in a faltering voice,

"Are you an angel?" still not knowing what he said.

"Oh, no, no; I am only a Pilgrim," she replied.

"May I sit by you a little?" said the man. He sat down, drawing long breaths, as though he had gone through great fatigue; and looked about with wondering eyes. "You will wonder, but I do not know where I am," he said. "I feel as if I must he dreaming. This is not where I expected to come. I looked for something very different; do you think there can have been any— mistake?"

"Oh, never that," she said; "there are no mistakes here."

Then he looked at her again, and said,—

"I perceive that you belong to this country, though you say you are a pilgrim. I should be grateful if you would tell me. Does one live—here? And is this all? Is there no—no—but I don't know what word to use. All is so strange, different from what I expected."

"Do you know that you have died?"

"Yes—yes, I am quite acquainted with that," he said, hurriedly; as if it had been an idea he disliked to dwell upon. "But then I expected—Is there no one to tell you where to go, or what you are to be? or to take any notice of you?"

The little Pilgrim was startled by this tone. She did not understand its meaning, and she had not any word to say to him. She looked at him with as much bewilderment as he had shown when he approached her, and replied, faltering,—

"There are a great many people here; but I have never heard if there is anyone to tell you—"

"What does it matter how many people there are if you know none of them?" he said.

"We all know each other," she answered him but then paused and hesitated a little, because this was what had been said to her, and of herself she was not assured of it, neither did she know at all how to deal with this stranger, to whom she had not any commission. It seemed that he had no one to care for him, and the little Pilgrim had a sense of compassion, yet of trouble in her heart; for what could she say? And it was very strange to her to see one who was not content here.

"Ah, but there should be someone to point out the way, and tell us which is our circle, and where we ought to go," he said. And then he too was silent for a while, looking about him as all were fain to do on their first arrival, finding everything so strange. There were people coming in at every moment, and some were met at the very threshold, and some went away alone with peaceful faces, and there were many groups about talking together in soft voices; but no one interrupted the other, and though so many were there, each voice was as clear as if it had spoken alone, and there was no tumult of sound as when many people assemble together in the lower world.

The little Pilgrim wondered to find herself with the woman resting upon her on one side, and the man seated silent on the other, neither having, it appeared, any guide but only herself, who knew so little. How was she to lead them in the paths which she did not know?—and she was exhausted by the agitation of her struggle with the woman whom she felt to be her charge. But in this moment of silence she had time to remember the face of the Lord, when he gave her this commission, and her

111

heart was strengthened. The man all this time sat and watched, looking eagerly all about him, examining the faces of those who went and came: and sometimes he made a little start as if to go and speak to someone he knew; but always drew back again and looked at the little Pilgrim, as if he had said, "This is the one who will serve me best." He spoke to her again after a while and said, "I suppose you are one of the guides that show the way."

"No," said the little Pilgrim, anxiously. "I know so little! It is not long since I came here. I came in the early morning—"

"Why, it is morning now. You could not come earlier than it is now. You mean yesterday."

"I think," said the Pilgrim, "that yesterday is the other side; there is no yesterday here."

He looked at her with the keen look he had, to understand her the better; and then he said,—

"No division of time! I think that must be monotonous. It will be strange to have no night; but I suppose one gets used to everything. I hope though there is something to do. I have always lived a very busy life. Perhaps this is just a little pause before we go—to be—to have—to get our—appointed place."

He had an uneasy look as he said this, and looked at her with an anxious curiosity, which the little Pilgrim did not understand.

"I do not know," she said softly, shaking her head. "I have so little experience. I have not been told of an appointed place."

The man looked at her very strangely.

"I did not think," he said, "that I should have found such ignorance here. Is it not well known that we must all appear before the judgment-seat of God?"

There words seemed to cause a trembling on the still air, and the woman on the other side raised herself suddenly up, clasping her hands and some of those who had just entered heard the words, and came and crowded about the little Pilgrim, some standing, some falling down upon their knee, all with their faces turned towards her. She who had always been so simple and small, so little used to teach; she was frightened with the sight of all these strangers crowding, hanging upon her lips, looking to her for knowledge. She knew not what to do or what to say. The tears came into her eyes.

"Oh," she said, "I do not know anything about a judgment-seat. I know that our Father is here, and that when we are in trouble we are taken to him to be comforted, and that our dear Lord our Brother is among us every day, and everyone may see him. Listen," she said, standing up suddenly among them, feeling strong as an angel. "I have seen him! though I am nothing, so little as you see, and often silly, never clever as some of you are, I have seen him! and so will all of you. There is no more that I know of," she said softly, clasping her hands. "When you see him it comes into your heart what you must do."

And then there was a murmur of voices about her, some saying that was best, and some wondering if that were all, and some crying if he would but come now—while the little Pilgrim stood among them with her face shining, and they all looked at her, asking her to tell them more, to show them how to find him. But this was far above what she could do, for she too was not much more than a stranger, and had little strength. She would not go back a step, nor desert those who were so anxious to know, though her heart fluttered almost as it had used to do before she died, what with her longing to tell them, and knowing that she had no more to say.

But in that land it is never permitted that one who stands bravely and fails not shall be left without succor; for it is no longer needful there to stand even to death, since all dying is over, and all souls are tested. When it was seen that the little Pilgrim was thus surrounded by so many that questioned her, there suddenly came about her many others from the brightness out of which she had come, who, one going to one hand, and one to another, safely led them into the ways in which their course lay: so that the Pilgrim was free to lead forth the woman who had been given her in charge, and whose path lay in a dim, but pleasant country, outside of that light and gladness in which the Pilgrim's home was.

"But," she said, "you are not to fear or be cast down, because he goes likewise by these ways, and there is not a corner in all this land but he is to be seen passing by; and he will come and speak to you, and lay his hand upon you; and afterwards everything will be clear, and you will know what you are to do."

"Stay with me till he comes,—oh, stay with me," the woman cried, clinging to her arm.

"Unless another is sent," the little Pilgrim said. And it was nothing to her that the air was less bright there, for her mind was full of light, so that, though her heart still fluttered a little with all that had passed, she had no longing to return, nor to shorten the way, but went by the lower road sweetly, with the stranger hanging upon her, who was stronger and taller than she. Thus they went on, and the Pilgrim told her all she knew, and everything that came into her heart. And so full was she of the great things she had to say, that it was a surprise to her, and left her trembling, when suddenly the woman took away her clinging hand, and flew forward with arms outspread and a cry of joy. The little Pilgrim stood still to see, and on the path before them was a child, coming towards them singing, with a look such as is never seen but upon the faces of children who have come here early, and who behold the face of the Father, and have never known fear nor sorrow. The woman flew and fell at the child's feet, and he put his hand upon her, and raised her up, and called her "mother." Then he smiled upon the little Pilgrim, and led her away.

"Now she needs me no longer," said the Pilgrim; and it was a surprise to her, and for a moment she wondered in herself if it was known that this child should come so suddenly and her work be over; and also how she was to return again to the sweet place among the flowers from which she had come. But when she turned to look if there was any way, she found one standing by such as she had not yet seen. This was a youth, with a face just touched with manhood, as at the moment when the boy ends, when all is still fresh and pure in the heart; but he was taller and greater than a man.

"I am sent," he said, "little sister, to take you to the Father; because you have been very faithful, and gone beyond your strength."

And he took the little Pilgrim by the hand, and she knew he was an angel; and immediately the sweet air melted about them into light, and a hush came upon her of all thought and all sense, attending till she should receive the blessing, and her new name, and see what is beyond telling, and hear and understand.

2: The Little Pilgrim Goes up Higher

When the little Pilgrim came out of the presence of the Father, she found herself in the street of a great city. But what she saw and heard when she was with Him it is not given to the tongue of mortal to say, for it is beyond words, and beyond even thought. As the mystery of love is not to be spoken but to be felt, even in the lower earth, so, but much less, is that great mystery of the love of the Father to be expressed in sound. The little Pilgrim was very happy when she went into that sacred place, but there was a great awe upon her, and it might even be said that she was afraid; but when she came out again she feared nothing, but looked with clear eyes upon all she saw, loving them, but no more overawed by them, having seen that which is above all. When she came forth again to her common life—for it is not permitted save for those who have attained the greatest heights to dwell there—she had no longer need of any guide, but came alone, knowing where to go, and walking where it pleased her, with reverence and a great delight in seeing and knowing all that was around, but no fear. It was a great city, but it was not like the great cities which she had seen.

She understood as she passed along how it was that those who had been dazzled but by a passing glance had described the walls and the pavement as gold. They were like what gold is, beautiful and clear, of a lovely colour, but softer in tone than metal ever was, and as cool and fresh to walk upon and to touch as if they had been velvet grass. The buildings were all beautiful, of every style and form that it is possible to think of, yet in great harmony, as if every man had followed his own taste, yet all had been so combined and grouped by the master architect that each individual feature enhanced the effect of the rest. Some of the houses were greater and some smaller, but all of them were rich in carvings and pictures and lovely decorations, and the effect was as if the richest materials had been employed, marbles and beautiful sculptured stone, and wood of beautiful tints, though the little Pilgrim knew that these were not like the marble and stone she had once known, but heavenly representatives of them, far better than they.

There were people at work upon them, building new houses and making additions, and a great many painters painting upon them the history of the people who lived there, or of others who were worthy that commemoration. And the streets were full of pleasant sound, and of crowds going and coming, and the commotion of much business, and many things to do. And this movement, and the brightness of the air, and the wonderful things that were to be seen on every side, made the Pilgrim gay, so that she could have sung with pleasure as she went along. And all who met her smiled, and every group exchanged greetings as they passed along, all knowing each other.

Many of them, as might be seen, had come there, as she did, to see the wonders of the beautiful city; and all who lived there were ready to tell them whatever they desired to know, and show them the finest houses and the greatest pictures. And this gave a feeling of holiday and pleasure which was delightful beyond description, for all the busy people about were full of sympathy with the strangers, bidding them welcome, inviting them into their houses, making the warmest fellowship. And friends were meeting continually on every side; but the Pilgrim had no sense that she was forlorn in being alone, for all were friends; and it pleased her to watch the others, and see how one turned this way and one another, every one finding something that delighted him above all other things.

She herself took a great pleasure in watching a painter, who was standing upon a balcony a little way above her, painting upon a great *fresco*: and when he saw this he asked her to come up beside him and see his work. She asked him a great many questions about it, and why it was that he was working only at the draperies of the figures, and did not touch their faces, some of which were already finished and seemed to be looking at her, as living as she was, out of the wall, while some were merely outlined as yet. He told her that he was not a great painter to do this, or to design the great work, but that the master would come presently, who had the chief responsibility. "For we have not all the same genius," he said, "and if I were to paint this head it would not have the gift of life as that one has; but to stand by and see him put it in, you cannot think what a happiness that is; for one knows every touch, and just what effect it will have, though one could not do it one's self; and it is a wonder and a delight perpetual that it should be done."

The little Pilgrim looked up at him and said, "That is very beautiful to say. And do you never wish to be like him—to make the lovely, living faces as well as the other parts?"

"Is not this lovely too?" he said; and showed her how he had just put in a billowy robe, buoyed out with the wind, and sweeping down from the shoulders of a stately figure in such free and graceful folds that she would have liked to take it in her hand and feel the silken texture; and then he told her how absorbing it was to study the mysteries of color and the differences of light. "There is enough in that to make one happy," he said. "It is thought by some that we will all come to the higher point with work and thought: but that is not my feeling; and whether it is so or not what does it matter, for our Father makes no difference: and all of us are necessary to everything that is done: and it is almost more delight to see the master do it than to do it with one's own hand. For one thing, your own work may rejoice you in your heart, but always with a little trembling because it is never so perfect as you would have it—whereas in your master's work you have full content, because his idea goes beyond yours, and as he makes every touch you can feel 'That is right—that is complete—that is just as it ought to be.' Do you understand what I mean?" he said, turning to her with a smile.

"I understand it perfectly," she cried, clasping her hands together with the delight of accord. "Don't you think that is one of the things that are so happy here? you understand at half a word."

"Not everybody," he said, and smiled upon her like a brother; "for we are not all alike even here."

"Were you a painter?" she said, "in—in the other—"

"In the old times. I was one of those that strove for the mastery, and sometimes grudged—We remember these things at times," he said gravely, "to make us more aware of the blessedness of being content."

"It is long since then?" she said with some wistfulness; upon which he smiled again.

"So long," he said, "that we have worn out most of our links to the world below. We have all come away, and those who were after us for generations. But you are a newcomer."

"And are they all with you? are you all—together? do you live—as in the old time?"

Upon this the painter smiled, but not so brightly as before.

"Not as in the old time," he said, "nor are they all here. Some are still upon the way, and of some we have no certainty, only news from time to time. The angels are very good to us. They never miss an occasion to bring us news; for they go everywhere, you know."

"Yes," said the little Pilgrim, though indeed she had not known it till now; but it seemed to her as if it had come to her mind by nature and she had never needed to be told.

"They are so tender-hearted," the painter said; "and more than that, they are very curious about men and women. They have known it all from the beginning, and it is a wonder to them. There is a friend of mine, an angel, who is more wise in men's hearts than anyone I know; and yet he will say to me sometimes, 'I do not understand you,—you are wonderful.' They like to find out all we are thinking. It is an endless pleasure to them, just as it is to some of us to watch the people in the other worlds."

"Do you mean—where we have come from?" said the little Pilgrim.

"Not always there. We in this city have been long separated from that country, for all that we love are out of it."

"But not here?" the little Pilgrim cried again, with a little sorrow—a pang that she knew was going to be put away—in her heart.

"But coming! coming!" said the painter, cheerfully; "and some were here before us, and some have arrived since. They are everywhere."

"But some in trouble—some in trouble!" she cried, with the tears in her eyes.

"We suppose so," he said, gravely; "for some are in that place which once was called among us the place of despair."

"You mean—" and though the little Pilgrim had been made free of fear, at that word which she would not speak, she trembled, and the light grew dim in her eyes.

"Well!" said her new friend, "and what then? The Father sees through and through it as he does here; they cannot escape him: so that there is Love near them always. I have a son," he said, then sighed a little, but smiled again, "who is there."

The little Pilgrim at this clasped her hands with a piteous cry.

"Nay, nay," he said, "little sister; my friend I was telling you of, the angel, brought me news of him just now. Indeed there was news of him through all the city. Did you not hear all the bells ringing? But perhaps that was before you came. The angels who know me best came one after another to tell me, and our Lord himself came to wish me joy. My son had found the way."

The little Pilgrim did not understand this, and almost thought that the painter must be mistaken or dreaming. She looked at him very anxiously and said,—

"I thought that those unhappy—never came out any more."

The painter smiled at her in return, and said,—

"Had you children in the old time?"

She paused a little before she replied.

119

"I had children in love," she said, "but none that were born mine."

"It is the same," he said, "it is the same; and if one of them had sinned against you, injured you, done wrong in any way, would you have cast him off, or what would you have done?"

"Oh!" said the little Pilgrim again, with a vivid light of memory coming into her face, which showed she had no need to think of this as a thing that might have happened, but knew. "I brought him home. I nursed him well again. I prayed for him night and day. Did you say cast him off? when he had most need of me? then I never could have loved him," she cried.

The painter nodded his head, and his hand with the pencil in it, for he had turned from his picture to look at her.

"Then you think you love better than our Father?" he said; and turned to his work, and painted a new fold in the robe, which looked as if a soft air had suddenly blown into it, and not the touch of a skilful hand.

This made the Pilgrim tremble, as though in her ignorance she had done something wrong. After that there came a great joy into her heart. "Oh, how happy you have made me!" she cried. "I am glad with all my heart for you and your son—"Then she paused a little and added, "But you said he was still there."

"It is true; for the land of darkness is very confusing, they tell me, for want of the true light, and our dear friends the angels are not permitted to help: but if one follows them, that shows the way. You may be in that land yet on your way hither. It was very hard to understand at first," said the painter; "there are some sketches I could show you. No one has ever made a picture of it, though many have tried; but I could show you some sketches— if you wish to see."

To this the little Pilgrim's look was so plain an answer that the painter laid down his pallet and his brush, and left his work, to show them to her as he had promised. They went down from the balcony and along the street until they came to one of the great palaces, where many were coming and going. Here they walked through some vast halls, where students were working at easels, doing every kind of beautiful work: some painting pictures, some preparing drawings, planning houses and palaces. The Pilgrim would have liked to pause at every moment to see one lovely thing or another; but the painter walked on steadily till he came to a room which was full of sketches, some of them like pictures in little, with many figures,—some of them only a representation of a flower, or the wing of a bird. "These are all the master's," he said; "sometimes the sight of them will be enough to put something great into the mind of another. In this corner are the sketches I told you of."

There were two of them hanging together upon the wall, and at first it seemed to the little Pilgrim as if they represented the flames and fire of which she had read, and this made her shudder for the moment. But then she saw that it was a red light like a stormy sunset, with masses of clouds in the sky, and a low sun very fiery and dazzling, which no doubt to a hasty glance must have looked, with its dark shadows and high lurid lights, like the fires of the bottomless pit.

But when you looked down you saw the reality what it was. The country that lay beneath was full of tropical foliage, but with many stretches of sand and dry plains, and in the foreground was a town, that looked very prosperous and crowded, though the figures were very minute, the subject being so great; but no one to see it would have taken it for anything but a busy and wealthy place, in a thunderous atmosphere, with a storm coming on. In the next there was a section of a street with a great banqueting hall open to the view, and many people sitting about the table. You could see that there was a great deal of laughter and conversation going on, some very noisy groups, but others that sat more quietly in corners and conversed, and some who sang, and every kind of entertainment.

The little Pilgrim was very much astonished to see this, and turned to the painter, who answered her directly, though she had not spoken. "We used to think differently once. There are some who are there and do not know it. They think only it is the old life over again, but always worse, and they are led on in the ways of evil; but they do not feel the punishment until they begin to find out where they are and to struggle, and wish for other things."

The little Pilgrim felt her heart beat very wildly while she looked at this, and she thought upon the rich man in the parable, who, though he was himself in torment, prayed that his brother might be saved, and she said to herself, "Our dear Lord would never leave him there who could think of his brother when he was himself in such a strait." And when she looked at the painter he smiled upon her, and nodded his head. Then he led her to the other corner of the room where there were other pictures. One of them was of a party seated round a table and an angel looking on. The angel had the aspect of a traveller, as if he were passing quickly by and had but paused a moment to look, and one of the men glancing up suddenly saw him.

The picture was dim, but the startled look upon this man's face, and the sorrow on the angel's, appeared out of the misty background with such truth that the tears came into the little Pilgrim's eyes, and she said in her heart, "Oh that I could go to him and help him!" The other sketches were dimmer and dimmer. You seemed to see out of the darkness, gleaming lights, and companies of revellers, out of which here and there was one trying to escape. And then the wide plains in the night, and the white vision of the angel in the distance, and here and there by different paths a fugitive striving to follow. "Oh, sir," said the little Pilgrim, "how did you learn to do it? You have never been there."

"It was the master, not I; and I cannot tell you if he has ever been there. When the Father has given you that gift, you can go to many places, without leaving the one where you are. And then he has heard what the angels say."

"And will they all get safe at the last? and even that great spirit, he that fell from heaven—"

The painter shook his head and said, "It is not permitted to you and me to know such great things. Perhaps the wise will tell you if you ask them: but for me I ask the Father in my heart and listen to what he says."

"That is best!" the little Pilgrim said; and she asked the Father in her heart: and there came all over her such a glow of warmth and happiness that her soul was satisfied. She looked in the painter's face and laughed for joy. And he put out his hands as if welcoming someone, and his countenance shone; and he said,—

"My son had a great gift. He was a master born, though it was not given to me. He shall paint it all for us so that the heart shall rejoice; and you will come again and see."

After that it happened to the little Pilgrim to enter into another great palace where there were many people reading, and some sitting at their desks and writing, and some consulting together, with many great volumes stretched out open upon the tables. One of these who was seated alone looked up as she paused wondering at him, and smiled as everyone did, and greeted her with such a friendly tone that the Pilgrim, who always had a great desire to know, came nearer to him and looked at the book, then begged his pardon, and said she did not know that books were needed here. And then he told her that he was one of the historians of the city where all the records of the world were kept, and that it was his business to work upon the great history, and to show what was the meaning of the Father in everything that had happened, and how each event came in its right place.

"And do you get it out of books?" she asked; for she was not learned, nor wise, and knew but little, though she always loved to know.

"The books are the records," he said; "and there are many here that were never known to us in the old days; for the angels love to look into these things, and they can tell us much, for they saw it; and in the great books they have kept there is much put down that was never in the books we wrote, for then we did not know. We found out about the kings and the state, and tried to understand what great purposes they were serving; but even these we did not know, for those purposes were too great for us, not knowing the end from the beginning, and the hearts of men were too great for us. We comprehended the evil sometimes, but never fathomed the good. And how could we know the lesser things which were working out God's way? for some of these even the angels did not know; and it has happened to me that our Lord himself has come in sometimes to tell me of one that none of us had discovered."

"Oh," said the little Pilgrim, with tears in her eyes, "I should like to have been that one!—that was not known even to the angels, but only to Himself!"

The historian smiled. "It was my brother," he said.

The Pilgrim looked at him with great wonder. "Your brother, and you did not know him!"

And then he turned over the pages and showed her where the story was.

"You know," he said, "that we who live here are not of your time, but have lived and lived here till the old life is far away and like a dream. There were great tumults and fightings in our time, and it was settled by the prince of the place that our town was to be abandoned, and all the people left to the mercy of an enemy who had no mercy. But every day as he rode out he saw at one door a child, a little fair boy, who sat on the steps, and sang his little song like a bird. This child was never afraid of anything,— when the horses pranced past him, and the troopers pushed him aside, he looked up into their faces and smiled. And when he had anything, a piece of bread, or an apple, or a plaything, he shared it with his playmates; and his little face, and his pretty voice, and all his pleasant ways, made that corner bright. He was like a flower growing there; everybody smiled that saw him."

"I have seen such a child," the little Pilgrim said.

"But we made no account of him," said the historian. "The Lord of the place came past him every day, and always saw him singing in the sun by his father's door. And it was a wonder then, and it has been a wonder ever since, why, having resolved upon it, that prince did not abandon the town, which would have changed all his fortune after. Much had been made clear to me since I began to study, but not this: till the Lord himself came to me and told me. The prince looked at the child till he loved him, and he reflected how many children there were like this that would be murdered, or starved to death, and he could not give up the little singing boy to the sword. So he remained; and the town was saved, and he became a great king. It was so secret that even the angels did not know it. But without that child the history would not have been complete."

"And is he here?" the little Pilgrim said.

"Ah," said the historian, "that is more strange still; for that which saved him was also to his harm. He is not here. He is Elsewhere."

The little Pilgrim's face grew sad; but then she remembered what she had been told.

"But you know," she said, "that he is coming?"

"I know that our Father will never forsake him, and that everything that is being accomplished in him is well."

"Is it well to suffer? Is it well to live in that dark stormy country? Oh, that they were all here, and happy like you!"

He shook his head a little and said,—

"It was a long time before I got here; and as for suffering that matters little. You get experience by it. You are more accomplished and fit for greater work in the end. It is not for nothing that we are permitted to wander; and sometimes one goes to the edge of despair—"

She looked at him with such wondering eyes that he answered her without a word.

"Yes," he said, "I have been there."

And then it seemed to her that there was something in his eyes which she had not remarked before. Not only the great content that was everywhere, but a deeper light, and the air of a judge who knew both good and evil, and could see both sides, and understood all, both to love and to hate.

"Little sister," he said, "you have never wandered far; it is not needful for such as you. Love teaches you, and you need no more; but when we have to be trained for an office like this, to make the way of the Lord clear through all the generations, reason is that we should see everything, and learn all that man is and can be. These things are too deep for us; we stumble on, and know not till after. But now to me it is all clear."

She looked at him again and again while he spoke, and it seemed to her that she saw in him such great knowledge and tenderness as made her glad; and how he could understand the follies that men had done, and fathom what real meaning was in them, and disentangle all the threads. He smiled as she gazed at him, and answered as if she had spoken.

"What was evil perishes, and what was good remains; almost everywhere there is a little good. We could not understand all if we had not seen all and shared all."

"And the punishment too," she said, wondering more and more.

He smiled so joyfully that it was like laughter.

"Pain is a great angel," he said. "The reason we hated him in the old days was because he tended to death and decay; but when it is towards life he leads, we fear him no more. The welcome thing of all in the land of darkness is when you see him first and know who he is; for by this you are aware that you have found the way."

The little Pilgrim did nothing but question with her anxious eyes, for this was such a wonder to her, and she could not understand. But he only sat musing with a smile over the things he remembered. And at last he said,—

"If this is so interesting to you, you shall read it all in another place, in the room where we have laid up our own experiences, in order to serve for the history afterwards. But we are still busy upon the work of the earth. There is always something new to be discovered. And it is essential for the whole world that the chronicle should be full. I am in great joy because it was but just now that our Lord told me about that child. Everything was imperfect without him, but now it is clear."

"You mean your brother? And you are happy though you are not sure if he is happy?" the little Pilgrim said.

"It is not to be happy that we live," said he; and then, "We are all happy so soon as we have found the way."

She would have asked him more, but that he was called to a consultation with some others of his kind, and had to leave her, waving his hand to her with a tender kindness which went to her heart. She looked after him with great respect, scarcely knowing why; but it seemed to her that a man who had been in the land of darkness, and made his way out of it, must be more wonderful than any other. She looked round for a little upon the great library, full of all the books that had ever been written, and where people were doing their work, examining and reading and making extracts, everyone with looks of so much interest, that she almost envied them,—though it was a generous delight in seeing people so happy in their occupation, and a desire to associate herself somehow in it, rather than any grudging of their satisfaction, that was in her mind.

She went about all the courts of this palace alone, and everywhere saw the same work going on, and everywhere met the same kind looks. Even when the greatest of all looked up from his work and saw her, he would give her a friendly greeting and a smile; and nobody was too wise to lend an ear to the little visitor, or to answer her questions. And this was how it was that she began to talk to another, who was seated at a great table with many more, and who drew her to him by something that was in his looks, though she could not have told what it was. It was not that he was kinder than the rest, for they were all kind. She stood by him a little, and saw how he worked and would take something from one book and something from another, putting them ready for use. And it did not seem any trouble to do this work, but only pleasure, and the very pen in his hand was like a winged thing, as if it loved to write. When he saw her watching him, he looked up and showed her the beautiful book out of which he was copying, which was all illuminated with lovely pictures.

"This is one of the volumes of the great history," he said. "There are some things in it which are needed for another, and it is a pleasure to work at it. If you will come here you will be able to see the page while I write."

Then the little Pilgrim asked him some questions about the pictures, and he answered her, describing and explaining them; for they were in the middle of the history, and she did not understand what it was. When she said, "I ought not to trouble you, for you are busy," he laughed so kindly that she laughed too for pleasure. And he said,—

"There is no trouble here. When we are not allowed to work, as sometimes happens, that makes us not quite so happy, but it is very seldom that it happens so."

"Is it for punishment?" she said.

And then he laughed out with a sound which made all the others look up smiling; and if they had not all looked so tenderly at her, as at a child who has made such a mistake as it is pretty for the child to make, she would have feared she had said something wrong; but she only laughed at herself too, and blushed a little, knowing that she was not wise: and to put her at her ease again, he turned the leaf and showed her other pictures, and the story which went with them, from which he was copying something. And he said,—

"This is for another book, to show how the grace of the Father was beautiful in some homes and families. It is not the great history, but connected with it; and there are many who love that better than the story which is more great."

Then the Pilgrim looked in his face and said,—

"What I want most is, to know about your homes here."

"It is all home here," he said, and smiled; and then, as he met her wistful looks, he went on to tell her that he and his brothers were not always there. "We have all our occupations," he said, "and sometimes I am sent to inquire into facts that have happened, of which the record is not clear; for we must omit nothing; and sometimes we are told to rest and take in new strength; and sometimes—"

"But oh, forgive me," cried the little Pilgrim, "you had some who were more dear to you than all the world in the old time?"

And the others all looked up again at the question, and looked at her with tender eyes, and said to the man whom she questioned,—"Speak!"

He made a little pause before he spoke, and he looked at one here and there, and called to them,—

"Patience, brother," and "Courage, brother." And then he said, "Those whom we loved best are nearly all with us; but some have not yet come."

"Oh," said the little Pilgrim, "but how then do you bear it, to be parted so long—so long?"

Then one of those to whom the first speaker had called out "Patience" rose, and came to her smiling; and he said,—

"I think every hour that perhaps she will come, and the joy will be so great, that thinking of that makes the waiting short: and nothing here is long, for it never ends; and it will be so wonderful to hear her tell how the Father has guided her, that it will be a delight to us all; and she will be able to explain many things, not only for us, but for all; and we love each other so that this separation is as nothing in comparison with what is to come."

It was beautiful to hear this, but it was not what the little Pilgrim expected, for she thought they would have told her of the homes to which they all returned when their work was over, and a life which was like the life of the old time; but of this they said nothing, only looking at her with smiling eyes, as at the curious questions of a child. And there were many other things she would have asked, but refrained when she looked at them, feeling as if she did not yet understand; when one of them broke forth suddenly in a louder voice, and said,—

"The little sister knows only the little language and the beginning of days. She has not learned the mysteries, and what Love is, and what life is."

And another cried, "It is sweet to hear it again;" and they all gathered round her with tender looks, and began to talk to each other, and tell her, as men will tell of the games of their childhood, of things that happened, which were half-forgotten, in the old time.

After this the little Pilgrim went out again into the beautiful city, feeling in her heart that everything was a mystery, and that the days would never be long enough to learn all that had yet to be learned, but knowing now that this too was the little language, and pleased with the sweet thought of so much that was to come. For one had whispered to her as she went out that the new tongue, and every explanation, as she was ready for it, would come to her through one of those whom she loved best, which is the usage of that country. And when the stranger has no one there that is very dear, then it is an angel who teaches the greater language, and that is what happens often to the children who are brought up in that heavenly place.

When she reached the street again, she was so pleased with this thought that it went out of her mind to ask her way to the great library, where she was to read the story of the historian's journey through the land of darkness; indeed she forgot that land altogether, and thought only of what was around her in the great city, which is beyond everything that eye has seen, or that ear has heard, or that it has entered into the imagination to conceive. And now it seemed to her that she was much more familiar with the looks of the people, and could distinguish between those who belonged to the city and those who were visitors like herself; and also could tell which they were who had entered into the mysteries of the kingdom, and which were, like herself, only acquainted with the beginning of days.

And it came to her mind, she could not tell how, that it was best not to ask questions, but to wait until the beloved one should come, who would teach her the first words. For in the meantime she did not feel at all impatient or disturbed by her want of knowledge, but laughed a little at herself to suppose that she could find out everything, and went on looking round her, and saying a word to every one she met, and enjoying the holiday looks of all the strangers, and the sense she had in her heart of holiday too. She was walking on in this pleasant way, when she heard a sound that was like silver trumpets, and saw the crowd turn towards an open space in which all the beautiful buildings were shaded with fine trees, and flowers were springing at the very edge of the pavements. The strangers all hastened along to hear what it was, and she with them, and some also of the people of the place. And as the little Pilgrim found herself walking by a woman who was of these last, she asked her what it was.

And the woman told her it was a poet who had come to say to them what had been revealed to him, and that the two with the silver trumpets were angels of the musicians' order, whose office it was to proclaim everything that was new, that the people should know. And many of those who were at work in the palaces came out and joined the crowd, and the painter who had showed the little Pilgrim his picture, and many whose faces she began to be acquainted with. The poet stood up upon a beautiful pedestal all sculptured in stone, and with wreaths of living flowers hung upon it—and when the crowd had gathered in front of him, he began his poem.

He told them that it was not about this land, or anything that happened in it, which they knew as he did, but that it was a story of the old time, when men were walking in darkness, and when no one knew the true meaning even of what he himself did, but had to go on as if blindly, stumbling and groping with their hands. And "Oh, brethren," he said, "though all is more beautiful and joyful here where we know, yet to remember the days when we knew not, and the ways when all was uncertain, and the end could not be distinguished from the beginning, is sweet and dear; and that which was done in the dim twilight should be celebrated in the day; and our Father himself loves to hear of those who, having not seen, loved, and who learned without any teacher, and followed the light, though they did not understand."

And then he told them the story of one who had lived in the old time; and in that air, which seemed to be made of sunshine, and amid all those stately palaces, he described to them the little earth which they had left behind—the skies that were covered with clouds, and the ways that were so rough and stony, and the cruelty of the oppressor, and the cries of those that were oppressed. And he showed the sickness and the troubles, and the sorrow and danger; and how Death stalked about, and tore heart from heart; and how sometimes the strongest would fail, and the truest fall under the power of a lie, and the tenderest forget to be kind; and how evil things lurked in every corner to beguile the dwellers there; and how the days were short and the nights dark, and life so little that by the time a man had learned something it was his hour to die. "What can a soul do that is born there?" he cried; "for war is there and fighting, and perplexity and darkness; and no man knows if that which he does will be for good or evil, or can tell which is the best way, or know the end from the beginning; and those he loves the most are a mystery to him, and their thoughts beyond his reach. And clouds are between him and the Father, and he is deceived with false gods and false teachers, who make him to love a lie."

The people who were listening held their breath, and a shadow like a cloud fell on them, and they remembered and knew that it was true. But the next moment their hearts rebelled, and one and another would have spoken, and the little Pilgrim herself had almost cried out and made her plea for the dear earth which she loved; when he suddenly threw forth his voice again like a great song. "Oh, dear mother earth," he cried; "oh, little world and great, forgive thy son! for lovely thou art and dear, and the sun of God shines upon thee, and the sweet dews fall; and there were we born, and loved and died, and are come hence to bless the Father and the Son. For in no other world, though they are so vast, is it given to any to know the Lord in the darkness, and follow him groping, and make way through sin and death, and overcome the evil, and conquer in his name."

At which there was a great sound of weeping and of triumph, and the little Pilgrim could not contain herself, but cried out too in joy as if for a deliverance. And then the poet told his tale. And as he told them of the man who was poor and sorrowful and alone, and how he loved and was not loved again, and trusted and was betrayed, and was tempted and drawn into the darkness, so that it seemed as if he must perish; but when hope was almost gone, turned again from the edge of despair, and confronted all his enemies, and fought and conquered—the people followed every word with great outcries of love and pity and wonder. For each one as he listened remembered his own career and that of his brethren in the old life, and admired to think that all the evil was past, and wondered that out of such tribulation and through so many dangers all were safe and blessed here.

And there were others that were not of them, who listened, some seated at the windows of the palaces and some standing in the great square,—people who were not like the others, whose bearing was more majestic, and who looked upon the crowd all smiling and weeping, with wonder and interest, but had no knowledge of the cause, and listened as it were to a tale that is told. The poet and his audience were as one, and at every period of the story there was a deep breathing and pause, and everyone looked at his neighbour, and some grasped each other's hands as they remembered all that was in the past; but the strangers listened and gazed and observed all, as those who listen and are instructed in something beyond their knowledge.

The little Pilgrim stood all this time not knowing where she was, so intent was she upon the tale; and as she listened it seemed to her that all her own life was rolling out before her, and she remembered the things that had been, and perceived how all had been shaped and guided, and trembled a little for the brother who was in danger, yet knew that all would be well.

The woman who had been at her side listened too with all her heart, saying to herself, as she stood in the crowd, "He has left nothing out! The little days they were so short, and the skies would change all in a moment and one's heart with them. How he brings it all back!" And she put up her hand to dry away a tear from her eyes, though her face all the time was shining with the recollection. The little Pilgrim was glad to be by the side of a woman after talking with so many men, and she put out her hand and touched the cloak that this lady wore, and which was white and of the most beautiful texture, with gold threads woven in it, or something that looked like gold.

"Do you like," she said, "to think of the old time?"

The woman turned and looked down upon her, for she was tall and stately, and immediately took the hand of the little Pilgrim into hers, and held it without answering, till the poet had ended and come down from the place where he had been standing. He came straight through the crowd to where this lady stood, and said something to her. "You did well to tell me," looking at her with love in his eyes,—not the tender sweetness of all those kind looks around, but the love that is for one. The little Pilgrim looked at them with her heart beating, and was very glad for them, and happy in herself; for she had not seen this love before since she came into the city, and it had troubled her to think that perhaps it did not exist any more. "I am glad," the lady said, and gave him her other hand; "but here is a little sister who asks me something, and I must answer her. I think she has but newly come."

"She has a face full of the morning," the poet said. It did the little Pilgrim good to feel the touch of the warm, soft hand; and she was not afraid, but lifted her eyes and spoke to the lady and to the poet. "It is beautiful what you said to us. Sometimes in the old time we used to look up to the beautiful skies and wonder what there was above the clouds; but we never thought that up here in this great city you would be thinking of what we were doing, and making beautiful poems all about us. We thought that you would sing wonderful psalms, and talk of things high, high above us."

"The little sister does not know what the meaning of the earth is," the poet said. "It is but a little speck, but it is the centre of all. Let her walk with us, and we will go home, and you will tell her, Ama, for I love to hear you talk."

"Will you come with us?" the lady said.

And the little Pilgrim's heart leaped up in her, to think she was now going to see a home in this wonderful city; and they went along, hand in hand, and though they were three together, and many were coming and going, there was no difficulty, for every one made way for them. And there was a little murmur of pleasure as the poet passed, and those who had heard his poem made obeisance to him, and thanked him, and thanked the Father for him that he was able to show them so many beautiful things. And they walked along the street which was shining with color, and saw as they passed how the master painter had come to his work, and was standing upon the balcony where the little Pilgrim had been, and bringing out of the wall, under his hand, faces which were full of life, and which seemed to spring forth as if they had been hidden there.

"Let us wait a little and see him working," the poet said; and all round about the people stopped on their way, and there was a soft cry of pleasure and praise all through the beautiful street. And the painter with whom the little Pilgrim had talked before came, and stood behind her as if he had been an old friend, and called out to her at every new touch to mark how this and that was done. She did not understand as he did, but she saw how beautiful it was, and she was glad to have seen the great painter, as she had been glad to hear the great poet. It seemed to the little Pilgrim as if everything happened well for her, and that no one had ever been so blessed before. And to make it all more sweet, this new friend, this great and sweet lady, always held her hand, and pressed it softly when something more lovely appeared; and even the pictured faces on the wall seemed to beam upon her, as they came out one by one like the stars in the sky.

Then the three went on again, and passed by many more beautiful palaces, and great streets leading away into the light, till you could see no further; and they met with bands of singers who sang so sweetly that the heart seemed to leap out of the Pilgrim's breast to meet with them, for above all things this was what she had loved most. And out of one of the palaces there came such glorious music that everything she had seen and heard before seemed as nothing in comparison. And amid all these delights they went on and on, but without wearying, till they came out of the streets into lovely walks and alleys, and made their way to the banks of a great river, which seemed to sing, too, a soft melody of its own.

And here there were some fair houses surrounded by gardens and flowers that grew everywhere, and the doors were all open, and within everything was lovely and still, and ready for rest if you were weary. The little Pilgrim was not weary; but the lady placed her upon a couch in the porch, where the pillars and the roof were all formed of interlacing plants and flowers; and there they sat with her, and talked, and explained to her many things. They told her that the earth though so small was the place in all the world to which the thoughts of those above were turned. "And not only of us who have lived there, but of all our brothers in the other worlds; for we are the race which the Father has chosen to be the example.

In every age there is one that is the scene of the struggle and the victory, and it is for this reason that the chronicles are made, and that we are all placed here to gather the meaning of what has been done among men. And I am one of those," the lady said, "that go back to the dear earth and gather up the tale of what our little brethren are doing. I have not to succor like some others, but only to see and bring the news; and he makes them into great poems, as you have heard; and sometimes the master painter will take one and make of it a picture; and there is nothing that is so delightful to us as when we can bring back the histories of beautiful things."

"But, oh," said the little Pilgrim, "what can there be on earth so beautiful as the meanest thing that is here?"

Then they both smiled upon her and said, "It is more beautiful than the most beautiful thing here to see how, under the low skies and in the short days, a soul will turn to our Father. And sometimes," said Ama, "when I am watching, one will wander and stray, and be led into the dark till my heart is sick; then come back and make me glad. Sometimes I cry out within myself to the Father, and say, 'O my Father, it is enough!' and it will seem to me that it is not possible to stand by and see his destruction. And then while you are gazing, while you are crying, he will recover and return, and go on again. And to the angels it is more wonderful than to us, for they have never lived there. And all the other worlds are eager to hear what we can tell them. For no one knows except the Father how the battle will turn, or when it will all be accomplished; and there are some who tremble for our little brethren. For to look down and see how little light there is, and how no one knows what may happen to him next, makes them afraid who never were there."

The little Pilgrim listened with an intent face, clasping her hands, and said,—

"But it never could be that our Father should be overcome by evil. Is not that known in all the worlds?"

Then the lady turned and kissed her; and the poet broke forth in singing, and said, "Faith is more heavenly than heaven; it is more beautiful than the angels. It is the only voice that can answer to our Father. We praise him, we glorify him, we love his name; but there is but one response to him through all the worlds, and that is the cry of the little brothers, who see nothing and know nothing, but believe that he will never fail."

At this the little Pilgrim wept, for her heart was touched; but she said,—

"We are not so ignorant; for we have our Lord who is our Brother, and he teaches us all that we require to know."

Upon this the poet rose and lifted up his hands and sang again a great song; it was in the other language which the little Pilgrim still did not understand, but she could make out that it sounded like a great proclamation that He was wise as he was good, and called upon all to see that the Lord had chosen the only way: and the sound of the poet's voice was like a great trumpet sounding bold and sweet, as if to tell this to those who were far away.

"For you must know," said the Lady Ama, who all the time held the Pilgrim's hand, "that it is permitted to all to judge according to the wisdom that has been given them. And there are some who think that our dear Lord might have found another way, and that wait, sometimes with trembling, lest he should fail;

but not among us who have lived on earth, for we know. And it is our work to show to all the worlds that his way never fails, and how wonderful it is, and beautiful above all that heart has conceived. And thus we justify the ways of God, who is our Father. But in the other worlds there are many who will continue to fear until the history of the earth is all ended and the chronicles are made complete."

"And will that be long?" the little Pilgrim cried, feeling in her heart that she would like to go to all the worlds and tell them of our Lord, and of his love, and how the thought of him makes you strong; and it troubled her a little to hear her friends speak of the low skies, and the short days, and the dimness of that dear country which she had left behind, in which there were so many still whom she loved.

Upon this Ama shook her head, and said that of that day no one knew, not even our Lord, but only the Father; and then she smiled and answered the little Pilgrim's thought. "When we go back," she said, "it is not as when we lived there; for now we see all the dangers of it and the mysteries which we did not see before. It was by the Father's dear love that we did not see what was around us and about us while we lived there, for then our hearts would have fainted; and that makes us wonder now that anyone endures to the end."

"You are a great deal wiser than I am," said the little Pilgrim; "but, though our hearts had fainted, how could we have been overcome? For He was on our side."

At this neither of them made any reply at first, but looked at her; and at length the poet said that she had brought many thoughts back to his mind, and how he had himself been almost worsted when one like her came to him and gave strength to his soul. "For that He was on our side was the only thing she knew," he said, "and all that could be learned or discovered was not worthy of naming beside it. And this I must tell when next I speak to the people, and how our little sister brought it to my mind."

And then they paused from this discourse, and the little Pilgrim looked round upon the beautiful houses and the fair gardens, and she said,—

"You live here? and do you come home at night?—but I do not mean at night, I mean when your work is done. And are they poets like you that dwell all about in these pleasant places, and the—"

She would have said the children, but stopped, not knowing if perhaps it might be unkind to speak of the children when she saw none there.

Upon this the lady smiled once more, and said,—

"The door stands open always, so that no one is shut out, and the children come and go when they will. They are children no longer, and they have their appointed work like him and me."

"And you are always among those you love?" the Pilgrim said; upon which they smiled again and said, "We all love each other;" and the lady held her hand in both of hers, and caressed it, and softly laughed and said, "You know only the little language. When you have been taught the other you will learn many beautiful things."

She rested for some time after this, and talked much with her new friends; and then there came into the heart of the little Pilgrim a longing to go to the place which was appointed for her, and which was her home, and to do the work which had been given her to do. And when the lady saw this she rose and said that she would accompany her a little upon her way. But the poet bid her farewell and remained under the porch, with the green branches shading him, and the flowers twining round the pillars, and the open door of this beautiful house behind him.

When she looked back upon him he waved his hand to her as if bidding her God-speed, and the lady by her side looked back too and waved her hand, and the little Pilgrim felt tears of happiness come to her eyes; for she had been wondering with a little disappointment to see that the people in the city, except those who were strangers, were chiefly alone, and not like those in the old world where the husband and wife go together. It consoled her to see again two who were one. The lady pressed her hand in answer to her thought, and bade her pause a moment and look back into the city as they passed the end of the great street out of which they came. And then the Pilgrim was more and more consoled, for she saw many who had before been alone now walking together hand in hand.

"It is not as it was," Ama said. "For all of us have work to do which is needed for the worlds, and it is no longer needful that one should sit at home while the other goes forth; for our work is not for our life as of old, or for ourselves, but for the Father who has given us so great a trust. And, little sister, you must know that though we are not so great as the angels, nor as many that come to visit us from the other worlds, yet we are nearer to him. For we are in his secret, and it is ours to make it clear."

The little Pilgrim's heart was very full to hear this; but she said,—

"I was never clever, nor knew much. It is better for me to go away to my little border-land, and help the strangers who do not know the way."

"Whatever is your work is the best," the lady said; "but though you are so little you are in the Father's secret too, for it is nature to you to know what the others cannot be sure of, that we must have the victory at the last: so that we have this between us, the Father and we. And though all are his children, we are of the kindred of God, because of our Lord who is our Brother." And then the Lady Ama kissed her, and bade her when she returned to the great city, either for rest or for love, or because the Father sent for her, that she should come to the house by the river. "For we are friends for ever," she said, and so threw her white veil over her head, and was gone upon her mission, whither the little Pilgrim did not know.

And now she found herself at a distance from the great city, which shone in the light with its beautiful towers, and roofs, and all its monuments, softly fringed with trees, and set in a heavenly firmament. And the Pilgrim thought of those words that described this lovely place as a bride adorned for her husband, and did not wonder at him who had said that her streets were of gold and her gates of pearl, because gold and pearls and precious jewels were as nothing to the glory and the beauty of her. The little Pilgrim was glad to have seen these wonderful things, and her mind was like a cup running over with almost more than it could contain. It seemed to her that there never could be a time when she should want for wonder and interest and delight, so long as she had this to think of.

Yet she was not sorry to turn her back upon the beautiful city, but went on her way singing in unutterable content, and thinking over what the lady had said, that we were in God's secret, more than all the great worlds above and even the angels, because of knowing how it is that in darkness and doubt, and without any open vision, a man may still keep the right way. The path lay along the bank of the river which flowed beside her and made the air full of music, and a soft air blew across the running stream and breathed in her face and refreshed her, and the birds sang in all the trees. And as she passed through the villages the people came out to meet her, and asked of her if she had come from the city, and what she had seen there. And everywhere she found friends, and kind voices that gave her greeting.

But some would ask her why she still spoke the little language, though it was sweet to their ears; and others when they heard it hastened to call from the houses and the fields some among them who knew the other tongue but a little, and who came and crowded round the little Pilgrim, and asked her many questions both about the things she had been seeing and about the old time. And she perceived that the village folk were a simple folk, not learned and wise like those she had left; and that though they lived within sight of the great city, and showed every stranger the beautiful view of it, and the glory of its towers, yet few among them had travelled there; for they were so content with their fields, and their river, and the shade of their trees, and the birds singing, and their simple life, that they wanted no change; though it pleased them to receive the little Pilgrim, and they brought her into their villages rejoicing, and called every one to see her.

And they told her that they had all been poor and laboured hard in the old time, and had never rested; so that now it was the Father's good pleasure that they should enjoy great peace and consolation among the fresh-breathing fields and on the river-side, so that there were many who even now had little occupation except to think of the Father's goodness, and to rest. And they told her how the Lord himself would come among them, and sit down under a tree, and tell them one of his parables, and make them all more happy than words could say; and how sometimes he would send one out of the beautiful city, with a poem or tale to say to them, and bands of lovely music, more lovely than anything beside, except the sound of the Lord's own voice.

"And what is more wonderful, the angels themselves come often and listen to us," they said, "when we begin to talk and re-mind each other of the old time, and how we suffered heat and cold, and were bowed down with labour, and bending over the soil, and how sometimes the harvest would fail us, and some-times we had not bread, and sometimes would hush the children to sleep because there was nothing to give them; and how we grew old and weary, and still worked on and on."

"We are those who were old," a number of them called out to her, with a murmuring sound of laughter, one looking over another's shoulder. And one woman said, "The angels say to us, 'Did you never think the Father had forsaken you and the Lord forgotten you?'" And all the rest answered as in a chorus, "There were moments that we thought this; but all the time we knew that it could not be."

"And the angels wonder at us," said another. All this they said, crowding one before another, every one anxious to say some-thing, and sometimes speaking together, but always in accord. And then there was a sound of laughter and pleasure, both at the strange thought that the Lord could have forgotten them, and at the wonder of the angels over their simple tales. And im-mediately they began to remind each other, and say, "Do you remember?" and they told the little Pilgrim a hundred tales of the hardships and troubles they had known, all smiling and radiant with pleasure; and at every new account the others would applaud and rejoice, feeling the happiness all the more for the evils that were past. And some of them led her into their gardens to show her their flowers, and to tell her how they had begun to study and learn how colours were changed and form perfected, and the secrets of the growth and of the germ, of which they had been ignorant. And others arranged themselves in choirs, and sang to her delightful songs of the fields, and accompanied her out upon her way, singing and answering to each other.

The difference between the simple folk and the greatness of the others made the little Pilgrim wonder and admire; and she loved them in her simplicity, and turned back many a time to wave her hand to them, and to listen to the lovely simple singing as it went further and further away. It had an evening tone of rest and quietness, and of protection and peace. "*He leadeth me by the green pastures and beside the quiet waters,*" she said to herself; and her heart swelled with pleasure to think that it was those who had been so old, and so weary and poor, who had this rest to console them for all their sorrows.

And as she went along, not only did she pass through many other villages, but met many on the way who were travelling towards the great city, and would greet her sweetly as they passed, and sometimes stop to say a pleasant word, so that the little Pilgrim was never lonely wherever she went. But most of them began to speak to her in the other language, which was as beautiful and sweet as music, but which she could not understand; and they were surprised to find her ignorant of it, not knowing that she was but a newcomer into these lands. And there were many things that could not be told but in that language, for the earthly tongue had no words to express them. The little Pilgrim was a little sad not to understand what was said to her, but cheered herself with the thought that it should be taught to her by one whom she loved best.

The way by the riverside was very cheerful and bright, with many people coming and going, and many villages, some of them with a bridge across the stream, some withdrawn among the fields, but all of them bright and full of life, and with sounds of music, and voices, and footsteps: and the little Pilgrim felt no weariness, and moved along as lightly as a child, taking great pleasure in everything she saw, and answering all the friendly greetings with all her heart, yet glad to think that she was approaching ever nearer to the country where it was ordained that she should dwell for a time and succour the strangers, and receive those who were newly arrived. And she consoled herself with the thought that there was no need of any language but that which she knew.

As this went through her mind, making her glad, she suddenly became aware of one who was walking by her side, a lady who was covered with a veil white and shining like that which Ama had worn in the beautiful city. It hung about this stranger's head so that it was not easy to see her face, but the sound of her voice was very sweet in the pilgrim's ear, yet startled her like the sound of something which she knew well, but could not remember. And as there were few who were going that way, she was glad and said, "Let us walk together, if that pleases you." And the stranger said, "It is for that I have come," which was a reply which made the little Pilgrim wonder more and more, though she was very glad and joyful to have this companion upon her way. And then the lady began to ask her many questions, not about the city, or the great things she had seen, but about herself, and what the dear Lord had given her to do.

"I am little and weak, and I cannot do much," the little Pilgrim said. "It is nothing but pleasure. It is to welcome those that are coming, and tell them. Sometimes they are astonished and do not know. I was so myself. I came in my sleep, and understood nothing. But now that I know, it is sweet to tell them that they need not fear."

"I was glad," the lady said, "that you came in your sleep; for sometimes the way is dark and hard, and you are little and tender. When your brother comes you will be the first to see him, and show him the way."

"My brother! is he coming?" the little Pilgrim cried. And then she said with a wistful look, "But we are all brethren, and you mean only one of those who are the children of our Father. You must forgive me that I do not know the higher speech, but only what is natural, for I have not yet been long here."

"He whom I mean is called—" and here the lady said a name which was the true name of a brother born whom the Pilgrim loved above all others. She gave a cry, and then she said, trembling, "I know your voice, but I cannot see your face. And what you say makes me think of many things. No one else has covered her face when she has spoken to me. I know you, and yet I cannot tell who you are."

The woman stood for a little without saying a word, and then very softly, in a voice which only the heart heard, she called the little Pilgrim by her name.

"*Mother*," cried the Pilgrim, with such a cry of joy that it echoed all about in the sweet air, and flung herself upon the veiled lady, and drew the veil from her face, and saw that it was she. And with this sight there came a revelation which flooded her soul with happiness. For the face which had been old and feeble was old no longer, but fair in the maturity of day; and the figure that had been bent and weary was full of a tender majesty, and the arms that clasped her about were warm and soft with love and life. And all that had changed their relations in the other days and made the mother in her weakness seem as a child, and transferred all protection and strength to the daughter, was gone for ever and the little Pilgrim beheld in a rapture one who was her sister and equal, yet ever above her,—more near to her than any, though all were so near,—one of whom she herself was a part, yet another, and who knew all her thoughts and the way of them before they arose in her.

And to see her face as in the days of her prime, and her eyes so clear and wise, and to feel once more that which is different from the love of all, that which is still most sweet where all is sweet, the love of one, was like a crown to her in her happiness. The little Pilgrim could not think for joy, nor say a word, but held this dear mother's hands and looked in her face, and her heart soared away to the Father in thanks and joy. They sat down by the roadside under the shade of the trees,—while the river ran softly by, and everything was hushed out of sympathy and kindness,—and questioned each other of all that had been and was to be. And the little Pilgrim told all the little news of home, and of the brothers and sisters and the children that had been born, and of those whose faces were turned towards this better country; and the mother smiled and listened and would have heard all over and over, although many things she already knew. "But why should I tell you, for did not you watch over us and see all we did, and were not you near us always?" the little Pilgrim said.

"How could that be?" said the mother; "for we are not like our Lord, to be everywhere. We come and go where we are sent. But sometimes we knew, and sometimes saw, and always loved. And whenever our hearts were sick for news it was but to go to him, and he told us everything. And now, my little one, you are as we are, and have seen the Lord. And this has been given us, to teach our child once more, and show you the heavenly language, that you may understand all, both the little and the great."

Then the Pilgrim lifted her head from her mother's bosom, and looked in her face with eyes full of longing. "You said 'we,'" she said.

The mother did nothing but smile; then lifted her eyes and looked along the beautiful path of the river to where someone was coming to join them. And the little Pilgrim cried out again, in wonder and joy; and presently found herself seated between them, her father and her mother, the two who had loved her most in the other days. They looked more beautiful than the angels and all the great persons whom she had seen; for still they were hers and she was theirs more than all the angels and all the blessed could be. And thus she learned that though the new may take the place of the old, and many things may blossom out of it like flowers, yet that the old is never done away.

And then they sat together, telling of everything that had befallen, and all the little tender things that were of no import, and all the great changes and noble ways, and the wonders of heaven above—and the earth beneath, for all, were open to them, both great and small; and when they had satisfied their souls with these, her father and mother began to teach her the other language, smiling often at her faltering tongue, and telling her the same thing over and over till she learnt it; and her father called her his little foolish one, as he had done in the old days; and at last, when they had kissed her and blessed her, and told her how to come home to them when she was weary, they gave her, as the Father had permitted them, with joy and blessing, her new name.

The little Pilgrim was tired with happiness and all the wonder and pleasure; and as she sat there in the silence; leaning upon those who were so dear to her, the soft air grew sweeter and sweeter about her, and the light faded softly into a dimness of tender indulgence and privilege for her, because she was still little and weak. And whether that heavenly suspense of all her faculties was sleep or not she knew not, but it was such as in all her life she had never known. When she came back to herself, it was by the sound of many voices calling her, and many people hastening past and beckoning to her to join them.

"Come, come," they said, "little sister: there has been great trouble in the other life, and many have arrived suddenly and are afraid. Come, come, and help them,—come and help them!"

And she sprang up from her soft seat, and found that she was no longer by the riverside, or within sight of the great city, or in the arms of those she loved, but stood on one of the flowery paths of her own border-land, and saw her fellows hastening towards the gates where there seemed a great crowd. And she was no longer weary, but full of life and strength; and it seemed to her that she could take them up in her arms, those trembling strangers, and carry them straight to the Father, so strong was she, and light, and full of force.

And above all the gladness she had felt, and all her pleasure in what she had seen, and more happy even than the meeting with those she loved most, was her happiness how, as she went along as light as the breeze to receive the strangers. She was so eager that she began to sing a song of welcome as she hastened on. "Oh, welcome, welcome!" she cried; and as she sang she knew it was one of the heavenly melodies which she had heard in the great city; and she hastened on, her feet flying over the flowery ways, thinking how the great worlds were all watching, and the angels looking on, and the whole universe waiting till it should be proved to them that the dear Lord, the Brother of us all, had chosen the perfect way, and that over all evil and the sorrow he was the Conqueror alone.

And the little Pilgrim's voice, though it was so small, echoed away through the great firmament to where the other worlds were watching to see what should come, and cheered the anxious faces of some great lords and princes far more great than she, who were of a nobler race than man; for it was said among the stars that when such a little sound could reach so far, it was a token that the Lord had chosen aright, and that his method must be the best. And it breathed over the earth like someone saying Courage! to those whose hearts were failing; and it dropped down, down, into the great confusions and traffic of the Land of Darkness, and startled many, like the cry of a child calling and calling, and never ceasing, "Come! and come! and come!"

3: THE LITTLE PILGRIM IN THE SEEN AND UNSEEN

The little Pilgrim, whose story has been told in another place, and who had arrived but lately on the other side, among those who know trouble and sorrow no more, was one whose heart was always full of pity for the suffering. And after the first rapture of her arrival, and of the blessed work which had been given to her to do, and all the wonderful things she had learned of the new life, there returned to her in the midst of her happiness so many questions and longing thoughts that They were touched by them who have the care of the younger brethren, the simple ones of heaven. These questions did not disturb her peace or joy, for she knew that which is so often veiled on earth,—that all is accomplished by the will of the Father, and that nothing can happen but according to His appointment and under His care. And she was also aware that the end is as the beginning to Him who knows all, and that nothing is lost that is in His hand.

But though she would herself have willingly borne the sufferings of earth ten times over for the sake of all that was now hers, yet it pierced her soul to think of those who were struggling in darkness, and whose hearts were stifled within them by all the bitterness of the mortal life. Sometimes she would be ready to cry out with wonder that the Lord did not hasten His steps and go down again upon the earth to make all plain; or how the Father himself could restrain His power, and did not send down ten legions of angels to make all that was wrong right, and turn all that was mournful into joy.

'It is but for a little time,' said her companions. 'When we have reached this place we remember no more the anguish.' 'But to them in their trouble it does not seem a little time,' the Pilgrim said. And in her heart there rose a great longing. Oh that He would send me! that I might tell my brethren,—not like the poor man in the land of darkness, of the gloom and misery of that distant place, but a happier message, of the light and brightness of this, and how soon all pain would be over. She would not put this into a prayer, for she knew that to refuse a prayer is pain to the Father, if in His great glory any pain can be. And then she reasoned with herself and said, 'What can I tell them, except that all will soon be well? and this they know, for our Lord has said it; but I am like them, and I do not understand.'

One fair morning while she turned over these thoughts in her mind there suddenly came towards her one whom she knew as a sage, of the number of those who know many mysteries and search into the deep things of the Father. For a moment she wondered if perhaps he came to reprove her for too many questionings, and rose up and advanced a little towards him with folded hands and a thankful heart, to receive the reproof if it should be so,—for whether it were praise or whether it were blame, it was from the Father, and a great honour and happiness to receive. But as he came towards her he smiled and bade her not to fear. 'I am come,' he said, 'to tell you some things you long to know, and to show you some things that are hidden to most. Little sister, you are not to be charged with any mission—'

'Oh, no,' she said, 'oh, no. I was not so presuming—'

'It is not presuming to wish to carry comfort to any soul; but it is permitted to me to open up to you, so far as I may, some of the secrets. The secrets of the Father are all beautiful, but there is sorrow in them as well as joy; and Pain, you know, is one of the great angels at the door.'

'Is his name Pain? and I took him for Consolation!' the little Pilgrim said.

'He is not Consolation; he is the schoolmaster whose face is often stern. But I did not come to tell you of him whom you know; I am going to take you—back,' the wise man said.

'Back!' She knew what this meant, and a great pleasure, yet mingled with fear, came into her mind. She hesitated, and looked at him, and did not know how to accept, though she longed to do so, for at the same time she was afraid. He smiled when he saw the alarm in her face.

'Do you think,' he said, 'that you are to go this journey on your own charges? Had you insisted, as some do, to go at all hazards, you might indeed have feared. And even now I cannot promise that you will not feel the thorns of the earth as you pass; but you will be cared for, so that no harm can come.'

'Ah,' she said wistfully, 'it is not for harm—' and could say nothing more.

He laid his hand upon her arm, and he said, 'Do not fear; though they see you not, it is yet sweet for a moment to be there, and as you pass, it brings thoughts of you to their minds.'

For these two understood each other, and knew that to see and yet not be seen is only a pleasure for those who are most like the Father, and can love without thought of love in return.

When he touched her, it seemed to the little Pilgrim suddenly that everything changed round her, and that she was no longer in her own place, but walking along a weary length of road. It was narrow and rough, and the skies were dim; and as she went on by the side of her guide she saw houses and gardens which were to her like the houses that children build, and the little gardens in which they sow seeds and plant flowers, and take them up again to see if they are growing. She turned to the Sage, saying, 'What are—?' and then stopped and gazed again, and burst out into something that was between laughing and tears. 'For it is home,' she cried, 'and I did not know it! dear home!' Her heart was remorseful, as if she had wounded the little diminished place.

'This is what happens with those who have been living in the king's palaces,' he said with a smile.

'But I love it dearly, I love it dearly!' the little Pilgrim said, stretching out her hands as if for pardon. He smiled at her, consoling her; and then his face changed and grew very grave.

'Little sister,' he said, 'you have come not to see happiness but pain. We want no explanation of the joy, for that flows freely from the heart of the Father, and all is clear between us and Him; but that which you desire to know is why trouble should be. Therefore you must think of Him and be strong, for here is what will rend your heart.'

The little Pilgrim was seized once more with mortal fear. 'Oh friend,' she cried, 'I have done with pain. Must I go and see others suffering and do nothing for them?'

'If anything comes into your heart to do or say, it will be well for them,' the Sage replied: and he took her by the hand and led her into a house she knew. She began to know them all now, as her vision became accustomed to the atmosphere of the earth. She perceived that the sun was shining, though it had appeared so dim, and that it was a clear summer morning, very early, with still the colors of the dawn in the east. When she went indoors, at first she saw nothing, for the room was darkened, the windows all closed, and a miserable watch-light only burning. In the bed there lay a child whom she knew. She knew them all,—the mother at the bedside, the father near the door, even the nurse who was flitting about disturbing the silence.

Her heart gave a great throb when she recognised them all; and though she had been glad for the first moment to think that she had come just in time to give welcome to a little brother stepping out of earth into the better country, a shadow of trouble and pain enveloped her when she saw the others and remembered and knew. For he was their beloved child; on all the earth there was nothing they held so dear. They would have given up their home and all they possessed, and become poor and homeless and wanderers with joy, if God, as they said, would have but spared their child. She saw into their hearts and read all this there; and knowing them, she knew it without even that insight. Everything they would have given up and rejoiced, if but they might have kept him. And there he lay, and was about to die. The little Pilgrim forgot all but the pity of it, and their hearts that were breaking, and the vacant place that was soon to be. She cried out aloud upon the Father with a great cry. She forgot that it was a grief to Him in His great glory to refuse.

There came no reply; but the room grew light as with a reflection out of heaven, and the child in the bed, who had been moving restlessly in the weariness of ending life, turned his head towards her, and his eyes opened wide, and he saw her where she stood. He cried out, 'Look! mother, mother!' The mother, who was on her knees by the bedside, lifted her head and cried, 'What is it, what is it, Oh my darling?' and the father, who had turned away his face not to see the child die, came nearer to the bed, hoping they knew not what. Their faces were paler than the face of the dying, upon which there was light; but no light came to them out of the hidden heaven. 'Look! she has come for me,' he said; but his voice was so weak they could not hear him, nor take any comfort. At this the little Pilgrim put out her arms to him, forgetting in her joy the poor people who were mourning, and cried out, 'Oh, but I must go with him! I must take him home!' For this was her own work, and she thought of her wonderings and her questions no more.

Someone touched her on the shoulder, and she looked round; and behind her was a great company of the dear children from the better country, whom the Father had sent, and not her,—lest he should grieve for those he had left behind,—to come for the child and show him the way. She paused for a moment, scarcely willing to give him up; but then her companion touched her and pointed to the other side. Ah, that was different! The mother lay by the side of the bed, her face turned only to the little white body which her child had dropped from him as he came out of his sickness,—her eyes wild with misery, without tears; her feverish mouth open, but no cry in it. The sword of the angel had gone through and through her. She did not even writhe upon it, but lay motionless, cut down, dumb with anguish. The father had turned round again and leaned his head upon the wall.

All was over,—all over! The love and the hope of a dozen lovely years, the little sweet companion, the daily joy, the future trust—all—over—as if a child had never been born. Then there rose in the stillness a great and exceeding bitter cry, 'God!' that was all, pealing up to heaven, to the Father, whom they could not see in their anguish, accusing Him, reproaching Him who had done it. Was He their enemy that He had done it? No man was ever so wicked, ever so cruel but he would have spared them their boy,—taken everything and spared them their boy; but God, God! The little Pilgrim stood by and wept. She could do nothing but weep, weep, her heart aching with the pity and the anguish. How were they to be told that it was not God, but the Father; that God was only His common name, His name in law, and that He was the Father. This was all she could think of; she had not a word to say. And the boy had shaken his little bright soul out of the sickness and the weakness with such a look of delight! He knew in a moment! But they—oh, when, when would they know?

Presently she sat outside in the soft breathing airs and little morning breezes, and dried her aching eyes. And the Sage who was her companion soothed her with kind words. 'I said you would feel the thorns as you passed,' he said. 'We cannot be free of them, we who are of mankind.'

'But oh,' she cried amid her tears, 'why,—why? The air of the earth is in my eyes, I cannot see. Oh, what pain it is, what misery! Was it because they loved him too much, and that he drew their hearts away?'

The Sage only shook his head at her, smiling. 'Can one love too much?' he said.

'Oh brother, it is very hard to live and to see another—I am confused in my mind,' said the little Pilgrim, putting her hand to her eyes. 'The tears of those that weep have got into my soul. To live and see another die,—that was what I was saying; but the child lives like you and me. Tell me, for I am confused in my mind.'

'Listen!' said the Sage; and when she listened she heard the sound of the children going back with a great murmur and ringing of pleasant voices like silver bells in the air, and among them the voice of the child asking a thousand questions, calling them by their names. The two pilgrims listened and laughed to each other for love at the sound of the children. 'Is it for the little brother that you are troubled?' the Sage said in her ear.

Then she was ashamed, and turned from the joyful sounds that were ascending ever higher and higher to the little house that stood below, with all its windows closed upon the light. It was wrapped in darkness though the sun was shining, the windows closed as if they never would open more, and the people within turning their faces to the wall, covering their eyes that they might not see the light of day. 'Oh miserable day!' they were saying; 'Oh dark hour! Oh life that will never smile again!' She sat between earth and heaven, her eyes smiling, but her mouth beginning to quiver once more. 'Is it to raise their thoughts and their hearts?' she said.

'Little sister,' said he, 'when the Father speaks to you, it is not for me nor for another that He speaks. And what He says to you is—'

'Ah,' said the little Pilgrim, with joy, 'it is for myself, myself alone! As if I were a great angel, as if I were a saint. It drops into my heart like the dew. It is what I need, not for you, though I love you, but for me only. It is my secret between me and

Him.'

Her companion bowed his head. 'It is so. And thus has He spoken to the little child. But what He said or why He said it, is not for you or me to know. It is His secret; it is between the little one and his Father. Who can interfere between these two? Many and many are there born on earth whose work and whose life are ordained elsewhere,—for there is no way of entrance into the race of man which is the nature of the Lord, but by the gates of birth; and the work which the Father has to do is so great and manifold that there are multitudes who do but pass through those gates to ascend to their work elsewhere. But the Father alone knows whom he has chosen. It is between the child and Him. It is their secret; it is as you have said.'

The little Pilgrim was silent for a moment, but then turned her head from the bright shining of the skies and the voices of the children which floated farther and farther off, and looked at the house in which there was sorrow and despair. She pointed towards it, and looked at him who was her instructor, and had come to show her how these things were.

'They are to blame,' he said; 'but none will blame them. The little life is hard. The Father, though He is very near, seems far off; and sometimes even His word is as a dream. It is to them as if they had lost their child. Can you not remember?—that was what we said. We have lost—'

Then the little Pilgrim, musing, began to smile, but wept again as she thought of the father and the mother. 'If we were to go,' she said, 'hand in hand, you and I, and tell them that the Father had need of him, that it was not for the little life but for the great and beautiful world above that the child was born; and that he had got great promotion and was gone with the princes and the angels according as was ordained? And why should they mourn? Let us go and tell them—'

He shook his head. 'They could not see us; they would not know us. We should be to them as dreams. If they do not take comfort from our Lord, how could they take comfort from you and me? We could not bring them back their child. They want

155

their child, not only to know that all is well with him,—for they know that all is well with him,—but what they want is their child. They are to blame; but who shall blame them? Not any one that is born of woman. How can we tell them what is the Father's secret and the child's?'

'And yet we could tell them why it must be so?' said the little Pilgrim. 'For they prayed and besought the Lord. Oh brother, I have no understanding. For the Lord said, "Ask, and it shall be given you;" and they asked, yet they are refused.'

'Little sister, the Father must judge between His children; and he must first be heard who is most concerned. While they were praying, the Father and the child talked together and said what we know not; but this we know, that his heart was satisfied with that which was said to him. Must not the Father do what is best for the child He loves, whatever the other children may say? Nay, did not our own fathers do this on earth, and we submitted to them; how much more He who sees all?'

The little Pilgrim stole softly from his side when he had done speaking, and went back into the darkened house, and saw the mother where she sat weeping and refusing to be comforted, in her sorrow perceiving not heaven nor any consolation, nor understanding that her child had gone joyfully to his Father and her Father, as his soul had required, and as the Lord had willed. Yet though she had not joy but only anguish in her faith, and though her eyes were darkened that she could not see, yet the woman ceased not to call upon God, God, and to hold by Him who had smitten her. And the father of the child had gone into his chamber and shut the door, and sat dumb, opening not his mouth, thinking upon his delightsome boy, and how they had walked together and talked together, and should do so again nevermore.

And in their hearts they reproached their God, the giver of all, and accused the Lord to His face, as if He had deceived them, yet clung to Him still, weeping and upbraiding, and would not let Him go. The little Pilgrim wept too, and said many things to them which they could not hear. But when she saw that though they were in darkness and misery, God was in all their thoughts, she bethought herself suddenly of what the poet had said in the celestial city, and of the songs he sang, which were a wonder to the Angels and Powers, of the little life and the sorrowful earth, where men endured all things, yet overcame by the name of the Lord. When this came into her mind, she rose up again softly with a sacred awe, and wept not, but did them reverence; for without any light or guidance in their anguish they yet wavered not, died not, but endured, and in the end would overcome. It seemed to her that she saw the great beautiful angels looking on, the great souls that are called to love and to serve, but not to suffer like the little brethren of the earth; and that among the princes of heaven there was reverence and awe, and even envy of those who thus had their garments bathed in blood, and suffered loss and pain and misery, yet never abandoned their life and the work that had been given them to do.

As she came forth again comforted, she found the Sage standing with his face lifted to heaven, smiling still at the sound, though faint and distant, of the children all calling to each other and shouting together as they reached the gate. 'Oh, hush!' she said; 'let not the mother hear them! for it will make her heart more bitter to think she can never hear again her child's voice.'

'But it is her child's voice,' he said; then very gently, 'they are to blame; but no one will be found to blame them either in earth or heaven.'

The earth pilgrims went far after this, yet more softly than when they first left their beautiful country,—for then the little Pilgrim had been glad, believing that as all had been made clear to her in her own life, so that all that concerned the life of man should be made clear; but this was more hard and encompassed with pain and darkness, as that which is in the doing is always more hard to understand than that which is accomplished. And she learned now what she had not understood, though her companion warned her, how sharp are those thorns of earth that pierce the wayfarer's foot, and that those who come back cannot help but suffer because of love and fellow-feeling. And she learned that though she could smile and give thanks to the Father in the recollection of her own griefs that were past, yet those that are present are too poignant, and to look upon others in their hour of darkness makes His ways more hard to comprehend than even when the sorrow is your own.

While she mused thus, there was suddenly revealed to her another sight. They had gone far before they came to this new scene. Night had crept over the skies all gray and dark; and the sea came in with a whisper which sounded to some like the hush of peace, and to some like the voice of sorrow and moaning, and to some was but the monotony of endless recurrence, in which was no soul. The skies were dark overhead, but opened with a clear shining of light which had no colour, towards the west,—for the sun had long gone down, and it was night. The two travellers perceived a woman who came out of a house all lit with lamps and firelight, and took the lonely path towards the sea. And the little Pilgrim knew her, as she had known the father and mother in the darkened house, and would have joined her with a cry of pleasure; but she remembered that the friend could not see her or hear her, being wrapped still in the mortal body, and in a close enveloping mantle of thoughts and cares.

The Sage made her a sign to follow, and these two tender companions accompanied her who saw them not, walking darkling by the silent way. The heart of the woman was heavy in her breast. It was so sore by reason of trouble, and for all the bitter wounds of the past, and all the fears that beset her life to come, that she walked, not weeping because of being beyond tears, but as it were bleeding, her thoughts being in her little way like those of His upon whose brow there once stood drops as it were of blood; and out of her heart there came a moaning which was without words.

If words had been possible, they would have been as His also, who said, '*Father, forgive them, for they know not what they do.*' For those who had wounded her were those whom in all the world she loved most dear; and the quivering of anguish was in her as she walked, seeking the darkness and the silence, and to hide herself, if that might be, from her own thoughts. She went along the lonely path with the stinging of her wounds so keen and sharp that all her body and soul were as one pain. Greater grief hath no man than this, to be slain and tortured by those whom he loves. When her soul could speak, this was what it said 'Father, forgive them! Father, save them!' She had no strength for more.

This the heavenly pilgrims saw,—for they stood by her as in their own country, where every thought is clear, and saw her heart. But as they followed her and looked into her soul—with their hearts, which were human too, wrung at the sight of hers in its anguish—there suddenly became visible before them a strange sight such as they had never seen before. It was like the rising of the sun; but it was not the sun. Suddenly into the heart upon which they looked there came a great silence and calm. There was nothing said that even they could hear, nor done that they could see; but for a moment the throbbing was stilled, and the anguish calmed, and there came a great peace. The woman in whom this wonder was wrought was astonished, as they were. She gave a low cry in the darkness for wonder that the pain had gone from her in an instant, in the twinkling of an eye. There was no promise made to her that her prayer would be granted, and no new light given to guide her for the time to come; but her pain was taken away. She stood hushed, and lifted her eyes; and the gray of the sea, and the low cloud that was like a canopy above, and the lightening of colourless light towards the west, entered with their great quiet into her heart. '*Is this the peace that passeth all understanding?*' she said to herself, confused with the sudden calm. In all her life it had never so happened to her before,—to be healed of her grievous wounds, yet without cause; and while no change was wrought, yet to be put to rest.

'It is our Brother,' said the little Pilgrim, shedding tears of joy. 'It is the secret of the Lord,' said the Sage; but not even they had seen Him passing by.

They walked with her softly in the silence, in the sound of the sea, till the wonder in her was hushed like the pain, and talked with her, though she knew it not. For very soon questions arose in her heart. 'And oh,' she said, 'is this the Lord's reply?' with thankfulness and awe; but because she was human, and knew so little, and was full of impatience, 'Oh, and is this *all?*' was what she next said. 'I asked for *them*, and Thou hast given to *me*—' then the voice of her heart grew louder, and she cried, with the sound of the pain coming back, 'I ask one thing, and Thou givest another. I asked no blessing for me. I asked for them, my Lord, my God. Give it to them—to them!' with disappointment rising in her heart. The little Pilgrim laid her hand upon the woman's arm,—for she was afraid lest our Lord might be displeased, forgetting (for she was still imperfect) that He sees all that is in the soul, and understands and takes no offence,— and said quickly, 'Oh, be not afraid; He will save them too. The blessing will come for them too.'

'At His own time,' said the Sage, 'and in His own way.'

These thoughts rose in the woman's soul. She did not know that they were said to her, nor who said them, but accepted them as if they had come from her own thoughts. For she said to herself, 'This is what is meant by the answer of prayer. It is not what we ask; yet what I ask is according to Thy will, my Lord. It is not riches, nor honours, nor beauty, nor health, nor long life, nor anything of this world. If I have been impatient, this is my punishment,—that the Lord has thought, not of them, but of me. But I can bear all, Oh my Lord! that and a thousand times more, if Thou wilt but think of them and not of me!'

Nevertheless she returned to her home stilled and comforted; for though her trouble returned to her and was not changed, yet for a moment it had been lifted from her, and *the peace which passeth all understanding* had entered her heart.

'But why, then,' said the little Pilgrim to her companion, when the friend was gone, 'why will not the Father give to her what she asks? for I know what it is. It is that those whom she loves should love Him and serve Him; and that is His will too, for He would have all love Him, He who loves all.'

'Little sister,' said her companion, 'you asked me why He did not let the child remain upon the earth.'

'Ah, but that is different,' she cried; 'oh, it is different! When you said that the secret was between the child and the Father I knew that it was so; for it is just that the Father should consider us first one by one, and do for us what is best. But it is always best to serve Him. It is best to love him; it is best to give up all the world and cleave to Him, and follow wherever He goes. No man can say otherwise than this,—that to follow the Lord and serve Him, that is well for all, and always the best!'

She spoke so hotly and hastily that her companion could find no room for reply. But he was in no haste; he waited till she had said what was in her heart. Then he replied, 'If it were even so, if the Father heard all prayers, and put forth His hand and forced those who were far off to come near—'

The little Pilgrim looked up with horror in her face, as if he had blasphemed, and said, 'Forced! not so; not so!'

'Yet it must be so,' he said, 'if it is against their desire and will.'

'Oh, not so; not so!' she cried, 'but that He should change their hearts.'

'Yet that too against their will,' he said.

The little Pilgrim paused upon the way; and her heart rose against her companion, who spoke things so hard to be received, and that seemed to dishonour the work of the Lord. But she remembered that it could not be so, and paused before she spoke, and looked up at him with eyes that were full of wonder and almost of fear. 'Then must they perish?' she said, 'and must her heart break?' and her voice sank low for pity and sorrow. Though she was herself among the blessed, yet the thorns and briers of the earth caught at her garments and pierced her tender feet.

'Little sister,' said the Sage, 'to us who are born of the earth it is hard to remember that the child belongs not first to the parents, nor the husband to the wife, nor the wife to the husband, but that all are the children of the Father. And He is just; He will not neglect the little one because of those prayers which the father and the mother pour forth to Him, although they cry with anguish and with tears. Nor will He break His great law and violate the nature He has made, and compel His own child to what it wills not and loves not. The woman is comforted in the breaking of her heart; but those whom she loves, are not they also the children of the Father, who loves them more than she does? And each is to Him as if there were not another in the world. Nor is there any other in the world,—for none can come between the Father and the child.'

A smile came upon the little Pilgrim's face, yet she trembled. 'It is dim before me,' she said, 'and I cannot see clearly. Oh, if the time would but hasten, that our Lord might come, and all struggles be ended, and the darkness vanish away!'

'He will come when all things are ready,' said the Sage; and as they went upon their way be showed her other sights, and the mysteries of the heart of man, and the great patience of our Lord.

It happened to them suddenly to perceive in their way a man returning home. These are words that are sweet to all who have lived upon the earth and known its ways; but far, far were they from that meaning which is sweet. The dark hours had passed, and men had slept; and the night was over. The sun was rising in the sky, which was keen and clear with the pleasure of the morning. The air was fresh with the dew, and the birds awaking in the trees, and the breeze so sweet that it seemed to blow from heaven; and to the two travellers it seemed almost in the joy of the new day as if the Lord had already come.

But here was one who proved that it was not so. He had not slept all the night, nor had night been silent to him nor dark, but full of glaring light and noise and riot; his eyes were red with fever and weariness, and his soul was sick within him, and the morning looked him in the face and upbraided him as a sister might have upbraided him, who loved him. And he said in his heart, as one had said of old, that all was vanity; that it was vain to live, and evil to have been born; that the day of death was better than the day of birth, and all was delusion, and love but a word, and life a lie. His footsteps on the road seemed to sound all through the sleeping world; and when he looked the morning in the face he was ashamed, and cursed the light.

The two went after him into a silent house, where everybody slept. The light that had burned for him all night was sick like a guilty thing in the eye of day, and all that had been prepared for his repose was ghastly to him in the hour of awaking, as if prepared not for sleep but for death. His heart was sick like the watch-light, and life flickered within him with disgust and disappointment. For why had he been born, if this were all?—for all was vanity. The night and the day had been passed in pleasure, and it was vanity; and now his soul loathed his pleasures, yet he knew that was vanity too, and that next day he would resume them as before. All was vain,—the morning and the evening, and the spirit of man and the ways of human life. He looked himself in the face and loathed this dream of existence, and knew that it was naught. So much as it had cost to be born, to be fed, and guarded and taught and cared for, and all for this! He said to himself that it was better to die than to live, and never to have been than to be.

As these spectators stood by with much pity and tenderness looking into the weariness and sickness of this soul, there began to be enacted before them a scene such as no man could have seen, which no one was aware of save he who was concerned, and which even to him was not clear in its meanings, but rather like a phantasmagoria, a thing of the mists; yet which was great and solemn as is the council of a king in which great things are debated for the welfare of the nations. The air seemed in a moment to be full of the sound of footsteps, and of something more subtle, which the Sage and the Pilgrim knew to be wings; and as they looked, there grew before them the semblance of a court of justice, with accusers and defenders; but the judge and the criminal were one. Then was put forth that indictment which he had been making up in his soul against life and against the world; and again another indictment which was against himself. And then the advocates began their pleadings.

Voices were there great and eloquent, such as are familiar in the courts above, which sounded forth in the spectators' ears earnest as those who plead for life and death. And these speakers declared that sin only is vanity, that life is noble and love sweet, and every man made in the image of God, to serve both God and man; and they set forth their reasons before the judge and showed him mysteries of life and death; and they took up the counter-indictment and proved to him how in all the world he had sought but himself, his own pleasure and profit, his own will, not the will of God, nor even the good desire of humble nature, but only that which pleased his sick fancies and his self-loving heart.

And they besought him with a thousand arguments to return and choose again the better way. 'Arise,' they cried, 'thou, miserable, and become great; arise, thou vain soul, and become noble. Take thy birthright, Oh son, and behold the face of the Father.' And then there came a whispering of lower voices, very penetrating and sweet, like the voices of women and children, who murmured and cried, 'Oh father! Oh brother! Oh love! Oh my child!' The man who was the accused, yet who was the judge, listened; and his heart burned, and a longing arose within him for the face of the Father and the better way.

But then there came a clang and clamour of sound on the other side; and voices called out to him as comrade, as lover, as friend, and reminded him of the delights which once had been so sweet to him, and of the freedom he loved; and boasted the right of man to seek what was pleasant and what was sweet, and flouted him as a coward whose aim was to save himself, and scorned him as a believer in old wives' tales and superstitions that men had outgrown. And their voices were so vehement and full of passion that by times they mastered the others, so that it was as if a tempest raged round the soul which sat in the midst, and who was the offender and yet the judge of all.

The two spectators watched the conflict, as those who watch the trial upon which hangs a man's life. It seemed to the little Pilgrim that she could not keep silent, and that there were things which she could tell him which no one knew but she.

She put her hand upon the arm of the Sage and called to him, 'Speak you, speak you! he will hear you; and I too will speak, and he will not resist what we say.' But even as she said this, eager and straining against her companion's control, the strangest thing ensued. The man who was set there to judge himself and his life; he who was the criminal, yet august upon his seat, to weigh all and give the decision; he before whom all those great advocates were pleading,—a haze stole over his eyes. He was but a man, and he was weary, and subject to the sway of the little over the great, the moment over the life, which is the condition of man.

While yet the judgment was not given or the issue decided, while still the pleadings were in his ears, in a moment his head dropped back upon his pillow, and he fell asleep. He slept like a child, as if there was no evil, nor conflict, nor danger, nor questions, more than how best to rest when you are weary, in all the world. And straightway all was silent in the place. Those who had been conducting this great cause departed to other courts and tribunals, having done all that was permitted them to do. And the man slept, and when it was noon woke and remembered no more.

The Sage led the little Pilgrim forth in a great confusion, so that she could not speak for wonder. But he said, 'This sleep also was from the Father; for the mind of the man was weary, and not able to form a judgment. It is adjourned until a better day.'

The little Pilgrim hung her head and cried, 'I do not understand. Will not the Lord interfere? Will not the Father make it clear to him? Is he the judge between good and evil? Is it all in his own hand?'

The Sage spoke softly, as if with awe. He said, 'This is the burden of our nature, which is not like the angels. There is none in heaven or on earth that can take from him what is his right and great honor among the creatures of God. The Father respects that which He has made. He will force no child of His. And there is no haste with Him; nor has it ever been fathomed among us how long He will wait, or if there is any end. The air is full of the coming and going of those who plead before the sons of men; and sometimes in great misery and trouble there will be a cause won and a judgment recorded which makes the universe rejoice. And in everything at the end it is proved that our Lord's way is the best, and that all can be accomplished in His name.'

The little Pilgrim went on her way in silence, knowing that the longing in her heart which was to compel them to come in, like that king who sent to gather his guests from the highways and the hedges, could not be right, since it was not the Father's way, yet confused in her soul, and full of an eager desire to go back and wake that man and tell him all that had been in her heart while she watched him sitting on his judgment-seat. But there came recollections wafted across her mind as by breezes of the past, of scenes in her earthly life when she had spoken without avail, when she had said all that was in her heart and failed, and done harm when she had meant to do good. And slowly it came upon her that her companion spoke the truth, and that no man can save his brother; but each must sit and hear the pleadings and pronounce that judgment which is for life or death. 'But oh,' she cried, 'how long and how bitter it is for those who love them, and must stand by and can give no aid!'

Then her companion unfolded to her the patience of the Lord, and how He is not discouraged, nor ever weary, but opens His great assizes year by year and day by day; and how the cause was argued again, as she had seen it, before the souls of men, sometimes again and again and over and over, till the pleadings of the advocates carried conviction, and the judge perceived the truth and consented to it. He showed her that this was the great thing in human life, and that though it was not enough to make a man perfect, yet that he who sinned against his will was different from the man who sinned with his will; and how in all things the choice of the man for good or evil was all in all. And he led her about the world so that she could see how everywhere the heavenly advocates were travelling, entering into the secret places of the souls, and pleading with each man to his face.

And the little Pilgrim looked on with pitying and tender eyes, and it seemed to her that the heart of the judge, before whom that great question was debated, leaned mostly to the right, and acknowledged that the way of the Lord was the best way; but either that sleep overpowered him and weariness, or the other voices deafened his ears, or something betrayed him that he forgot the reasons of the wise and the judgment of his own soul. At first it comforted her to see how something nobler in every man would answer to the pleadings; and then her heart failed her, to perceive that notwithstanding this the judge would leave his seat without a decision, and all would end in vanity. 'And oh, friend,' she cried, 'what shall be done to those who see and yet refuse?'—her heart being wrung by the disappointment and the failure. But her companion smiled still, and he said, 'They are the children of the Father. Can a woman forget her child that she should not have compassion on the son of her womb? She may forget; yet will not He forget.' And thus they went on and on.

But time would not suffice to tell what these two pilgrims saw as they wandered among the ways of men. They saw poverty and misery and pain, which came of the evil which man had done upon the earth, and were his punishment, and could be cured by nothing but by the return of each to his Father, and the giving up of all self-worship and self-seeking and sin. But amid all the confusion and among those who had fallen the lowest they found not one who was forsaken, whose name the Father had forgotten, or who was not made to pause in his appointed moment, and to sit upon his throne and hear the pleadings before him of the great advocates of God, reasoning of temperance and righteousness and judgment to come.

But once before they returned to their home, a great thing befell them; and they beheld that court sit, and the pleadings made, for the last time upon earth, which was a sight more solemn and terrible than anything they had yet seen. They found themselves in a chamber where sat a man who had lived long and known both good and evil, and fulfilled many great offices, so that he was famed and honoured among men. He was a man who was wise in all the learning of the earth, standing but a little way below those who have begun the higher learning in the world beyond, and lifting up his head as if he would reach the stars. The travellers stood by him in his beautiful house, which was as the palace of wisdom, and saw him in the midst of all his honors.

The lamps were lit within, and the night was sweet without, breathing of rest and happy ease, and riches and knowledge, as if they would endure forever. And the man looked round on all he had, and all he had achieved, and everything which he possessed, to enjoy it. For of wisdom and of glory he had his fill, and his soul was yet strong to take pleasure in what was his, and he looked around him like God, and said that everything was good; so that the little Pilgrim gazed, and wondered whether this could indeed be one of the brethren of the earth, or if he was one who had wandered hither from another sphere.

But as the thought arose, she heard, and lo! the steps of the pleaders and the sound of their entry. They came slowly like a solemn procession, more grave and awful in their looks than any she had seen, for they were great and the greatest of all, such as come forth but rarely when the last word is to be said. The words they said were few; but they stood round him reminding him of all that had been, and of what must be, and of many things which were known but to God and him alone, and calling upon him yet once more before time should come to an end and life be lost. But the sound of their voices in his ear was but as some great strain of music which he had heard many times and knew and heeded not. He turned to the goods which he had laid up for many years, and all the knowledge he had stored, and said to himself, 'Soul, take thine ease.' And to the heavenly advocates he smiled and replied that life was strong and wisdom the master of all.

Then there came a chill and a shiver over all, as if the earth had been stopped in her career or the sun fallen from the sky; and the little Pilgrim, looking on, could see the heavenly pleaders come forth with bowed heads and the door of hope shut to, and a whisper which crept about from sea to sea and said, 'In vain! in vain!' And as they went forth from the gates an icy breath swept in, and the voice of the Death-Angel saying, 'Thou fool, this night thy soul shall be required of thee!' The sound went through her heart as if it had been pierced by a sword, and she gave a cry of anguish, for she could not bear that a brother should be lost. But when she looked up at the face of her companion, though it was pale with the pity and the terror of that which had been thus accomplished, there was still upon it a smile; and he said, 'Not yet; not yet. The Father loves not less, but more than ever.' 'Oh friend,' she cried, 'will there ever come a moment when the Father will forget? *Is* there any place where He cannot go?'

Then he who was wise turned towards her, and a great light came upon his face; and he said, 'We have searched the records, and heard all witnesses from the beginnings of time; but we have never found the boundary of His mercy, and there is no country known to man that is without his presence. And never has it been known that He has shut His ear to those who called upon Him, or forgotten one who is His. The heavenly pleaders may be silenced, but never our Lord, who pleads for all; and heaven and earth may forget, yet will He never forget who is the Father of all. And every child of His is to Him as if there was none other in the world.'

Then the little Pilgrim lifted her face and beheld that radiance which is over all, which is the love that lights the world, both angels and the great spheres above and the little brethren who stumble and struggle and weep; and in that light there was no darkness at all, but everything shone as in the morning, sweet yet terrible, but ever clear and fair. And immediately, ere she was aware, the rough roads of the earth were left far behind, and she had returned to her place, and to her peaceful state, and to the work which had been given her,—to receive the wanderers and to bid them a happy welcome as the doors opened and they entered into their inheritance. And thus her soul was satisfied, though she knew now nothing more than she had known always,—that the eye of the Father is over all, and that He can neither forget nor forsake.

4: On the Dark Mountains

When the little Pilgrim had been thus permitted to see the secret workings of God in earthly places, and among the brethren who are still in the land of hope,—these being things which the angels desire to look into, and which are the subject of story and of song not only in the little world below, but in the great realms above,—her heart for a long time reposed and was satisfied, and asked no further question. For she had seen what the dealings of the Father were in the hearts of men, and how till the end came He did not cease to send His messengers to plead in every heart, and to hold a court of justice that no man might be deceived, but each know whither his steps were tending, and what was the way of wisdom.

After this it was permitted to her to read in the archives of the heavenly country the story of one, who, neglecting all that the advocates of God could say, had found himself, when the little life was completed, not upon the threshold of a better country, but in the midst of the Land of Darkness,—that region in which the souls of men are left by God to their own devices, and the Father stands aloof, and hides His face and calls them not, neither persuades them more. Over this story the little Pilgrim had shed many tears; for she knew well, being enlightened in her great simplicity by the heavenly wisdom, that it was pain and grief to the Father to turn away His face; and that no one who has but the little heart of a man can imagine to himself what that sorrow is in the being of the great God.

And a great awe came over her mind at the thought, which seemed well-nigh a blasphemy, that He could grieve; yet in her heart, being His child, she knew that it was true. And her own little spirit throbbed through and through with longing and with desire to help those who were thus utterly lost. 'And oh!' she said, 'if I could but go! There is nothing which could make a child afraid, save to see them suffer. What are darkness and terror when the Father is with you? I am not afraid—if I might but go!' And by reason of her often pleading, and of the thought that was ever in her mind, it was at last said that one of those who knew might instruct her, and show her by what way alone the travellers who come from that miserable land could approach and be admitted on high.

'I know,' she said, 'that between us and them there is a gulf fixed, and that they who would come from thence cannot come, neither can anyone—'

But here she stopped in great dismay, for it seemed that she had thus answered her own longing and prayer.

The guide who had come for her smiled upon her and said, 'But that was before the Lord had ended His work. And now all the paths are free wherever there is a mountain-pass or a river-ford; the roads are all blessed, and they are all open, and no barriers for those who will.'

'Oh,' she cried, 'dear friend, is that true for all?'

He looked away from her into the depths of the lovely air, and he replied: 'Little sister, our faith is without bounds, but not our knowledge. I who speak to you am no more than a man. The princes and powers that are in high places know more than I; but if there be any place where a heart can stir and cry out to the Father and He take no heed,—if it be only in a groan, if it be only with a sigh,—I know not that place, yet many depths I know.' He put out his hand and took hers after a pause; and then he said, 'There are some who are stumbling upon the dark mountains. Come and see.'

As they passed along, there were many who paused to look at them, for he had the mien of a great prince, a lord among men; and his face still bore the trace of sorrow and toil, and there was about him an awe and wonder which was more than could be put in words. So that those who saw him understood as he went by, not who he was, nor what he had been, but that he had come out of great tribulation, of sorrow beyond the sorrows of men. The sweetness of the heavenly country had soothed away his care, and taken the cloud from his face; but he was as yet unaccustomed to smile,—though when he remembered and looked round him and saw that all was well, his countenance lightened like the morning sky, and his eyes woke up in splendour like the sun rising. The little Pilgrim did not know who her brother was, but yet gave thanks to God for him, she knew not why.

How far they went cannot be estimated in words, for distance matters little in that place; but at the end they came to a path which sloped a little downwards to the edge of a delightful moorland country, all brilliant with the hues of the mountain flowers. It was like a flowery plateau high among the hills, in a region where are no frosts to check the glow of the flowers, or scorch the grass. It spread far around in hollows and ravines and softly swelling hills, with the rush over them of a cheerful breeze full of mountain scents and sounds; and high above them rose the mountain heights of the celestial world, veiled in those blue breadths of distance which are heaven itself when man's fancy ascends to them from the low world at their feet.

All the little earth can do in color and mists, and travelling shadows fleet as the breath, and the sweet steadfast shining of the sun, was there, but with a ten-fold splendor. They rose up into the sky, every peak and jagged rock all touched with the light and the smile of God, and every little blossom on the turf rejoicing in the warmth and freedom and peace. The heart of the little Pilgrim swelled, and she cried out, 'There is nothing so glorious as the everlasting hills. Though the valleys and the plains are sweet, they are not like them. They say to us, lift up your heart!'

Her guide smiled, but he did not speak. His smile was full of joy, but grave, like that of a man whose thoughts are bent on other things; and he pointed where the road wound downwards by the feet of these triumphant hills. She kept her eyes upon them as she moved along. Those heights rose into the very sky, but bore upon them neither snow nor storm. Here and there a whiteness like a film of air rounded out over a peak; and she recognized that it was one of those angels who travel far and wide with God's commissions, going to the other worlds that are in the firmament as in a sea. The softness of these films of white was like the summer clouds that she used to watch in the blue of the summer sky in the little world which none of its children can cease to love; and she wondered now whether it might not sometimes have been the same dear angels whose flight she had watched unknowing, higher than thought could soar or knowledge penetrate.

Watching those floating heavenly messengers, and the heights of the great miraculous mountains rising up into the sky, the little Pilgrim ceased to think whither she was going, although she knew from the feeling of the ground under her feet that she was descending, still softly, but more quickly than at first, until she was brought to herself by the sensation of a great wind coming in her face, cold as from a sudden vacancy. She turned her head quickly from gazing above to what was before her, and started with a cry of wonder. For below lay a great gulf of darkness, out of which rose at first some shadowy peaks and shoulders of rock, all falling away into a gloom which eyes accustomed to the sunshine could not penetrate.

Where she stood was the edge of the light,—before her feet lay a line of shadow slowly darkening out of daylight into twilight, and beyond into that measureless blackness of night; and the wind in her face was like that which comes from a great depth below of either sea or land,—the sweep of the current which moves a vast atmosphere in which there is nothing to break its force. The little Pilgrim was so startled by these unexpected sensations that she caught the arm of her guide in her sudden alarm, and clung to him, lest she should fall into the terrible darkness and the deep abyss below.

'There is nothing to fear,' he said; 'there is a way. To us who are above there is no danger at all; and it is the way of life to those who are below.'

'I see nothing,' she cried, 'save a few points of rock, and the precipice,—the pit which is below. Oh, tell me what is it? Is it where the fires are, and despair dwells? I did not think that was true. Let me go and hide myself and not see it, for I never thought that was true.'

'Look again,' said the guide.

The little Pilgrim shrank into a crevice of the rock, and uncovering her eyes, gazed into the darkness; and because her nature was soft and timid there came into her mind a momentary fear. Her heart flew to the Father's footstool, and cried out to Him, not any question or prayer, but only 'Father, Father!' and this made her stand erect, and strengthened her eyes, so that the gloom even of hell could no more make her afraid. Her guide stood beside with a steadfast countenance, which was grave, yet full of a solemn light.

And then all at once he lifted up his voice, which was sonorous and sweet like the sound of an organ, and uttered a shout so great and resounding that it seemed to come back in echoes from every hollow and hill. What he said the little Pilgrim could not understand; but when the echoes had died away and silence followed, something came up through the gloom,—a sound that was far, far away, and faint in the long distance; a voice that sounded no more than an echo. When he who had called out heard it, he turned to the little Pilgrim with eyes that were liquid with love and pity; 'Listen,' he said, 'there is someone on the way.'

'Can we help them?' cried the little Pilgrim; her heart bounded forward like a bird. She had no fear. The darkness and the horrible way seemed as nothing to her. She stretched out her arms as if she would have seized the traveller and dragged him up into the light.

He who was by her side shook his head, but with a smile. 'We can but wait,' he said. 'It is forbidden that anyone should help; for this is too terrible and strange to be touched even by the hands of angels. It is like nothing that you know.'

'I have been taught many things,' said the little Pilgrim, humbly. 'I have been taken back to the dear earth, where I saw the judgment-seat, and the pleaders who spoke, and the man who was the judge, and how each is judge for himself.'

'You have seen the place of hope,' said her guide, 'where the

Father is and the Son, and where no man is left to his own ways. But there is another country, where there is no voice either from God or from good spirits, and where those who have refused are left to do as seems good in their own eyes.'

'I have read,' said the little Pilgrim, with a sob, 'of one who went from city to city and found no rest.'

Her guide bowed his head very gravely in assent. 'They go from place to place,' he said, 'if haply they might find one in which it is possible to live. Whether it is order or whether it is license, it is according to their own will. They try all things, ever looking for something which the soul may endure. And new cities are founded from time to time, and a new endeavour ever and ever to live, only to live. For even when happiness fails and content, and work is vanity and effort is naught, it is something if a man can but endure to live.'

The little Pilgrim looked at him with wistful eyes, for what he said was beyond her understanding. 'For us,' she said, 'life is nothing but joy. Oh, brother, is there then condemnation?'

'It is no condemnation; it is what they have chosen,—it is to follow their own way. There is no longer anyone to interfere. The pleaders are all silent; there is no voice in the heart. The Father hinders them not, nor helps them, but leaves them.' He shivered as if with cold; and the little Pilgrim felt that there breathed from the depths of darkness at their feet an icy wind which touched her hands and feet and chilled her heart. She shivered too, and drew close to the rock for shelter, and gazed at the awful cliffs rising out of the gloom, and the paths that disappeared at her feet, leading down, down into that abyss; and her heart failed within her to think that below there were souls that suffered, and that the Father and the Son were not there. He, the All-loving, the All-present,—how could it be that He was not there?

'It is a mystery,' said the man who was her guide, and who answered to her thought. 'When I set my foot upon this blessed land I knew that there, even there, He is. But in that country His face is hidden, and even to name His name is anguish,—for then only do men understand what has befallen them, who can say that name no more.'

'That is death indeed,' she cried; and the wind came up silent with a wild breath that was more awful than the shriek of a storm; for it was like the stifled utterances of all those miserable ones who have no voice to call upon God, and know not where He is nor how to pronounce His name.

'Ah,' said he, 'if we could have known what death was! We had believed in death in the time of all great illusions, in the time of the gentle life, in the day of hope. But in the land of darkness there are no illusions; and every man knows that though he should fling himself into the furnace of the gold, or be cut to pieces by the knives, or trampled under the dancers' feet, yet that it will be but a little more pain, and that death is not, nor any escape that way.'

'Oh, brother!' she cried, 'you have been there!'

He turned and looked upon her; and she read as in a book things which tongue of man cannot say,—the anguish and the rapture, the unforgotten pang of the lost, the joy of one who has been delivered after hope was gone.

'I have been there; and now I stand in the light, and have seen the face of the Lord, and can speak His blessed name.' And with that he burst forth into a great melodious cry, which was not like that which he had sent into the dark depths below, but mounted up like the sounding of silver trumpets and all joyful music, giving a voice to the sweet air and the fresh winds which blew about the hills of God. But the words he said were not comprehensible to his companion, for they were in the sweet tongue which is between the Father and His child, and known to none but to them alone.

Yet only to hear the sound was enough to transport all who listened, and to make them know what joy is and peace. The little Pilgrim wept for happiness to hear her brother's voice; but in the midst of it her ear was caught by another sound,—a faint cry which tingled up from the darkness like a note of a muffled bell,—and she turned from the joy and the light, and flung out her arms and her little voice towards him who was stumbling upon the dark mountains. And 'Come,' she cried, 'come, come!' forgetting all things save that one was there in the darkness, while here was light and peace.

'It is nearer,' said her guide, hearing, even in the midst of his triumph song, that faint and distant cry; and he took her hand and drew her back, for she was upon the edge of the precipice, gazing into the black depths, which revealed nothing save the needles of the awful rocks and sheer descents below. 'The moment will come,' he said, 'when we can help; but it is not yet.'

Her heart was in the depths with him who was coming, whom she knew not save that he was coming, toiling upwards towards the light; and it seemed to her that she could not contain herself, nor wait till he should appear, nor draw back from the edge, where she might hold out her hands to him and save him some single step, if no more. But presently her heart returned to her brother who stood by her side, and who was delivered, and with whom it was meet that all should rejoice, since he had fought and conquered, and reached the land of light. 'Oh,' she said, 'it is long to wait while he is still upon these dark mountains. Tell me how it came to you to find the way.'

He turned to her with a smile, though his ear too was intent, and his heart fixed upon the traveller in the darkness, and began to tell her his tale to beguile the time of waiting, and to hold within bounds the pity that filled her heart. He told her that he was one of many who came from the pleasant earth together, out of many countries and tongues; and how they had gone here and there each man to a different city; and how they had crossed each other's paths coming and going, yet never found rest for their feet; and how there was a little relief in every change, and one sought that which another left; and how they wandered round and round over all the vast and endless plain, until at length in revolt from every other way, they had chosen a spot upon the slope of a hill, and built there a new city, if perhaps something better might be found there; and how it had been built with towers and high walls, and great gates to shut it in, so that no stranger should find entrance; and how every house was a palace, with statues of marble, and pillars so precious with beautiful work, and arches so lofty and so fair that they were better than had they been made of gold,—yet gold was not wanting, nor diamond stones that shone like stars, and everything more beautiful and stately than heart could conceive.

'And while we built and laboured,' he said, 'our hearts were a little appeased. And it was called the city of Art, and all was perfect in it, so that nothing had ever been seen to compare with it for beauty; and we walked upon the battlements and looked over the plain and viewed the dwellers there, who were not as we. And we went on to fill every room and every hall with carved work in stone and beaten gold, and pictures and woven tissues that were like the sun-gleams and the rainbows of the pleasant earth. And crowds came around envying us and seeking to enter; but we closed our gates and drove them away. And it was said among us that life would now become as of old, and everything would go well with us as in the happy days.'

The little Pilgrim looked up into his face, and for pity of his pain (though it was past) almost wished that *that* could have come true.

'But when the work was done,' he said, and for a moment no more.

'Oh, brother! when the work was done?' 'You do not know what it is,' he said, 'to be ten times more powerful and strong, to want no rest, to have fire in your veins, to have the craving in your heart above everything that is known to man. When the work was done, we glared upon each other with hungry eyes, and each man wished to thrust forth his neighbour and possess all to himself. And then we ceased to take pleasure in it, notwithstanding that it was beautiful; and there were some who would have beaten down the walls and built them anew; and some would have torn up the silver and gold, and tossed out the fair statues and the adornments in scorn and rage to the meaner multitudes below. And we who were the workers began to contend one against another to satisfy the gnawings of the rage that was in our hearts. For we had deceived ourselves, thinking once more that all would be well; while all the time nothing was changed, and we were but as the miserable ones that rushed from place to place.'

Though all this wretchedness was over and past, it was so terrible to think of that he paused and was silent awhile. And the little Pilgrim put her hand upon his arm in her great pity, to soothe him, and almost forgot that there was another traveller not yet delivered upon the way. But suddenly at that moment there came up through the depths the sound of a fall, as if the rocks had crashed from a hundred peaks, yet all muffled by the great distance, and echoing all around in faint echoes, and rumblings as in the bosom of the earth; and mingled with them were far-off cries, so faint and distant that human ears could not have heard them, like the cries of lost children, or creatures wavering and straying in the midst of the boundless night. This time she who was watching upon the edge of the gloom would have flung herself forward altogether into it, had not her companion again restrained her.

'One has stumbled upon the mountains; but listen, listen, little sister, for the voices are many,' he said. 'It is not one who comes, but many; and though he falls he will rise again.' And once more he shouted aloud, bending down against the rocks, so that they caught his voice; and the sweet air from the skies came behind him in a great gust like a summer storm, and carried it into all the echoing hollows of the hills. And the little Pilgrim knew that he shouted to all who came to take courage and not to fear. And this time there rose upwards many faint and wavering sounds that did not stir the air, but made it tingle with a vibration of the great distance and the unknown depths; and then again all was still. They stood for a time intent upon the great silence and darkness which swept up all sight and sound, and then the little Pilgrim once more turned her eyes towards her companion, and he began again his wonderful tale.

'He who had been the first to found the city, and who was the most wise of any, though the rage was in him like all the rest, and the disappointment and the anguish, yet would not yield. And he called upon us for another trial, to make a picture which should be the greatest that ever was painted; and each one of us, small or great, who had been of that art in the dear life, took share in the rivalry and the emulation, so that on every side there was a fury and a rush, each man with his band of supporters about him struggling and swearing that his was the best. Not that they loved the work or the beauty of the work, but to keep down the gnawing in their hearts, and to have something for which they could still fight and storm, and for a little forget.'

'I was one who had been among the highest.' He spoke not with pride, but in a low and deep voice which went to the heart of the listener, and brought the tears to her eyes. It was not like that of the painter in the heavenly city, who rejoiced and was glad in his work, though he was but as a humble workman, serving those who were more great. But this man had the sorrow of greatness in him, and the wonder of those who can do much, to find how little they can do.

'My veins,' he said, 'were filled with fire, and my heart with the rage of a great desire to be first, as I had been first in the days of the gentle life. And I made my plan to be greater than all the rest, to paint a vast picture like the world, filled with all the glories of life. In a moment I had conceived what I should do, for my strength was as that of a hundred men; and none of us could rest or breathe till it was accomplished, but flung ourselves upon this new thing as upon water in the desert. Oh, my little sister, how can I tell you; what words can show forth this wonderful thing? I stood before my great canvas with all those who were of my faction pressing upon me, noting every touch I made, shouting, and saying, "He will win! he will win!" when lo! there came a mystery and a wonder into that place. I had arranged men and women before me according to all the devices of art, to serve as my models, that nature might be in my picture, and life; but when I looked I saw them not, for between them and me had come a Face.'

The eyes of the little Pilgrim dropped with tears. She held

out her hands towards him with a sympathy which no words could say.

'Often had I painted that Face in the other life, sometimes with awe and love, sometimes with scorn,—for hire and for bread, and for pride and for fame. It is pale with suffering, yet smiles; the eyes have tears in them, yet light below, and all that is there is full of tenderness and of love. There is a crown upon the brow, but it is made of thorns. It came before me suddenly, while I stood there, with the men shouting close to my ear urging me on, and fierce fury in my heart, and the rage to be first, and to forget. Where my models were, there it came. I could not see them, nor my groups that I had planned, nor anything but that Face. I called out to my men. "Who has done this?" but they heard me not, nor understood me, for to them there was nothing there save the figures I had set,—a living picture all ready for the painter's hand.

'I could not bear it, the sight of that Face. I flung my tools away; I covered my eyes with my hands. But those who were about me pressed on me and threatened; they pulled my hands from my eyes. "Coward!" they cried, and "Traitor, to leave us in the lurch! Now will the other side win and we be shamed. Rather tear him limb from limb, fling him from the walls!" The crowd came round me like an angry sea; they forced my pencils back into my hands. "Work," they cried, "or we will tear you limb from limb." For though they were upon my side, it was for rivalry, and not out of any love for me.' He paused for a moment, for his heart was yet full of the remembrance, and of joy that it was past.

'I looked again,' he said, 'and still it was there. Oh Face divine,—the eyes all wet with pity, the lips all quivering with love! And neither pity nor love belonged to that place, nor any succor, nor the touch of a brother, nor the voice of a friend. "Paint," they cried, "or we will tear you limb from limb!" and fire came into my heart. I pushed them from me on every side with the strength of a giant. And then I flung it on the canvas, crying I know not what,—not to them, but to Him. Shrink not from me, little sister, for I blasphemed. I called Him Impostor, Deceiver, Galilean; and still with all my might, with all the fury of my soul, I set Him there for every man to see, not knowing what I did. Everything faded from me but that Face; I saw it alone. The crowd came round me with shouts and threats to drag me away but I took no heed. They were silenced, and fled and left me alone, but I knew nothing; nor when they came back with others and seized me, and flung me forth from the gates, was I aware what I had done. They cast me out and left me upon the wild without a shelter, without a companion, storming and raving at them as they did at me. They dashed the great gates behind me with a clang, and shut me out. And I turned and defied them, and cursed them as they cursed me, not knowing what I had done.'

'Oh, brother!' murmured the little Pilgrim, kneeling, as if she had accompanied him all the way with her prayers, but could not now say more.

'Then I saw again,' he went on, not hearing her in the great force of that passion and wonder which was still in his mind, 'that vision in the air. Wherever I turned, it was there,—His eyes wet with pity, His countenance shining with love. Whence came He? What did He in that place, where love is not, where pity comes not?'

'Friend,' she cried, 'to seek you there!'

Her companion bowed his head in deep humbleness and joy. And again he lifted his great voice and intoned his song of praise. The little Pilgrim understood it, but by fragments,—a line that was more simple that came here and there. And it praised the Lord that where the face of the Father was hidden; and where love was not, nor compassion, nor brother had pity on brother, nor friend knew the face of friend; and all succour was stayed, and every help forbidden,—yet still in the depths of the darkness and in the heart of the silence, He who could not forget nor forsake was there. The voice of the singer was like that of one of the great angels, and many of the inhabitants of the blessed country began to appear, gathering in crowds to hear this great music, as the little sister thought; and she herself listened with all her heart, wondering and seeing on the faces of those dear friends whom she did not know an expectation and a hope which were strange to her, though she could always understand their love and their joy.

But in the middle of this great song there came again another sound to her ear,—a sound which pierced through the music like lightning through the sky, though it was but the cry of one distraught and fainting; a cry out of the depths not even seeking help, a cry of distress too terrible to be borne. Though it was scarcely louder than a sigh, she heard it through all the music, and turned and flew to the edge of the precipice whence it came. And immediately the darkness seemed to move as with a pulse in a great throb, and something came through the wind with a rush, as if part of the mountain had fallen—and lo! at her feet lay one who had flung himself forward, his arms stretched out, his face to the ground, as if he had seized and grasped in an agony the very soil. He lay there, half in the light and half in the shadow, gripping the rocks with his hands, burrowing into the cool herbage above and the mountain flowers; clinging, catching hold, despairing, yet seizing everything he could grasp,—the tender grass, the rolling stones.

The little Pilgrim flung herself down upon her knees by his side, and grasped his arm to help, and cried aloud for aid; and the song of the singer ceased, and there was silence for a moment, so that the breath of the fugitive could be heard panting, and his strong struggle to drag himself altogether out of that abyss of darkness below. She thought of nothing, nor heard nor saw anything but the strain of that last effort which seemed to shake the very mountains; until suddenly there seemed to rise all around the hum and murmur as of a great multitude, and looking up, she saw every little hill and hollow, and the glorious plain beyond as far as eye could see, crowded with countless throngs; and on the high peaks above, in the full shining of the sun, came bands of angels, and of those great beings who are more mighty than men.

And the eyes of all were fixed upon the man who lay as one dead upon the ground, and from the lips of all came a low murmur of rapture and delight, that spread like the hum of the bees, like the cooing of the doves, like the voice of a mother over her child; and the same sound came to her own lips unawares, and she murmured 'welcome' and 'brother' and 'friend,' not knowing what she said; and looking to the others, whispered, 'Hush! for he is weak'—and all of them answered with tears, with 'hush' and 'welcome' and 'friend' and 'brother' and 'beloved,' and stood smiling and weeping for joy. And presently there came softly into the blessed air the ringing of the great silver bells, which sound only for victory and great happiness and gain. And there was joy in heaven; and every world was stirred. And throughout the firmament, and among all the lords and princes of life, it was known that the impossible had become true, and the name of the Lord had proved enough, and love had conquered even despair.

'Hush!' she said, 'for he is weak.' And because it was her blessed service to receive those who had newly arrived in that heavenly country, and to soothe and help them so that like newborn children they should be able to endure and understand the joy, she knelt by him on the ground and tried to rouse him, though with trembling, for never before had she stood by one who was newly come out of the land of despair. 'Let the sun come upon him,' she said; 'let him feel the brightness of the light,'—and with her soft hands she drew him out of the shade of the twilight to where the brightness of the day fell like a smile upon the flowers. And then at last he stirred, and turned round and opened his eyes, for the genial warmth had reached him. But his eyes were heavy and dazzled with the light; and he looked round him as if confused from beneath his heavy eyelids. 'And where am I?' he said; 'and who are you?' 'Oh, brother!' said the little Pilgrim, and told him in his ear the name of that heavenly place, and many comforting and joyful things. But he understood her not, and still gazed about him with dazzled eyes, for his face was still towards the darkness, and fear was upon him lest this place should prove no more than a delusion, and the darkness return, and the anguish and pain.

Then he who had been her guide, and told her his tale, came forward and stood by the side of the newly come. And 'Brother,' he said, 'look upon me, for you know me, and know from whence I come.'

The stranger looked dimly with his heavy eyes. And he replied, 'It is as a dream that I know you, and know from whence you came. And the dream is sweet to lie here, and think that I am at peace. Deceive me not, oh! deceive me not with dreams that are sweet; but let me go upon my way and find the end, if there is any end, or if any good can be.'

'What shall we do,' cried the little Pilgrim, 'to persuade him that he has arrived and is safe, and dreams no more?'

And they stood round him wondering, and troubled to find how little they could do for him, and that the light entered so slowly into his soul. And he lay on the bank like one left for death, so weary and so worn with all the horrors of the way that his heart was faint within him, and peace itself seemed to him but an illusion. He lay silent while they watched and waited, then turned himself upon the grass, which was as soft to the weary wayfarer as angels' wings; and then the sunshine caught his eye, as if he had been a newborn babe awakened to the light. He put out his hand to it, and touched the ground that was golden with those heavenly rays, and gathered himself up till he felt it upon his face, and opened wide his dazzled eyes, then shaded them with trembling hands, and said to himself, 'It is the sun; it is the sun!'

But still he did not dare to believe that the danger and the toil were over, nor could he listen, nor understand what the brethren said. While they all stood around and watched and waited, wondering each how the newcomer should be satisfied, there suddenly arose a sound with which they were all acquainted,— the sound of One approaching. The faces of the blessed were all around like the stars in the sky,—multitudes whom none could count or reckon; but He who came was seen of none, save him to whom He came. The weary man rose up with a great cry, then fell again upon his knees, and flung his arms wide in the wonder and the joy. And 'Lord,' he cried, 'was it Thou? Lord, it was Thou! Thine was the face. And Thou hast brought me here!'

The watchers knew not what the other voice said, for what is said to each newcomer is the secret of the Lord. But when they looked again, the man stood upright upon his feet, and his face was full of light; and though he trembled with weakness and with weariness, and with exceeding joy, yet the confusion and the fear were gone from him. And he had no longer any suspicion of them, as if they might betray him, but held out his trembling hands and cried, 'Friends,—you are friends? and you spoke to me and called me brother? And am I here? And am I here?' For to name the name of that blessed country was not needful any longer, now that he had seen the Lord.

Then a great band and guard of honour, of angels and principalities and powers, surrounded him, and led him away to the holy city, and to the presence of the Father, who had permitted and had not forbidden what the Lord had done. And all the companies of the blessed followed after with wonder and gladness and triumph, because the great love of the Lord had drawn out of the darkness even those who were beyond hope.

The little Pilgrim saw them depart from her with love and joy, and sat down upon the rocky edge and sang her own song of peace; for her fear was gone, and she was ready to do her service there upon the verge of the precipice as among the flowers and the sunshine, where her own place was. 'From the depths,' she said, 'they come, they come!—from the land of darkness, where no love is. For Thy love, Oh Lord, is more than the darkness and the depths. And where hope is not, there Thy pity goes.' She sat and sang to herself like a happy child, for her heart had fathomed the awful gloom which baffles angels and men; and she had learned that though hope comes to an end and light fails, and the feet of the ambassadors are stayed on the mountains, and the voice of the pleaders is silenced, and darkness swallows up the world, yet Love never fails. As she sang, the pity in her heart grew so strong, and her desire to help the lost, that she rose up and stepped forth into the awful gloom, and had it been permitted, in her gentleness and weakness would have gone forth to the deeps and had no fear.

The ground gave way under her feet, so dreadful was the precipice; but though her heart beat with the horror of it, and the whirl of the descent and the darkness which blinded her eyes, yet had she no hurt. And when her foot touched the rock, and that sinking sense of emptiness and vacancy ceased, she looked around and saw the path by which that traveller had come. For when the eyes are used to the darkness, the horror of the gloom was no longer like a solid thing, but moved into shades of darker and less dark, so that she saw where the rocks stood, and how they sank with edges that cut like swords down and ever down into the abysses; and how here a deep ravine was rent between them, and there were breaks and scars as though someone had caught the jagged points with wounded hand or foot, struggling up the perpendicular surface towards the little ray of light, like a tiny star which shone as on immeasurable heights to show where life was.

As she travelled deeper and deeper, it was a wonder to see how far that little ray penetrated down and down through gulfs of darkness, blue and cold like the shimmer of a diamond, and even when it could be seen no more, sent yet a shadowy refraction, a line of something less black than the darkness, a lightening amid the gloom, a something indefinable which was hope.

The rocks were more cruel than imagination could conceive,—sometimes pointed and sharp like knives, sometimes smooth and upright as a wall with no hold for the climber, sometimes moving under the touch, with stones that rolled and crushed the bleeding feet; and though the solid masses were distinguishable from the lighter darkness of the air, yet it could only be in groping that the travellers by that way could find where any foothold was. The traveller who came from above, and who had the privilege of her happiness, sank down as if borne on wings, yet needed all her courage not to be afraid of the awful rocks that rose all above and around her, perpendicular in the gloom. And the great blast of an icy wind swept upwards like something flying upon great wings, so tremendous was the force of it, whirling from the depths below, sucked upwards by the very warmth of the life above; so that the little Pilgrim herself caught at the rocks that she might not be swept again towards the top, or dashed against the stony pinnacles that stood up on every side. She was glad when she found a little platform under her feet for a moment where she could rest, and also because she had come, not from curiosity to see that gulf, but with the hope and desire to meet someone to whom she could be of a little comfort or help in the terrors of the way.

While she stood for a moment to get her breath, she became sensible that some living thing was near; and putting out her hand she felt that there was round her something that was like a bastion upon a fortified wall, and immediately a hand touched hers, and a soft voice said, 'Sister, fear not! for this is the watch-tower, and I am one of those who keep the way.' She had started and trembled indeed, not that she feared, but because the delicate fabric of her being was such that every movement of the wind, and even those that were instinctive and belonged to the habits of another life, betrayed themselves in her. And 'Oh,' she said, 'I knew not that there were any watch-towers, or any one to help, but came because my heart called me, if perhaps I might hold out my hand in the darkness, and be of use where there was no light.'

'Come and stand by me,' said the watcher; and the little Pilgrim saw that there was a whiteness near to her, out of which slowly shaped the face of a fair and tender woman, whom she knew not, but loved. And though they could scarcely see each other, yet they knew each other for sisters, and kissed and took comfort together, holding each other's hands in the midst of the awful gloom. And the little Pilgrim questioned in low and hushed tones, 'Is it to help that you are here?'

'To help when that may be; but rather to watch, and to send the news and make it known that one is coming, that the bells of joy may be sounded, and all the blessed may rejoice.'

'Oh,' said the little Pilgrim, 'tell me your name, that I may do you honour,—for to gain such high promotion can be given only to the great who are made perfect, and to those who love most.'

'I am not great,' said the watcher; 'but the Lord, who considers all, has placed me here, that I may be the first to see when one comes who is in the dark places below. And also because there are some who say that love is idolatry, and that the Father will not have us long for our own, therefore am I permitted to wait and watch and think the time not long for the love I bear him. For he is mine; and when he comes I will ascend with him to the dear country of the light, and some other who loves enough will be promoted in my place.'

'I am not worthy,' said the little Pilgrim. 'It is a great promotion; but oh, that we might be permitted to help, to put out a hand, or to clear the way!'

'Nay, my little sister,' said the watcher, 'but patience must have its perfect work; and for those who are coming help is secret. They must not see it nor know it, for the land of darkness is beyond hope. The Father will not force the will of any creature He has made, for He respects us in our nature, which is His image. And when a man will not, and will not till the day is over, what can be done for him? He is left to his will, and is permitted to do it as it seems good in his eyes. A man's will is great, for it is the gift of God. But the Lord, who cannot rest while one is miserable, still goes secretly to them, for His heart yearns after them. And by times they will see His face, or some thought of old will seize upon them. And some will say, "To perish upon the dark mountains is better than to live here." And I have seen,' said the watcher, 'that the Lord will go with them all the way— but secretly, so that they cannot see Him. And though it grieves His heart not to help, yet will He not,—for they have become the creatures of their own will, and by that must they attain.'

She put out her hand to the newcomer and drew her to the side of the rocky wall, so that they felt the sweep of the wind in their faces; but were not driven before it. 'And come,' she said, 'for two of us together will be like a great light to those who are in the darkness. They will see us like a lamp, and it will cheer them, though they know not why we are here. Listen!' she cried. And the little Pilgrim, holding fast the hand of the watcher, listened and looked down upon the awful way; and underneath the sweep of the icy wind was a small sharp sound as of a stone rolling or a needle of rock that broke and fell, like the sounds that are in a wood when some creature moves, though too far off for footstep to sound. 'Listen!' said the watcher; and her face so shone with joy that the little Pilgrim saw it clearly, like the shining of the morning in the midst of the darkness. 'He comes!'

'Oh, sister!' she cried, 'is it he whom you love above all the rest? Is it he?'

The watcher smiled and said, 'If it is not he, yet is it a brother; if it is not he now, yet his time will come. And in every one who passes, I hope to see his face; and the more that come, the more certain it is that he will come. And the time seems not long for the love I bear him. And it is for this that the Lord has so considered me. Listen! for someone comes.'

And there came to these watchers the strangest sight; for there flew past them while they gazed a man who seemed to be carried upon the sweep of the wind. In the midst of the darkness they could see the faint white in his face, with eyes of flame and lips set firm, whirled forward upon the wind, which would have dashed him against the rocks; but as he whirled past, he caught with his hand the needles of the opposite peaks, and was swung high over a great chasm, and landed upon a higher height, high over their heads. And for a moment they could hear, like a pulsation through the depths, the hard panting of his breath; then, with scarcely a moment for rest, they heard the sound of his progress onward, as if he did battle with the mountain, and his own swiftness carried him like another wind. It had taken less than a moment to sweep him past, quicker than the flight of a bird, as sudden as a lightning flash.

The little Pilgrim followed him with her eager ears, wondering if he would leap thus into the country of light and take heaven by storm, or whether he would fall upon the heavenly hills, and lie prostrate in weariness and exhaustion, like him to whom she had ministered. She followed him with her ears, for the sound of his progress was with crashing of rocks and a swift movement in the air; but she was called back by the pressure of the hand of the watcher, who did not, like the little Pilgrim, follow him who thus rushed through space as far as there was sound or sight of him, but had turned again to the lower side, and was gazing once more, and listening for the little noises in the gulf below. The little Pilgrim remembered her friend's hope, and said softly, 'It was not he?' And the watcher clasped her hand again, and answered, 'It was a dear brother. I have sounded the silver bells for him; and soon we shall hear them answering from the heights above. And another time it will be he.'

And they kissed each other because they understood each the other in her heart.

And then they talked together of the old life when all things began; and of the wonderful things they had learned concerning the love of the Father and the Son; and how all the world was held by them and penetrated through and through by threads of love, so that it could never fail. And the darkness seemed light round them; and they forgot for a little that the wind was not as a summer breeze. Then once more the hand of the watcher pressed that of her companion, and bade her hush and listen; and they sat together holding their breath, straining their ears. Then heard they faint sounds which were very different from those made by him who had been driven past them like an arrow from a bow,—first as of something falling, but very far away, and a faint sound as of a foot which slipped. The listeners did not say a word to each other; they sat still and listened, scarcely drawing their breath.

The darkness had no voice; it could not be but that some traveller was there, though hidden deep, deep in the gloom, only betrayed by the sound. There was a long pause, and the watcher held fast the little Pilgrim's hand, and betrayed to her the longing in her heart; for though she was already blessed beyond all blessedness known on earth, yet had she not forgotten the love that had begun on earth, but was forevermore. She murmured to herself and said, 'If it is not he, it is a brother; and the more that come, the more sure it is that he will come. Little sister, is there one for whom you watch?'

'There is no one,' the Pilgrim said,—'but all.'

'And so care I for all,' cried the watcher; and she drew her companion with her to the edge of the abyss, and they sat down upon it low among the rocks to escape the rushing of the wind. And they sang together a soft song; 'For if he should hear us,' she said, 'it may give him courage.' And there they sat and sang; and the white of their garments and of their heavenly faces showed like a light in the deep gloom, so that he who was toiling upwards might see that speck above him, and be encouraged to continue upon his way.

Sometimes he fell, and they could hear the moan he made,— for every sound came upwards, however small and faint it might be,—and sometimes dragged himself along, so that they heard his movement up some shelf of rock. And as the Pilgrim looked, she saw other and other dim whitenesses along the ravines of the dark mountains, and knew that she was not the only one, but that many had come to watch and look for the coming of those who had been lost.

Time was as nothing to these heavenly watchers; but they knew how long and terrible were the moments to those upon the way. Sometimes there would be silence like the silence of long years; and fear came upon them that the wayfarer had turned back, or that he had fallen, and lay suffering at the bottom of some gulf, or had been swept by the wind upon some icy peak and dashed against the rocks. Then *anon*, while they listened and held their breath, a little sound would strike again into the silence; bringing back hope; and again and again all would be still. The little Pilgrim held her companion's hand; and the thought went through her mind that were she watching for one whom she loved above the rest, her heart would fail. But the watcher answered her as if she had spoken, and said, 'Oh, no, oh, no; for if it is not he, it is a brother; and the Lord give them joy!' But they sang no more, their hearts being faint with suspense and with eagerness to hear every sound.

Then in the great chill of the silence, suddenly, and not far off, came the sound of one who spoke. He murmured to himself and said, 'Who can continue on this terrible way? The night is black like hell, and there comes no morning. It was better in the land of darkness, for still we could see the face of man, though not God.' The muffled voice shook at that word, and then was still suddenly, as though it had been a flame and the wind had blown it out. And for a moment there was silence; until suddenly it broke forth once more,—

'What is this that has come to me that I can say the name of God? It tortures no longer, it is as balm. But He is far off and hears nothing. He called us and we answered not. Now it is we who call, and He will not hear. I will lie down and die. It cannot be that a man must live and live forever in pain and anguish. Here will I lie, and it will end. Oh Thou whose face I have seen in the night, make it possible for a man to die!'

The watcher loosed herself from her companion's clasp, and stood upright upon the edge of the cliff, clasping her hands together and saying low, as to herself, 'Father, Father!' as one who cannot refrain from that appeal, but who knows the Father loves best, and that to intercede is vain; and longing was in her face and joy. For it was he, and she knew that he could not now fail, but would reach to the celestial country and to the shining of the sun; yet that it was not hers to help him, nor any man's, nor angel's. But the little Pilgrim was ignorant, not having been taught; and she committed herself to those depths, though she feared them, and though she knew not what she could do. And once more the dense air closed over her, and the vacancy swallowed her up, and when she reached the rocks below, there lay something at her feet which she felt to be a man; but she could not see him nor touch him, and when she tried to speak, her voice died away in her throat and made no sound.

Whether it was the wind that caught it and swept it quite away, or that the well of that depth profound sucked every note upwards, or whether because it was not permitted that either man or angel should come out of their sphere, or help be given which was forbidden, the little Pilgrim knew not,—for never had it been said to her that she should stand aside where need was. And surprise which was stronger than the icy wind, and for a moment a great dismay, took hold upon her,—for she understood not how it was that the bond of silence should bind her, and that she should be unable to put forth her hand to help him whom she heard moaning and murmuring, but could not see. And scarcely could her feet keep hold of the awful rock, or her form resist the upward sweep of the wind; but though he saw her not nor she him, yet could not she leave him in his weakness and misery, saying to herself that even if she could do nothing, it must be well that a little love should be near.

Then she heard him speak again, crouching under the rock at her feet; and he said faintly to himself, 'That was no dream. In the land of darkness there are no dreams nor voices that speak within us. On the earth they were never silent struggling and crying; but there—all blank and still. Therefore it was no dream. It was One who came and looked me in the face; and love was in His eyes. I have not seen love, oh, for so long! But it was no dream. If God is a dream I know not, but love I know. And He said to me, "Arise and go." But to whom must I go? The words are words that once I knew, and the face I knew. But to whom, to whom?'

The little Pilgrim cried aloud, so that she thought the rocks must be rent by the vehemence of her cry, calling like the other, 'Father, Father, Father!' as if her heart would burst; and it was like despair to think that she made no sound, and that the brother could not hear her who lay thus fainting at her feet. Yet she could not stop, but went on crying like a child that has lost its way; for to whom could a child call but to her father, and all the more when she cannot understand? And she called out and said that God was not His name save to strangers, if there are any

194

strangers, but that His name was Father, and it was to Him that all must go. And all her being thrilled like a bird with its song, so that the very air stirred; yet no voice came. And she lifted up her face to the watcher above, and beheld where she stood holding up her hands a little whiteness in the great dark. But though these two were calling and calling, the silence was dumb. And neither of them could take him by the hand nor lift him up, nor show him, far, far above, the little diamond of the light, but were constrained to stand still and watch, seeing that he was one of those who are beyond hope.

After she had waited a long time, he stirred again in the dark and murmured to himself once more, saying low, 'I have slept and am strong. And while I was sleeping He has come again; He has looked at me again. And somewhere I will find Him. I will arise and go; I will arise and go—'

And she heard him move at her feet and grope over the rock with his hands; but it was smooth as snow with no holding, and slippery as ice. And the watcher stood above and the Pilgrim below, but could not help him. He groped and groped, and murmured to himself, ever saying, 'I will arise and go.' And their hearts were wrung that they could not speak to him nor touch him nor help him. But at last in the dark there burst forth a great cry, 'Who said it?' and then a sound of weeping, and amid the weeping, words. 'As when I was a child, as when hope was—I will arise and I will go—to my Father, to my Father! for now I remember, and I know.'

The little Pilgrim sank down into a crevice of the rocks in the weakness of her great joy. And something passed her mounting up and up; and it seemed to her that he had touched her shoulder or her hand unawares, and that the dumb cry in her heart had reached him, and that it had been good for him that a little love stood by, though only to watch and to weep. And she listened and heard him go on and on; and she herself ascended higher to the watch-tower. And the watcher was gone who had waited there for her beloved, for she had gone with him, as the Lord had promised her, to be the one who should lead him to the holy city and to see the Father's face. And it was given to the little Pilgrim to sound the silver bells and to warn all the bands of the blessed, and the great angels and lords of the whole world, that from out the land of darkness and from the regions beyond hope another had come.

She remained not there long, because there were many who sought that place that they might be the first to see if one beloved was among the travellers by that terrible way, and to welcome the brother or sister who was the most dear to them of all the children of the Father. But it was thus that she learned the last lesson of all that is in heaven and that is in earth, and in the heights above and in the depths below, which the great angels desire to look into, and all the princes and powers. And it is this: that there is that which is beyond hope yet not beyond love; and that hope may fail and be no longer possible, but love cannot fail,—for hope is of men, but love is the Lord; and there is but one thing which to Him is not possible, which is to forget; and that even when the Father has hidden His face and help is forbidden, yet there goes He secretly and cannot forbear.

But if there were any deep more profound, and to which access was not, either from the dark mountains or by any other way, the Pilgrim was not taught, nor ever found any knowledge, either among the angels who know all things, or among her brothers who were the children of men.

5: THE LAND OF DARKNESS

I found myself standing on my feet, with the tingling sensation of having come down rapidly upon the ground from a height. There was a similar feeling in my head, as of the whirling and sickening sensation of passing downwards through the air, like the description Dante gives of his descent upon Geryon. My mind, curiously enough, was sufficiently disengaged to think of that, or at least to allow swift passage for the recollection through my thoughts. All the aching of wonder, doubt, and fear which I had been conscious of a little while before was gone. There was no distinct interval between the one condition and the other, nor in my fall (as I supposed it must have been) had I any consciousness of change. There was the whirling of the air, resisting my passage, yet giving way under me in giddy circles, and then the sharp shock of once more feeling under my feet something solid, which struck, yet sustained. After a little while the giddiness above and the tingling below passed away, and I felt able to look about me and discern where I was. But not all at once; the things immediately about me impressed me first, then the general aspect of the new place.

First of all the light, which was lurid, as if a thunder-storm were coming on. I looked up involuntarily to see if it had begun to rain; but there was nothing of the kind, though what I saw above me was a lowering canopy of cloud, dark, threatening, with a faint reddish tint diffused upon the vaporous darkness. It was, however, quite sufficiently clear to see everything, and there was a good deal to see. I was in a street of what seemed a great and very populous place. There were shops on either side, full apparently of all sorts of costly wares. There was a continual current of passengers up and down on both sides of the way, and in the middle of the street carriages of every description, humble and splendid. The noise was great and ceaseless; the traffic continual. Some of the shops were most brilliantly lighted, attracting one's eyes in the sombre light outside, which, however, had just enough of day in it to make these spots of illumination look sickly.

Most of the places thus distinguished were apparently bright with the electric or some other scientific light; and delicate machines of every description, brought to the greatest perfection, were in some windows, as were also many fine productions of art, but mingled with the gaudiest and coarsest in a way which struck me with astonishment. I was also much surprised by the fact that the traffic, which was never stilled for a moment, seemed to have no sort of regulation. Some carriages dashed along, upsetting the smaller vehicles in their way, without the least restraint or order, either, as it seemed, from their own good sense or from the laws and customs of the place.

When an accident happened, there was a great shouting, and sometimes a furious encounter; but nobody seemed to interfere. This was the first impression made upon me. The passengers on the pavement were equally regardless. I was myself pushed out of the way, first to one side, then to another, hustled when I paused for a moment, trodden upon and driven about. I retreated soon to the doorway of a shop, from whence with a little more safety I could see what was going on. The noise made my head ring. It seemed to me that I could not hear myself think. If this were to go on forever, I said to myself, I should soon go mad.

'Oh, no,' said someone behind me, 'not at all. You will get used to it; you will be glad of it. One does not want to hear one's thoughts; most of them are not worth hearing.'

I turned round and saw it was the master of the shop, who had come to the door on seeing me. He had the usual smile of a man who hoped to sell his wares; but to my horror and astonishment, by some process which I could not understand, I saw that he was saying to himself, 'What a d——d fool! here's another of those cursed wretches, d—— him!' all with the same smile. I started back, and answered him as hotly, 'What do you mean by calling me a d——d fool? fool yourself, and all the rest of it. Is this the way you receive strangers here?'

'Yes,' he said with the same smile, 'this is the way; and I only describe you as you are, as you will soon see. Will you walk in and look over my shop? Perhaps you will find something to suit you if you are just setting up, as I suppose.'

I looked at him closely, but this time I could not see that he was saying anything beyond what was expressed by his lips: and I followed him into the shop, principally because it was quieter than the street, and without any intention of buying,—for what should I buy in a strange place where I had no settled habitation, and which probably I was only passing through?

'I will look at your things,' I said, in a way which I believe I had, of perhaps undue pretension. I had never been over-rich, or of very elevated station; but I was believed by my friends (or enemies) to have an inclination to make myself out something more important than I was. 'I will look at your things, and possibly I may find something that may suit me; but with all the *ateliers* of Paris and London to draw from, it is scarcely to be expected that in a place like this—'

Here I stopped to draw my breath, with a good deal of confusion; for I was unwilling to let him see that I did not know where I was.

'A place like this,' said the shop-keeper, with a little laugh which seemed to me full of mockery, 'will supply you better, you will find, than—any other place. At least you will find it the only place practicable,' he added. 'I perceive you are a stranger here.'

'Well, I may allow myself to be so, more or less. I have not had time to form much acquaintance with—the place; what—do you call the place?—its formal name, I mean,' I said with a great desire to keep up the air of superior information. Except for the first moment, I had not experienced that strange power of looking into the man below the surface which had frightened me. Now there occurred another gleam of insight, which gave me once more a sensation of alarm. I seemed to see a light of hatred and contempt below his smile; and I felt that he was not in the least taken in by the air which I assumed.

'The name of the place,' he said, 'is not a pretty one. I hear the gentlemen who come to my shop say that it is not to be named to ears polite; and I am sure your ears are very polite.' He said this with the most offensive laugh, and I turned upon him and answered him, without mincing matters, with a plainness of speech which startled myself, but did not seem to move him, for he only laughed again. 'Are you not afraid,' I said, 'that I will leave your shop and never enter it more?'

'Oh, it helps to pass the time,' he said; and without any further comment began to show me very elaborate and fine articles of furniture. I had always been attracted to this sort of thing, and had longed to buy such articles for my house when I had one, but never had it in my power. Now I had no house, nor any means of paying so far as I knew, but I felt quite at my ease about buying, and inquired into the prices with the greatest composure.

'They are just the sort of thing I want. I will take these, I think; but you must set them aside for me, for I do not at the present moment exactly know—'

'You mean you have got no rooms to put them in,' said the master of the shop. 'You must get a house directly, that's all. If you're only up to it, it is easy enough. Look about until you find something you like, and then—take possession.'

'Take possession'—I was so much surprised that I stared at him with mingled indignation and surprise—'of what belongs to another man?' I said.

I was not conscious of anything ridiculous in my look. I was indignant, which is not a state of mind in which there is any absurdity; but the shopkeeper suddenly burst into a storm of laughter. He laughed till he seemed almost to fall into convulsions, with a harsh mirth which reminded me of the old image of the crackling of thorns, and had neither amusement nor warmth in it; and presently this was echoed all around, and looking up, I saw grinning faces full of derision bent upon me from every side, from the stairs which led to the upper part of the house and from the depths of the shop behind,—faces with pens behind their ears, faces in workmen's caps, all distended from ear to ear, with a sneer and a mock and a rage of laughter which nearly sent me mad. I hurled I don't know what imprecations at them as I rushed out, stopping my ears in a paroxysm of fury and mortification. My mind was so distracted by this occurrence that I rushed without knowing it upon someone who was passing, and threw him down with the violence of my exit; upon which I was set on by a party of half a dozen ruffians, apparently his companions, who would, I thought, kill me, but who only flung me, wounded, bleeding, and feeling as if every bone in my body had been broken, down on the pavement, when they went away, laughing too.

I picked myself up from the edge of the causeway, aching and sore from head to foot, scarcely able to move, yet conscious that if I did not get myself out of the way, one or other of the vehicles which were dashing along would run over me. It would be impossible to describe the miserable sensations, both of body and mind, with which I dragged myself across the crowded pavement, not without curses and even kicks from the passers-by, and avoiding the shop from which I still heard those shrieks of devilish laughter, gathered myself up in the shelter of a little projection of a wall, where I was for the moment safe. The pain which I felt was as nothing to the sense of humiliation, the mortification, the rage with which I was possessed.

There is nothing in existence more dreadful than rage which is impotent, which cannot punish or avenge, which has to restrain itself and put up with insults showered upon it. I had never known before what that helpless, hideous exasperation was; and I was humiliated beyond description, brought down—I, whose inclination it was to make more of myself than was justifiable—to the aspect of a miserable ruffian beaten in a brawl, soiled, covered with mud and dust, my clothes torn, my face bruised and disfigured,—all this within half an hour or there about of my arrival in a strange place where nobody knew me or could do me justice! I kept looking out feverishly for someone with an air of authority to whom I could appeal.

Sooner or later somebody must go by, who, seeing me in such a plight, must inquire how it came about, must help me and vindicate me. I sat there for I cannot tell how long, expecting every moment that were it but a policeman, somebody would notice and help me; but no one came. Crowds seemed to sweep by without a pause,—all hurrying, restless; some with anxious faces, as if any delay would be mortal; some in noisy groups intercepting the passage of the others. Sometimes one would pause to point me out to his comrades with a shout of derision at my miserable plight, or if by a change of posture I got outside the protection of my wall, would kick me back with a coarse injunction to keep out of the way. No one was sorry for me; not a look of compassion, not a word of inquiry was wasted upon me; no representative of authority appeared. I saw a dozen quarrels while I lay there, cries of the weak, and triumphant shouts of the strong; but that was all.

I was drawn after a while from the fierce and burning sense of my own grievances by a querulous voice quite close to me. 'This is my corner,' it said. 'I've sat here for years, and I have a right to it. And here you come, you big ruffian, because you know I haven't got the strength to push you away.'

'Who are you?' I said, turning round horror-stricken; for close beside me was a miserable man, apparently in the last stage of disease. He was pale as death, yet eaten up with sores. His body was agitated by a nervous trembling. He seemed to shuffle along on hands and feet, as though the ordinary mode of locomotion was impossible to him, and yet was in possession of all his limbs. Pain was written in his face. I drew away to leave him room, with mingled pity and horror that this poor wretch should be the partner of the only shelter I could find within so short a time of my arrival. I who—It was horrible, shameful, humiliating; and yet the suffering in his wretched face was so evident that I could not but feel a pang of pity too. 'I have nowhere to go,' I said. 'I am—a stranger. I have been badly used, and nobody seems to care.'

'No,' he said, 'nobody cares; don't you look for that. Why should they? Why, you look as if you were sorry for *me!* What a joke!' he murmured to himself,—'what a joke! Sorry for someone else! What a fool the fellow must be!'

'You look,' I said, 'as if you were suffering horribly; and you say you have come here for years.'

'Suffering! I should think I was,' said the sick man; 'but what is that to you? Yes; I've been here for years,—oh, years! that means nothing,—for longer than can be counted. Suffering is not the word. It's torture; it's agony! But who cares? Take your leg out of my way.'

I drew myself out of his way from a sort of habit, though against my will, and asked, from habit too, 'Are you never any better than now?'

He looked at me more closely, and an air of astonishment

202

came over his face. 'What d'ye want here,' he said, 'pitying a man? That's something new here. No; I'm not always so bad, if you want to know. I get better, and then I go and do what makes me bad again, and that's how it will go on; and I choose it to be so, and you needn't bring any of your d——d pity here.'

'I may ask, at least, why aren't you looked after? Why don't you get into some hospital?' I said.

'Hospital!' cried the sick man, and then he too burst out into that furious laugh, the most awful sound I ever had heard. Some of the passers-by stopped to hear what the joke was, and surrounded me with once more a circle of mockers.

'Hospitals! perhaps you would like a whole Red Cross Society, with ambulances and all arranged?' cried one. 'Or the *Misericordia*!' shouted another. I sprang up to my feet, crying, 'Why not?' with an impulse of rage which gave me strength. Was I never to meet with anything but this fiendish laughter? 'There's some authority, I suppose,' I cried in my fury. 'It is not the rabble that is the only master here, I hope.' But nobody took the least trouble to hear what I had to say for myself. The last speaker struck me on the mouth, and called me an accursed fool for talking of what I did not understand; and finally they all swept on and passed away.

I had been, as I thought, severely injured when I dragged myself into that corner to save myself from the crowd; but I sprang up now as if nothing had happened to me. My wounds had disappeared; my bruises were gone. I was as I had been when I dropped, giddy and amazed, upon the same pavement, how long—an hour?—before? It might have been an hour, it might have been a year, I cannot tell. The light was the same as ever, the thunderous atmosphere unchanged. Day, if it was day, had made no progress; night, if it was evening, had come no nearer,—all was the same.

As I went on again presently, with a vexed and angry spirit, regarding on every side around me the endless surging of the crowd, and feeling a loneliness, a sense of total abandonment and solitude, which I cannot describe, there came up to me a man of remarkable appearance. That he was a person of importance, of great knowledge and information, could not be doubted. He was very pale, and of a worn but commanding aspect. The lines of his face were deeply drawn; his eyes were sunk under high arched brows, from which they looked out as from caves, full of a fiery impatient light. His thin lips were never quite without a smile; but it was not a smile in which any pleasure was. He walked slowly, not hurrying, like most of the passengers. He had a reflective look, as if pondering many things. He came up to me suddenly, without introduction or preliminary, and took me by the arm.

'What object had you in talking of these antiquated institutions?' he said. And I saw in his mind the gleam of the thought, which seemed to be the first with all, that I was a fool, and that it was the natural thing to wish me harm, just as in the earth above it was the natural thing, professed at least, to wish well,—to say, Good-morning, good-day, by habit and without thought. In this strange country the stranger was received with a curse, and it woke an answer not unlike the hasty 'Curse you, then, also!' which seemed to come without any will of mine through my mind. But this provoked only a smile from my new friend. He took no notice. He was disposed to examine me, to find some amusement perhaps—how could I tell?—in what I might say.

'What antiquated things?'

'Are you still so slow of understanding? What were they—hospitals? The pretences of a world that can still deceive itself. Did you expect to find them here?'

'I expected to find—how should I know?' I said, bewildered—'some shelter for a poor wretch where he could be cared for, not to be left there to die in the street. Expected! I never thought. I took it for granted—'

'To die in the street!' he cried with a smile and a shrug of his shoulders. 'You'll learn better by and by. And if he did die in the street, what then? What is that to you?'

'To me!' I turned and looked at him, amazed; but he had somehow shut his soul, so that I could see nothing but the deep eyes in their caves, and the smile upon the close-shut mouth. 'No more to me than to anyone. I only spoke for humanity's sake, as—a fellow-creature.'

My new acquaintance gave way to a silent laugh within himself, which was not so offensive as the loud laugh of the crowd, but yet was more exasperating than words can say. 'You think that matters? But it does not hurt you that he should be in pain. It would do you no good if he were to get well. Why should you trouble yourself one way or the other? Let him die—if he can—That makes no difference to you or me.'

'I must be dull indeed,' I cried,—'slow of understanding, as you say. This is going back to the ideas of times beyond knowledge—before Christianity—' As soon as I had said this I felt somehow—I could not tell how—as if my voice jarred, as if something false and unnatural was in what I said. My companion gave my arm a twist as if with a shock of surprise, then laughed in his inward way again.

'We don't think much of that here, nor of your modern pretences in general. The only thing that touches you and me is what hurts or helps ourselves. To be sure, it all comes to the same thing,—for I suppose it annoys you to see that wretch writhing; it hurts your more delicate, highly-cultivated consciousness.'

'It has nothing to do with my consciousness,' I cried angrily; 'it is a shame to let a fellow-creature suffer if we can prevent it.'

'Why shouldn't he suffer?' said my companion. We passed as he spoke some other squalid, wretched creatures shuffling among the crowd, whom he kicked with his foot, calling forth a yell of pain and curses. This he regarded with a supreme contemptuous calm which stupefied me. Nor did any of the passers-by show the slightest inclination to take the part of the sufferers. They laughed, or shouted out a gibe, or what was still more wonderful, went on with a complete unaffected indifference, as if all this was natural. I tried to disengage my arm in horror and dismay, but he held me fast with a pressure that hurt me. 'That's the question,' he said. 'What have we to do with it? Your fictitious consciousness makes it painful to you. To me, on the contrary, who take the view of nature, it is a pleasurable feeling. It enhances the amount of ease, whatever that may be, which I enjoy. I am in no pain. That brute who is'—and he flicked with a stick he carried the uncovered wound of a wretch upon the roadside—'makes me more satisfied with my condition. Ah! you think it is I who am the brute? You will change your mind by and by.'

'Never!' I cried, wrenching my arm from his with an effort, 'if I should live a hundred years.'

'A hundred years,—a drop in the bucket!' he said with his silent laugh. 'You will live forever, and you will come to my view; and we shall meet in the course of ages, from time to time, to compare notes. I would say goodbye after the old fashion, but you are but newly arrived, and I will not treat you so badly as that.' With which he parted from me, waving his hand, with his everlasting horrible smile.

'Goodbye!' I said to myself, 'goodbye! why should it be treating me badly to say goodbye—'

I was startled by a buffet on the mouth. 'Take that!' cried someone, 'to teach you how to wish the worst of tortures to people who have done you no harm.'

'What have I said? I meant no harm; I repeated only what is the commonest civility, the merest good manners.'

'You wished,' said the man who had struck me,—'I won't repeat the words: to me, for it was I only that heard them, the awful company that hurts most, that sets everything before us, both past and to come, and cuts like a sword and burns like fire. I'll say it to yourself, and see how it feels. God be with you! There! it is said, and we all must bear it, thanks, you fool and accursed, to you.'

And then there came a pause over all the place, an awful stillness,—hundreds of men and women standing clutching with desperate movements at their hearts as if to tear them out, moving their heads as if to dash them against the wall, wringing their hands, with a look upon all their convulsed faces which I can never forget. They all turned to me, cursing me with those horrible eyes of anguish. And everything was still; the noise all stopped for a moment, the air all silent, with a silence that could be felt. And then suddenly out of the crowd there came a great piercing cry; and everything began again exactly as before.

While this pause occurred, and while I stood wondering, bewildered, understanding nothing, there came over me a darkness, a blackness, a sense of misery such as never in all my life—though I have known troubles enough—I had felt before. All that had happened to me throughout my existence seemed to rise pale and terrible in a hundred scenes before me,—all momentary, intense, as if each was the present moment. And in each of these scenes I saw what I had never seen before. I saw where I had taken the wrong instead of the right step, in what wantonness, with what self-will it had been done; how God (I shuddered at the name) had spoken and called me, and even entreated, and I had withstood and refused.

All the evil I had done came back, and spread itself out before my eyes; and I loathed it, yet knew that I had chosen it, and that it would be with me forever. I saw it all in the twinkling of an eye, in a moment, while I stood there, and all men with me, in the horror of awful thought. Then it ceased as it had come, instantaneously, and the noise and the laughter, and the quarrels and cries, and all the commotion of this new bewildering place, in a moment began again. I had seen no one while this strange paroxysm lasted. When it disappeared, I came to myself, emerging as from a dream, and looked into the face of the man whose words, not careless like mine, had brought it upon us. Our eyes met, and his were surrounded by curves and lines of anguish which were terrible to see.

'Well,' he said with a short laugh, which was forced and harsh, 'how do you like it? that is what happens when—If it came often, who could endure it?' He was not like the rest. There was no sneer upon his face, no gibe at my simplicity. Even now, when all had recovered, he was still quivering with something that looked like a nobler pain. His face was very grave, the lines deeply drawn in it; and he seemed to be seeking no amusement or distraction, nor to take any part in the noise and tumult which was going on around.

'Do you know what that cry meant?' he said. 'Did you hear that cry? It was someone who saw—even here once in a long time, they say, it can be seen—'

'What can be seen?'

He shook his head, looking at me with a meaning which I could not interpret. It was beyond the range of my thoughts. I came to know after, or I never could have made this record. But on that subject he said no more. He turned the way I was going, though it mattered nothing what way I went, for all were the same to me. 'You are one of the newcomers?' he said; 'you have not been long here—'

'Tell me,' I cried, 'what you mean by *here*. Where are we? How can one tell who has fallen—he knows not whence or where? What is this place? I have never seen anything like it. It seems to me that I hate it already, though I know not what it is.'

He shook his head once more. 'You will hate it more and more,' he said; 'but of these dreadful streets you will never be free, unless—' And here he stopped again.

'Unless—what? If it is possible, I will be free of them, and that before long.'

He smiled at me faintly, as we smile at children, but not with derision.

'How shall you do that? Between this miserable world and all others, there is a great gulf fixed. It is full of all the bitterness and tears that come from all the universe. These drop from them, but stagnate here. We, you perceive, have no tears, not even at moments—' Then, 'You will soon be accustomed to all this,' he said. 'You will fall into the way. Perhaps you will be able to amuse yourself to make it passable. Many do. There are a number of fine things to be seen here. If you are curious, come with me and I will show you. Or work,—there is even work. There is only one thing that is impossible, or if not impossible—' And here he paused again and raised his eyes to the dark clouds and lurid sky overhead. 'The man who gave that cry! if I could but find him! he must have seen—'

'What could he see?' I asked. But there arose in my mind something like contempt. A visionary! who could not speak plainly, who broke off into mysterious inferences, and appeared to know more than he would say. It seemed foolish to waste time, when evidently there was still so much to see, in the company of such a man; and I began already to feel more at home. There was something in that moment of anguish which had wrought a strange familiarity in me with my surroundings. It was so great a relief to return out of the misery of that sharp and horrible self-realization, to what had come to be, in comparison, easy and well known. I had no desire to go back and grope among the mysteries and anguish so suddenly revealed. I was glad to be free from them, to be left to myself, to get a little pleasure perhaps like the others.

While these thoughts passed through my mind, I had gone on without any active impulse of my own, as everybody else did; and my latest companion had disappeared. He saw, no doubt, without any need for words, what my feelings were. And I proceeded on my way. I felt better as I got more accustomed to the place, or perhaps it was the sensation of relief after that moment of indescribable pain.

As for the sights in the streets, I began to grow used to them. The wretched creatures who strolled or sat about with signs of sickness or wounds upon them disgusted me only, they no longer called forth my pity. I began to feel ashamed of my silly questions about the hospital. All the same, it would have been a good thing to have had some receptacle for them, into which they might have been driven out of the way. I felt an inclination to push them aside as I saw other people do, but was a little ashamed of that impulse too; and so I went on. There seemed no quiet streets, so far as I could make out, in the place. Some were smaller, meaner, with a different kind of passengers, but the same hubbub and unresting movement everywhere. I saw no signs of melancholy or seriousness; active pain, violence, brutality, the continual shock of quarrels and blows, but no pensive faces about, no sorrowfulness, nor the kind of trouble which brings thought. Everybody was fully occupied, pushing on as if in a race, pausing for nothing.

The glitter of the lights, the shouts, and sounds of continual going, the endless whirl of passers-by, confused and tired me after a while. I went as far out as I could go to what seemed the outskirts of the place, where I could by glimpses perceive a low horizon all lurid and glowing, which seemed to sweep round and round. Against it in the distance stood up the outline, black against that red glow, of other towers and house-tops, so many and great that there was evidently another town between us and the sunset, if sunset it was. I have seen a western sky like it when there were storms about, and all the colours of the sky were heightened and darkened by angry influences.

The distant town rose against it, cutting the firmament so that it might have been tongues of flame flickering between the dark solid outlines; and across the waste open country which lay between the two cities, there came a distant hum like the sound of the sea, which was in reality the roar of that other multitude. The country between showed no greenness or beauty; it lay dark under the dark overhanging sky. Here and there seemed a cluster of giant trees scathed as if by lightning, their bare boughs standing up as high as the distant towers, their trunks like black columns without foliage. Openings here and there, with glimmering lights, looked like the mouths of mines; but of passengers there were scarcely any. A figure here and there flew along as if pursued, imperfectly seen, a shadow only a little darker than the space about. And in contrast with the sound of the city, here was no sound at all, except the low roar on either side, and a vague cry or two from the openings of the mine,—a scene all drawn in darkness, in variations of gloom, deriving scarcely any light at all from the red and gloomy burning of that distant evening sky.

A faint curiosity to go forwards, to see what the mines were, perhaps to get a share in what was brought up from them, crossed my mind. But I was afraid of the dark, of the wild uninhabited savage look of the landscape; though when I thought of it, there seemed no reason why a narrow stretch of country between two great towns should be alarming. But the impression was strong and above reason. I turned back to the street in which I had first alighted, and which seemed to end in a great square full of people. In the middle there was a stage erected, from which someone was delivering an oration or address of some sort. He stood beside a long table, upon which lay something which I could not clearly distinguish, except that it seemed alive, and moved, or rather writhed with convulsive twitchings, as if trying to get free of the bonds which confined it.

Round the stage in front were a number of seats occupied by listeners, many of whom were women, whose interest seemed to be very great, some of them being furnished with note-books; while a great unsettled crowd coming and going, drifted round,—many, arrested for a time as they passed, proceeding on their way when the interest flagged, as is usual to such open-air assemblies. I followed two of those who pushed their way to within a short distance of the stage, and who were strong, big men, more fitted to elbow the crowd aside than I, after my rough treatment in the first place, and the agitation I had passed through, could be. I was glad, besides, to take advantage of the explanation which one was giving to the other. 'It's always fun to see this fellow demonstrate,' he said, 'and the subject today's a capital one. Let's get well forward, and see all that's going on.'

'Which subject do you mean?' said the other; 'the theme or the example?' And they both laughed, though I did not seize the point of the wit.

'Well, both,' said the first speaker. 'The theme is nerves; and as a lesson in construction and the calculation of possibilities, it's fine. He's very clever at that. He shows how they are all strung to give as much pain and do as much harm as can be; and yet how well it's all managed, don't you know, to look the reverse. As for the example, he's a capital one—all nerves together, lying, if you like, just on the surface, ready for the knife.'

'If they're on the surface I can't see where the fun is,' said the other.

'Metaphorically speaking. Of course they are just where other people's nerves are; but he's what you call a highly organised nervous specimen. There will be plenty of fun. Hush! he is just going to begin.'

'The arrangement of these threads of being,' said the lecturer, evidently resuming after a pause, 'so as to convey to the brain the most instantaneous messages of pain or pleasure, is wonderfully skilful and clever. I need not say to the audience before me, enlightened as it is by experiences of the most striking kind, that the messages are less of pleasure than of pain. They report to the brain the stroke of injury far more often than the thrill of pleasure; though sometimes that too, no doubt, or life could scarcely be maintained. The powers that be have found it necessary to mingle a little sweet of pleasurable sensation, else our miserable race would certainly have found some means of procuring annihilation. I do not for a moment pretend to say that the pleasure is sufficient to offer a just counterbalance to the other.

None of my hearers will, I hope, accuse me of inconsistency. I am ready to allow that in a previous condition I asserted somewhat strongly that this was the case; but experience has enlightened us on that point. Our circumstances are now understood by us all in a manner impossible while we were still in a condition of incompleteness. We are all convinced that there is no compensation. The pride of the position, of bearing everything rather than give in, or making a submission we do not feel, of preserving our own will and individuality to all eternity, is the only compensation. I am satisfied with it, for my part.'

The orator made a pause, holding his head high, and there was a certain amount of applause. The two men before me cheered vociferously. 'That is the right way to look at it,' one of them said. My eyes were upon them, with no particular motive; and I could not help starting, as I saw suddenly underneath their applause and laughter a snarl of cursing, which was the real expression of their thoughts. I felt disposed in the same way to curse the speaker, though I knew no reason why.

He went on a little farther, explaining what he meant to do;

and then turning round, approached the table. An assistant, who was waiting, uncovered it quickly. The audience stirred with quickened interest, and I with consternation made a step forwards, crying out with horror. The object on the table, writhing, twitching to get free, but bound down by every limb, was a living man. The lecturer went forwards calmly, taking his instruments from their case with perfect composure and coolness. 'Now, ladies and gentlemen,' he said, and inserted the knife in the flesh, making a long clear cut in the bound arm. I shrieked out, unable to restrain myself. The sight of the deliberate wound, the blood, the cry of agony that came from the victim, the calmness of all the lookers-on, filled me with horror and rage indescribable.

I felt myself clear the crowd away with a rush, and spring on the platform, I could not tell how. 'You devil!' I cried, 'let the man go! Where is the police? Where is a magistrate? Let the man go this moment! fiends in human shape! I'll have you brought to justice!' I heard myself shouting wildly, as I flung myself upon the wretched sufferer, interposing between him and the knife. It was something like this that I said. My horror and rage were delirious, and carried me beyond all attempt at control.

Through it all I heard a shout of laughter rising from everybody round. The lecturer laughed; the audience roared with that sound of horrible mockery which had driven me out of myself in my first experience. All kinds of mocking cries sounded around me. 'Let him a little blood to calm him down.' 'Let the fool have a taste of it himself, doctor.' Last of all came a voice mingled with the cries of the sufferer whom I was trying to shield, 'Take him instead; curse him! take him instead.' I was bending over the man with my arms outstretched, protecting him, when he gave vent to this cry.

And I heard immediately behind me a shout of assent, which seemed to come from the two strong young men with whom I had been standing, and the sound of a rush to seize me. I looked round, half mad with terror and rage; a second more and I should have been strapped on the table too. I made one wild bound into the midst of the crowd; and struggling among the arms stretched out to catch me, amid the roar of the laughter and cries—fled—fled wildly, I knew not whither, in panic and rage and horror which no words could describe. Terror winged my feet. I flew, thinking as little of whom I met, or knocked down, or trod upon in my way, as the others did at whom I had wondered a little while ago.

No distinct impression of this headlong course remains in my mind, save the sensation of mad fear such as I had never felt before. I came to myself on the edge of the dark valley which surrounded the town. All my pursuers had dropped off before that time; and I have the recollection of flinging myself upon the ground on my face in the extremity of fatigue and exhaustion. I must have lain there undisturbed for some time. A few steps came and went, passing me; but no one took any notice, and the absence of the noise and crowding gave me a momentary respite. But in my heat and fever I got no relief of coolness from the contact of the soil. I might have flung myself upon a bed of hot ashes, so much was it unlike the dewy cool earth which I expected, upon which one can always throw one's self with a sensation of repose. Presently the uneasiness of it made me struggle up again and look around me. I was safe; at least the cries of the pursuers had died away, the laughter which made my blood boil offended my ears no more.

The noise of the city was behind me, softened into an indefinite roar by distance, and before me stretched out the dreary landscape in which there seemed no features of attraction. Now that I was nearer to it, I found it not so unpeopled as I thought. At no great distance from me was the mouth of one of the mines, from which came an indication of subterranean lights; and I perceived that the flying figures which I had taken for travellers between one city and another were in reality wayfarers endeavouring to keep clear of what seemed a sort of press-gang at the openings.

One of them, unable to stop himself in his flight, adopted the same expedient as myself, and threw himself on the ground close to me when he had got beyond the range of pursuit. It

214

was curious that we should meet there, he flying from a danger which I was about to face, and ready to encounter that from which I had fled. I waited for a few minutes till he had recovered his breath, and then, 'What are you running from?' I said. 'Is there any danger there?' The man looked up at me with the same continual question in his eyes,—Who is this fool?

'Danger!' he said. 'Are you so new here, or such a cursed idiot, as not to know the danger of the mines? You are going across yourself, I suppose, and then you'll see.'

'But tell me,' I said; 'my experience may be of use to you afterwards, if you will tell me yours now.'

'Of use!' he cried, staring; 'who cares? Find out for yourself. If they get hold of you, you will soon understand.'

I no longer took this for rudeness, but answered in his own way, cursing him too for a fool. 'If I ask a warning I can give one; as for kindness,' I said, 'I was not looking for that.'

At this he laughed, indeed we laughed together,—there seemed something ridiculous in the thought; and presently he told me, for the mere relief of talking, that round each of these pit-mouths there was a band to entrap every passer-by who allowed himself to be caught, and send him down below to work in the mine. 'Once there, there is no telling when you may get free,' he said; 'one time or other most people have a taste of it. You don't know what hard labor is if you have never been there. I had a spell once. There is neither air nor light; your blood boils in your veins from the fervent heat; you are never allowed to rest. You are put in every kind of contortion to get at it, your limbs twisted, and your muscles strained.'

'For what?' I said.

'For gold!' he cried with a flash in his eyes—'gold! There it is inexhaustible; however hard you may work, there is always more, and more!'

'And to whom does all that belong?' I said. 'To whoever is strong enough to get hold and keep possession,—sometimes one, sometimes another. The only thing you are sure of is that it will never be you.'

Why not I as well as another? was the thought that went through my mind, and my new companion spied it with a shriek of derision.

'It is not for you nor your kind,' he cried. 'How do you think you could force other people to serve *you*? Can you terrify them or hurt them, or give them anything? You have not learned yet who are the masters here.'

This troubled me, for it was true. 'I had begun to think,' I said, 'that there was no authority at all,—for every man seems to do as he pleases; you ride over one, and knock another down, or you seize a living man and cut him to pieces'—I shuddered as I thought of it—'and there is nobody to interfere.'

'Who should interfere?' he said. 'Why shouldn't every man amuse himself as he can? But yet for all that we've got our masters,' he cried with a scowl, waving his clinched fist in the direction of the mines; 'you'll find it out when you get there.'

It was a long time after this before I ventured to move, for here it seemed to me that for the moment I was safe,—outside the city, yet not within reach of the dangers of that intermediate space which grew clearer before me as my eyes became accustomed to the lurid threatening afternoon light. One after another the fugitives came flying past me,—people who had escaped from the armed bands whom I could now see on the watch near the pit's mouth. I could see too the tactics of these bands,—how they retired, veiling the lights and the opening, when a greater number than usual of travellers appeared on the way, and then suddenly widening out, throwing out flanking lines, surrounded and drew in the unwary. I could even hear the cries with which their victims disappeared over the opening which seemed to go down into the bowels of the earth.

By and by there came flying towards me a wretch more dreadful in aspect than any I had seen. His scanty clothes seemed singed and burned into rags; his hair, which hung about his face unkempt and uncared for, had the same singed aspect; his skin was brown and baked. I got up as he approached, and caught him and threw him to the ground, without heeding his struggles to get on. 'Don't you see,' he cried with a gasp, 'they may get me again.' He was one of those who had escaped out of the mines; but what was it to me whether they caught him again or not? I wanted to know how he had been caught, and what he had been set to do, and how he had escaped. Why should I hesitate to use my superior strength when no one else did? I kept watch over him that he should not get away.

'You have been in the mines?' I said.

'Let me go!' he cried. 'Do you need to ask?' and he cursed me as he struggled, with the most terrible imprecations. 'They may get me yet. Let me go!'

'Not till you tell me,' I cried. 'Tell me and I'll protect you. If they come near I'll let you go. Who are they, man? I must know.'

He struggled up from the ground, clearing his hot eyes from the ashes that were in them, and putting aside his singed hair. He gave me a glance of hatred and impotent resistance (for I was stronger than he), and then cast a wild terrified look back. The skirmishers did not seem to remark that anybody had escaped, and he became gradually a little more composed. 'Who are they?' he said hoarsely. 'They're cursed wretches like you and me; and there are as many bands of them as there are mines on the road; and you'd better turn back and stay where you are. You are safe here.'

'I will not turn back,' I said.

'I know well enough: you can't. You've got to go the round like the rest,' he said with a laugh which was like a sound uttered by a wild animal rather than a human voice. The man was in my power, and I struck him, miserable as he was. It seemed a relief thus to get rid of some of the fury in my mind. 'It's a lie,' I said; 'I go because I please. Why shouldn't I gather a band of my own if I please, and fight those brutes, not fly from them like you?'

He chuckled and laughed below his breath, struggling and cursing and crying out, as I struck him again, 'You gather a band! What could you offer them? Where would you find them? Are you better than the rest of us? Are you not a man like the rest?

217

Strike me you can, for I'm down. But make yourself a master and a chief—you!'

'Why not I?' I shouted again, wild with rage and the sense that I had no power over him, save to hurt him. That passion made my hands tremble; he slipped from me in a moment, bounded from the ground like a ball, and with a yell of derision escaped, and plunged into the streets and the clamour of the city from which I had just flown. I felt myself rage after him, shaking my fists with a consciousness of the ridiculous passion of impotence that was in me, but no power of restraining it; and there was not one of the fugitives who passed, however desperate he might be, who did not make a mock at me as he darted by. The laughing-stock of all those miserable objects, the sport of fate, afraid to go forwards, unable to go back, with a fire in my veins urging me on! But presently I grew a little calmer out of mere exhaustion, which was all the relief that was possible to me. And by and by, collecting all my faculties, and impelled by this impulse, which I seemed unable to resist, I got up and went cautiously on.

Fear can act in two ways: it paralyzes, and it renders cunning. At this moment I found it inspire me. I made my plans before I started, how to steal along under the cover of the blighted brushwood which broke the line of the valley here and there. I set out only after long thought, seizing the moment when the vaguely perceived band were scouring in the other direction intercepting the travellers. Thus, with many pauses, I got near to the pit's mouth in safety. But my curiosity was as great as, almost greater than my terror.

I had kept far from the road, dragging myself sometimes on hands and feet over broken ground, tearing my clothes and my flesh upon the thorns; and on that farther side all seemed so silent and so dark in the shadow cast by some disused machin-ery, behind which the glare of the fire from below blazed upon the other side of the opening, that I could not crawl along in the darkness, and pass, which would have been the safe way, but with a breathless hot desire to see and know, dragged myself to the very edge to look down. Though I was in the shadow, my eyes were nearly put out by the glare on which I gazed. It was not fire; it was the lurid glow of the gold, glowing like flame, at which countless miners were working. They were all about like flies,—some on their knees, some bent double as they stooped over their work, some lying cramped upon shelves and ledges. The sight was wonderful, and terrible beyond description. The workmen seemed to consume away with the heat and the glow, even in the few minutes I gazed.

Their eyes shrank into their heads; their faces blackened. I could see some trying to secret morsels of the glowing metal, which burned whatever it touched, and some who were being searched by the superiors of the mines, and some who were punishing the offenders, fixing them up against the blazing wall of gold. The fear went out of my mind, so much absorbed was I in this sight. I gazed, seeing farther and farther every moment into crevices and seams of the glowing metal, always with more and more slaves at work, and the entire pantomime of labor and theft, and search and punishment, going on and on,—the baked faces dark against the golden glare, the hot eyes taking a yellow reflection, the monotonous clamor of pick and shovel, and cries and curses, and all the indistinguishable sound of a multitude of human creatures. And the floor below, and the low roof which overhung whole myriads within a few inches of their faces, and the irregular walls all breached and shelved, were every one the same, a pandemonium of gold,—gold everywhere. I had loved many foolish things in my life, but never this; which was perhaps why I gazed and kept my sight, though there rose out of it a blast of heat which scorched the brain.

While I stooped over, intent on the sight, someone who had come up by my side to gaze too was caught by the fumes (as I suppose), for suddenly I was aware of a dark object falling prone into the glowing interior with a cry and crash which brought back my first wild panic. He fell in a heap, from which his arms shot forth wildly as he reached the bottom, and his cry was half anguish yet half desire. I saw him seized by half a dozen eager watchers, and pitched upon a ledge just under the roof, and tools thrust into his hands. I held on by an old shaft, trembling, unable to move. Perhaps I cried too in my horror,—for one of the overseers who stood in the centre of the glare looked up. He had the air of ordering all that was going on, and stood unaffected by the blaze, commanding the other wretched officials, who obeyed him like dogs. He seemed to me, in my terror, like a figure of gold, the image perhaps of wealth or Pluto, or I know not what, for I suppose my brain began to grow confused, and my hold on the shaft to relax. I had strength enough, however (for I cared not for the gold), to fling myself back the other way upon the ground, where I rolled backwards, downwards, I knew not how, turning over and over upon sharp ashes and metallic edges, which tore my hair and beard.—and for a moment I knew no more.

This fall saved me. I came to myself after a time, and heard the press-gang searching about. I had sense to lie still among the ashes thrown up out of the pit, while I heard their voices. Once I gave myself up for lost. The glitter of a lantern flashed in my eyes, a foot passed, crashing among the ashes so close to my cheek that the shoe grazed it. I found the mark after, burned upon my flesh; but I escaped notice by a miracle. And presently I was able to drag myself up and crawl away; but how I reached the end of the valley I cannot tell. I pushed my way along mechanically on the dark side. I had no further desire to see what was going on in the openings of the mines. I went on, stumbling and stupid, scarcely capable even of fear, conscious only of wretchedness and weariness, till at last I felt myself drop across the road within the gateway of the other town, and lay there with no thought of anything but the relief of being at rest.

When I came to myself, it seemed to me that there was a change in the atmosphere and the light. It was less lurid, paler, gray, more like twilight than the stormy afternoon of the other city. A certain dead serenity was in the sky,—black paleness, whiteness, everything faint in it. This town was walled, but the gates stood open, and I saw no defences of troops or other guardians. I found myself lying across the threshold, but pushed to one side, so that the carriages which went and came should not be stopped or I injured by their passage. It seemed to me that there was some thoughtfulness and kindness in this action, and my heart sprang up in a reaction of hope. I looked back as if upon a nightmare on the dreadful city which I had left, on its tumults and noise, the wild racket of the streets, the wounded wretches who sought refuge in the corners, the strife and misery that were abroad, and, climax of all, the horrible entertainment which had been going on in the square, the unhappy being strapped upon the table.

How, I said to myself, could such things be? Was it a dream? Was it a nightmare? Was it something presented to me in a vision,—a strong delusion to make me think that the old fables which had been told concerning the end of mortal life were true? When I looked back it appeared like an allegory, so that I might have seen it in a dream; and still more like an allegory were the gold mines in the valley, and the myriads who laboured there. Was it all true, or only a reflection from the old life mingling with the strange novelties which would most likely elude understanding on the entrance into this new? I sat within the shelter of the gateway on my awakening, and thought over all this. My heart was calm,—almost, in the revulsion from the terrors I had been through, happy.

I persuaded myself that I was but now beginning; that there had been no reality in these latter experiences, only a curious succession of nightmares, such as might so well be supposed to follow a wonderful transformation like that which must take place between our mortal life and—the world to come. The world to come! I paused and thought of it all, until the heart began to beat loud in my breast. What was this where I lay? Another world,—a world which was not happiness, not bliss? Oh, no; perhaps there was no world of bliss save in dreams. This, on the other hand, I said to myself, was not misery; for was not I seated here, with a certain tremulousness about me, it was true, after all the experiences which, supposing them even to have been but dreams, I had come through,—a tremulousness very comprehensible, and not at all without hope?

I will not say that I believed even what I tried to think. Something in me lay like a dark shadow in the midst of all my theories; but yet I succeeded to a great degree in convincing myself that the hope in me was real, and that I was but now beginning—beginning with at least a possibility that all might be well. In this half conviction, and after all the troubles that were over (even though they might only have been imaginary troubles), I felt a certain sweetness in resting there within the gateway, with my back against it. I was unwilling to get up again, and bring myself in contact with reality. I felt that there was pleasure in being left alone. Carriages rolled past me occasionally, and now and then some people on foot; but they did not kick me out of the way or interfere with my repose.

Presently as I sat trying to persuade myself to rise and pursue my way, two men came up to me in a sort of uniform. I recognized with another distinct sensation of pleasure that here were people who had authority, representatives of some kind of government. They came up to me and bade me come with them in tones which were peremptory enough; but what of that?—better the most peremptory supervision than the lawlessness from which I had come. They raised me from the ground with a touch, for I could not resist them, and led me quickly along the street into which that gateway gave access, which was a handsome street with tall houses on either side. Groups of people were moving about along the pavement, talking now and then with considerable animation; but when my companions were seen, there was an immediate moderation of tone, a sort of respect which looked like fear.

There was no brawling nor tumult of any kind in the street. The only incident that occurred was this: when we had gone some way, I saw a lame man dragging himself along with difficulty on the other side of the street. My conductors had no sooner perceived him than they gave each other a look and darted across, conveying me with them, by a sweep of magnetic influence, I thought, that prevented me from staying behind. He made an attempt with his crutches to get out of the way, hurrying on—and I will allow that this attempt of his seemed to me very grotesque, so that I could scarcely help laughing; the other lookers-on in the street laughed too, though some put on an aspect of disgust. 'Look, the tortoise!' someone said; 'does he think he can go quicker than the orderlies?'

My companions came up to the man while this commentary was going on, and seized him by each arm. 'Where were you going? Where have you come from? How dare you make an exhibition of yourself?' they cried. They took the crutches from him as they spoke and threw them away, and dragged him on until we reached a great grated door which one of them opened with a key, while the other held the offender (for he seemed an offender) roughly up by one shoulder, causing him great pain. When the door was opened, I saw a number of people within, who seemed to crowd to the door as if seeking to get out; but this was not at all what was intended.

My second companion dragged the lame man forwards, and pushed him in with so much violence that I could see him fall forwards on his face on the floor. Then the other locked the door, and we proceeded on our way. It was not till sometime later that I understood why.

In the meantime I was hurried on, meeting a great many people who took no notice of me, to a central building in the middle of the town, where I was brought before an official attended by clerks, with great books spread out before him. Here I was questioned as to my name and my antecedents and the time of my arrival, then dismissed with a nod to one of my conductors. He led me back again down the street, took me into one of the tall great houses, opened the door of a room which was numbered, and left me there without a word. I cannot convey to any one the bewildered consternation with which I felt myself deposited here; and as the steps of my conductor died away in the long corridor, I sat down, and looking myself in the face, as it were, tried to make out what it was that had happened to me. The room was small and bare. There was but one thing hung upon the undecorated walls, and that was a long list of printed regulations which I had not the courage for the moment to look at. The light was indifferent, though the room was high up, and the street from the window looked far away below.

I cannot tell how long I sat there thinking, and yet it could scarcely be called thought. I asked myself over and over again, Where am I? is it a prison? am I shut in, to leave this enclosure no more? what am I to do? how is the time to pass? I shut my eyes for a moment and tried to realize all that had happened to me; but nothing save a whirl through my head of disconnected thoughts seemed possible, and some force was upon me to open my eyes again, to see the blank room, the dull light, the vacancy round me in which there was nothing to interest the mind, nothing to please the eye,—a blank wherever I turned. Presently there came upon me a burning regret for everything I had left,—for the noisy town with all its tumults and cruelties, for the dark valley with all its dangers.

Everything seemed bearable, almost agreeable, in comparison with this. I seemed to have been brought here to make acquaintance once more with myself, to learn over again what manner of man I was. Needless knowledge, acquaintance unnecessary, unhappy! for what was there in me to make me to myself a good companion? Never, I knew, could I separate myself from that eternal consciousness; but it was cruelty to force the contemplation upon me. All blank, blank around me, a prison! And was this to last forever?

I do not know how long I sat, rapt in this gloomy vision; but at last it occurred to me to rise and try the door, which to my astonishment was open. I went out with a throb of new hope. After all, it might not be necessary to come back. There might be other expedients; I might fall among friends. I turned down the long echoing stairs, on which I met various people, who took no notice of me, and in whom I felt no interest save a desire to avoid them, and at last reached the street. To be out of doors in the air was something, though there was no wind, but a motionless still atmosphere which nothing disturbed. The streets, indeed, were full of movement, but not of life—though this seems a paradox.

The passengers passed on their way in long regulated lines,— those who went towards the gates keeping rigorously to one side of the pavement, those who came, to the other. They talked to each other here and there; but whenever two men in uniform, such as those who had been my conductors, appeared, silence ensued, and the wayfarers shrank even from the looks of these persons in authority. I walked all about the spacious town. Everywhere there were tall houses, everywhere streams of people coming and going, but no one spoke to me, or remarked me at all. I was as lonely as if I had been in a wilderness. I was indeed in a wilderness of men, who were as though they did not see me, passing without even a look of human fellowship, each absorbed in his own concerns. I walked and walked till my limbs trembled under me, from one end to another of the great streets, up and down, and round and round.

But no one said, How are you? Whence come you? What are you doing? At length in despair I turned again to the blank and miserable room, which had looked to me like a cell in a prison. I had wilfully made no note of its situation, trying to avoid rather than to find it, but my steps were drawn thither against my will. I found myself retracing my steps, mounting the long stairs, passing the same people, who streamed along with no recognition of me, as I desired nothing to do with them; and at last found myself within the same four blank walls as before.

Soon after I returned I became conscious of measured steps passing the door, and of an eye upon me. I can say no more than this. From what point it was that I was inspected I cannot tell; but that I was inspected, closely scrutinized by someone, and that not only externally, but by a cold observation that went through and through me, I knew and felt beyond any possibility of mistake. This recurred from time to time, horribly, at uncertain moments, so that I never felt myself secure from it. I knew when the watcher was coming by tremors and shiverings through all my being; and no sensation so unsupportable has it ever been mine to bear. How much that is to say, no one can tell who has not gone through those regions of darkness, and learned what is in all their abysses. I tried at first to hide, to fling myself on the floor, to cover my face, to burrow in a dark corner. Useless attempts! The eyes that looked in upon me had powers beyond my powers. I felt sometimes conscious of the derisive smile with which my miserable subterfuges were regarded. They were all in vain.

And what was still more strange was that I had not energy to think of attempting any escape. My steps, though watched, were not restrained in any way, so far as I was aware. The gates of the city stood open on all sides, free to those who went as well as to those who came; but I did not think of flight. Of flight! Whence should I go from myself? Though that horrible inspection was from the eyes of some unseen being, it was in some mysterious way connected with my own thinking and reflections, so that the thought came ever more and more strongly upon me, that from myself I could never escape. And that reflection took all energy, all impulse from me. I might have gone away when I pleased, beyond reach of the authority which regulated everything,— how one should walk, where one should live,—but never from my own consciousness. On the other side of the town lay a great plain, traversed by roads on every side. There was no reason why I should not continue my journey there; but I did not. I had no wish nor any power in me to go away.

In one of my long, dreary, companionless walks, unshared by any human fellowship, I saw at last a face which I remembered; it was that of the cynical spectator who had spoken to me in the noisy street, in the midst of my early experiences. He gave a glance round him to see that there were no officials in sight, then left the file in which he was walking, and joined me. 'Ah!' he said, 'you are here already,' with the same derisive smile with which he had before regarded me. I hated the man and his sneer, yet that he should speak to me was something, almost a pleasure.

'Yes,' said I, 'I am here.' Then, after a pause, in which I did not know what to say, 'It is quiet here,' I said.

'Quiet enough. Do you like it better for that? To do whatever you please with no one to interfere; or to do nothing you please, but as you are forced to do it,—which do you think is best?'

I felt myself instinctively glance round, as he had done, to make sure that no one was in sight. Then I answered, faltering, 'I have always held that law and order were necessary things; and the lawlessness of that—that place—I don't know its name—if there is such a place,' I cried, 'I thought it was a dream.'

He laughed in his mocking way. 'Perhaps it is all a dream; who knows?' he said.

'Sir,' said I, 'you have been longer here than I—'

'Oh,' cried he, with a laugh that was dry and jarred upon the air almost like a shriek, 'since before your forefathers were born!' It seemed to me that he spoke like one who, out of bitterness and despite, made every darkness blacker still. A kind of madman in his way; for what was this claim of age?—a piece of bravado, no doubt, like the rest.

'That is strange,' I said, assenting, as when there is such a hallucination it is best to do. 'You can tell me, then, whence all this authority comes, and why we are obliged to obey.'

He looked at me as if he were thinking in his mind how to hurt me most. Then, with that dry laugh, 'We make trial of all things in this world,' he said, 'to see if perhaps we can find something we shall like.—discipline here, freedom in the other place. When you have gone all the round like me, then perhaps you will be able to choose.'

'Have you chosen?' I asked.

He only answered with a laugh. 'Come,' he said, 'there is amusement to be had too, and that of the most elevated kind. We make researches here into the moral nature of man. Will you come? But you must take the risk,' he added with a smile which afterwards I understood.

We went on together after this till we reached the centre of the place, in which stood an immense building with a dome, which dominated the city, and into a great hall in the centre of that, where a crowd of people were assembled. The sound of human speech, which murmured all around, brought new life to my heart. And as I gazed at a curious apparatus erected on a platform, several people spoke to me.

'We have again,' said one, 'the old subject today.'

'Is it something about the constitution of the place?' I asked in the bewilderment of my mind. My neighbours looked at me with alarm, glancing behind them to see what officials might be near.

'The constitution of the place is the result of the sense of the inhabitants that order must be preserved,' said the one, who had spoken to me first. 'The lawless can find refuge in other places. Here we have chosen to have supervision, nuisances removed, and order kept. That is enough. The constitution is not under discussion.'

'But man is,' said a second speaker. 'Let us keep to that in which we can mend nothing. Sir, you may have to contribute your quota to our enlightenment. We are investigating the rise of thought. You are a stranger; you may be able to help us.'

'I am no philosopher,' I said with a panic which I could not explain to myself.

'That does not matter. You are a fresh subject.' The speaker made a slight movement with his hand, and I turned round to escape in wild, sudden fright, though I had no conception what could be done to me; but the crowd had pressed close round me, hemming one in on every side. I was so wildly alarmed that I struggled among them, pushing backwards with all my force, and clearing a space round me with my arms; but my efforts were vain. Two of the officers suddenly appeared out of the crowd, and seizing me by the arms, forced me forwards. The throng dispersed before them on either side, and I was half dragged, half lifted up upon the platform, where stood the strange apparatus which I had contemplated with a dull wonder when I came into the hall.

My wonder did not last long. I felt myself fixed in it, standing supported in that position by bands and springs, so that no effort of mine was necessary to hold myself up, and none possible to release myself. I was caught by every joint, sustained, supported, exposed to the gaze of what seemed a world of upturned faces; among which I saw, with a sneer upon it, keeping a little behind the crowd, the face of the man who had led me here. Above my head was a strong light, more brilliant than anything I had ever seen, and which blazed upon my brain till the hair seemed to singe and the skin shrink. I hope I may never feel such a sensation again. The pitiless light went into me like a knife; but even my cries were stopped by the framework in which I was bound. I could breathe and suffer, but that was all.

Then someone got up on the platform above me and began to speak. He said, so far as I could comprehend in the anguish and torture in which I was held, that the origin of thought was the question he was investigating, but that in every previous subject the confusion of ideas had bewildered them, and the rapidity with which one followed another. 'The present example has been found to exhibit great persistency of idea,' he said. 'We hope that by his means some clearer theory may be arrived at.' Then he pulled over me a great movable lens as of a microscope, which concentrated the insupportable light.

The wild, hopeless passion that raged within my soul had no outlet in the immovable apparatus that held me. I was let down among the crowd, and exhibited to them every secret movement of my being, by some awful process which I have never fathomed. A burning fire was in my brain; flame seemed to run along all my nerves; speechless, horrible, incommunicable fury raged in my soul. But I was like a child—nay, like an image of wood or wax—in the pitiless hands that held me. What was the cut of a surgeon's knife to this? And I had thought *that* cruel! And I was powerless, and could do nothing—to blast, to destroy, to burn with this same horrible flame the fiends that surrounded me, as I desired to do.

Suddenly, in the raging fever of my thoughts, there surged up the recollection of that word which had paralyzed all around, and myself with them. The thought that I must share the anguish did not restrain me from my revenge. With a tremendous effort I got my voice, though the instrument pressed upon my lips. I know not what I articulated save 'God,' whether it was a curse or a blessing. I had been swung out into the middle of the hall, and hung amid the crowd, exposed to all their observations, when I succeeded in gaining utterance. My God! my God! Another moment and I had forgotten them and all my fury in the tortures that arose within myself. What, then, was the light that racked my brain?

Once more my life from its beginning to its end rose up before me,—each scene like a spectre, like the harpies of the old fables rending me with tooth and claw. Once more I saw what might have been, the noble things I might have done, the happiness I had lost, the turnings of the fated road which I might have taken,—everything that was once so possible, so possible, so easy! but now possible no more. My anguish was immeasurable; I turned and wrenched myself, in the strength of pain, out of the machinery that held me, and fell down, down among all the curses that were being hurled at me,—among the horrible and miserable crowd. I had brought upon them the evil which I shared, and they fell upon me with a fury which was like that which had prompted myself a few minutes before; but they could do nothing to me so tremendous as the vengeance I had taken upon them. I was too miserable to feel the blows that rained upon me, but presently I suppose I lost consciousness altogether, being almost torn to pieces by the multitude.

While this lasted, it seemed to me that I had a dream. I felt the blows raining down upon me, and my body struggling upon the ground; and yet it seemed to me that I was lying outside upon the ground, and above me the pale sky which never brightened at the touch of the sun. And I thought that dull, persistent cloud wavered and broke for an instant, and that I saw behind a glimpse of that blue which is heaven when we are on the earth—the blue sky—which is nowhere to be seen but in the mortal life; which is heaven enough, which is delight enough, for those who can look up to it, and feel themselves in the land of hope. It might be but a dream; in this strange world who could tell what was vision and what was true?

The next thing I remember was that I found myself lying on the floor of a great room full of people with every kind of disease and deformity, some pale with sickness, some with fresh wounds, the lame, and the maimed, and the miserable. They lay round me in every attitude of pain, many with sores, some bleeding, with broken limbs, but all struggling, some on hands and knees, dragging themselves up from the ground to stare at me. They roused in my mind a loathing and sense of disgust which it is impossible to express. I could scarcely tolerate the thought that I—I! should be forced to remain a moment in this lazar-house.

The feeling with which I had regarded the miserable creature who shared the corner of the wall with me, and who had cursed me for being sorry for him, had altogether gone out of my mind. I called out, to whom I know not, adjuring someone to open the door and set me free; but my cry was answered only by a shout from my companions in trouble. 'Who do you think will let you out?' 'Who is going to help you more than the rest?' My whole body was racked with pain; I could not move from the floor, on which I lay. I had to put up with the stares of the curious, and the mockeries and remarks on me of whoever chose to criticise. Among them was the lame man whom I had seen thrust in by the two officers who had taken me from the gate. He was the first to jibe. 'But for him they would never have seen me,' he said. 'I should have been well by this time in the fresh air.' 'It is his turn now,' said another. I turned my head as well as I could and spoke to them all.

'I am a stranger here,' I cried. 'They have made my brain burn with their experiments. Will nobody help me? It is no fault of mine, it is their fault. If I am to be left here uncared for, I shall die.'

At this a sort of dreadful chuckle ran round the place. 'If that is what you are afraid of, you will not die,' somebody said, touching me on my head in a way which gave me intolerable pain. 'Don't touch me,' I cried. 'Why shouldn't I?' said the other, and pushed me again upon the throbbing brain. So far as my sensations went, there were no coverings at all, neither skull nor skin upon the intolerable throbbing of my head, which had been exposed to the curiosity of the crowd, and every touch was agony; but my cry brought no guardian, nor any defence or soothing. I dragged myself into a corner after a time, from which some other wretch had been rolled out in the course of a quarrel; and as I found that silence was the only policy, I kept silent, with rage consuming my heart.

Presently I discovered by means of the new arrivals which kept coming in, hurled into the midst of us without thought or question, that this was the common fate of all who were repulsive to the sight, or who had any weakness or imperfection which offended the eyes of the population. They were tossed in among us, not to be healed, or for repose or safety, but to be out of sight, that they might not disgust or annoy those who were more fortunate, to whom no injury had happened; and because in their sickness and imperfection they were of no use in the studies of the place, and disturbed the good order of the streets. And there they lay one above another,—a mass of bruised and broken creatures, most of them suffering from injuries which they had sustained in what would have been called in other regions the service of the State. They had served like myself as objects of experiments. They had fallen from heights where they had been placed in illustration of some theory.

They had been tortured or twisted to give satisfaction to some question. And then, that the consequences of these proceedings might offend no one's eyes, they were flung into this receptacle, to be released if chance or strength enabled them to push their way out when others were brought in, or when their importunate knocking wearied some watchman, and brought him angry and threatening to hear what was wanted. The sound of this knocking against the door, and of the cries that accompanied it, and the rush towards the opening when anyone was brought in, caused a hideous continuous noise and scuffle which was agony to my brain.

Everyone pushed before the other; there was an endless rising and falling as in the changes of a feverish dream, each man
as he got strength to struggle forwards himself, thrusting back
his neighbours, and those who were nearest to the door beating
upon it without cease, like the beating of a drum without cadence or measure, sometimes a dozen passionate hands together,
making a horrible din and riot. As I lay unable to join in that
struggle, and moved by rage unspeakable towards all who could,
I reflected strangely that I had never heard when outside this
horrible continual appeal of the suffering. In the streets of the
city, as I now reflected, quiet reigned. I had even made compari-
sons on my first entrance, in the moment of pleasant anticipation which came over me, of the happy stillness here with the
horror and tumult of that place of unrule which I had left.

When my thoughts reached this point I was answered by the
voice of someone on a level with myself, lying helpless like me
on the floor of the lazar-house. 'They have taken their precautions,' he said; 'if they will not endure the sight of suffering, how
should they hear the sound of it? Every cry is silenced there.'

'I wish they could be silenced within too,' I cried savagely; 'I
would make them dumb had I the power.'

'The spirit of the place is in you,' said the other voice.

'And not in you?' I said, raising my head, though every movement was agony; but this pretence of superiority was more than
I could bear.

The other made no answer for a moment; then he said faintly,
'If it is so, it is but for greater misery.'

And then his voice died away, and the hubbub of beating and
crying and cursing and groaning filled all the echoes. They cried,
but no one listened to them. They thundered on the door, but
in vain. They aggravated all their pangs in that mad struggle to
get free. After a while my companion, whoever he was, spoke
again.

'They would rather,' he said, 'lie on the roadside to be kicked
and trodden on, as we have seen; though to see that made you
miserable.'

'Made me miserable! You mock me,' I said. 'Why should a man be miserable save for suffering of his own?'

'You thought otherwise once,' my neighbor said.

And then I remembered the wretch in the corner of the wall in the other town, who had cursed me for pitying him. I cursed myself now for that folly. Pity him! was he not better off than I? 'I wish,' I cried, 'that I could crush them into nothing, and be rid of this infernal noise they make!'

'The spirit of the place has entered into you,' said that voice.

I raised my arm to strike him; but my hand fell on the stone floor instead, and sent a jar of new pain all through my battered frame. And then I mastered my rage and lay still, for I knew there was no way but this of recovering my strength,—the strength with which, when I got it back, I would annihilate that reproachful voice and crush the life out of those groaning fools, whose cries and impotent struggles I could not endure. And we lay a long time without moving, with always that tumult raging in our ears. At last there came into my mind a longing to hear spoken words again. I said, 'Are you still there?'

'I shall be here,' he said, 'till I am able to begin again.'

'To begin! Is there here, then, either beginning or ending? Go on; speak to me; it makes me a little forget my pain.'

'I have a fire in my heart,' he said; 'I must begin and begin— till perhaps I find the way.'

'What way?' I cried, feverish and eager; for though I despised him, yet it made me wonder to think that he should speak riddles which I could not understand.

He answered very faintly, 'I do not know.' The fool! then it was only folly, as from the first I knew it was. I felt then that I could treat him roughly, after the fashion of the place—which he said had got into me. 'Poor wretch!' I said, 'you have hopes, have you? Where have you come from? You might have learned better before now.'

'I have come,' he said, 'from where we met before. I have come by the valley of gold. I have worked in the mines. I have served in the troops of those who are masters there. I have lived in this town of tyrants, and lain in this lazar-house before. Everything has happened to me, more and worse than you dream of.'

'And still you go on? I would dash my head against the wall and die.'

'When will you learn,' he said with a strange tone in his voice, which, though no one had been listening to us, made a sudden silence for a moment, it was so strange; it moved me like that glimmer of the blue sky in my dream, and roused all the sufferers round with an expectation—though I know not what. The cries stopped; the hands beat no longer. I think all the miserable crowd were still, and turned to where he lay. 'When will you learn—that you have died, and can die no more?'

There was a shout of fury all around me. 'Is that all you have to say?' the crowd burst forth; and I think they rushed upon him and killed him, for I heard no more until the hubbub began again more wild than ever, with furious hands beating, beating against the locked door.

After a while I began to feel my strength come back. I raised my head. I sat up. I began to see the faces of those around me, and the groups into which they gathered; the noise was no longer so insupportable,—my racked nerves were regaining health. It was with a mixture of pleasure and despair that I became conscious of this. I had been through many deaths; but I did not die, perhaps could not, as that man had said. I looked about for him, to see if he had contradicted his own theory. But he was not dead. He was lying close to me, covered with wounds; but he opened his eyes, and something like a smile came upon his lips. A smile,—I had heard laughter, and seen ridicule and derision, but this I had not seen. I could not bear it. To seize him and shake the little remaining life out of him was my impulse; but neither did I obey that.

Again he reminded me of my dream—was it a dream?—of the opening in the clouds. From that moment I tried to shelter him, and as I grew stronger and stronger and pushed my way to the door, I dragged him along with me. How long the struggle was I cannot tell, or how often I was balked, or how many darted through before me when the door was opened. But I did not let him go; and at last, for now I was as strong as before,—stronger than most about me,—I got out into the air and brought him with me. Into the air! it was an atmosphere so still and motionless that there was no feeling of life in it, as I have said; but the change seemed to me happiness for the moment. It was freedom. The noise of the struggle was over; the horrible sights were left behind. My spirit sprang up as if I had been born into new life. It had the same effect, I suppose, upon my companion, though he was much weaker than I, for he rose to his feet at once with almost a leap of eagerness, and turned instantaneously towards the other side of the city.

'Not that way,' I said; 'come with me and rest.'

'No rest—no rest—my rest is to go on;' and then he turned towards me and smiled and said, 'Thanks'—looking into my face. What a word to hear! I had not heard it since—A rush of strange and sweet and dreadful thoughts came into my mind. I shrank and trembled, and let go his arm, which I had been holding; but when I left that hold I seemed to fall back into depths of blank pain and longing. I put out my hand again and caught him. 'I will go,' I said, 'where you go.'

A pair of the officials of the place passed as I spoke. They looked at me with a threatening glance, and half paused, but then passed on. It was I now who hurried my companion along. I recollected him now. He was a man who had met me in the streets of the other city when I was still ignorant, who had convulsed me with the utterance of that name which, in all this world where we were, is never named but for punishment,—the name which I had named once more in the great hall in the midst of my torture, so that all who heard me were transfixed with that suffering too. He had been haggard then, but he was more haggard now. His features were sharp with continual pain; his eyes were wild with weakness and trouble, though there was a meaning in them which went to my heart. It seemed to me that in his touch there was a certain help, though he was weak and tottered, and every moment seemed full of suffering.

Hope sprang up in my mind,—the hope that where he was so eager to go there would be something better, a life more liveable than in this place. In every new place there is new hope. I was not worn out of that human impulse. I forgot the nightmare which had crushed me before,—the horrible sense that from myself there was no escape,—and holding fast to his arm, I hurried on with him, not heeding where. We went aside into less frequented streets, that we might escape observation. I seemed to myself the guide, though I was the follower. A great faith in this man sprang up in my breast. I was ready to go with him wherever he went, anywhere—anywhere must be better than this. Thus I pushed him on, holding by his arm, till we reached the very outmost limits of the city. Here he stood still for a moment, turning upon me, and took me by the hands.

'Friend,' he said, 'before you were born into the pleasant earth I had come here. I have gone all the weary round. Listen to one who knows: all is harder, harder, as you go on. You are stirred to go on by the restlessness in your heart, and each new place you come to, the spirit of that place enters into you. You are better here than you will be farther on. You were better where you were at first, or even in the mines, than here. Come no farther. Stay; unless—' but here his voice gave way. He looked at me with anxiety in his eyes, and said no more.

'Then why,' I cried, 'do you go on? Why do you not stay?'

He shook his head, and his eyes grew more and more soft. 'I am going,' he said, and his voice shook again. 'I am going—to try—the most awful and the most dangerous journey—' His voice died away altogether, and he only looked at me to say the rest.

'A journey? Where?'

I can tell no man what his eyes said. I understood, I cannot tell how; and with trembling all my limbs seemed to drop out of joint and my face grow moist with terror. I could not speak any more than he, but with my lips shaped, How? The awful thought made a tremor in the very air around. He shook his head slowly as he looked at me, his eyes, all circled with deep lines, looking out of caves of anguish and anxiety; and then I remembered how he had said, and I had scoffed at him, that the way he sought was one he did not know. I had dropped his hands in my fear; and yet to leave him seemed dragging the heart out of my breast, for none but he had spoken to me like a brother, had taken my hand and thanked me. I looked out across the plain, and the roads seemed tranquil and still.

There was a coolness in the air. It looked like evening, as if somewhere in those far distances there might be a place where a weary soul might rest; and I looked behind me, and thought what I had suffered, and remembered the lazar-house and the voices that cried and the hands that beat against the door, and also the horrible quiet of the room in which I lived, and the eyes which looked in at me and turned my gaze upon myself. Then I rushed after him, for he had turned to go on upon his way, and caught at his clothes, crying, 'Behold me, behold me! I will go too!'

He reached me his hand and went on without a word; and I with terror crept after him, treading in his steps, following like his shadow. What it was to walk with another, and follow, and be at one, is more than I can tell; but likewise my heart failed me for fear, for dread of what we might encounter, and of hearing that name or entering that presence which was more terrible than all torture. I wondered how it could be that one should willingly face *that* which racked the soul, and how he had learned that it was possible, and where he had heard of the way.

And as we went on I said no word, for he began to seem to me a being of another kind, a figure full of awe; and I followed as one might follow a ghost. Where would he go? Were we not fixed here forever, where our lot had been cast? And there were still many other great cities where there might be much to see, and something to distract the mind, and where it might be more possible to live than it had proved in the other places. There might be no tyrants there, nor cruelty, nor horrible noises, nor dreadful silence. Towards the right hand, across the plain, there seemed to rise out of the gray distance a cluster of towers and

roofs like another habitable place; and who could tell that something better might not be there?

Surely everything could not turn to torture and misery. I
dragged on behind him, with all these thoughts hurrying through
my mind. He was going—I dare to say it now, though I did not
dare then—to seek out a way to God; to try, if it was possible,
to find the road that led back,—that road which had been open
once to all. But for me, I trembled at the thought of that road. I
feared the name, which was as the plunging of a sword into my
inmost parts. All things could be borne but that. I dared not even
think upon that name. To feel my hand in another man's hand
was much, but to be led into that awful presence, by awful ways,
which none knew—how could I bear it? My spirits failed me,
and my strength. My hand became loose in his hand; he grasped
me still, but my hold failed, and ever with slower and slower
steps I followed, while he seemed to acquire strength with every
winding of the way. At length he said to me, looking back upon
me, 'I cannot stop; but your heart fails you. Shall I loose my hand
and let you go?'

'I am afraid; I am afraid!' I cried.

'And I too am afraid; but it is better to suffer more and to
escape than to suffer less and to remain.'

'Has it ever been known that one escaped? No one has ever
escaped. This is our place,' I said; 'there is no other world.'

'There are other worlds; there is a world where every way
leads to One who loves us still.'

I cried out with a great cry of misery and scorn. 'There is no
love!' I said.

He stood still for a moment and turned and looked at me. His
eyes seemed to melt my soul. A great cloud passed over them,
as in the pleasant earth a cloud will sweep across the moon; and
then the light came out and looked at me again, for neither
did he know. Where he was going all might end in despair and
double and double pain. But if it were possible that at the end
there should be found that for which he longed, upon which his
heart was set! He said with a faltering voice, 'Among all whom

I have questioned and seen, there was but one who found the way. But if one has found it, so may I. If you will not come, yet let me go.'

'They will tear you limb from limb; they will burn you in the endless fires,' I said. But what is it to be torn limb from limb, or burned with fire? There came upon his face a smile, and in my heart even I laughed to scorn what I had said.

'If I were dragged every nerve apart, and every thought turned into a fiery dart,—and that is so,' he said,—'yet will I go, if but perhaps I may see Love at the end.'

'There is no love!' I cried again with a sharp and bitter cry; and the echo seemed to come back and back from every side, No love! no love! till the man who was my friend faltered and stumbled like a drunken man; but afterwards he recovered strength and resumed his way.

And thus once more we went on. On the right hand was that city, growing ever clearer, with noble towers rising up to the sky, and battlements and lofty roofs, and behind a yellow clearness, as of a golden sunset. My heart drew me there; it sprang up in my breast and sang in my ears, Come, and come. Myself invited me to this new place as to a home. The others were wretched, but this will be happy,—delights and pleasures will be there. And before us the way grew dark with storms, and there grew visible among the mists a black line of mountains, perpendicular cliffs, and awful precipices, which seemed to bar the way. I turned from that line of gloomy heights, and gazed along the path to where the towers stood up against the sky. And presently my hand dropped by my side, that had been held in my companion's hand; and I saw him no more.

I went on to the city of the evening light. Ever and ever, as I proceeded on my way, the sense of haste and restless impatience grew upon me, so that I felt myself incapable of remaining long in a place, and my desire grew stronger to hasten on and on; but when I entered the gates of the city this longing vanished from my mind. There seemed some great festival or public holiday going on there. The streets were full of pleasure-parties, and in

240

every open place (of which there were many) were bands of dancers, and music playing; and the houses about were hung with tapestries and embroideries and garlands of flowers. A load seemed to be taken from my spirit when I saw all this,—for a whole population does not rejoice in such a way without some cause.

And to think that after all I had found a place in which I might live and forget the misery and pain which I had known, and all that was behind me, was delightful to my soul. It seemed to me that all the dancers were beautiful and young, their steps went gayly to the music, their faces were bright with smiles. Here and there was a master of the feast, who arranged the dances and guided the musicians, yet seemed to have a look and smile for new-comers too. One of these came forwards to meet me, and received me with a welcome, and showed me a vacant place at the table, on which were beautiful fruits piled up in baskets, and all the provisions for a meal. 'You were expected, you perceive,' he said. A delightful sense of well-being came into my mind. I sat down in the sweetness of ease after fatigue, of refreshment after weariness, of pleasant sounds and sights after the arid way. I said to myself that my past experiences had been a mistake, that this was where I ought to have come from the first, that life here would be happy, and that all intruding thoughts must soon vanish and die away.

After I had rested, I strolled about, and entered fully into the pleasures of the place. Wherever I went, through all the city, there was nothing but brightness and pleasure, music playing, and flags waving, and flowers and dancers and everything that was most gay. I asked several people whom I met what was the cause of the rejoicing; but either they were too much occupied with their own pleasures, or my question was lost in the hum of merriment, the sound of the instruments and of the dancers' feet.

When I had seen as much as I desired of the pleasure out of doors, I was taken by some to see the interiors of houses, which were all decorated for this festival, whatever it was, lighted up with curious varieties of lighting, in tints of different colours. The doors and windows were all open; and whosoever would could come in from the dance or from the laden tables, and sit down where they pleased and rest, always with a pleasant view out upon the streets, so that they should lose nothing of the spectacle. And the dresses, both of women and men, were beautiful in form and colour, made in the finest fabrics, and affording delightful combinations to the eye. The pleasure which I took in all I saw and heard was enhanced by the surprise of it, and by the aspect of the places from which I had come, where there was no regard to beauty nor anything lovely or bright.

Before my arrival here I had come in my thoughts to the conclusion that life had no brightness in these regions, and that whatever occupation or study there might be, pleasure had ended and was over, and everything that had been sweet in the former life. I changed that opinion with a sense of relief, which was more warm even than the pleasure of the present moment; for having made one such mistake, how could I tell that there were not more discoveries awaiting me, that life might not prove more endurable, might not rise to something grander and more powerful? The old prejudices, the old foregone conclusion of earth that this was a world of punishment, had warped my vision and my thoughts.

With so many added faculties of being, incapable of fatigue as we were, incapable of death, recovering from every wound or accident as I had myself done, and with no foolish restraint as to what we should or should not do, why might not we rise in this land to strength unexampled, to the highest powers? I rejoiced that I had dropped my companion's hand, that I had not followed him in his mad quest. Sometime, I said to myself, I would make a pilgrimage to the foot of those gloomy mountains, and bring him back, all racked and tortured as he was, and show him the pleasant place which he had missed.

In the meantime the music and the dance went on. But it began to surprise me a little that there was no pause, that the festival continued without intermission. I went up to one of those who seemed the masters of ceremony, directing what was going on. He was an old man, with a flowing robe of brocade, and a chain and badge which denoted his office. He stood with a smile upon his lips, beating time with his hand to the music, watching the figure of the dance.

'I can get no one to tell me,' I said, 'what the occasion of all this rejoicing is.'

'It is for your coming,' he replied without hesitation, with a smile and a bow.

For the moment a wonderful elation came over me. 'For my coming!' But then I paused and shook my head. 'There are others coming besides me. See! they arrive every moment.'

'It is for their coming too,' he said with another smile and a still deeper bow; 'but you are the first as you are the chief.'

This was what I could not understand; but it was pleasant to hear, and I made no further objection. 'And how long will it go on?' I said.

'So long as it pleases you,' said the old courtier.

How he smiled! His smile did not please me. He saw this, and distracted my attention. 'Look at this dance,' he said; 'how beautiful are those round young limbs! Look how the dress conceals yet shows the form and beautiful movements! It was invented in your honour. All that is lovely is for you. Choose where you will, all is yours. We live only for this; all is for you.' While he spoke, the dancers came nearer and nearer till they circled us round, and danced and made their pretty obeisances, and sang, 'All is yours; all is for you;' then breaking their lines, floated away in other circles and processions and endless groups, singing and laughing till it seemed to ring from every side, 'Everything is yours; all is for you.'

I accepted this flattery I know not why, for I soon became aware that I was no more than others, and that the same words were said to every newcomer. Yet my heart was elated, and I threw myself into all that was set before me. But there was always in my mind an expectation that presently the music and the dancing would cease, and the tables be withdrawn, and a pause come. At one of the feasts I was placed by the side of a lady very fair and richly dressed, but with a look of great weariness in her eyes. She turned her beautiful face to me, not with any show of pleasure, and there was something like compassion in her look. She said, 'You are very tired,' as she made room for me by her side.

'Yes,' I said, though with surprise, for I had not yet acknowledged that even to myself. 'There is so much to enjoy. We have need of a little rest.'

'Of rest!' said she, shaking her head, 'this is not the place for rest.'

'Yet pleasure requires it,' I said, 'as much as—' I was about to say pain; but why should one speak of pain in a place given up to pleasure? She smiled faintly and shook her head again. All her movements were languid and faint; her eyelids drooped over her eyes. Yet when I turned to her, she made an effort to smile. 'I think you are also tired,' I said.

At this she roused herself a little. 'We must not say so; nor do I say so. Pleasure is very exacting. It demands more of you than anything else. One must be always ready—'

'For what?'

'To give enjoyment and to receive it.' There was an effort in her voice to rise to this sentiment, but it fell back into weariness again.

'I hope you receive as well as give,' I said.

The lady turned her eyes to me with a look which I cannot forget, and life seemed once more to be roused within her, but not the life of pleasure; her eyes were full of loathing and fatigue and disgust and despair. 'Are you so new to this place,' she said, 'and have not learned even yet what is the height of all misery and all weariness; what is worse than pain and trouble, more dreadful than the lawless streets and the burning mines, and the torture of the great hall and the misery of the lazar-house—'

'Oh, lady,' I said, 'have you been there?'

She answered me with her eyes alone; there was no need of more. 'But pleasure is more terrible than all,' she said; and I knew

244

in my heart that what she said was true.

There is no record of time in that place. I could not count it by days or nights; but soon after this it happened to me that the dances and the music became no more than a dizzy maze of sound and sight which made my brain whirl round and round, and I too loathed what was spread on the table, and the soft couches, and the garlands, and the fluttering flags and ornaments. To sit forever at a feast, to see forever the merrymakers turn round and round, to hear in your ears forever the whirl of the music, the laughter, the cries of pleasure! There were some who went on and on, and never seemed to tire; but to me the endless round came at last to be a torture from which I could not escape.

Finally, I could distinguish nothing,—neither what I heard nor what I saw; and only a consciousness of something intolerable buzzed and echoed in my brain. I longed for the quiet of the place I had left; I longed for the noise in the streets, and the hubbub and tumult of my first experiences. Anything, anything rather than this! I said to myself; and still the dancers turned, the music sounded, the bystanders smiled, and everything went on and on. My eyes grew weary with seeing, and my ears with hearing. To watch the newcomers rush in, all pleased and eager, to see the eyes of the others glaze with weariness, wrought upon my strained nerves. I could not think, I could not rest, I could not endure.

Music forever and ever,—a whirl, a rush of music, always going on and on; and ever that maze of movement, till the eyes were feverish and the mouth parched; ever that mist of faces, now one gleaming out of the chaos, now another, some like the faces of angels, some miserable, weary, strained with smiling, with the monotony, and the endless, aimless, never-changing round. I heard myself calling to them to be still—to be still! to pause a moment. I felt myself stumble and turn round in the giddiness and horror of that movement without repose. And finally, I fell under the feet of the crowd, and felt the whirl go over and over me, and beat upon my brain, until I was pushed and thrust out of the way lest I should stop the measure. There I lay, sick, satiate, for I know not how long,—loathing everything around me, ready to give all I had (but what had I to give?) for one moment of silence. But always the music went on, and the dancers danced, and the people feasted, and the songs and the voices echoed up to the skies.

How at last I stumbled forth I cannot tell. Desperation must have moved me, and that impatience which after every hope and disappointment comes back and back,—the one sensation that never fails. I dragged myself at last by intervals, like a sick dog, outside the revels, still hearing them, which was torture to me, even when at last I got beyond the crowd. It was something to lie still upon the ground, though without power to move, and sick beyond all thought, loathing myself and all that I had been and seen. For I had not even the sense that I had been wronged to keep me up, but only a nausea and horror of movement, a giddiness and whirl of every sense. I lay like a log upon the ground.

When I recovered my faculties a little, it was to find myself once more in the great vacant plain which surrounded that accursed home of pleasure,—a great and desolate waste upon which I could see no track, which my heart fainted to look at, which no longer roused any hope in me, as if it might lead to another beginning, or any place in which yet at the last it might be possible to live. As I lay in that horrible giddiness and faintness, I loathed life and this continuance which brought me through one misery after another, and forbade me to die. Oh that death would come,—death, which is silent and still, which makes no movement and hears no sound! that I might end and be no more! Oh that I could go back even to the stillness of that chamber which I had not been able to endure!

Oh that I could return,—return! to what? To other miseries and other pain, which looked less because they were past. But I knew now that return was impossible until I had circled all the dreadful round; and already I felt again the burning of that desire that pricked and drove me on,—not back, for that was impossible. Little by little I had learned to understand, each step printed upon my brain as with red-hot irons: not back, but on, and on—to greater anguish, yes; but on, to fuller despair, to experiences more terrible,—but on, and on, and on. I arose again, for this was my fate. I could not pause even for all the teachings of despair.

The waste stretched far as eyes could see. It was wild and terrible, with neither vegetation nor sign of life. Here and there were heaps of ruin, which had been villages and cities; but nothing was in them save reptiles and crawling poisonous life and traps for the unwary wanderer. How often I stumbled and fell among these ashes and dust-heaps of the past! Through what dread moments I lay, with cold and slimy things leaving their trace upon my flesh! The horrors which seized me, so that I beat my head against a stone,—why should I tell? These were nought; they touched not the soul. They were but accidents of the way.

At length, when body and soul were low and worn out with misery and weariness, I came to another place, where all was so different from the last that the sight gave me a momentary solace. It was full of furnaces and clanking machinery and endless work. The whole air round was aglow with the fury of the fires; and men went and came like demons in the flames, with red-hot melting metal, pouring it into moulds and beating it on anvils. In the huge workshops in the background there was a perpetual whir of machinery, of wheels turning and turning, and pistons beating, and all the din of labour, which for a time renewed the anguish of my brain, yet also soothed it,—for there was meaning in the beatings and the whirlings.

And a hope rose within me that with all the forces that were here, some revolution might be possible,—something that would change the features of this place and overturn the worlds. I went from workshop to workshop, and examined all that was being done, and understood,—for I had known a little upon the earth, and my old knowledge came back, and to learn so much more filled me with new life. The master of all was one who never rested, nor seemed to feel weariness nor pain nor pleasure. He had everything in his hand. All who were there were his workmen or his assistants or his servants. No one shared with him in his councils. He was more than a prince among them; he was as a god.

And the things he planned and made, and at which in armies and legions his workmen toiled and labored, were like living things. They were made of steel and iron, but they moved like the brains and nerves of men. They went where he directed them, and did what he commanded, and moved at a touch. And though he talked little, when he saw how I followed all that he did, he was a little moved towards me, and spoke and explained to me the conceptions that were in his mind, one rising out of another, like the leaf out of the stem and the flower out of the bud. For nothing pleased him that he did, and necessity was upon him to go on and on.

'They are like living things,' I said; 'they do your bidding, whatever you command them. They are like another and a stronger race of men.'

'Men!' he said, 'what are men? The most contemptible of all things that are made,—creatures who will undo in a moment what it has taken millions of years, and all the skill and all the strength of generations to do. These are better than men. They cannot think or feel. They cannot stop but at my bidding, or begin unless I will. Had men been made so, we should be masters of the world.'

'Had men been made so, you would never have been,—for what could genius have done or thought?—you would have been a machine like all the rest.'

'And better so!' he said, and turned away; for at that moment, watching keenly as he spoke the action of a delicate combination of movements, all made and balanced to a hair's breadth, there had come to him suddenly the idea of something which made it a hundredfold more strong and terrible. For they were terrible, these things that lived yet did not live, which were his slaves and moved at his will. When he had done this, he looked at me, and a smile came upon his mouth; but his eyes smiled not, nor ever changed from the set look they wore. And the words he spoke were familiar words, not his, but out of the old life. 'What a piece of work is a man!' he said; 'how noble in reason, how infinite in faculty! in form and moving how express and admirable! And yet to me what is this quintessence of dust?' His mind had followed another strain of thought, which to me was bewildering, so that I did not know how to reply. I answered like a child, upon his last word.

'We are dust no more,' I cried, for pride was in my heart,— pride of him and his wonderful strength, and his thoughts which created strength, and all the marvels he did; 'those things which hindered are removed. Go on; go on! you want but another step. What is to prevent that you should not shake the universe, and overturn this doom, and break all our bonds? There is enough here to explode this gray fiction of a firmament, and to rend those precipices, and to dissolve that waste,—as at the time when the primeval seas dried up, and those infernal mountains rose.'

He laughed, and the echoes caught the sound and gave it back as if they mocked it. 'There is enough to rend us all into shreds,' he said, 'and shake, as you say, both heaven and earth, and these plains and those hills.'

'Then why,' I cried in my haste, with a dreadful hope piercing through my soul—'why do you create and perfect, but never employ? When we had armies on the earth, we used them. You have more than armies; you have force beyond the thoughts of man, but all without use as yet.'

'All,' he cried, 'for no use! All in vain!—in vain!'

'Oh master!' I said, 'great and more great in time to come, why?—why?'

He took me by the arm and drew me close.

'Have you strength,' he said, 'to bear it if I tell you why?'

I knew what he was about to say. I felt it in the quivering of my veins, and my heart that bounded as if it would escape from my breast; but I would not quail from what he did not shrink to utter. I could speak no word, but I looked him in the face and waited—for that which was more terrible than all.

He held me by the arm, as if he would hold me up when the shock of anguish came. 'They are in vain,' he said, 'in vain—because God rules over all.'

His arm was strong; but I fell at his feet like a dead man.

How miserable is that image, and how unfit to use! Death is still and cool and sweet. There is nothing in it that pierces like a sword, that burns like fire, that rends and tears like the turning wheels. Oh life, Oh pain, Oh terrible name of God in which is all succour and all torment! What are pangs and tortures to that, which ever increases in its awful power, and has no limit nor any alleviation, but whenever it is spoken penetrates through and through the miserable soul? Oh God, whom once I called my Father! Oh Thou who gavest me being, against whom I have fought, whom I fight to the end, shall there never be anything but anguish in the sound of Thy great name?

When I returned to such command of myself as one can have who has been transfixed by that sword of fire, the master stood by me still. He had not fallen like me, but his face was drawn with anguish and sorrow like the face of my friend who had been with me in the lazar-house, who had disappeared on the dark mountains. And as I looked at him, terror seized hold upon me, and a desire to flee and save myself, that I might not be drawn after him by the longing that was in his eyes.

The master gave me his hand to help me to rise, and it trembled, but not like mine.

'Sir,' I cried, 'have not we enough to bear? Is it for hatred, is it for vengeance, that you speak that name?'

'Oh friend,' he said, 'neither for hatred nor revenge. It is like a fire in my veins; if one could find Him again!'

'You, who are as a god, who can make and destroy,—you, who could shake His throne!'

He put up his hand. 'I who am His creature, even here—and still His child, though I am so far, so far—' He caught my hand in his, and pointed with the other trembling. 'Look! your eyes are more clear than mine, for they are not anxious like mine.

Can you see anything upon the way?'

The waste lay wild before us, dark with a faintly-rising cloud, for darkness and cloud and the gloom of death attended upon that name. I thought, in his great genius and splendour of intellect, he had gone mad, as sometimes may be. 'There is nothing,' I said, and scorn came into my soul; but even as I spoke I saw—I cannot tell what I saw—a moving spot of milky whiteness in that dark and miserable wilderness, no bigger than a man's hand, no bigger than a flower. 'There is something,' I said unwillingly; 'it has no shape nor form. It is a gossamer-web upon some bush, or a butterfly blown on the wind.'

'There are neither butterflies nor gossamers here.'

'Look for yourself, then!' I cried, flinging his hand from me. I was angry with a rage which had no cause. I turned from him, though I loved him, with a desire to kill him in my heart, and hurriedly took the other way. The waste was wild; but rather that than to see the man who might have shaken earth and hell thus turning, turning to madness and the awful journey. For I knew what in his heart he thought; and I knew that it was so. It was something from that other sphere; can I tell you what? A child perhaps—Oh thought that wrings the heart!—for do you know what manner of thing a child is? There are none in the land of darkness. I turned my back upon the place where that whiteness was. On, on, across the waste! On to the cities of the night! On, far away from maddening thought, from hope that is torment, and from the awful Name!

A Christmas Tale

How to account for this strange adventure, or what explanation to put upon it, I cannot tell, but it began after a very prosaic fashion—rather more commonplace even that the circumstances under which the Laureate meditated his *Legend of Godiva*, After a long drive to a little country station, I found to my dismay, that I had missed the train.

Missed the train! There was not another till twelve o'clock at noon of the next day, and it was then the afternoon between two and three o'clock; for the place in which I was so fortunate as to find myself, was one of the smallest of country stations on a "branch line." It seems extremely odd, looking bock upon it, that there should have been such an unreasonable time to wait; but it did not puzzle, it only discomfited me at the time.

And there was not even a single house, save the half-built little railway house itself, where dwelt the station-master, at this inhospitable station; so I had to be directed by that functionary, and by his solitary porter, how to get to Witcherley village, which lay a mile and a half off across the fields. It was summer, but there had been a great deal of rain, and the roads, as I knew by my morning's experience, were "heavy"—yet I set off with singular equanimity on my journey across the fields. Altogether I took the business very coolly, and made up my mind to it. It is astonishing how easily one can manage this in a certain frame of mind.

It was rather a pretty country—especially when the sun came glancing down over it, finding out all the rain upon the leaves—

when it was only *I* that found them out instead of the sun. When pushing down a deep lane, my hat caught the great overhanging bough of a hawthorn, and shook over me a sparkling shower of water-drops, big and cool like so many diamonds. I cannot say that I entirely enjoyed the impromptu baptism, and the wet matted brambles underfoot were full of treacherous surprises, and the damp path under that magnificent seam of red-brown earth, which had caught my eye half a mile off, caught my foot now with unexampled tenacity. Notwithstanding, the road was pretty; a busy little husbandman of a breeze began to rustle out the young corn, and raise the feeble stalks which had been "laid" by the rain; and everything grew lustily in the refreshed and sweetened atmosphere, through which the birds raised their universal twitter. There appeared white gable-ends, bits of orchard closely planted, a church-spire rising through the trees, and over the next stile I leaped into the extreme end of the little village street of Witcherley—a very rural little village indeed, lying, though within a mile and a half of a railway station, secure and quiet among the old Arcadian fields.

Facing me was a great iron gate, extremely ornamental, as things were made a hundred years ago, with a minute porter's-lodge shut tip, plainly intimating that few carriages rolled up that twilight avenue, to which entrance was given by a little postern-door at the side. The avenue was narrow, but the trees were great and old, and hid all appearance of the house to which they led. Then came three thatched cottages flanking at a little distance the moss-grown wall which extended down the road from the manor-house gates; and then the path mode a sharp turn round the abrupt corner of a gable which projected into it, the grey wall of which was lightened by one homely bow-window in the upper story, but nothing more. This being the Witcherley Arms, I went no further, though some distant cottages, grey, silent, and rude, caught my eye a little way on.

The Witcherley Arms, indeed, was the hamlet of Witcherley—it was something between an inn and a farmhouse, with long low rooms, small windows, and an irregular and rambling extent of building, which it was hard to assign any use for, and which seemed principally filled up with long passages leading to closets and cupboards and laundries in a prodigal and strange profusion. A few rude steps led to the door, within which, on one side, was a little bar, and on the other the common room of the inn. Just in front of the house, surrounded by a little plot of grass, stood a large old elm-tree, with the sign swung high among its branches; opposite was the gate of a farmyard, and the dull walls of a half square of barns and offices; behind, the country seemed to swell into a bit of rising-ground, covered with the woods of the manor-house; but the prospect before was of a rude district broken up by solitary roads, crossing the moorland, and apparently leading nowhere. One leisurely country-cart stood near the door, the horse standing still with dull patience, and that indescribable quiet consciousness that it matters nothing to any one how long the bumpkin stays inside, or the peaceable brute without, which is only to be found in the extreme and undisturbed seclusion of very rural districts.

I confess I entered the Witcherley Arms with a little dismay, and no great expectations of its comfort or good cheer. The public room was large enough, lighted with two casement windows, with a low unequal ceiling and a sanded floor. Two small tables in the windows, and one long one placed across the room behind, with a bristly supply of hard high-backed wooden chairs, were all the furniture. A slow country fellow in a smock frock, the driver of the cart, drank his beer sullenly at one of the smaller tables. The landlord loitered about between the open outer door and the "coffee-room," and I took my seat at the head of the big table, and suggested dinner to the open-eyed country maid.

She was more startled than I expected by the idea. Dinner! there was boiled bacon in the house, she knew, and ham and eggs were practicable. I was not disposed to be fastidious under present circumstances, so the cloth was spread, and the boiled bacon set before me, preparatory to the production of the more savoury dish. To have a better look at me, the landlord came in and established himself beside the bumpkin in the window. These worthies were not at all of the ruffian kind, but, on the contrary, perfectly honest-looking, obtuse, and leisurely: their dialect was strange to my ear, and their voices confused; but I could make out that what they did talk about was the " Squire."

Of course, the most natural topic in the world in a place so primitive; and I, examining my bacon, which was not inviting, paid little attention to them. By-and-by, however, the landlord loitered out again to the door; and there my attention was attracted at once by a voice without, as different as possible from their mumbling rural voices. This was followed immediately by a quick alert footstep, and then entered the room an old gentleman, little, carefully dressed, precise and particular, in a blue coat with gilt buttons, a spotless white cravat, Hessian boots, and hair of which I could not say with certainty whether it was grey or powdered. He came in as a monarch comes into a humble corner of his dominions. There could be no doubt about his identity—this was the squire.

Hodge at the window pulled his forelock reverentially; the old gentleman nodded to him, but turned his quick eye upon me—strangers were somewhat unusual at the Witcherley Arms—and then my boiled bacon, which I still only looked at! The squire drew near with suave and compassionating courtesy: I told him my story—I had missed the train. The train was entirely a new institution in this primitive corner of the country. The old gentleman evidently did not half approve of it, and treated my detention something in the light of a piece of retributive justice. "Ah, haste, haste! nothing else will please us nowadays," he said, shaking his head with dignity: "the good old coach, now, would have carried you comfortably, without the risk of a day's waiting or a broken limb; but novelty carries the day."

I did not say that the railway was, after all, not so extreme a novelty in other parts of the world as in Witcherley, and I was rewarded for my forbearance. "If you do not mind waiting half an hour, and walking half a mile," added the squire immediately, "I think I can promise you a better dinner than anything you have here—a plain country table, sir, nothing more, and a house of the old style; but better than honest Giles's bacon, to which I see you don't take very kindly. He will give you a good bed, though—a clean, comfortable bed. I have slept myself, sir, on occasion, at the Witcherley Arms."

When he said this, some recollection or consciousness came for an instant across the old gentleman's countenance; and the landlord, who stood behind him, and who was also an old man, uttered what seemed to me a kind of suppressed groan. The squire heard it, and turned around upon him quickly.

"If your gable-room is not otherwise occupied tonight," said the old gentleman—"mind I do not say it will, or is likely to be—put the gentleman into it, Giles."

The landlord groaned again a singular affirmative, which roused my curiosity at once. Was it haunted? or what could there be of tragical or mysterious connected with the gable-room?

However, I had only to make my acknowledgements, and accept with thanks the squire's proposal, and we set out immediately for the manor-house. My companion looked hale, active, and light of foot—scarcely sixty—a comely, well-preserved old gentleman, with a clear frosty complexion, blue eyes, without a cloud, features somewhat high and delicate, and altogether, in his refined and particular way, looked like the head of a long-lived patriarchal race, who might live a hundred years. He paused, however, when we got to the corner, to look to the north over the broken country on which the sunshine slanted as the day began to wane. It was a wild solitary prospect, as different as possible from the softer scenes through which I had come to Witcherley. Those broken bits of road, rough cart-tracks over the moor, with heaps of stones piled here and there, the intention of which one could not decide upon; fir-trees, all alone and by themselves, growing singly at the angles of the road—sometimes the long horizontal gleam of water in a deep cutting—sometimes a green bit of moss, prophetic of pitfall and quagmire—and no visible moving thing upon the whole scene. The picture to me was somewhat desolate. My new friend, however, gazed upon it with a lingering eye, sighed, did not say anything—but, turning round with a little vehemence, took some highly-flavoured snuff from a small gold box, and seemed, under cover of this innocent stimulant, to shake off some emotion. As he did so, looking back I saw the inmates of the Witcherley Arms at the door, in a little crowd gazing at him. The landscape must have been as familiar to him as he was to these good people. I began to grow very curious. Was anything going to happen to the old squire?

The old squire, however, was of the class of men who enjoy conversation, and relish a good listener. He led me down through the noiseless road, past the three cottages, to the manorial gates, with a pleasant little stream of remark and explanation, a little jaunty wit, a little caustic observation, great natural shrewdness, and some little knowledge of the world. Entering in by that little side-door to the avenue, was like coming out of daylight into sudden night. The road was narrow—the trees tall, old, and of luxuriant growth. I did not wonder that his worship was proud of them, but, for myself, should have preferred something less gloomy. The line was long, too, and wound upwards by an irregular ascent; and the thick dark foliage concealed, till we had almost reached it, the manor-house, which turned its turreted gable-end towards us, by no means unlike the Witcherley Arms.

It was a house of no particular date or character—old, irregular, and somewhat picturesque—built of the grey limestone of the district, spotted over with lichens, and covering here and there the angle of a wall with an old growth of exuberant ivy—ivy so old, thick, and luxuriant, that there was no longer any shapeliness or distinctive character in the big, blunt, glossy leaves. A small lawn before the door, graced with one clipped yew-tree, was the only glimpse of air or daylight, so far as I could see, about the house; for the trees closed in on every side, as if to shut it out entirely from all chance of seeing or being seen. The big hall-door opened from without, and I followed the squire with no small curiosity into the noiseless house, in which I could not hear a single domestic sound. Perhaps drawing-rooms were not in common use at Witcherley—at all events we went at once to the dining-room, a large long apartment, with an ample fireplace at the upper end—three long windows on one side, and a curious embayed alcove in the corner, projecting from the room like an afterthought of the builder.

To this pretty recess you descended by a single step from the level of the dining-room, and it was lighted by a broad, Elizabethan oriel window, with a cushioned seat all round, fastened to the wall. We went here, naturally passing by the long dining-table, which occupied the almost entire mid-space of the apartment. These three long dining-room windows looked out upon the lawn and the clipped yew-tree—the oriel looked upon nothing, but was closely overshadowed by a group of lime-trees casting down a tender, cold, green light through their delicate wavering leaves. There were old panel portraits on the walls, old crimson hangings,—a carpet, of which all the colours were blended and indistinguishable with old age. The chairs in the recess were covered with embroidery as faded as the carpet; everything bore the same tone of antiquity.

At the same time, everything appeared in the most exemplary order, well-preserved and graceful—without a trace of wealth, and with many traces of frugality, yet undebased by any touch of shabbiness. And as the squire placed himself in the stiff elbow-chair in this pleasant little alcove, and cast his eye with becoming dignity down the long line of the room, I could not but recognise a pleasant and suitable congeniality between my host and his house.

Presently a grave middle-aged man-servant entered the room, and busied himself very quietly spreading the table—the squire in the meantime entering upon a polite and good-humoured catechetical examination of myself; but pausing now and then to address a word to Joseph, which Joseph answered with extreme brevity and great respectfulness. There was nothing inquisitive or disagreeable in the squire's inquiries; on the contrary, they were pleasant indications of the kindly interest which an old man often shows in a young one unexpectedly thrown into his path. I was by no means uninterested, meanwhile, in the slowly-completed arrangements of the dinner-table, all accomplished so quietly.

When Joseph had nearly finished his operations, a tall young fellow in a shooting-coat, sullen, loutish, and down-looking, lounged into the room, and threw himself into an easy-chair. He did not bear a single feature of resemblance to the courtly old *beau* beside me, yet was his son notwithstanding beyond all controversy—the heir of the house. Then came the earlier instalments of the dinner; and simultaneously with the silver tureen appeared an old lady, who dropped me a noiseless curt-sey, and took her seat at the head of the table, without a word. I could make nothing whatever of this mistress of the house. She was dressed in some faded rich brocaded dress, entirely harmonising with the carpets and the embroidered chairs, and wore a large faint brooch at her neck, with a half-obliterated miniature, set round with dull yellow pearls. She sent me soup, and carved the dishes placed before her in a noiseless, seemingly motionless way, which there was no comprehending; and was either the most mechanical automaton in existence, or a person stunned and petrified.

The young squire sat opposite myself, one person only at the long vacant side of the table, with his back to the three windows. An uneasy air of shame, sullenness, and half-resentment hung about him, and he, too, never spoke. In spite, however, of this uncomfortable companionship, the squire, in his place at the foot of the table, kept up his pleasant, lively, vivacious stream of conversation without the slightest damp or restraint,—gave forth his old-fashioned formal witticisms—his maxims of the old world, his dignified country-gentleman reflections upon the errors of the new. Silent at the presiding shadow at the head— silent the lout in the middle. The old servant, grave, solemn, and almost awe-stricken, moved silently about behind; yet, little assisted by my own discomposed and embarrassed responses, there was quite a lively sound of conversation at the table, kept up by the brave old squire.

With the conclusion of the dinner, and with another little

noiseless curtsey, the old lady disappeared as she came. I had not heard the faintest whisper of her voice during the whole time, nor observed her looking at anyone; and it was almost a relief to hear her dress rustle softly as she glided out of the room. It seemed to me, however, that our attendant took an unnecessarily long time in arranging the few plates of fruit and placing the wine upon the table; and lingered with visible anxiety, casting stealthy looks of mingled awe and sympathy at his master, and exercising a watchful and jealous observation of the young squire. The old squire, however, took no notice, for his part, of the sullenness of his heir, or the watch of Joseph, but pared his apple briskly, and went on with his description of a celebrated old house in the neighbourhood, which, if I had another day to spare, I would find it very much worth my while to see. "At another time," said the old gentleman, "I might have offered you my own services as guide and *cicerone*; but present circumstances make that impracticable; however, I advise you sincerely, go yourself and see."

As he said these words, there seemed a simultaneous start of consciousness on the part of the young man and of the servant. Joseph's napkin fell out of his hands, and he hurried from the room without picking it up; while the young squire, with an evidently irrestrainable motion, pushed back his chair from the table, grew violently red, drank half-a-dozen glasses of wine in rapid succession, and cast a furtive and rapid glance at his father, who, perfectly lively and at his ease, talked on without a moment's discomposure. Then the young man rose up suddenly, walked away from the table, tossed the fallen napkin into the fireplace with his foot, came back again, grasped the back of his chair, cleared his throat, and, turning his flushed face towards his father without lifting his eyes, seemed trying in vain to invent words for something which he had to say.

Whatever it was, it would not bear words. The young Hercules, a fine, manly, full-grown figure, stood exactly opposite me, with his down-looking eyes; but all that he seemed able to articulate was a beginning—"I say, father; father, I say."

"No occasion for saying another word about the matter, my boy," said the old gentleman. "I understand you perfectly—come back as early as you please tomorrow, and you'll find all right, and everything prepared for you. You may rely upon me."

Not another word was exchanged between them; the lout plunged his hands into his pockets, and left the room as resentful, sullen, and ashamed as ever, yet with an air of relief. The squire leaned back in his chair for an instant, and sighed—but whether it was over a household mystery, or the excellence of the wine which he held up to the light, it was impossible to tell, for he resumed what he was saying immediately, and rounded off a handsome little sentence about the advantages of travel to young men.

At this point Joseph entered once more, with looks still more awe-stricken and anxious, on pretence of finding his napkin. "And now that we are alone," said the squire, calling him, "we may as well be comfortable. Take the wine, Joseph, into the oriel. We call it the oriel, though the word is a misnomer; but family customs, sir, family customs, grow strong and flourish in an old house. It has been named so since my earliest recollection, and for generations before that."

"And for generations after, no doubt," said I. "Your grandchildren—"

"*My* grandchildren!" exclaimed the old man with a look of dismay; "but, my good sir, you are perfectly excusable—perfectly excusable," he continued, recovering himself; "you are not aware of my family history, and the traditions of the house. But I observe that you have shown some surprise at various little incidents—understand me, I beg—shown surprise in the most decorous and natural manner consistent with perfect good-breeding. I should be uneasy did you suppose I implied anything more. The fact is, you have come among us at a family crisis. Be seated—and to understand it, you ought to know the history of the house."

I took my seat immediately, with haste and a little excitement. The squire's elbow-chair had already been placed by Joseph on the other side of the small carved oak table—the wine with its dull ruby glow, and the old-fashioned tall glasses, small goblets, long-stalked and ornamented, stood between us; and overhead a morsel of inquisitive blue sky, looked into through the close interlacing of those tremulous delicate lime-tree leaves.

The squire took his seat, paused again, sighed; and then turning round towards the dining-room proper, which began to grow dim as twilight came on, cast a look somewhat melancholy, yet fall of dignified satisfaction, upon the array of family portraits, and began his tale.

"We are an old family," said the old gentleman; " I do not need to say to any one acquainted with this district, or with the untitled gentry of the North of England, how long and how unbroken has been our lineal succession. Witcherley Manor-house, has descended for centuries, without a single lapse, from father to son; and you will observe, sir, one of the distinguishing peculiarities of our race, and the reason of my amazement when you spoke unguardedly of grandchildren, the offspring of every marriage in this house is one son."

The words were said so solemnly that I started—"One son!"

"One son," continued the squire with dignity, "enough to carry on the race and preserve its honours—nothing to divide or encumber. In fact, I feel that the existence of the family depends on this wise and benevolent arrangement of nature. If I have a regret," said the old man mildly, with a natural sigh, "regarding the approaching marriage of my boy, it is because, he has chosen his wife, contrary to the usage of our house, out of a neighbouring and very large family—yet I ought to have more confidence in the fortunes of the race."

Being somewhat surprised, not to say dumbfoundered, by these reflections, I thought it better to make no remark upon them, and prudently held my peace.

"We were once rich, sir," continued the squire, with a smile, "but that is a period beyond the memory of man. Three centuries ago, an ancestor of mine, a man of curious erudition, a disciple of the Rosy Cross, lost a large amount of the gold he had in search of the mysterious power of making the baser metals into gold. There he hangs, sir, looking down upon us, a most remarkable man. I would call him the founder of our race, but that such a statement would be untrue, and would abridge our ascertained genealogy by many generations; he was, however, the founder of everything remarkable in our history. In the pursuit of science he was so unfortunate as to risk and lose a large portion of his family inheritance—everything, in short, but the manor-house and lands of Witcherley—I am not ashamed to say a small estate."

I bent my head to the old man with involuntary respect, as he bowed to me over his wine in his stately old pride and truthfulness; but I made no other interruption, and he immediately resumed his tale.

"In the ordinary course of nature, as people call it, with younger children to be provided for, and daughters to be portioned, the house of Witcherley, sir, must long ago have come to a conclusion. But my ancestor was a wise man; he had purchased his wisdom at no small cost, and knew how to make use of it, and he left to us who came after him the most solemn heirloom of the house, a family vow—a vow which each successive father among us is pledged to administer to his son, and which, I am proud to say, has never been broken in the entire known history of the race."

"I beg your pardon. I should be grieved to make any impertinent inquiries," said I—for the squire came to a sudden pause, and my curiosity was strongly excited—"but might I ask what that was?"

The old gentleman filled his glass and sipped it slowly. The daylight had gradually faded through the soft green lime-leaves; but still the waning rays were cooled and tinted by the verdant medium through which they came. I thought there was a tinge of pallor on my companion's face; but he sat opposite, in his elbow-chair, with the most perfect calmness, sipping his wine.

"It depends entirely," he said with deliberation, "upon the providential natural arrangement of succession, which I have already told you of. The family vow is no longer binding upon that Squire of Witcherley who has more than one child—one son."

"And that contingency, has it never happened?" cried I, with eagerness.

"It threatened to happen, sir, on one occasion," said the squire. "My own grandfather married a wife with some fortune, who brought him a daughter. I am grieved to say of so near a relation that his mind was degenerate. Instead of showing any disappointment, he made an exhibition of unseemly satisfaction at the thought of escaping the fate of his race. He took down the old gateway, sir, and erected the piece of foolishness in iron which disfigure my avenue. But it was short-lived—short-lived. Providence stepped in, and withdrew from him both wife and child; and it was only by a second marriage late in life that he escaped the terrible calamity of being the last of his line. No, I am proud to say that contingency has never occurred, nor that vow been broken, for three hundred years."

"And the vow?" I grew quite excited, and leaned over the little table to listen, with a thrill of expectation. The squire cleared his throat, kept his eyes fixed upon the table, and answered me slowly. It was not nervousness, but pure solemnity; and it impressed me accordingly.

"Sir," he said, at last raising his head, " the lands of Witcherley are insufficient to support two households. When the heir is of age, and is disposed to marry, according to the regulation of the family the father ceases; one generation passes away, and another begins. Sir, my son is on the eve of marriage; *he* will be Squire of Witcherley tomorrow."

I started to my feet in sudden alarm; then seated myself again, half subdued, half appalled by the composure of the old man. "I beg your pardon," I said, faltering; "I have misunderstood you, of course. You give up a portion of your authority—a share of your throne. Oh, by no means unusual, I understand."

"You do not understand *me*," said the squire, "nor the ways of this house. I spoke nothing of share or portion; there is no such

264

thing possible at Witcherley. I said, simply, the father ceased and the son succeeded. These were my words. On these lands there can be but one squire."

I could not listen in quietness. I rose from my chair again in dismay and apprehension. "You mean to withdraw—to leave the house—to abdicate?" I gasped, scarcely knowing what I said.

"Sir," said the squire, looking up with authority, "I mean to *cease*."

It is impossible to give the smallest idea of the horror of these words, spoken in this strange silent house in the dark room, with its line of long dull windows letting in a colourless ghostly twilight, and the tremulous limes quivering at the oriel. I cried aloud, yet it was only in a whisper: "Why—what—how is this! Murder—suicide! Good heaven, what do you mean?"

"Be seated, sir," said my companion, authoritatively. "I trust I speak to a gentleman, and a man of honour. Do *I* betray any unseemly agitation? The means are our secret—the fact is as I tell you. Tomorrow, air, my son will be Squire of Witcherley, and I shall have fulfilled the vow and the destiny of my race."

How I managed to sit down quietly again in this ghastly half-light at the domestic table of a man who had just made a state-ment so astounding, and under a roof where the implements of murder might be waiting, or the draught of the suicide prepared, I cannot tell: yet I did so, overawed by the quietness of my com-panion, in presence of whom, though my head throbbed and my veins swelled, it seemed impossible to say a word. I sat looking at him in silence, revolving a hundred wild schemes of rescue. In England, and the nineteenth century! It was not possible; yet I could not help the shuddering sense of reality, which crept upon me. "And your son?" I exclaimed, abruptly, with a renewed sense of horror—the son's sullen and guilty shame returning in strong confirmation before my eyes.

"My son," said the squire, with again a natural sigh—"yes. I confess it has hitherto been the father who has taken the initia-tive in this matter; but my boy knew his rights. I was perhaps dil-atory. Yes—yes, it is all perfectly right, and I have not the smallest reason to complain."

"But what—what?—for heaven's sake, tell me! You are not about to do anything?—what are you about to do?" cried I.

"Sir, you are excited," said the squire. "I am about to do nothing which I am not quite prepared for. Pardon me for reminding you. You are a stranger—you are in the country—and in this quiet district we keep early hours. Do me the favour to ring for lights; the bell is close to your hand; and as our avenue is of the darkest, Joseph will guide to the postern."

I rang the bell, as I was desired, with passive obedience. I was struck dumb with amaze and bewilderment, half angry at this sudden dismissal, and half disposed to remain in spite of it; but I *was* a stranger, indebted to my companion's courtesy for my introduction here, and without the slightest claim upon him. Lights appeared, as if by magic, in an instant, and Joseph lingered waiting for orders. "Take your lantern and light the gentleman to the end of the avenue," said the squire, coming briskly out of the recess, and arranging for himself a chair and a newspaper at the table. Then he held out his hand to me, shook mine heartily, and dismissed me with the condescending but authoritative bow of a monarch. I muttered something about remaining—about service and assistance—but the old gentleman took no further notice of me, and sat down to his newspaper with dignified impenetrability.

Having no resource but to follow Joseph, I went out with no small amount of discomposure. And looking back to the placid old figure at the table, with his lamp and his paper, and struck with the overwhelming incongruity of ideas, the mysterious horror of the story, and the composed serenity of the scene, went out after my guide in perfect bewilderment, ready to believe that my senses had deceived me—that my host laboured under some extraordinary delusion—anything rather than that this was true.

The avenue was black as midnight; darkness was no description of the pitchy gloom of this narrow path, with its crowd of overshadowing trees; and not even the wavering light of Joseph's lantern, cast upon the ground at my feet, secured me from frequent collisions with the big boles of those gigantic elms. The wind too, unlike a summer breeze, came chill and ghostly up the confined road, and rain was beginning to fall. I presume the old servant scarcely heard my questions, amid the universal rustle of the leaves and patter of the rain. He did not answer, at all events, except by directions and injunctions to take care. I caught him by the arm at last, when we came to the door. "Do you know of anything that is about to happen—quick—tell me!" I cried, my excitement coming to a climax. The lantern almost fell from Joseph's hand, but I could not see his face.

"A many things happen nowadays," said Joseph, "but I reckon master wants me more nor you, sir, if that be all."

"Your master! it is your master I am concerned about," cried I. "You look like an old servant—do you know what all this mean? Is the old man safe? If there's any danger, tell me, and I'll go back with you and watch all night."

"Danger! the squire's in his own house," said Joseph, "and not a servant in it but's been there for twenty years. Thank you all the same; but mind your own business, young gentleman, and ride betimes in the morning, and never think on't again, whate'er ye may have heard tonight."

Saying which, Joseph closed abruptly in my face the postern-door, at which we had been standing, and through the open ironwork of the closed gates I saw his light gleam hastily, as he hurried up the avenue. His manner and words excited instead of subduing my agitated curiosity. I stood irresolute in the rain and the darkness, gazing through the iron gate, which now I could distinguish only by touch, and could not see, though I was close to it. What was to be done? What could I do? Just then I heard a horse's hoofs upon the road, and turned round eagerly, with the intention of addressing the passenger, whoever it might be. Raising my eyes, though it was impossible to see anything, I cried, "Hold—wait—let me speak to you!" when, with an effect, like a suddenly displayed lantern, the moon broke out through the clouds.

My eyes had been straining, in the darkness, to the unseen face; now, when this fitful illumination revealed it, I started back in confusion. It was the same ashamed sullen resentful face which had lowered upon me at the squire's table—his son—and instead of pausing when he perceived me, the young man touched his horse smartly with his whip, and plunged away, at a heavy gallop, into the night. I think this last incident filled up the measure of my confused and bewildering excitement. I turned from the gate at once, and pushed book towards the Witcherley Arms.

Reaching them, I went in with the full intention of rousing the country, and returning in force, to gain an entrance to the manor-house, and save the old man in his own despite. But when I went into the dull public room, with its two flaring melancholy candles, its well-worn country paper, which one clown was spelling over, and another listening to—when, in my haste and heat, I came within this cheerless, lifeless atmosphere, heard the fall of the monotonous slow voices, and saw the universal stagnation of life, my excitement relaxed in spite of myself. In this scene, so coldly, dully commonplace—in this ordinary, unvaried stream of existence, it was impossible: there was no room for mysteries and horrors here.

Yet within the little bar on the other side of the passage, the landlord and his wife were peering out at me with a half-scared curiosity, and holding consultations together in an excited and uneasy restlessness, something like my own. Stimulated once more by seeing this, I hastened up to them, and though they both retreated before me, and made vain attempts to conceal their curiosity and eagerness, my own mind Was too much roused to be easily deceived. I asked hastily if there was any constabulary force in the neighbourhood—soldiers, county police, protectors of the peace.

The woman uttered a faint exclamation of terror; but the landlord, with a certain stupid adroitness, which I could not help remarking, took up my question. "Polis! Lord a' mercy! the gentleman's been robbed. I'se a constable mysel'."

"I have not been robbed; but I suspect you know more than

I do," cried I, impatiently. "Your old squire is in some mysterious danger. If you're a constable, rouse half-a-dozen men in the neighbourhood, and come up with me to the manor-house—if you're a constable! I should say, if you're a man, make haste and follow me. Do you hear? At this very moment the old man may be in peril of his life."

"What's wrong, sir? what's wrong? It cannot be robbers, for robbers could ne'er reach to the manor-house," said the wife, interposing. "Bless and preserve us! is't the Russians or the French, or the pitmen, or what's wrong? and if he's off and away to the manor, who'll mind his own house?"

"I am sure you know what I mean," cried I. "Your old master is in danger. I cannot tell you what danger. You know better than I do. Can you look on quietly, and see the squire lose his life?"

"I know nought about the squire's life," said Giles sullenly, after a pause; "and no more do you, sir, that's a stranger to Witcherley ways. The squire's got his own about him that won't see wrong to him. It's no ado o' mine, and it's no ado o' yours; and I'm not agoing on a fool's errand for any man, let alone a strange gentleman I never set eyes on afore. Do you think I'd go and anger the squire in his own house, because summat skeared a traveller? I'm not agoing to do no such foolishness. If the squire takes notions, what's that to a stranger like you, that'll maybe never see him again?"

"Takes notions?" I caught at this new idea with infinite relief. "What do you mean? *Does* the squire take notions? Is it all a delusion of his? Is that what you mean?"

"Sir, it's in the family; they're queer, that's what they are," said the woman, answering me eagerly, while her husband hung back, and made no response. "It comes strange to the likes of you; for it takes a deal of studyin' to larn Witcherley ways."

"Witcherley ways—in the family—a delusion—a monomania," said I to myself. Certainly this looked the most reasonable explanation. Yes, to be sure; everybody had heard of such. I received the idea eagerly, and calmed down at once. After all, the wonder was, that it had never struck me before; and then the confusion of the young man—the anxiety of Joseph. No doubt, they trembled for the exhibition of this incipient madness—no doubt, they were afraid of the narrative with which the unfortunate old gentleman was sure to horrify a new listener. I became quite "easy in my mind" as I revolved all this. Monomaniacs, too, are so gravely reasonable in most oases, and have so much method in their madness.

I returned to the dull public-room with restored composure, and thinking it all over, in the lifeless silence, in this place where it seemed impossible that anything could happen, could almost have laughed at myself for my own fears. By-and-by the house was shut up, and I transferred my quarters to the gable-room, which I was to occupy for the night It was a well-sized apartment, somewhat bare, but very clean, and sufficiently comfortable, very much like the best bedroom of a humble country inn, which it was.

The bow-window—the only window in the room—looked out into sheer darkness, a heavy visible gloom; the night was somewhat wild, and dismal with wind and rain, and, in spite of the homely comfort of my surroundings, I have seldom spent a more miserable night. Dreary old stories revived out of the oblivion of childhood; tales of the creeping stream of blood from some closed door, the appalling pistol-shot, the horror of the death-gasp and cry, forced themselves on my memory; and when I slept, it was only to see visions of the squire, or of someone better known to me in his place, standing in ghastly solitude with the knife or the poison, struggling with assassins, or stretched upon a horrible deathbed, red with murder.

Through these feverish fancies came the rounds of the night; the creeping silence, which, like the darkness, was not negative, but positive; the dismal creaking of the sign among the great boughs of the elm-tree; the rush of rain against the window; the moaning and sobbing echoes of the wind. These terrors, however, waking and sleeping, did not make me watch for and start up to meet the earliest dawn, as might have been supposed; on the contrary, I fell into a heavy slumber as the morning broke, and slept late and long, undisturbed by the early sounds of rustical awakening. When I roused myself at last, it was ten o'clock—a pale, wet, melancholy morning, the very ghost and shadow of the more dismal night.

I cannot tell whether the story of the evening was the first thing which occurred to my mind when I awoke. Indeed, I rather think not, but that a more everyday and familiar apprehension, the dread of once more losing the train, was the earliest thought which occupied me, despite all the horrors of the night. But my mind immediately rebounded with excitement and eagerness into the former channel, when I looked out from my window. Immediately under it, in the pale drizzle of rain, stood the squire's son, dressed as his father had been, in a blue coat with gilt buttons, but new, and of the latest fashion, and with a white favour on the breast. His face was flushed with rude half-concealed exultation; his manner seemed arrogant and authoritative, but still he had not lost the down-looking, sullen, resentful shame of the previous night. He was putting money in the hand of Giles, who stood by with a scowl upon his face, and touched his hat with a still more sullen unwillingness.

Several other men, a heaving little rustic crowd, lingered around, eyeing the young man askance with looks of soared and unfriendly curiosity. "Let them drink our health, and see that the bells are rung." I heard only these words distinctly, and the young squire strode away towards the manor-house. When he was out of sight, my phlegmatic landlord threw his money vehemently on the ground with an expression of disgust, and shook his clenched hand after the disappearing figure; but thinking better of it by-and-by, and relenting towards the honest coin, picked it up deliberately, piece by piece, and hastily disappeared within the house. My *toilette* did not occupy me much after this incident, and as soon as I had hastily completed it, I hurried downstairs. Giles was in the passage, giving directions, intermixed with a low growl of half-spoken curses. When he saw me, he suddenly stopped, and retreated within his little bar. I followed him anxiously. "What has happened?—what of the squire?"

"The squire?—it's none o' my business—nor yours neither. Mind your breakfast and your train, young gentleman, and don't you bother about Witcherley—Missus, you're wanted! —I've enow on my own hands."

Saying which Giles fled, and left me unanswered and unsatisfied. Turning to his wife, who appeared immediately with my breakfast, I found her equally impracticable. She, poor woman, seemed able for nothing but to wring her hands, wipe her eyes with an apron, and answer to my eager inquiries, "Don't you meddle in it—don't you, then! Lord! it's Witcherley ways."

It was impossible to bear this tantalising bewilderment. I took my hat, and rushed out, equally indifferent to train and breakfast. The same bumpkins stood still loitering in the highroad, in the rain; and, soared and awe-stricken as they seemed, were still able to divert the main subject of their slow thoughts, with some dull observation of myself, as I rushed past. I did not pause, however, to ask any fruitless questions of this mazed chorus of spectators, but hurried along the road to the little postern-gate.

To my surprise, I found the great gates open, and another little circle of bystanders, children and women, standing by. I hastened up the dark avenue, when the rain pattered and the leaves rustled in the pallid daylight, as they had done in the blank night. Everything remained exactly as it was yesterday, when I passed up this same tortuous road with the squire. I rushed on with growing excitement, unable to restrain myself. The hall-door stood slightly ajar. I pushed it open, and entered with a hasty step, which echoed upon the paved hall as though the house were vacant. Roused from a corner by the sound, Joseph rose and came forward to meet me. The poor fellow looked very grave and solemn, and had been sitting in forlorn solitude, reading in this chilly uninhabited hall. But at sight of me the cautiousness of suspicion seemed to inspire Joseph. He quickened his pace, and came forward resolutely, keeping himself between me and the dining-room door.

"I want to see your master—your master!—beg him to see

me for a moment; I will not detain him," said I.

"My master ?" Joseph paused and looked at me earnestly, as if to ascertain how much or how little I knew.

"My master, sir, was married this morning. I couldn't make so bold as to disturb him; perhaps you could call another day."

"Married! Now, Joseph," said I, trying what an appeal would do, "you know it is in vain to attempt deceiving me; your master's son is married, but I do not want him: I want to see the old squire."

"There's no old squire, sir," said Joseph, with a husky voice, "there ain't. I tell you true; you're dreaming. My master's a young gentleman, and married this morning. It's no good coming here," cried the old servant, growing excited, "to make trouble, and disturb a quiet house. My master's a young gentleman—younger than yourself; there can be but one squire."

"Joseph, what do you mean?" cried I. "Do you forget what I saw and heard— do you forget that I was here and dined with your old master last night? Where is he? What have you done with him? I'll rouse the country. I'll have you all indicted for murder, every soul in the house. Where is the old squire?"

He laid his hand upon my shoulder fiercely, trembling himself, however, as he did so, with the tremor of weakness. "Will you hold your tongue—will you be quiet—will you leave this house?"

"No," cried I, raising my voice, and shaking the old man off—"No, I'll ascertain the truth before I move a step. I will not leave the house. Here, go call your new master; I'll wait for him where I sate with his father yesterday. His father, poor old man, what have you done with him? I will not move a step till I search this mystery out."

I pushed my way as I spoke into the dining-room, Joseph following and opposing me feebly. The appearance of the silent untenanted room moved me with a new and mysterious thrill of horror. There it lay unaltered, undisturbed, in the very same formal arrangement as when I left it last night; the portraits looking darkly from the walls, the tender lime-leaves flickering round the oriel, the long vacant dining-table shining dully in the sub-dued light. Every chair stood as it had stood yesterday—the very newspaper lay upon the table. But where was the old squire?

I turned round upon Joseph suddenly—"He sat there, just there, last night. You are as conscious of it as I am. I want to know where he is now."

A kind of hysteric sob of terror escaped from the old servant's breast. He retreated hastily, covering his eyes with his hand, yet casting looks of horror at the vacant elbow-chair. "I'll go, sir— I'll go— I'll call my master," he said, with a cracked unsteady voice; and he went out of the room, not daring, as I fancied, to turn his back upon the ghostly empty seat. I, in my excite-ment, paced up and down the room, with all my private sense of wrong and horror, and all my public sentiment of justice, giving authority to my step. It did not occur to me that I had no right to enter another man's house after this fashion, or that I ran any risk in doing so. I was excited beyond the reach of all personal consideration. I thought of nothing but the old squire; here only last night I had sat at his table, joined him in conversation, and listened to his story, and where—where—ghastly confirmation to that tale of horror—where was he now?

I had heard Joseph's step, timid and yet hasty, shuffle up the great echoing staircase; bat as I stood still to listen, now the si-lence crept and stagnated around me without a human sound to break it. Nothing but the rain outside, the wet leaves against the window, not even the familiar pulse of a clock to soften the painful stillness. My thoughts were of the blackest. I concluded no better than that murder, cowardly and base, was in this house, which I, alone and unsupported, had come to beard, accuse, and defy in its own stronghold. But, fired with excitement, I feared nothing—thought of nothing but a possible spectacle of hor-ror concealed within one of these unknown rooms, and of the question perpetually on my lips, Where is the squire?

At length, as I listened, a foot sounded upon the stair, heavy, sometimes rapid, sometimes hesitating, the true step of guilt. I felt assured it was the son, the parricide! My heart beat with choking rapidity, a cold dew rose upon my forehead, and I turned to the door to face the newcomer with the fervour and zeal of an avenger. Now for the solution of this horrible mystery! And now a suspicious uncertain hand tries the door doubtfully—now it creaks upon its hinges—now——

My dearest friend! you cannot be half or a hundredth part so much disappointed as I was; for as the door creaked, and the guilty step advanced, and my heart beat with wild expectation, I awoke—

I am ashamed to confess the humiliating truth—awoke to find myself in my own crimson easy-chair, after dinner, with the fire glowing into the cosy twilight, and so dark avenue or lonely manor-house within a score of miles. Under the circumstances, I am grieved to add that the deepest mystery, a gloom which I fear I may never be able to penetrate, still hangs darkly over the ways of Witcherley, and the fate of the old squire.

Had Joseph's young master come only five minutes sooner—but late is inexorable; and though I have made investigations through a primitive nook of country, and missed a train with resignation in the pursuit of knowledge, I have never fallen upon that rainy pathway across the field, nor come to the Witcherley Arms again.

"Dies Iræ" The Story of a Spirit in Prison

He that works me good with unmoved face, Does it but half; he chills me while he aids,—
My benefactor, not my Brother-man.

—Coleridge.

PART 1

I had been very ill. I knew that. Strange whisperings had from time to time penetrated to my brain that were not intended for me to hear, and I knew from them that those in waiting upon me had given up all hope of my recovery.

At first I had rebelled, bitterly, clamorously. Still, as I appeared to lie, speechless, helpless, life was at fever heat in my brain, and my soul was rising up in fierce rebellion. In the full tide of youth and health to be singled out from the multitude to ... die! There was surely injustice, cruel injustice, in it. "*Threescore and ten years*," I quoted, and I had but lived twenty-five. Never yet had I been denied anything that life could give, and now the common blessing of life itself was to be taken from me at a stroke.

I knew, I did not deny that I knew, that Death had never been a respecter of ages; but "All men think all men mortal but themselves": and that it should be I against whom the decree had gone forth—it was incredible.

That phase had passed; my fruitless wrath had spent itself; a few salt tears had gathered, and lain in the hollow cups of my eyes, and those that watched had looked more sadly than before upon me.

"Hush! she is dying!" I heard them say, as the first cock crew.

So the "Supreme Moment" was at hand; and, strangely enough, I was now beyond caring for it. Probably I was too weak to care.

"It must be very near," I thought, as I saw my good pastor kneel by my bedside, a look of intense earnestness contracting his features.

"She must not die. She shall not die. There is much for her to do on earth yet."

What did he mean? Was it work that I had left undone, and was he going to wrestle for my soul from out the very grip of death, as had done Luther, centuries ago, for his friend?

Ah! I was weary . . . too weary to think more. Through dimming sight I could just see the hospital nurse, a kindly dark-eyed woman, who seemed all eyes and cap and spotless linen, move round me as in a dream. Was she praying now too? And my cousin, whom they had brought four hundred miles, because I had no nearer relative, was she too sinking on her knees? . . . I was growing faint . . . fainter the air was stifling! . . I was struggling . . . panting . . . striving . . . Free! . . . drawing, it seemed to me, a long, long breath.

Where was I?

Halfway through the room, halfway to the roof, turning with amazed eyes to look on the scene upon which I had just closed my eyes.

There, was the kneeling pastor, with folded upraised hands and supplicating speech; there the nurse, with bent head but professional watchfulness; my little fair-haired cousin, her head buried on her hands; strangest of all, there lay a figure outstretched under a snowy counterpane, that it was impossible to help recognising as myself. For one moment I saw distinctly the white, drawn face, sharpening in the death-agony, the closed eyes, the cup-like hollows filled with the cruel tears I had shed, the white hand on the counterpane. . . . A moment and all was

277

dark I knew no more.

★★★★★★

Had I been asleep, or was I awake now?

I was in the open air, a great sense of space, of breath, of life about me.

Behind me lay a valley stretching into the dim distance, encompassed with white mist. Shadows of human beings were faintly discernible in its midst, moving to and fro, and a very distant hum of voices penetrated the air. Here and there I could see figures emerging from its white cloud; sometimes in little bands of three and four—sometimes alone. Was that the earth that lay so close to an encircling world? . . .

Yes, and it lay behind me now. What was beyond? I looked up with eager inquiry.

Before me rose in a long incline the green slope of a hillside that, through shaded ways, led to a level overshadowed by an amphitheatre of hills—hills whose peaks rose like great white crystals, roseate, golden-tipped, losing themselves in colour.

With bated breath and a strange thrill of expectancy, I asked myself, if perchance my feet had wandered to the threshold of Paradise; if these golden heights were where saints and angels congregated—where they "*summered high in bliss upon the hills of God.*"

Nor did I fear that I had been deceived, when down the turf-clad path there moved towards me one, half-goddess, half-woman.

Where had I seen or heard of beauty such as hers before? Surely in some dream. Ah! I knew. . . . How often had I repeated with untiring delight—

Her robe, ungirt from clasp to hem
No wrought flowers did adorn; . . .
Her hair, that lay along her back,
Was yellow, like ripe corn.

There, in all the glory of the poet's picturing, she stood: a Blessed Damozel; and her soft slow steps were surely bringing her to me.

She was close to me. I was looking up into the blue depths of her eyes.

Yes:

They were deeper than the depths
Of water stilled at even.

But they were filled with a soft sadness that brought a shapeless fear to mingle with my wonder.

Was she sad for me, this Blessed Damozel? Her whole mien was one of gracious pity. . . . Was it for me? . . . A faint feeling began to gather at my heart. The "hills of God" seemed very far away.

PART 2

We were slowly climbing the steep, the Blessed Damozel and I. Her hand clasped mine in familiar touch. Her words of welcome had been sweet to my soul, for in saying them, through the depth of sorrow in her eyes there had shone the purest light of love.

"You . . . love me!" I had said, surprised into speech.

"I have loved you," she had murmured, "all your life upon the earth."

"Then I will fear no evil," I had answered, reassured, and clung to her outstretched hand.

As we went I pointed to the crystal heights on which the glory lay.

"I know them. I have read of them. They are the 'hills of God.' Are we going there?"

She lifted a reverent gaze to the far-off peaks.

"These are the 'hills of Holiness,'" she answered, and with averted gaze pursued her way.

The old faint fear crept coldly round my heart, and my gaze went fearfully forward. Visions of Paradise were slowly melting away from me. In their place the *Dies Iræ* began to repeat itself in my brain.

That Day of Wrath! that dreadful day! . . .

What was before me? . . . What awaited me? . . .

Halfway up the slope a murmur behind made me turn curiously. A little company was just emerging from the mist-filled valley, and following in our steps. My guide looked behind.

"Shall we wait for them?" she asked, and drew me aside into the shade of a grove of trees.

Before long they were nearing us. A little woman led by the hand by a fair guide somewhat like my own, but of a very different type of beauty. The flowing hair was dark, the figure fuller, and there was a very marked difference in her expression. It was of one that triumphed, and in her large dark eyes a light of victory shone. A little company followed them. A widow with streaming eyes, leading by the hand a boy and girl; a maiden, pale-faced and worn; a hard-featured woman, speaking volubly to a deaf audience, but with tears in her eyes.

"Who is she?" I asked, my gaze going back to the small central figure.

"A little maiden lady of seventy years, who left the world this morning. No, she does not look her years. It is the 'youth of the soul' that is on her face—immortal youth."

"And those who are with her, are they all dead? They somehow look different."

"No; these are the forms of those who have loved her, and whose souls are longing after her so powerfully, that, unknown to themselves, they are here with her, testifying unconsciously to her love and sweet charity while among them."

"Did . . . did no one come with me?" I asked, shamed, I knew not why, before the question was well framed.

"She had seventy years of life, you only twenty-five," my friend answered, very sorrowfully. Her love would evidently fain cover a multitude of sins.

At this moment the group stopped almost opposite to us. The little face had the beauty of a child rather than that of an old woman.

"*She* has possessed her soul in innocency," I said, involuntarily. "But what does it all mean? I suppose she was kind to those people, but . . ."

"Keep your gaze fixed steadily upon her, and you will one by one see the different scenes of her life stand out in clear relief. I see them now, and as she moves up to higher planes, they will stand out in bolder and still bolder relief to every eye."

I steadied my gaze, and this is what I saw:—

I saw her as a girl seated at a piano, painfully imparting the most elementary knowledge of its use to a perplexed girl as old as herself.

"The girl has to win her bread by teaching. She is trying to fit her for the battle. She has no money. She is giving time . . . and love."

The scene had melted away.

Round her was a little house of mean appearance. She was "on household cares intent." A fretful woman was extended on a sofa, speaking in querulous tones.

I looked to my guide.

"The sick woman is a worn out music-teacher, homeless, sick. She is no relative, not even a friend, has but the claim of weakness and want. The little maiden lady had very small means. She argued with herself that the only way by which she could help her was to do without any service herself, and to use the cost of service in housing and clothing this poor woman. Like Dr Johnson's dependants, the music-mistress too often used her opportunities to grumble at her benefactress. But she is worshipping her today."

The woman of voluble speech was indeed on her knees before the little lady. I could hear her murmured thanks, and the troubled protest in response.

When I looked again, she was in other surroundings. The young widow and the boy and girl, whose figures were now fading into the mist, were clustered round her, younger and poorer.

"When the querulous old music-mistress died," spoke my guide, "the little lady vowed that she would still share her home with the homeless. Out of the crowd came this young widow,

281

penniless, with a boy and girl to rear. These are the mourners whose true sorrow follows her. The widow's gratitude was not confined to words. Look at the home she made for her."

I saw a bright and happy household, holding the head in loving reverence, and she growing old among them.

"Now," said my guide, bringing me back to the present, "she will have her reward."

At this moment her guide stopped, her face wreathed with smiles, took a crown she had been carefully carrying, and stooping over her with infinite tenderness, placed it on her brows.

She turned her face towards me, alight with soft surprise, and I saw plainly written in letters of gold:—

"*I was a stranger, and ye took me in.*"

Then they passed away, to where sweet strains of music called. We were alone, I with the tears gathered thick in my eyes.

"And I," looking round in bewilderment—"I have loved none, helped none, except through others; denied myself for none. What of me? . . . Ah! God will for Christ's sake forgive me. I died trusting in Him."

"God will for Christ's sake forgive you," said my sweet Damozel, solemnly, "but . . ."

"But what? Sweet Damozel, answer me," for my guide was pursuing her way with sorrowful mien.

"Yet one thing thou lackest," . . . she quoted.

"'One thing thou lackest,'" I repeated after her. "'*Sell all that thou hast, and give to the poor.*' But that. . . . we were told that was not meant literally."

"Its 'spirit' giveth life."

"Its 'Spirit'!" . . .

"Its spirit is Love, and Love is Everlasting Life."

I was deeply bewildered.

"But"—a strange fear beginning to gather round my heart—"the pains of hell, they at least were an invention of narrow-minded men, of whom Calvin was the chief: not even for the wicked do they exist!"

"I can believe in no hell," I went on passionately, finding my guide slow to answer, "for with it there could be no heaven. I for one," daringly, being deeply imbued with the latest sentiments I had listened to on earth—"I could not be happy in the highest heaven if I knew there was one poor soul imprisoned in a hell."

I thought for a moment that my Blessed Damozel was breathing a prayer for me, so sad was the expression of her uplifted eyes, and slowly but surely the terrors of the Unknown began to encompass me about.

The air was growing colder, purer, more difficult of breath, and an excessive light was blinding me. We had reached the level.

It was, as I had seen from afar, an amphitheatre encircled by high hills; at first it seemed to be closed in entirely, but on looking closer and with straining gaze, I saw openings to right and to left.

With a flash of memory, words that had been familiar to me from childhood repeated themselves in my brain.

"And He set the sheep on His right hand, and the goats on His left."

"Where . . . do they lead?" I asked, with a strange sinking of the heart.

"To God," answered my guide, solemnly.

Oh, Day of Wrath! . . . Oh, Dreadful Day! . . . rhymed on in my brain.

"Come!" said my guide; and, with a terror growing ever greater at my heart, I followed to where, as I gazed on the two parting roads, there, out of the light a shape slowly formed itself, terrible in its beauty to any erring child of earth, for its beauty was the beauty of Holiness.

I fell prostrate at its feet. I closed my eyes in the dust. All my complacency fell from me as a garment; all the fair colouring with which I had clothed myself in imagination, melted like a breath before that pure presence. Petty self-deceivings, multiplied self-excusings, they were as if they had never been.

I had but one cry:—

God have mercy upon me, ...
Christ have mercy upon me"

Through the silence, and as if it were afar off, I heard the voice of my Blessed Damozel pleading for me.

"Lord, have pity upon her. She has sinned in ignorance."

. . . . God have mercy upon me

"She is yet of tender years. Only a third of the days allotted to man upon the earth have been granted to her."

. . . . Christ have mercy upon me.

Strangely enough, although I lay prostrate as before, I could as plainly see my pleader and my Judge as if I had been standing upright before them; and although I did not once open my lips, a voice that yet seemed mine took up speech against me, almost without my will.

Mea culpa! mea culpa!. . .

"She brings none with her, it is true, but she lived in a charmed circle. Great wealth of this world's goods were bequeathed to her. She has known no poverty."

. . . . God have mercy upon me.

"She has known no sorrow."

. . . . Christ have mercy upon me.

"And," she went on, with pleading earnestness, "she has known no love."

Then I knew, from the light on my sweet guide's face, that this last plea had somehow brought amelioration of my sentence.

"Come!" she whispered low, and I kissed the hem of her garment as she gently raised me.

"Where . . . are you leading me?" I asked in a new humility, when we had gone some distance. "But I know," . . . for she was slow to answer. "To Outer Darkness."

She stopped short, and wound her arms round my neck.

"It is indeed Outer Darkness," she answered, and made my

284

spirit to fail with her word. "But, my love, you go on a quest that will end in victory, . . . on a high and holy quest."

"What quest?" raising weary eyes.

"The quest after Love."

"Ah! you said I had never known that. I thought I had."

"It is one thing to love, another to be loved. On earth we too often crave for the second, and so miss the first. Yet the first is of God; the second of self."

"And when I find Love, shall I be safe?" sorrowfully enough.

Her eyes were very sad. "When you have ceased to ask after safety, you may come within reach of Love."

"Alas! you talk in riddles."

"Till the riddle is solved, you will not see God, for . . . 'God is Love.'"

I was sorely bewildered, and grievously faint at heart.

"Wherever I go, will you go with me?" I asked, clinging to her in a loneliness that was growing and growing in me.

"You will come back to me," she answered, her eyes filling slowly with tears as she bent over me. "From the day that you were born, I have had you in my care. Now I may keep you but a very little longer. Ah! I am sad exceedingly for you, for I too have trodden every step of the way. I, like you, came hither trusting in the Christ, but with the very first lessons of the 'Religion of Love' unlearned; and only when you have conquered, shall I be free to live the wider life that lies beyond."

"There is a wider life beyond?"

"Yes!" the joy of all the ages future shining in her eyes, till she was transfigured to a beauty that thrilled me through and through, "a wider life beyond and beyond, and for ever beyond. We shall share it together."

"I shall never be like you!" I cried, in despair.

"My love, you will one day awake in His likeness, . . so shall I, . . . and we shall be satisfied."

But now and for me that Outer Darkness beckoned. Already I imagined that shadows were falling around us.

She read my thought.

"I shall wait for you at Dawn," she whispered.

"Have I then only one long night of horror and of pain before me?" I asked, with conscious relief.

"We count no time here. A night is as a thousand years; a thousand years as a night."

"You mean that Life is so intense, time is lost sight of."

"Yes."

"Why have you changed the word in the passage? why night instead of day?"

"There is no day where you go," she answered. "It is always night there."

I began to tremble exceedingly.

"But you will watch for me at Dawn?" in accents that were now piteous entreaty. "You will not fail me?"

"I shall watch with open arms for you at Dawn," she answered, and therewith fell on my neck and kissed me, mingling her tears with mine.

I thought I heard a sob, but it might have been my own sobbing breath, for my fears had overcome me, and I lay like a child in her arms, holding her fast.

As in a dream I felt the arms loosening slowly from round me, and then my own tenderly unclasped. I seemed to cling with all my might.

"Oh, Blessed Damozel! "I cried, "have pity! . . . Stay!" . . .

But it was of no avail. She was gone. I was alone, and swooning for fear and grief.

PART 3

When I awoke, the shadows of night were indeed around me. Straining my gaze into their depths, I could distinguish blacker shadows of massive buildings rising higher and higher on every hand; buildings on buildings, dark, gloomy, with endless passages winding in and out among them—passages narrow, foul, and overshadowed with such darkness as lay on my very soul; for surely it was not the darkness of Nature alone that brooded over that ghostly city.

From a height I looked down on it with ever-quickening gaze. Could these be human beings that crowded storey after storey of the towering masses of stone, and swarmed in swaying multitudes in every darkened passage? They did indeed seem to take shape to my curious gaze. Figures of old and young, sickly infants, and tottering old women, men and women of all ages, mixed in a motley crowd; and ever and *anon*, to my shrinking ear, from the whole came up a confused wailing of many voices, sounding, it seemed to me, every note of pain, from the feeble wail of infancy to that of torture unendurable, while loud-mouthed curses, that made my very flesh creep for fear, mingled from time to time with the sounds.

It is, I think, Jean Paul Richter who has recorded his belief that of all Hells the Hell of sound is the worst; and I knew then, as I had never known before, what he meant. It was no long time till, after listening to cry after cry, I put my hands to my ears in the vain endeavour to escape from it all. But no device of earth availed here. There was no closing of the ears. The increasing wail waxed ever louder and more bitter; I even grew to distinguish a horrible laughter mingling itself with it, till, when at last a terror-filled shriek rang and rang through the darkened air, I could bear it no longer. I threw myself on my knees and added my cry to theirs.

"God in Heaven, what have they done, to be so tormented?" I cried. "Is there no mercy in heaven or earth to help them?"

A voice, stern, resolute, sounded in my ear. It bade me rise; and looking up, I found by my side one of terrible aspect, awful in a majesty that made me cower before him.

"Who art thou?" I did not dare to ask, but he had read and answered my thought.

"I am the Avenging Angel," he answered.

"To these poor people," I said, with an indignant thrill.

"Of these poor people," he answered.

And although I knew not what he meant, I shrank before him.

"You are ... their ..."

But even as I spoke, another of those terror laden shrieks rent the air and startled me out of all self-control.

"What does it mean?" I sobbed, in almost equal terror.

"It means that cruelty is rampant, and there is none to check it; that lust is unbridled, and the innocent flee before it; that avarice stalks unheeded throughout the land, leaving famine and desolation behind. Look and learn."

They were words my Blessed Damozel had used; but they were repeated now with a sternness of tone that made me tremble as before a judge. No compassion shone in the eyes of the Avenging Angel as he bent them on me.

I turned my gaze where he directed, and found that by some strange means he had contrived to throw a strong light down on a pair of figures in the far depth of the valley—a pair clasped in each other's arms; a husband and wife. The woman was wan and worn to a shadow; the man scarcely better.

"Avarice has been on their track for years," said my guide. "She is slowly dying, but she has possessed her soul in patience. She will be at rest tonight."

"But why are they here at all? What sin did they commit?"

There was no answer. The thoughts of the Avenging Angel were far from me.

"Tomorrow at dawn I shall set her free, and she shall sleep till then. But . . . '*woe to him by whom the offence cometh.*'"

Why should all the graciousness pass from his face when he turned to me? Why should I have to shrink again into the attitude of a culprit? I did not dare to ask the question I was longing to have answered. Did death reign here as in the world? for no such possibility had entered my imagination. But questioning was lost sight of in a new terror.

A cry as of a hunted animal rent the air and startled me into a new agony of fear.

"What? . . . what is that?"

For answer the strange light fell with lurid gleam on a fleeing maiden of tender years and a monster in human shape pursuing.

My heart stood still, then leapt with sudden horror.

"O God, he gains on her! . . . Stop him! . . . You are an angel! Oh . . ."

My shrieks were mingling with the maiden's as I fell on my face to shut out the hideous horror.

It was long before I raised streaming eyes to my companion.

"You could have helped, you would not move."

"I am her Avenger," he answered, grimly.

"You will hurl her destroyer to the lowest hell," I said.

"Nay, not him alone."

"On whom will vengeance fall?" I asked, eagerly.

"These are the hidden things of God," he answered, solemnly. "Each goeth to his own place."

Each to his own place, and I was here. What had such scenes as those I was witnessing to do with me? . . .

Even as we spoke a great hum of angry voices was coming again within hearing, swelling as it rose and rose, ever nearer, and bringing with it a new horror before which my spirit quailed. Was there to be no rest for me through all this weary night? I shrank before the ever-growing tumult: children crying, women shrilly calling, men cursing.

"Oh, I cannot bear more! . . . The night is hideous with sound. A moment, I pray you, of rest. Shut out the sounds from my ears but for one brief moment. Let me dream, were it only for a moment, that I am again back in my old home, all barbarous sounds shut out. . . . I am a weak and tenderly reared girl. . . . Such sights and sounds as I have seen and heard tonight, I have never even dreamt of. What, . . . what is happening now? . . . Ah, spare me! No more light, I pray. But, my God, what is that? . . ."

"Cruelty rampant: the victims are at its mercy."

"Is there none to help? none to answer to such cries?"

"The few help; the many disregard. But the Lord will avenge," solemnly, "and I am His servant."

He was awful as he spoke, for the valley rang with execrations, strange oaths, piteous weeping.

I went back to my pleading.

"A moment of respite, I pray you, . . . I am sick at heart." . . .

What was happening? A strange light was spreading far and wide in a large semicircle, leaving the valley below in deeper gloom than before. The night was become light about us. I gazed as one in a dream at fair gardens stretching down gentle slopes, at stately mansions, at delicate women and strong-limbed men, strolling through softly carpeted rooms or lounging on low settees. Children like to little angels played merrily, and soft laughter welled out to us.

As I looked, recognition slowly came to me. I had got my prayer.

"It is what I left behind!" I cried, in rapture. "Ah, how good it was!"

For a brief moment I gazed, forgetting all the horrors I had gone through. Alas! it was only for a moment. My guide touched me on the shoulder.

"How good it was!" I repeated, ere I responded.

His face was sterner than before as he looked down on me. Slowly raising his hand with an ominous gesture, he pointed to the deep Valley of Shadow I had for the moment been allowed to forget.

"And what of them?" he asked.

I followed his gaze. I was growing truly bewildered.

"What! . . . Do they lie so near?"

"So near that although those in the Valley cannot climb to those who '*dwell at ease*,' yet those dwellers at ease can go to the weary and tormented and save them if they will."

"If they will!" I cried, indignantly.

"Who would rest if they could help that struggling multitude?" . . .

. . . A curious thing was happening. Slowly the mists enshrouding the Valley were rolling away before my eyes, and as they lifted themselves, the place was assuming a strangely familiar shape. Were not these the towers and fastnesses of my own town rising out of the crowd? Was that streak of grey not the river with its bridges, that separated the old town from the new?

Could it be? Was that Valley of wicked strife and dire poverty and cruel disease indeed the picturesque valley in the midst of my childhood's home? Was this the Valley of Shadow unspeakable I had been contemplating?

It was night. The gas lit streets were swarming with a swaying multitude, the crowded houses still poured forth their inmates. . They were recognisable for such men and women and children as I had grown up among. At this moment the old town clock I had known from a child tolled out the hour, I counted the strokes mechanically.

"Twelve o'clock! . . . Midnight!" I said, without thinking.

"Midnight!" repeated my guide, as the last stroke died away. "It is now the 'Day of Rest.'"

Oh! hideous mockery. "And that is . . ."

"The town where you and they were born."

"And these are . . ."

"Your sisters . . . and brothers."

"It has been a morbid dream," I cried. "I have had a nightmare."

But almost before I had dared to uplift my voice, the mists fell as before on all around. I was standing alone with my guide on the mountain-side. Below us stretched the darkened Valley like a Lake of Gloom in the heart of the pretty town: worse than all, that wail of all the weary, that cry of all the suffering, was filling again the void.

"Where are the watchmen?" I asked, with a tone of earth in my voice, which my guide must have recognised.

"In the fray," answered my guide, "adding to it, saving some, too late for others. They perhaps are least likely to think your dream morbid."

And, indeed, with that weary, weary wail in my ears, it was difficult to repeat my words.

"My God, it is too awful! "I cried in despair, for sight was now being added to sound; and when I would fain have closed both eyes and ears, it was to find as before that no such escape was possible. "It is too awful! It is hell indeed!"

And so saying, I sank to earth.

"No happiness was possible for you in Heaven, while one poor spirit lay in Hell," gibed a mocking voice in my ear.

Without looking up, I knew that my stern guide was gone, and that his place had been taken by an imp of darkness, who was grinning at my discomfiture.

"Beautiful dreamer of fair sentiments!" reviled another voice. "Imaginative sympathy is so fine a thing. And so easy." . . .

"Learn what this meaneth," spoke one solemnly in passing; "'*I will have mercy, and not sacrifice.*'". . .

. . ."'*And though I bestow all my goods to feed the poor, . . . and have not Love,*'" quoted another sorrowfully, "'*it profiteth me nothing.*'". . .

PART 4

"*One night is as a thousand years.*"

I was in the arms of my Blessed Damozel, sobbing my heart out on her breast.

"At last. . . . At last the day had dawned and set me free, and, as I had never doubted she would be, there, waiting on the fair hillside, had stood my sweet and Blessed Lady, the first rays of sunshine lying on her golden hair, her white arms outstretched, her eyes full of tenderest sympathy, and deep with unforgotten sorrow.

I could not speak. I could not bring before her mind one picture of the horrors I had undergone. I could only cling to her neck and sob, . . . and sob.

"I know it all," she whispered. "I too have gone every step of the way."

It seemed too cruel. She too, my Blessed Damozel.

"No! Not cruel, love." . . . Did ever saint or angel say that word as did my sweet lady? It fell as balm on the wounded spirit. "Not cruel. I . . . listen, love," . . . for indeed I was refusing to listen—"I would go through every pang of that time to gain what I have gained."

It was a spiritless questioning I undertook.

"What was your gain?"

"The Crown of Life: Love," she answered.

I had forgotten. It was a quest after Love I had been supposed to be sent forth on. I had not even once remembered it.

"I . . . have gained nothing," I answered.

"Ah, yes, you have." . . .

"What?"

"Knowledge." . . .

I was too weary for answer. I dropped my head upon her fair bosom. She understood, and presently we reclined on the slope together, I held fast in her arms, the soft air of summer wrapping us round, the trill of birds in our ear, the clear trickling of a brook close by. But what were they all to the loving embrace that held me: tender, true, for all the Eternity that lay before us?

We were *"as the angels of God."*

PART 5

"A thousand years is as a day."

It had seemed no more than a day, a too short day, till again the shadows were falling thick around me, and I stood alone with reluctant feet at the entrance to that world of darkness I had learned to name hell.

A force it was useless to resist was impelling me forward, and yet it was only to be met by sounds and sights that as strongly seemed to force me back at every step. Ah, for a door of escape! . . . And yet. . . . One glimmer of intelligence shone like a star in a dark firmament, where all was blackness before.

My Blessed Damozel had trodden every step of the way— nay, Christ Himself had trodden it. . . . I could never be as Christ, or even as my sweet lady, but there might be for me also sweet to be gained by the bitter.

I was moving ever down the slope, nearer and nearer to the black masses of people, deeper into the shadow of gloom, till I was at length myself one of the multitude that swayed this way and that, in the narrow alleys and in the open squares.

Caught into the stream, I had small time given me to think. There at my feet was a little child, disfigured, marred in visage, probably all that was criminal in embryo, but still a child, weak, helpless; and a reeling madman, emerging from the darkness, had his foot raised to kick. With the old cry of pain, I sprang to interpose, but it was only to discover what I had for the moment forgotten, that I was not now of Earth.

I could interpose no human body between; the child fell with a moan, and a passer-by lifted it, while another promptly implanted a blow on the drunken wretch, which he was too insensible to feel, I turned and fled. The old horrors of my night were indeed begun. It was as if all the peaceful homes were hidden from my sight, and light, a strange lurid light, that of itself lent a horrible clearness to the pictures, was poured down on every revolting sight that a city at its lowest can show. Nothing that was not of Earth, and already familiar to me through the newspaper columns of the day; it was only that the light detached them from the whole, and for a time I was made to see them, and only them, in a succession of horrors that was agonising.

Yes, they were all familiar.

That, before which I shrieked, would tomorrow be reported as a murder *"under peculiarly revolting circumstances;"* that which made me sicken to the verge of unconsciousness would be included in the annual statistics of the Society for Prevention of Cruelty to Children as one of the ten thousand cases that had been brought under their notice; and this, where I had stood at the girl's elbow, and wept, and implored her to turn from the temptation before her, would be mentioned as a sad case of suicide.

That fair young girl had moved me greatly. A cloud rested on her brain. Temporary illness had some months before stopped the weekly wage for which she worked, and, in her need, she had fallen behind in her payments. The burden of debt had ever since pressed heavily upon her; in the enfeebled state of her health, it had taken undue hold of her imagination, till now, with darkened vision, she stood like a creature at bay, on the brink of the Unknown.

"Help will come tomorrow," I had pleaded.

"There have been a great many tomorrows," had been her answer, "and no help came."

"They do not know," I pleaded, for the girl looked fiercely up at the gardened slopes where the helpers lay.

"They do not seek to know."

"Oh yes, they do. If I had known," . . .

"They know that we are here, and that we have not bread. They know that where there is not bread there is hunger, and sickness, and bitterness, and loss of self-restraint."

"They do not know that you have not bread."

But as I spoke, my confidence melted from me. I remembered that it was only the week before my illness, that I had sat at my comfortable drawing-room fire, brooding over the latest results of inquiries in East London. Twenty-five, if not thirty *per cent*, of the people living that day below the Poverty Line, one in four not knowing where 'Daily Bread' was to come from: one in every ten ' Very poor,' This very girl must have been one of these. I had had a week to do it in. Why had I not gone down on the spot into the dark gully, on whose banks we had builded our pleasant homes—why had I not gone down, and putting my arms round her, said to her, "Sister, you must know no more want, while I am here to share with you"?

O God, if I had but done it, if I could but do it now! No one could possibly object to charity like that; they could not say it was "demoralising." For that had been my great "problem" in these now far-off days. I laughed my problem to scorn as I stood close to my poor sister.

"Sweet, my love," I said to her, my whole heart going out in a strange yearning that it had never known before, "have patience but a little while. I know good women over there who would be shocked beyond measure if they thought you were on the point of taking away your own life, because of hunger, and cold, and misery. Let me but have time to go to them, and awake them from their slumber, and you will see what life can be yet."

She smiled bitterly at what she thought was her own better nature speaking.

"Ah, yes, I know well," she answered, with impatience in her voice, and her eye alight with a pained bewilderment, "that if I could bring myself to be a beggar and go from door to door, I should gather half-crowns in plenty; but '*to beg I am ashamed.*' . . Yet bread I must have or I cannot live. And my work does not suffice. My flesh fails for very weariness before I have coppers enough to buy more food to give strength for more work. Why should I go on? . . . I have none to care whether I live or die. . . . There is rest here!". . . pointing to the flood below.

"Oh, it is awful!" I said. "So much given, and yet blood at our doors."

"It is not money we want," she answered, almost fiercely, her intellect waking up with sudden flash to its clearest. "Yes, indeed, showers of half-crowns are falling, and the scramble for them is not good to see. More and more joining the clamouring crowd." . , . She suddenly laughed a horrible laugh. "Four coffins finding their way to one man's deathbed, sent by four different societies!—one will be enough for me. . . . Ah! I am sick, sick, weary of it all. The scramble for the falling coins, the 'crumbs from the rich man's table,' and those who have no heart or too much pride for the scramble . . . dying. Listen!" her eye gleaming fire, as she laid her hand on an imaginary listener—or was vision lent to her, that she could see as well as hear me?— "I tell you, tell you truly, what we want is not money but . . . Love. One loving woman to one struggling sister; one loving brother to one fallen comrade in the fight.

"One and one alone: caring as a sister would care, not once leaving her till she sees all her wrongs righted, or till her weakness or poverty is a thing of the past. Ah!" looking up to the gardened slopes, passionate pity gathering in her eyes, "were I ever to become rich, would it be possible for me, I wonder, to forget it all; to forget my toiling sisters, going wearily home after hours of sunshine spent in close rooms, home to bare meals, too tired to be amused, if there were amusement provided; only too thankful if kindly sleep await them, instead of perplexing care, care of how the week's debts are to be met? Would it be possible for me to forget, I wonder, that there must be many and many doing as I have so often done, toiling in spirit with the weary car horses, feeling that life with them and with me was much the same: on and on: the whip of want, if one threatens to stop?

"Ah! if I were but one of these," again looking up to the gardens above, tears in her voice and gathering in her eyes, "I would take one at least from this sorry den and make her life so fair for her; and she should know no want any more, nor care any more,—just as if I were her true sister,—nor bitterness of dependence, for there is no bitterness where Love is, nor shame of beggary. But . . . it is easy to dream dreams. If I were as they, I should no doubt grow self absorbed and self-sufficient even as they. Ah! . . . what nonsense it all is! Only, if my dream came to pass, there could be no talk then of 'over lapping Charity!'" and she laughed a laugh that was not good to hear. "Oh!" raising her hands to her head, "I shall be glad when my ears are deafened that I cannot hear; the mockery of it all is too great."

And once more there settled down upon her brain the cloud I now knew myself powerless to combat.

"Let me be your sister," I would fain have said; but I knew, before the words were spoken, that it was in vain.

My punishment was, that I could not give her help. My love and longing had come all too late.

Yet I had deemed myself a follower of Him who said: "*Love one another, as I have loved you.*"

I sought excuses. It was truly the sin of ignorance. My youth! . . . Had I then been so young? If one is not to rise to gracious womanhood in twenty-five years, when will the awakening come? I had surely not been too young to know what women of my own age were suffering.

"How old are you?" I found myself asking.

"Twenty-five. My birthday falls tomorrow."

Twenty-five, and weary of life: weary of disappointment rather; for of life, bright, beautiful, young life, with its joy in colour and movement, this sister of mine had known nothing.

Just then one passed close by us, in satin and pearls, with rouged cheek and glittering white teeth, that laughed us to scorn.

She was a *Nana*, let loose as a scourge on the weaklings of the day, scattering fortunes as a child scatters *bonbons*, sending youths forth stripped penniless, as the fruit of a week's folly; but for herself, all the pleasures a life of sin could give were hers. My companion lifted her head at sound of the laughter, and shuddered as she passed. There was again a flash of sanity.

"I was once as beautiful as she."

"But you were not tempted. . . ."

"Never. This," pointing to the flowing tide, "is better than that."

I stooped to hide the blinding tears.

"Sister! . . ." I said, "I am not worthy. . . . Ah! . . ."

She had not heard me. Like a bird she had flashed through the gloom into the tide below, and the water had opened to receive her.

What angel would greet *her* as she emerged from the mist? I thanked heaven that she went into God's good keeping, and, as the shrill laughter of the woman of sin came again on the still air, once more I thanked God for her. Turning slowly back to the crowded maze, with weeping eyes and humbled heart, I was conscious of a curious change in myself. What was it? The lagging step was gone, the intense unwillingness to move forward. The bitter outcry that the burden laid upon me was more than I could bear was no more. In its place there had come a strong impulse forward into the heart of the crowd; a great longing to take some one of them to me, the weaker the better, and push the way for him or her and myself out from the shadow into the light. I had forgotten even my Blessed Damozel in the strong interest that had sprung up in my heart. . . . Yes! in my heart, . . . that was then the secret.

My heart was awake . . . at last! Awake in its own regal right,

. . . asking nothing, . . . giving all. . . .

"And if I love thee, what is that to thee?" rang down a century's length and was understood.

And pity as an emotion was swallowed up in pity as a motive.

Instead of closing my ears to the continuous wail of pain, my eyes to the saddening sights, my arms seemed to stretch themselves out in pure yearning towards that sorrowing multitude, my feet were swift to take me into the heart of it.

One loving woman to one struggling sister! . . . that at least was within reach: to have her and hold her, and care for her and love her . . . for ever! That at least, . . . what more the future might unfold . . . I could leave.

Alas! I had forgotten, ... I was not of earth, and could help have come from heaven, these poor souls had been helped long ere now. No such heaven opened before me as I had been picturing. It was to be my fate to wander sadly, helpless, prayerful, in ever-present pain of powerlessness, among that weary multitude—suffering with them, learning from them, feeling myself unworthy to tie the shoe-latchet of the least of them.

It was they who were to save me, not I them.

Part 6

The sorrow was all gone from my sweet lady's eyes as they rested lovingly on mine. For the day had dawned once more, the shadows had melted away from about me, and I was standing in the early sunshine, my hands in hers, in a strong grasp of new strength and comradeship. Was I dreaming, or was that the same light of triumph on her countenance which had so impressed me in the dark-eyed saint who had led the little old lady of seventy to her Lord, and was she triumphing for me? . . .

But my heart was too full of enlarged life to allow me to linger for more than a moment on this new impression. I hastened to share it with her.

"Sweet sister, . . . " I did not notice the new equality. . . . "I have found it. I know . . . what it is to love."

The grasp on my hands grew tighter.

"And although there," glancing back, "and for a little time, it is indeed sorrow, . . . for all eternity it will be joy."

Ah! the deep, deep joy that glowed in the eyes of my listener!

"They are coming, are they not, . . . one by one; all those who have one spark of the Divine in them? And I know now why you pleaded for me so earnestly as my excuse that I had not known poverty, for indeed '*Hardly shall they that have riches enter into the Kingdom.*' It is poverty that has taught many of these poor souls that lesson of self-forgetfulness, which I altogether failed in learning. And sorrow is teaching others; and all, ... all except that lowest grade of all, that one in every hundred, which none yet have had power to raise or help—all are living nearer to the lessons of life, than are many of the dwellers at ease on the hillside."

No word would she speak in answer, but her look was eloquent of triumph at every word I spoke, and pleaded for more, . . . more. . . .

"Yes, they are surely closer to each other in their struggling and striving, failing and winning, than are the rich they envy. It is true, they stretch out weary limbs at night, and aching frames are laid on hard couches; but often and often, even then, their hearts 'make holiday.' For often, too tired to sleep, they allow their minds to dwell on the hard task completed, the righteous debt paid, want once more tided over for someone dearer than self! Yes, through it all, round the hearts of the loving among them—and there are many such— there never ceases to play that warmth of tender feeling, that only stern workers know who toil for those they love.

"Ah! to stand in the breach for the weak! . . . above all, for the weak that we love! . . . . I have learned, sweet sister, from that struggling multitude, that there is no joy on earth to compare with that; there is, there can be, no joy in earth or heaven greater than that." . . .

Upon which my Blessed Damozel loosened suddenly her

grasp of my hands, put her arms round my neck, and our lips met in a kiss that was full of promise. It told that we were one in intent and purpose: that we loved one another, but we loved humanity more; and the joy of the future would be, that, hand in hand, we would go forth together, as "ministers of grace" to "do His pleasure."

"God bless all those who are trying to add to the sum of human happiness; God bless all those who are trying to lessen the sum of human pain," had prayed Sunday after Sunday the clergyman of our parish.

Ah! we should be henceforth among "*the blessed of God*."

When she drew it back, my Blessed Damozel's face shone with such beauty that I found myself saying in fresh wonderment, "How very beautiful you are!"

She smiled. "Come," she said.

And she led me to a lake clear as crystal.

"Look."

I bent and saw reflected in it two faces side by side. One was that of my companion, smiling back at me with a beauty that again filled me with a great sense of gladness. I loved beauty. I loved her beauty.

Then I turned to the other, and as I looked my wonder grew and grew; and as my wonder grew, the eyes in the looking-glass we had found grew larger and softer and softer, till they filled with tears.

I . . . cannot be . . . like that." . . .

"You are like that," whispered my sister; "for that is '*the beauty of Holiness.*'"

"But I am not holy!" said I, in still deeper amazement.

"Holiness is . . . an Infinite Sympathy for others," she whispered again. "You remember?" . . .

Yes, I remembered a sister on Earth had spoken that, and I had thought it very beautiful.

While I was still pondering I felt my companion turn from me, and wafted on the soft air, there came from the direction in which she turned a distant sound of rejoicing.

I raised my head and turned with her. "What . . . is it?" I asked.

"The '*Songs of them that triumph,*'" said my Blessed Damozel, her eye lighting, her body swaying forward; '*the Shouts of them that feast,*' Hark! they are calling to us, calling to you and to me. . . . Come."

With a long, long sigh I was awaking.

Awaking to what? To the twilight of a darkened chamber, to the far, far-off sound of familiar voices: now to the sight of a familiar face.

It was the hospital nurse. She took my hand.

I could hear her speak. I could catch what she was saying.

"She is conscious, I am sure. She pressed my hand."

Another far-off voice: our clergyman's. "It was prayer that brought her back. For a moment the soul seemed separate from the body, but I was intent she should not die; with her powers, her riches, her youth, she had so much to do in the world yet. . . . I *would* not let her go."

I struggled for utterance.

"So much to do in the world yet! One loving woman to one struggling sister, . . . to have her and hold her, . . . and care for her and love her,—above all, . . . to love her . . . forever." . . .

"She is wandering again," said the nurse.

Was I wandering? Am I wandering still? . . . Has it been a dream, a dream and nothing more?

★★★★★★

To Mr Blackwood—Windsor 11th January [1895]
I send the proof corrected but pray don't publish it unless you think you can risk it. I should much prefer not putting any name, but if you prefer that I should take the responsibility, as is quite right, put the initials only. It seems to me however that any name would spoil the effect. It is sure to be attributed to me. My "Little Pilgrim" has never had my name, but nobody ever doubted that it was mine; and this too would be better for being without a name, but I leave it to you—nothing more than initials in any case . . passage from the *Autobiography and Letters* of Mrs Oliphant attributed to the above story.

A Visitor and His Opinions

CHAPTER 1

He came round the corner of the cliff suddenly, no step or rustle as of a wayfarer betraying him before he appeared, with something indefinable in his pose, as if he had just descended from a height, and a quick look around as at an unknown landscape quite new to him. It was near Dover, on the road that leads by the sea past the castle heights towards the town. A man more than ordinarily tall, of an imposing personality so far as could be seen in the darkening air, clothed not like the usual wayfarers on that road, but in long dark-coloured garments scarcely definable, different from ordinary English dress, though it was scarcely possible to say in what way.

His sudden appearance was very startling, as heralded by no sound or step, to the one or two people going in the other direction who met him without any warning, and started aside a little to make way for him without well knowing why. The covering on his head was like a closefitting Spanish cap, but enveloped with filmy folds of something dark which made it resemble a turban—all vague, however, in the ever decreasing light. Something shone in the front of this cap, vague also, like a faint star among clouds, or the gleam of one of those little electric lamps that are now so much in use on the stage.

It flashed in the eyes of a man on the road and dazzled him so that he had almost fallen over the cliff, though the other with whom he was walking saw nothing at all, but asked, "What light? I saw no light," when his companion cried out. The passenger, however, neither paused nor questioned, but walked on, with an exceedingly light firm step, and a certain air of noting everything about him, though he did not stop to look either to the right or left. He went on into the town, keeping his way straight, crossing streets, and even the railway itself, without the faintest hesitation or alarm, with the air of one whom neither train nor heavy waggon could hurt, as if he could have wafted them all away by his breath or a wave of his hand. And this air of quietness, of calm assurance as if nothing could harm him, was very impressive, and made people turn to look after him as he went swiftly, lightly past them. Who was he? One knows that princes are not greater to look at, larger, stronger, more power-ful, or even more imposing in aspect, than other men; yet there is a certain tradition of grandeur lingering about the name, so that several people said, "He looks like a prince," as this man went by.

He went to the great hotel, the Lord Warden which we all know, and where, as he rose into the light ascending the steps, much curiosity was excited, and a sudden pause occurred in the little bustle of people coming and going. It was such a pause as might occur if somebody had suddenly said, "The Prince of Wales is coming": the porters and other attendants backed into corners, the manager came forward bowing low, and rubbing his hands nervously and the guests in the hotel drew aside in little clusters, gazing at the newcomer, who, though he had no-body to announce him, and came forward attended by no suite or servants, made this curious impression on all who saw him. He came up to the obsequious manager, with again one almost imperceptible flash of a look round, which took in everything as everybody felt—a true prince's look, which in a moment rec-ognises whoever there may, be who is known; but there did not seem to be anyone here known to this great personage.

He said a few words to the manager in a tone which was not German or any accent we are used to, but yet not English ei-ther—in a large sonorous voice which gave a thrill to everyone standing by. The manager bowed more and more, till he seemed almost doubled in two. "It is all right, sir—your Highness—my lord," he said: and instead of calling any inferior, took up suddenly a pair of silver candlesticks in which the candles had just been lighted for some other guest, and himself went mounting backwards very uncomfortably up the stair, showing the way. The prince, or whatever he was, smiled, and said, "Walk, sir, as nature intended you."

These words were heard by everybody, They were not very extraordinary in the way of words; but yet they were repeated in the most curious way from one to another, as if they had possessed the most remarkable meaning. "I heard him say it with my own ears," various people said afterwards, as if they had been made partakers of some great axiom of wisdom. It was to the best apartment in the house that the about stranger was led—a spacious sitting-room, with large windows looking out upon the Channel, which that night was "dirty," flustered by big waves with white tops which rose and fell, making a fine effect to those who viewed it from the security of the shore.

The room was dark, save for these two twinkling lights and the broad spaces of window through which shone the last of the twilight, and the clearness of a windy sky, and the glimmer and weltering light of the sea. "Your Highness had, I fear, a bad passage," said the manager: he paused a moment for a reply, and then added, "But the luggage and your Highness's servant arrived all right."

At the same time another figure appeared in the doorway between the sitting room and a bedroom opening from it. No doubt about this individual. A well-bred valet, gentleman's gentleman, grave, respectful, point-devise. He had a letter in his hand. "From Lord Hillesborough, sir," he said, at first with less awe than had been hitherto shown at the sight of the stranger; but on the second look at this majestic figure, half visible, with the light of the candles behind him, even Jerningham felt a thrill "I was to wait your—your Highness here," he said, faltering as he drew back within the door.

"You will have the goodness to call me Sir only; I am not

accustomed to titles," said the stranger. Sir! to be sure! that was what it was right to say to the Prince of Wales himself. Not accustomed to titles! Was he perhaps, then, a king *incognito?* It appeared more like that than anything else to these two persons, accustomed to all the laws of service. Highness, though it means a great deal to other men, would not mean much to a king. To him it would mean a derogation, a sort of disrespect, though unintentional. Sir was the title for him—spelt with an "e" at the end, and not pronounced exactly as the English monosyllable is. Sire—it was pronounced Seer the manager was aware, who knew a little of all the languages of the Continent.

He made a lower bow than ever, backing and bowing himself out of the room, murmuring "Yes, Sire," as he went. As for Jerningham, his soul owned a thrill of alarm to feel himself left alone with this wonderful person, king or potentate. "A gentleman of great distinction," he was told, had engaged him; a foreign gentleman, not accustomed to English ways. This is not a description which usually fills the English domestic with the graces of humility. It is difficult for him not to despise a personage, however exalted, who is ignorant of English ways. But, though there was an outlandish look about this one, for once Jerningham was really overawed. He retreated from the doorway, and began to occupy himself with unpacking his new master's luggage; but after a time his curiosity overcame him, and he peeped through the chink of the door to see what 'E was about.

And indeed nothing could be more curious than what he was about. He had taken the letter to read it, not to the light of the candles, which burned all by themselves as though nobody wanted them upon the table, but to the window, where he stood reading it in the dark. No, not exactly in the dark either—a soft light fell about him, showing the whiteness of the letter and the attitude of his head bent to read it; a light that seemed suffused over his figure and the very part of the carpet he stood upon, and to shine in the panes of the window against the darkness that was in them from outside. What was it? Had he a taper, then, or some travelling-lamp, or—what? At this point in Jerningham's curious self-inquiries his new master turned his head half round, and the man felt as if he were being looked at with a sort of mild observant smile, though it could only have been through the woodwork of the door, or the wall itself, which was impossible—for that barrier of physical obstruction was between the gazer in the one room and the sudden observation of the personage in the other.

The effect, however, was so real, that Jerningham retreated to the farther corner of the bedroom and turned his face to the wall, and covered it with his hands to escape the sudden sensation. Yet the look which he thought he felt (which was ridiculous, impossible!) was not a severe look but a smiling one,—a look full of indulgence, as if for the error of a child, though so penetrating. Jerningham persuaded himself afterwards that it was that dashed taper or lamp, or whatever it was, by which the prince was reading his letter, which caught a reflection in his own eye through the chink of the door. But anyhow he did not venture to pursue his own observations any further.

The letter thus read was remarkable in tone, being as it was a letter from an old and distinguished English peer to a man much younger than himself, and, though so remarkable in appearance, coming so suddenly and with so little pretension upon the scene. It was in the most respectful terms, almost more than his own native prince would have called forth from so eminent a subject, though there were no titles of honour employed:

> I have endeavoured to carry out your wishes in the most complete manner in my power, though our arrangements here are necessarily all so incomplete, so little perfect, that I fear you will scarcely be able to understand that I have really done everything I could, remembering your command that there was to be no shutting out of the common conditions of our life, and that your desire, which it is the highest pleasure and honour to me to obey, was to see these conditions in their most simple form. I wish I could hope that the sight would give you any satisfaction; but I await with the most eager anxiety your permission

to arrange my poor house here for your reception, with a trembling hope that perhaps the rural life amid which we live, though still so unlike everything you have ever known, will not seem to you so terrible and repulsive as I feel with humiliation that which you have now come into must be.

The man whom I have sent is likewise according to your command, neither better nor worse than the ordinary. I could have selected a man of higher character so far as our imperfect knowledge goes, but it appeared to me that this would not be according to the sentiment you had expressed nor the object which you pursue. With what anxiety, what hopes, and what fears, I follow your course in my thoughts, I will not attempt to express: and I should add with what sympathy—were the word such as I could venture to use in the comparison between your elevated nature and that which is the inheritance of one who is always your devoted and most humble servant,

Hillesborough.

Signed below this name was a cipher in strange lettering like a second name. The stranger put down the letter on the table, still with the same smile upon his lip which he had turned upon Jerningham—a look as of indulgence, understanding everything, not unaware of feebleness, of something mingled in the respect, perhaps of a tone of obsequiousness, perhaps of an overstrain of effort—but accepting all with a benignancy which had no criticism in it. Presently he took off the covering from his head, which had the most curious shadowy appearance in the half light, as if the filmy drapery round it were a pair of folded wings, and the soft light that fell round him came from between them like the shining of a star.

The last hypothesis was not unjustified, as he took something from among the folds which caused an instant displacement of the lights and shadows about him. What it looked like was a large diamond set in something dark and indefinite, with a white rim as of silver round this strange little lamp of light separating it from the darkness below and around. He put it down upon the table, replacing upon his head the hat or turban upon which the downy dark wings seemed to close more distinctly than ever. It appeared to be habitual to him to have his head covered. He turned back after he had done this to the from the window—the dark sea view tossing its waves, the spray dashing upon the rocks and piers, the long weltering of the ridges of sea as they rose and fell, the lights in the harbour sinking and rising, the shadow of the cliff wrapping everything in deeper darkness. It seemed to have a great fascination for him.

During the course of the evening he turned to it again and again, as if with a sensation of relief, perhaps feeling that nature and even storm were more congenial than the surroundings of man. But he was not disposed to separate himself so far as would appear from the life going on around him. He looked at the clothes which Jerningham had arranged for him, spreading them out on the bed, with again a smile. "This is the dress of England?" he said, with the little accent which not unpleasantly pointed him out as not an Englishman. Jerningham by this time had recovered his self-possession. "Not of England, sir," he said; "but for the evenin', as far as I've 'eard, the costoome of all the civilised world."

"Is it so?" said the prince, with an amused look. He added, "Is it much remarked when a stranger continues to wear the dress of his own country here?"

"Oh, not at all, sir," cried Jerningham, with a sort of patronage and condescension to ignorance. "There was the Indian princes at the Jubilee in all colours, and blazing with jewels, as the papers said. It was pecooliar, but it was admired. The ladies, they liked it," he added, perceiving that his new master, now that he saw him more closely, was still a young man. "If I might make so bold as to ask," he said, after a moment's silence, "what was your 'Ighness's country, sir?"

"I do not think," said the stranger, "that I will change my dress tonight. Do you belong to this country? have you relations with the people here? do you think you could act as my guide?"

"My last place was 'ere, sir," said Jerningham, in a slightly alarmed tone. "I was in the commandant's service; and though I've no relations, yet I can find my way about. There ain't, however, as you might say, very much to see in a place like this,— nothing except the castle, and—and the cliffs, and—" Jerningham ended abruptly, constrained by his new master's eye.

"Some thousands of people," said the prince. "I wish to see them. Can you guide me to the places where they live? Men— and women—are what I want to see."

Jerningham looked up with a sudden leer in his eye. "O—oh!" he said. His glance told that he divined in his master a hypocrite of the foulest tastes hidden under this guise of gravity, and that his mind was somewhat relieved by the discovery. He put his hand over his mouth to conceal his suppressed laugh. "I can show your 'Ighness—what we calls life, sir," he said.

His master looked at him with a mild severity which betrayed no anger, yet, if that were possible to a countenance so full of intelligence, something like a want of understanding. It was the look of an acute observer confronted with something which was a puzzle to him, and called all his faculties into exercise. The mean perplexes the noble as much as the noble disturbs the mean. He did not understand.

"We will go at once," he said.

"Lord!" said Jerningham to himself, "ain't he hot on it!" He was pleased to guide a prince to see life, but there were preliminaries which he felt ought not to be neglected. "If I might make so bold, sir," he said, "won't your 'Ighness dine first? After your 'Ighness's journey—"

"I will go at once," his master repeated, with the air of a man not accustomed to be contradicted; and turning round, walked towards the door.

"Sir!" said Jerningham. "The weather is a bit cold. Your 'Ighness will put on a big coat at least over your costoome!"

"Put on a coat yourself, my good fellow," said the prince, benignantly. "Thank you for thinking of my comfort. I shall not feel the cold."

He went out without another word, followed by Jerningham, struggling into a greatcoat behind him, with haste and difficulty, not daring to keep this wonderful person waiting. As they went downstairs the same phenomena occurred as before. The people about the hall of the big hotel, though they were people in some cases thinking no little of themselves, drew back upon each other with the same impulse as moved the busy porters and waiters, and left a clear path for the Stranger and his attendant. The manager bowed to the ground, rubbing his fat hands obsequiously, but caught at Jerningham as he passed with an eager demand, half in pantomime, half in a whisper, "Won't the prince dine?" Jerningham answered in the same way, "He'll do as he likes, and there's no orders." He was a little put out, as well as the manager, about this unordered dinner; for if the prince was not hungry after his journey, Jerningham was, though he had made no journey: and the valet was fond of taking his ease in his inn.

He hurried, however, after the tall figure which went on in front of him, towards the lights of the town. Dover is not a well-lighted town. The twinkles of lamps made the darkness visible, and almost increased the danger of the path across the railway and all the intricacies of the streets, though in the darker parts Jerningham grew curiously aware of a light that seemed diffused around them, of which he could not tell where it came from, but which certainly was there. The darkest corners were somehow lighted by it, so that even Jerningham did not stumble and kick his shins, and the prince marched forward as if he had known the way all his life; but the man could not tell where it came from, and afterwards got into so dazed a condition from the various surprising incidents of the night that he ceased to remember that strange preliminary, though at first he was constantly turning round, gazing about, and even looking overhead to discover where it came from.

When they came into a street full of flares of gas, many of them unprotected and waving in the breeze, and where all the traffic of a Saturday night was going on,—outside stalls and little booths with their set out of provisions, red-and-white joints of beef, high coloured in the flare, deep green piles of vegetables,—the prince walked up and down several times together, now on the lighted side, where all the people were hustling each other, now on the darker pavement opposite, where everything appeared as in a phantasmagoria, the waving flame of the coarse lights, the incessant movement of the shadows, the din of the cries filling the night air with uproar. This was not what Jerningham believed his master desired, and he would have led him by a cross street in another direction but for the wave of his hand, which stopped all explanation.

There was a man half lying in a wheelbarrow towards the middle of the road, in the way the carts and carriages which of passed infrequently. He had something to sell half crushed under him where he lay, but he was past thinking of anything to sell. Whether he was ill or drunk was a difficult question. Jerningham unhesitatingly gave it, however, in favour of the latter, especially when his master stopped beside this partially perceptible figure, which suddenly yet softly became quite visible, showing a face stupefied and sodden, though whether with work or beer, or the sleepiness of fatigue, it was impossible to say. The man was roused, but writhed and twisted himself uncomfortably, as unwilling to be so brought out of his half-unconsciousness; but it was he who spoke first, struggling up out of his prostrate condition, and crushing the shell-fish over which he was lying as he raised himself on his elbow. "Who are you? and what do you want with me?" he said.

"Get up," said the stranger, "and take me to your home."

"My 'ome?" said the seller of shell-fish: but he got clumsily to his feet. "Don't you shine your lantern into my eyes," he said, "I've got no 'ome."

"Take me to the place where you live," the master said again.

"What do you want with the place where I lives? I lives no where to speak of—where I can, one time one place, one time another; and no good for me to go there at all, if I don't sell my

312

winkles and get a somethin' to tide over Sunday. Hey! I say, don't turn on that blasted lantern. Come on, then, I'll go if I must, and you'll just hear what *she* says."

Jerningham found himself after this, with a humiliation not to be described, walking along the flaring street, a wretched barrow trundling in front of him, and a still more wretched man. He had dreamed of something very different,—oyster-bars and strange expensive drinks, and smiles—that could be purchased too. The man with the barrow might be what his master understood by life; but Jerningham's ideas were not of that kind. They went on to the veriest slums—not to the quarters lit with fitful luxury to which Jerningham had intended to introduce his master. And as they went there ran on a sort of monologue of grumbling talk from the costermonger who was their guide.

"Nice streets these are for a man to be trundling about at this hour o' the night, where there's not a soul to buy a penn'orth, and not a copper in my pocket, s'help me——! Oh, I knows better. Ye needn't ask me! I knows country roads that are deeper in the mud, and more quiet still; and I knows London. London's what I like. Ye can lose yourself There, and none knows if ye're a man or just a bit of the whole blasted thing as is a-going round and round. If ye drops it don't matter, and if ye goes on it's all the same."

"And what has brought you to this?" said the clear voice which sounded over the head of the crouched-up, shambling creature. He gave a side-look up towards his questioner's face, then blinked and shrank again.

"Where have you got your bull's-eye thing as blinds a man a-flashing in his eyes? What's brought me to this? How d'ye know as I wasn't always like this, crying winkles about the streets? Well, I wasn't, and that's the fact, however ye've found it out. It's a many things, if ye will know. My folks was very respectable once. I was put to school and went to church and all that, and wore as good clothes as—you do. Lord! but you've got queer clothes on: I never had no outlandish rig like that. You're a furreeneering chap, I suppose! and what do ye want putting questions to me?"

313

"I want to know what has brought you to this." The stranger had the calm of power in his voice. He made no explanations, and there was no capability of resistance in the individual whom he questioned,—at least in the present case.

"Well," said the man, defiantly; "chief thing, I suppose, is drink. I was a silly when I was young—thought a poor chap could be like a gentleman, and take his pleasure 'stead o' working, working like a mole. And then came bad company, and then—Lord! when anything's happened to you as makes you miserable, there's nothing like a drop o' drink. Good folks they think it's your bad 'eart, as if a man wisht to get dead drunk and tumble about the streets. What a man wants is to forget hisself and all his trouble; to get lifted up as if he could fly; to have a dazzle in his eyes that makes everything grand. If it makes ye miserable in the end, I'm not denyin' of it; but at fust beginning it's a prince it makes ye, as if ye could fly over all the world.

"And then there's other things," said the man, pausing upon his barrow, standing still as in a reflective mood. The stranger stood like a tower immovable by his side, pausing when he paused; while poor Jerningham, indignant beyond words, not only to be in such company but to be forced to stand and listen, drew back as far as he could from this ridiculous group. The light, whatever it was—concealed lantern or bull's-eye— shone upon the costermonger's face, lighting it up with a soft ray. "Lord! when I think what a fool I was!—I thought as I'd always be a young chap able to take my fling: and I thought as being a silly one day was nothing again' going straight the next Nor it ain't neither, that's a fact, still," he added, vehemently, "so long as a man can keep his 'ead."

"Then some men, you think," said the stranger, "do keep their heads."

The man paused a moment reflectively, and then he burst into a harsh laugh. "Fact," he said, shaking his head. "I don't know as many does. There's a fellow I know as makes believe, and lies low and gets the tin out of poor chaps like me when they has a shilling to spend. That's one thing as brought me to this pass, as you're so curious wanting to know. And then there's the missus—as aggravates a man with her tongue and her sharpness and naggin', till ye don't mind a bit what ye do."

"The missus—that means that you have a wife? how in this state of wretchedness could you bind another being to yours?"

"Wretchedness!" said the man, so stimulated by this reproach that he sprang to his barrow and pushed on so quickly that Jerningham, proudly paying no attention, was left behind, and had almost to run to keep up with his master's accompanying stride. "I wish you'd talk of what you know, master! She ain't no more wretched, I can tell you, for being along o' me. Wretched yourself! and ye ain't no 'appier than the rest of us, I'll go any money, if the truth was known! Bless you," he said, dropping out of his momentary indignation into more ordinary tones, "we weren't like this neither her nor me when we come together. I was a young chap, earning a good wage when I was steady, and she was a young lass as—as wasn't for any man to turn up his nose at.

"Lord! she was a tidy one when we come together first! and nice spoken when her back wasn't up: but always a bit hasty in the temper, ready to give ye a kiss or a blow, As for wretched, you keep them big words to yourself, master! Jyane, I believe, if you ast her, she'd rather have me and my barrow than many a man as drives his own cart: for I'm a good tempered one, I am, and takes a deal of worritin' afore I answers back; and as for liftin' my hand upon her, much less my boot, as some chaps do, that's a thing as never happens——'cept now and again, when I'm devilled with the drink."

"But how was it," said the stranger, "when you were once young and earning a good wage, and she once so tidy and pleasant,—how was it that you did not continue so? You knew that the drink would harm you, did you not? and you knew that your bad company would make you bad too? and you knew that quarrels would spoil your comfort, and idleness would stop your wages? How was it, then?—how was it?"

The costermonger stopped again: he sat down upon the shafts of his barrow to reflect. "Blessed if I know," he said. "Lord!

I've said all that to myself many a day, but it ain't done no sort of good. Always seems, somehow, as if the wrong thing was the most fun. Governor! don't you say you don't know that, for I knows human nature, and I wouldn't believe you,—not I."

"You thought it over, then?" said the questioner: there was no blame in his voice,—it was the voice of an inquirer anxious to know. "There were times when you stopped and regretted, and wished to turn back to the other way?"

"You don't speak like a parson," said the man. "I donow what kind of a bloke you are. You don' seem somehow as if you was a tryin' to ketch a chap up. Sartain sure as I thought it over many a day. And we've kissed and made friends, Jyane and me: and we've said we'd never do it no more: but, Lord, afore you're six steps from your own door there's a chap coming along as says, 'Hallo, Joe! goin' to work o' Monday mornin' like you was the boss his-self. Man! I'll not believe it of you. There's some fun agoin' on down the street. Come you along o' me.' And p'raps you stops a moment and jaws, and says he'd best go to work himself, 'stead of stoppin' them that means better: but, Lord! it always ends the same way," he added, starting off with his barrow again. "You thinks it's just for once, and you goes. And then you wishes you had cut your throat sooner.

"And then you feels as if you'd choke the missus afore she gets out one of her burnin' blazin' words. Well! one thing as I can say is this—that it ain't them as preaches as suffers for it, but you yourself. And that it ain't never done o' purpose as they thinks, but just as you says to yourself for once and accidental-like. Lord! don't you think I'd rather have a good coat to my back, and a good supper to go 'ome to, 'stead of wheelin' a bar-row full o' dashed winkles as I hain't sold and ain't likely to, and not a copper in my pockets to give the missus for tomorrow as is Sunday?—which is your fault, master, now I comes to think of it, draggin' me out of the market where I could have got rid of every shell o' them, sure as I'm alive."

"'Old your tongue," said Jerningham, glad of an opportunity to display his disgust. "You were lying there drunk and smashing the winkles when you were spoke to by—a gentleman as—didn't ought to touch with the tongs a drunken beast like you!"

"Ho!" cried the costermonger, quick as fire, letting down the shafts of the barrow, and turning upon his new assailant; "you're agoin' it too? but I ain't that low down as I'll take abuse from the likes of you."

Jerningham, who really was the person to be pitied, having his personal dignity so sadly disturbed by such associations, only saved himself by jumping back from the sudden blow levelled at him. But the costermonger's wrath lasted only for a moment. The prince laid his hand on the man's arm, and he calmed at once by an influence which he understood as little as it was contrary to the circumstances altogether. He took up the shafts of his barrow again in haste and silence. And the strange party proceeded without a word through one dark street after another. Yet it was not dark around them. The dark atmosphere of the night, and the thick air contaminated by all the emanations of the crowding miserable houses, seemed just then to be softly cleared, illuminated by a vague radiance scarcely enough to be called light,—something softly diffused coming from no point like a lamp or lantern, but moving with them, wrapping them in a tempered warmth and softness.

The tall figure of the stranger was the least revealed of the three. He moved like a shadow, towering over them—a presence always felt yet vaguely seen. Thus they came at last to the court, opening off a little dingy street, where the seller of shell-fish lived. It was a sort of square of dingy houses, each with light in its windows, which filled the ill-smelling enclosure with a sort of squalid cheerfulness, in which, late as it was, children were still playing, and women keeping up a noisy conversation from the doors. The din, the closeness, and the smells quite overcame Jerningham, who was not accustomed, as he said afterwards, to no such slums. He fell back, his devotion to his new master being insufficient to make up for the injury to his feelings. "I'll be handier here, sir, to call the police, in case you should meet with anything as is disagreeable," he said.

"Quite right. I approve your prudence—and thought for me," said the prince, looking upon him with that smile which made Jerningham so uncomfortable.

"I wish, sir,—I do wish as your 'Ighness would be guided by me, and not risk yourself in no such places," cried the valet in his irritation. His master only laughed: this was all the answer Jerningham received.

And then there rose a tumult in the court,—one of the women darted out from her door, a fury with wild hair flying, with a wild flutter of ragged clothes, and a shawl on her shoulders, from which she flung forth her arms, the heavy drapery lending force to her fierce gesticulations. "You've been at it again, you drunken beast! you blasted fool! you darned ass !—you! you! you!" with each an epithet, she cried. "He's got them all still in the barrow, as I gave him the money to buy for a last chance. And here he's back without a penny, and my last shillin' gone to the dogs like all the rest, and nothin' left to buy a bite for the children—and it Satterday night! Oh! oh! oh!" she burst out in a wild mingled outburst of rage and tears, flying at the throat of the man. The stranger stopped her in full career with his hand upon her shoulder, but she did not yield to his influence so quickly as the man.

She struggled under his touch, tore herself away, and once more flung herself upon her husband who had seated himself on his barrow, with screams of rage and misery. A mingled din of approval and disapproval came from the lookers-on. "I don't wonder at her, poor lass, after all as she's had to bear," said one woman, who seemed to be on the outlook also for an errant husband; but, "Lord! she's got to put up with it, and why can't she take it easy?" said a matron, amiably tipsy, on another door-step, "Jyane, Jyane, you'll be sorry after!" said a third, interfering; "and 'im never lifting a hand!"

The stranger drew near the group again. He put his hand once more on her shoulder, and drew her away. "Is this the woman," he said, "that was so tidy when they came together, and so nice-spoken? and that a man loved? And what has brought

318

her to this pass?"

The woman turned upon him, struggling still. "And who told you that?" she shrieked,—"for you don't know me, nor I you. Tidy—and that a man loved! Look at him now—is that a man?"

"What has brought you," he said, "to this pass ?—you that were once sweet and young."

The woman stared in his face, but could not see it, while hers was clear, the seat of many passions, convulsed and struggling. "Let me go!" she cried. "I'll tear his eyes out, and no person shall stop me. Young! I'm not old yet, to be treated like that. Oh! if I was once tidy and nice-spoken, who's done it? I'm better than he is. I thinks of my children, I'm not—so bad as he."

"What has brought you to this pass?" the prince repeated, with his voice of perfect calm.

The woman flung herself down upon the dirty pavement, and covered her face with her hands.

CHAPTER 2

Jerningham had much of the same sort of annoyance to bear during the first month or two of his service with the mysterious prince. He was made the purse-bearer, which was some slight compensation (indeed on that first never-forgotten Saturday night he was called to pay for the barrow of winkles, and thus smooth down the tumult of the moment between the costermonger and his wife). His master showed a singular indifference to money, which he never touched or had any dealings in, bidding Jerningham do what was necessary whenever there was any question of payment, with a confidence which seemed to proceed rather from a certain contempt for that medium than from any well-founded trust in the man who had been recommended to him as an ordinary man and nothing more. In this situation of dignity, however, the servant accompanied his master through many strange scenes.

He went with him to London, and to many places there where Jerningham would willingly have followed, or even led his lord with very different aims from those which the prince seemed to pursue. And, indeed, the prince's aims were not very easy to fathom. He was not a charity organiser, nor an almoner, nor a missionary. He gave, or rather ordered Jerningham to give, money freely on occasion; but this was certainly not his object. He went everywhere with the same inquiry on his lips, "What has brought you to this pass?" and he put it to everybody, sometimes in the most astonishing circumstances, addressing people who it might have been thought would have knocked him down for his impertinence, or at least resented it in some unequivocal way.

But though they might be angry at first, they always ended by telling some story of strange things unlike those appearances which met the eye. One of the persons, for instance, thus interrogated was the clergyman of a large parish, a man full of good deeds, who was very indignant with the words—"this pass?" What pass was the excellent rector in, whose hands were only too full of everybody else's business, who was the Providence of so many? He had looked contemptuously, indignantly at his questioner, with a scorn of him as an unauthorised busybody which was most natural. But then a spell had fallen over that good clergyman.

"How did I come to this pass? full of tickets and cases to examine, and subscriptions to be got? How can a man help it? You go out full of faith, and the first person you meet with cheats you, and turns your very heart. Then you rush to the other side and trust nobody; and the first thing you hear is that you have helped to starve some real sufferer. Then one gets wild for a time; and at the last you come to feel there's no confidence to be put in anything but figures and cases, and cut and dry machinery. There was a time when I was—a young fool; thinking everything was to be done by reasoning with them, and persuading them, and showing your affection. Ah, that's the grand principle still! the love of God, and the sympathy of our Lord. But then one drifts into the organisation tickets, and elections to hospitals, and so forth. Regret it? ah, that I do with all my heart! If I were a young man again I'd stick to the higher principle: but what can a poor parson do that has to make the best he can of his parish, and keep all his charities going?"

There was never any reproof in the prince's eyes: he heard this, and a hundred other strange avowals, with a calm which was never broken, and he was unwearied in hearing them, going about the world everywhere, inquiring from every man the secret of his divergence. He took no notes of these many and varied cases: of the women who began with protestations of having been deceived, then, in the light of his steadfast eyes, burst forth into wailing plaints of folly, of the heedless rush into temptation, the fall, half invited, half defied; or the merchant who had meant no harm, who had staked his friend's credit for something which only an accident prevented from becoming his friend's advantage instead of hurt; or the servant who borrowed from his master, meaning nothing but to repay. Over all these persons and hundreds more the light which it was so difficult to define suffused itself, never failing although the sun might.

Jerningham made out at last by much study that it proceeded from somewhere just over his master's head, for it lighted up the faces of those who were before him, and kept himself in a curious depth of shadow, so that the most earnest gaze fixed upon him could scarcely penetrate that dimness. There were many things in Jerningham's mind as he thus attended upon his master. A strong curiosity in the first place. He could not in any way fathom this man. It was not for charity he went about the world, though sometimes he would be very charitable—so charitable that Jerningham thought that it was nothing but proper in the circumstances to take toll: nor was it for any pleasure to himself that the valet could understand. For what was the good of collecting all these stories?

The prince never talked of them, so far as Jerningham knew; it was not for the sake of gossip. Nor did he seem to intend to write a book, for he never put pen to paper, never wrote a letter. The problem was one which could not be explained in any way. And there were a great many mysterious things about the master to whose service he had been sent by so unexceptionable a nobleman as the Earl of Hillesborough. He had evidently plenty of money, which was left in Jerningham's hands, and which he himself never looked at. The prince lived as if there were no such thing as money in the world. When there was anything to pay he looked at Jerningham, and that was all that was necessary. Jerningham had pretty pickings, it must be allowed.

He did not rob his master, nor permit anyone else to do it, but he took a percentage for his trouble: this appeared to him perfectly right and justifiable, He did not, indeed, intend to do anything of the kind when he began. He had always been honest, he said to himself, and he never meant to be otherwise. But a percentage, that was allowed everywhere when a man had so much trouble as he had—a trouble which had never been mentioned or thought of when he was engaged. Another thing was that, as the prince did not wear the beautiful clothes that had been provided for him, preferring his own "costoome," as Jerningham said, it seemed wiser that the valet should wear some of them than that they should be thrown away. Jerningham wore the coats to keep the moth out of them. He put on one on a certain day with this excellent object, and another day he put on another.

The prince was larger than he, and much taller, yet somehow they all fitted Jerningham. It could do them nothing but good should the master finally make up his mind to put them on, that they should be worn to air them now and then. With all these things Jerningham did very well for himself and harmed nobody, as he himself believed. It did not occur to him that his master might one day turn upon him with his usual inquiry, "What has brought you to this pass?" and that he might be compelled to reveal everything. This pass! he was in no pass! he was doing nothing wrong. And as for any interrogation from his master, he made very light of that. The prince did not observe any of these things. In short, Jerningham came by degrees, notwithstanding the mystery that surrounded him, to have on the whole a considerable deal of good-humoured contempt for his prince.

There was one thing, however, about which he continued to be so very curious that he felt no effort to be too great to find it out. And that was, as has been said before, the mysterious light which accompanied his master everywhere. It flashed upon him suddenly at last what it was. Going into the prince's room one evening in the twilight, he was astonished and blinded by the light which shone from a table at which his master had been sitting,—a light almost level with the table, proceeding from one central point. Jerningham drew near upon the tips of his toes, though the prince was not there. He saw then, to his amazement, that it was a jewel in a curious dark setting covered with strange signs—but it was not the setting or the signs that moved him. It was the diamond!—such a diamond as he had never in his life beheld before.

You may think he was not likely to have had much experience in diamonds; but Jerningham had been in good places all his life, and had seen a great deal of jewellery in his day, though never, never anything like this! It was of the size of a small watch, and as it lay there on the table seemed to represent wealth itself incarnate, fortune and all it brings—quite unprotected, within the reach of any chance person that might come into the room. A flood of indignation rushed through Jerningham's mind at the rashness of his master, who could go and leave such a prize as that open upon the table. He bent over it to look at it, but it so blazed into his eyes that they were dazzled and could see nothing. Lord! what a thing to see lying on a table within reach of your hand—worth thousands and thousands, enough to make a man comfortable for life: comfortable! more than that,—rich, like a prince.

Jerningham made a rapid calculation in his mind how a man—not himself! oh, not himself! but any man might dispose of such a thing. It would be difficult to do, for diamonds of that size are not common anywhere; but no doubt, at least in foreign parts, it could be done. And a man could get away to Holland or some such place before ever anybody knew anything about it. From London a man can get off anywhere, These thoughts flew through Jerningham's mind with a sort of rush of moral indignation to think how easily it might be done, and how any man could do it. He put out his hand, not without alarm, to touch the wonderful thing which was worth, he said to himself almost bitterly, far more than all a man even in a good service could lay up in his life; but as he was about cautiously to lift it he heard the prince's step returning to the room, and fled precipitately, fearing to be asked what he was doing there. This was all that happened the first time.

But it appeared that the prince, always a strange person in all his habits, had a fancy for reading by the light of his great diamond, and Jerningham saw it many times after this. He began vaguely to define also, after many questions with himself where his master had hitherto hidden it, to make out, putting one thing to another, that this blazing orb of light was in reality no other than the shining jewel which he had hitherto thought no bigger than a glow-worm, which shone among the filmy folds of the prince's headgear when he was out of doors.

This made it more wonderful still to think that it could contract and then magnify itself in this way; but Jerningham soon came to the conclusion that its contraction must be caused by some peculiarity in its setting, which partially covered it when worn, and subdued its size and splendour. His mind grew more and more full of this diamond as time went on. He had been so angry at the thought that some one might steal it and escape to Holland with it, that it would be wrong to imagine he had any intention of committing such a crime: and yet his mind was full of the diamond by night and by day.

One night, he could scarcely tell how, he found himself at a late hour in the prince's room. Among his other habits was one of walking late, and so far as Jerningham was aware, his master was out, though he had represented to himself that he had heard the bell, and that this was the reason why he made his way thither at so late an hour. He was curious to know also (he said to himself) whether the prince went out with so valuable an ornament in his hat, alone, and at night, which would have been so foolish a thing to do.

Jerningham's heart gave a jump when he saw the blaze of the jewel on the table. The rest of the room, the bed and the large space behind, lay in total darkness, but a luminous circle was drawn round the table upon which the diamond lay. He paused a moment, his heart beating loud, and then he drifted silently, moving, as he afterwards said, by some sort of compulsion, not by his own will at all, into this circle of light. His face was a sight to see as he came within the range of the illumination out of the shadowy gloom in which all things are softened. It was blazing with excitement, with eager cupidity, with that vehemence of desire which is so strong a passion—to have it, to possess it, even to take it into his hands! but he was also afraid. His master might come in upon him before he could escape. There might be some trap about the dreadful glorious thing itself. It almost blinded him as he looked down into its white flames. At last, in mingled greed and terror, he put out his hand——

Ah! Jerningham's shriek would have wakened the Seven Sleepers; and there was no one to be awakened here, but only a perfectly collected, self possessed looker-on, who had seen everything with a pair of serene open eyes from the bed. What the prince saw was a man fixed and immovable, his countenance contorted with alarm and horror, standing, not as if he held the diamond, but as if it held him, in the centre of the floor, the rays of the gem shining round him, his features convulsed, his whole soul gone forth in that wild shriek. He stood trying vainly to disengage his fingers from the paralysing grasp that seemed to him to have seized him, an image of fright and helplessness. "Jerningham," said his master, "is it you? and what has brought you to this pass?"

"Oh, let me go, sir!" he cried. "I'm a fool; I'm a thief. I don't mind what you call me. Let me go; let me go! Your 'Ighness, I'd ask you on my bended knees, if I could bend a knee or move a finger! Oh, let me go!"

"What did you want with my diamond?" the prince said.

"Want with it? It was your 'Ighness's fault leaving of it there, where a man couldn't help seeing it. Want with it,—oh Lord! But I don't want nothing now but to be let free and never trouble nobody any more."

"What would you have done with it?" said the prince, in his calm tones, "had you got it safely away?"

"Oh Lord!—oh Lord!—only let me free of it for one moment! I'd have sold it," cried Jerningham, feeling the words forced from him, and understanding now in his trouble how it was that everyone had answered these questions—a thing he had never understood before.

"To whom? not to any honest dealer, who would know its value."

"I'd have gone—to Holland. I'd have found some o' those fellows out. It mightn't have been its value," cried Jerningham, "but it would have been a fortune to me. Oh, your 'Ighness! don't pull the brains and the eyes out of a poor man's head, but let me go!"

"And what would your life have been afterwards? You would have trembled to see me come in wherever you were and ask for my diamond. You would have been afraid to be seen by any one who knew you. You would have wandered from place to place, and tried every coarse pleasure which you cannot indulge in because you have your character to think of now; and you would have found them all bitter in your mouth."

"Very likely, sir; very likely, sir," cried Jerningham in his distress. "It's true; it's true. I've thought of all that. I knows it as well as any man. Sir, I'll never ask you for a character nor nothing if your 'Ighness will let me free."

"You thought of all that?" said the master, in his absolute calm.

"I did; I did! I knows it all. But what's the good of knowing when a thing drags you as if your soul was coming out of your body? It's your 'Ighness's fault for leaving it there."

"Then you will do it again tomorrow if I let you free."

"Oh, never, s'help me—oh, never! Yes, perhaps I will. A man never can tell what he'll do. I can't tell you a lie though I want to;—perhaps I will. It's stronger nor me. Oh, your 'Ighness; oh, for the love of God, let me free!"

Jerningham was in torture. The blood in his veins seemed to be turned into fire; sparks came from his broadcloth; his temples throbbed as if some dreadful machinery had been set going within; and the blaze of the diamond in his eyes was like those flames which he had heard of all his life as the reward of those who steal and lie. But suddenly in a moment he felt a dark still shadow over him. The machinery in his head stopped; the flare in his face was subdued; a cool hand touched his; and the cruel thing that held him loosed its clutches. This was what the sensation was—not that the diamond was taken from him by his master's hand, which was the fact, but as if it had been constrained to let him go. A sudden sense of relief ran through Jerningham's frame, but along with that—was it possible?—a regret,—a pang as of something which had all but been his, yet never would be his again.

The prince put it down on the table on the same spot as before. "You are sorry," he said, "that you have not succeeded. You forget already how it punished you. You would try again."

"No, your 'Ighness; no, your 'Ighness," said Jerningham. The sense of relief was in all his veins, and yet it was dreadful to him to give it up, and have no further hope of it. There ran through his mind like an arrow the thought, that after he was dismissed there might be a very good chance of coming back privately, and, with gloves or handkerchiefs wrapped round his hands or something, managing better another time. He did not entertain the thought, but it flashed through him all the same. He stood back in the shade an abashed and penitent sinner, notwithstanding this flash of thought.

"I asks no warning, sir, after what have 'appened; no board-wages nor nothing. I'm thankful to your 'Ighness for a-letting of me off. I asks no character. Mr Jones of the hotel will see, sir, as I leaves everything right, and not a pin out of its place. I'm—I'm a good servant, sir," said Jerningham. He paused for a moment, his intromissions with his master's garments and his percentages jumping up suddenly into his face. Then he added, "I mayn't be strong to resist a great temptation as has been left before my eyes; but I'm a good servant, sir, and nobody can speak different."

"You intended, then, to go away?" said the prince, with a smile. "No; you need not go away. I shall not dismiss you. You will, perhaps, attempt to do this again? Well, you know before-hand what the issue will be, and I need not say any more. We understand each other, I think? in this and also in the other little ways——

"What other little ways, sir?" said Jerningham, holding his head high; but it was very difficult to keep any pretence up in the presence of his master. "If your 'Ighness is satisfied, sir, so am I," he added, lowering his eyes and his tone.

The prince's laugh was not unkindly, yet it rung into Jerningham's very heart, and stung him much more than a lecture. "I am satisfied—that we understand each other," he said, and dismissed the culprit with a wave of his hand.

And this was how the strange incident ended. A master that had no respect for himself as a master; that could find out an attempt at robbery and never dismiss the man; that left the most valuable property about, and all his money in Jerningham's hands, notwithstanding that he knew Jerningham to be a rogue—as if it didn't matter,—as if nothing mattered! "Lord! I'd have turned him neck and crop out o' the 'ouse. I'd have in with him into the hands of the police sooner than look at him. He shouldn't never 'ave 'ad a day's grace from me!" Jerningham said to himself, putting himself in his master's place; but he was on the whole relieved to be going to bed as if nothing had happened, with his character safe, and no longer any necessity for flying to Holland or elsewhere in order to realise his ill-gotten gains.

It was shortly after this that the prince went for the first time to Hillesborough, though, as the reader may recollect, it was Lord Hillesborough who had arranged everything for him on his arrival in England. He was received with great state as became the highest rank—indeed, though he never stood upon his greatness, and his title was never fully announced, he had at the same time never hesitated to accept the name of Prince as natural and befitting his condition. When the old earl came out to the door to meet him, their rencounter was considered by many persons to be both curious and touching. Lord Hillesborough had travelled much in his life; he had been all over the world— everywhere, people said, without knowing very well what that word meant.

He had penetrated far into the East, he had gone through Africa (as was said; for much less was known of Africa in those days than now). As for Europe and such little holiday journeyings as are to be accomplished there, he thought nothing of them; and that he should have met in his wanderings a mysterious prince whom nobody knew, yet who was every inch a prince, bearing his superiority in every feature and action, was a very natural thing.

But it was strange and pathetic, as people say, to see that very old man, full of dignities and honours, bowing low before the stranger, who greeted him with the warmest cordiality, but no such demonstrations of respect. Lord Hillesborough hurried down the steps to open the carriage door with his own aged ivory hands. He murmured something about so poor a means of conveyance, though his carriage was good enough for the queen herself. The prince smiled in the most gracious and affectionate manner; he put his hand to his heart, his lips, and his forehead by way of greeting; finally, when he got out he put an arm round the old gentleman like a son, and seemed to raise him thus like a feather up the flight of majestic steps, which were usually a great strain upon Lord Hillesborough's limbs and breath. "I am glad to arrive at your house, my old friend," he said. "And I am honoured above all honours to see you here," said the old man.

The prince drew the old earl's arm within his own—and those who were watching saw, as if some air of youth and strength had blown that way, his countenance clear like the sun, and light come into his eyes. See what friendship does, they said, even to so old a man! For he no longer looked old when this glorious young prince,—so more than common tall, so splendid in his bearing, in his strange yet noble dress, and with—now clearly shining and displayed—a diamond bigger than the *Koh-i-noor* shining through the filmy folds of his head-dress,—had him by the hand.

There was a party of some eminence assembled at Hillesborough, presumably to meet the prince, though, so far as I am aware, the name of this illustrious *convive* had not been mentioned directly to any of them. The old earl had spoken, however, to some, of a friend whom he expected, who was making a sort of voyage of discovery in England, a member of a very old princely race, "of a civilisation much anterior to ours," he said. What did he mean? a Brahmin prince from India—perhaps a sacred *Llama* from Thibet,—"one of old Hillesborough's swans, who are mere geese," a witty member of the party said. But they did not laugh when they were presented to the mysterious and noble personage who appeared among them—though there was scarcely one who was not distinguished in one way or another—like an eagle among the lesser birds, rather than a swan.

He talked with them freely and upon all subjects, with an easy grace of utterance which was very surprising in a foreigner. And he was not a Hindoo: no dark nor even dusky blood ran in the veins which traversed visibly on his temples, in lines of blue, the milk-white of his complexion. He might have been an Anglo-Saxon for his fairness; but he was not an Anglo-Saxon,—the type was much higher, more intellectual, and finer than anything produced among our races.

There was a keen ethnographer among the party who was eager to identify him, yet entirely baffled by the prince's imperturbable and smiling incapacity for being questioned. He questioned a great deal himself on his own part, and knew almost everything about the private history of most of the people there, and this almost exclusively from themselves, for he encouraged no gossip. Day by day his fellow guests wondered more and more at him,—at his points of view, the opinions he expressed, and his curious spectator-attitude in respect to everything that went on. He blamed nothing, they observed, attacked nothing—had not a word to say about the foreign policy of England, nor her treatment of the distant States in which her sons had made their settlements. This was a thing that was eagerly expected from him at first. A foreigner himself, and evidently one from the far East or South, there was nothing so likely as that he should criticise the methods of Great Britain with those conquered or allied provinces, and the vast world of heathenism which she had more or less subdued.

But to the surprise especially of a Cabinet Minister, who was one of the party, he said nothing at all on this point. He did not even attempt to make out that his own race was more truly civilised than the British, and might with truth call them barbarians. He never spoke, indeed, of his own race at all. Sometimes he would exchange a recollection with Lord Hillesborough of some particular moment or occurrence through which they had passed together, and on these occasions named him apparently by a name which was quite unknown, and indeed never was caught by anyone, each hearer making of it a different sound—a word of a language which nobody had ever heard before.

The mysterious visitor caused great interest and excitement among the guests at Hillesborough. He was heard of through all the county; and people to whom it was half a day's journey came to call, with a sense that the very crown and climax of all old Lord Hillesborough's eccentricities was thus to be seen and taken account of. But the prince's visit was of still more importance to some of those who were most closely at hand.

CHAPTER 3

Lord Hillesborough had never married; but he was not without ties of family on that account. He had led a wild and wandering youth, and for the greater part of his middle age had been pursuing researches, which nobody could quite trace out, in distant parts of the universe, sometimes for years together dropping out of the knowledge of men. He had got beyond the climax of life when he returned and took for the first time possession of his ancestral place and honours. There he had neither been unaware of nor indifferent to the responsibilities of such a position. He had done all that a member of the House of Lords can to stimulate good legislation and control bad,—which is the highly important and useful office of that body,—taking care that the nation should have full time to think, and do nothing rashly or unadvisedly. He had taken up many schemes which seemed visionary to his colleagues and fellows, and some which were very practical and excellent. His estates were governed with great care under his own special supervision— no wrong being left without a remedy, and no poverty which could be helped being permitted to exist. Whatever was best in the way of leases and improvements to the farmers, and of good cottages, allotments, and indulgences to the labourers, existed on his land before the younger theorists had begun to speak of such schemes.

He was not altogether successful—what man is or can be?—and yet life was as tolerable at and about Hillesborough as it could well be made. He could not change the nature or the character of his surroundings. He that was unclean was unclean still, except now and then when a miracle would happen with, which Lord Hillesborough had nothing to do. He did not believe that allotments or anything else that he could do would save either men's souls or bodies; but when that divine something did come into an erring man's breast which makes him a good man—a miracle still daily accomplished among us, heaven be praised! which is greater than healing—the old lord acknowledged it with reverence however it came,—whether by means of the Methodist preacher in the village, or by the ministrations of an anachronism under the form of a modern brother of St Benedict, or by more intimate and secret help from heaven,—always allowing that this gift from God was beyond all allotments, and that to be made good was the one primary necessity of life.

This was a point in which he differed from most law-makers of today; and yet he was very modern in his way, and scorned no suggestion, even when coming from the least venerable quarter, which seemed to have any good in it. He was surrounded, in consequence, with what might be called a very high average of general wellbeing. More, perhaps, is scarcely to be looked for, whatever men may do or say.

I have said, however, that he did not want for the ties of a family, notwithstanding that he had never married, and had consequently no children of his own. His house was superintended and reigned over by his sister, Lady Elizabeth Camden, who had an only daughter, to whom the old gentleman was much attached; and it was the home of his nephew and heir, the son of a younger brother, who had been Lord Hillesborough's favourite in life. It was the evident and most commonplace conclusion that these two young persons, both so dear to the master of the house and both so deeply indebted to his bounty, should marry and carry on the lineage after him; but this most desirable and natural issue had been put aside sometime before, when it became evident that Arthur was not likely to turn out so well as had been hoped.

There were many excuses for him, people said. Why should he work either at school or college, when he knew there was no need whatever that he should do so, and when, without any exertion, he could have everything that is desirable in life? No doubt he would sow his wild oats, and settle down and marry some nice girl, and be as irreproachable as most of his fathers had been before him. Anyhow, he should not marry Lucy, Lady Elizabeth said, and she was a woman not given to changing her mind.

At the same time she had indicated, which perhaps was not so wise, the man who was to marry Lucy who was already an epitome of all the virtues, a man with very fine estates and a good deal of money, and universally approved of wherever he went. But, unfortunately, Lucy was not of her mother's opinion in this latter respect. Therefore, even in this admirably regulated house, with such a man as Lord Hillesborough at its head, all was not peace as it ought to have been. He was an example to the whole county, but it was not an example which was efficacious in his own house. And yet these two erring young people were both very fond of him, and considered him the best of men. They would have liked to please him; there was no opposition to him in either of their minds. Sometimes they were both in rebellion in different ways against Lady Elizabeth; but Uncle Hillesborough was to both the most loved and trusted of friends.

It was not long before this state of things was made very apparent to the prince. He fathomed it the first evening, when he saw the young people doing their utmost to entertain their guests, though nothing could have been more natural or delightful than the family affection between them, What might have been the confidences between him and Lord Hillesborough I cannot say—nor if there were any confidences; but it was not very long before this important and evidently most influential visitor, whose manners were such as gained everybody's trust, was sought by young Arthur with his tale, and a prayer for his intervention. "For one can see that Uncle Hillesborough thinks nothing too much to do for you," he said. "If Lord Hillesborough is so good, is not that a reason why I should be very cautious what I ask him?," said the prince, with a smile. But he soon was made aware very plainly what it was the young man had to ask. He listened patiently, and then he proceeded in his usual way to trace the trouble to its cause.

"What," he said, in the words he had already used so often, "has brought you to this pass?—for one like you, so young, so full of happiness, so well off, cannot have come to despair in a day. What has brought you to this pass?"

"Oh, I don't know," said the young man, with his hands in his pockets, swaying backward and forward against the light of the broad window—"nothing that was very bad. I got drawn in a bit with fellows I had known at school,—not for any harm, only for fun, don't you know. Everyone bets a little; and you never think when you begin that you can't stop just when you please. Then that leads to other things. When you get into your first hole, and see what an ass you've been, the thing you want most is not to think about it. It seems no use thinking about it when you can't mend it. Then fellows tell you how by risking a little more you have such a good chance of recovering yourself; and then you get awfully excited, and you heap on everything, and you feel sure you must win this time. Some fellows do, and set themselves straight, and then pull up, and are not a bit the worse for it.

"That's what I meant. They are actually the better for it, don't you know, getting such loads of experience; and, after all, nothing but experience ever teaches a man. Well! then when you have everything in the world hanging upon the chance of what is going to happen at a race meeting, or something else of that sort—don't you see your head's not any good for work or reading, and you can't bear home or being quiet. You have got *not* to think; and the only way not to think is to keep yourself in a whirl with—well, with other things; and so you get into what people call dissipation, without wanting to, without meaning to, just to keep yourself from thinking—"

The prince said nothing, but shook his head: there was perhaps a half smile on his face—or so at least the young man thought.

"What's the good of talking?" he said; "I can see you know it all quite well: and of course, however far off your country is, and however mysterious you make it, Uncle Hillesborough and you—human nature, I suppose, is the same there as here."

The prince did not make any reply to this: he continued to shake his head. "It seems to me," he said, "that if, instead of taking precautions against thinking, you had allowed yourself to think, all might have been mended at any moment before things came to this pass."

"I didn't come to a man like you," cried the youth, almost indignantly, "to be told that! Why, any old woman could have told me that! Don't you know how it draws you on? Oh, hang it all, you must know! You can't have come to know such lots of things, and to understand men so well, without finding that out. It draws you on; and in a kind of a way you like to be drawn on; and you think it's life, and all that; and after a while you can't bear the quiet of home, and the routine. You must have something to excite you, to fill up the gaps. I don't know why things that are called wrong should always be nicer than things that are called right. They make you spin, they keep you going. But it isn't because they're wicked you care for them; it's because they are fun."

"To me they seem very poor fun," the stranger said.

"Well, perhaps," said the youth, subdued. "You're above all that. I shouldn't suppose they would seem fun to you. I-shouldn't like it if they were. They're not always fun, to tell the truth, even to me; but they keep a fellow on. But you don't blame me badly, do you,—you that know what men are?" he added, after a pause, glancing up with a pleading look, like the insinuating plea of a child.

"Yes," said the prince, "I blame you: but still more, I wonder at you, selling your youth and all your chances and hopes for less than the mess of pottage! That was always something,—it satisfied a hunger of the moment; but yours are only the husks that the swine eat."

"Oh, I say! "cried the youth; then he paused, and said, penitently, with a drooping head, "I believe you're not far wrong. I have been a dreadful ass, that is the truth." He looked up again with his boyish insinuating plea. "But I've learned better now. I've bought my experience. Prince! if you will get Uncle Hillesborough to look over things this once, and start me straight, you shall see it will be very different another time."

"Will it be very different?" said the other. "If you had meant wrong the first time, and now meant right the second, I think there would be better hope: but you meant only fun, as you say; and how can you be sure that you will not mean fun again?"

"Oh, by Jove!" cried the young man, "I know better now! Fun's very well, but if it can only end in a revolver, one sees that won't pay. I'm up to a great many things now that I never thought of before. If you'll stand my friend, prince—"

"In any way, in every way that is permitted, I shall certainly stand your friend," the stranger said, in his grave tones but with his benignant look.

Young Arthur could not burst out with his schoolboy exuberance, "Oh, thank you; thank you awfully!" as he had intended. He was silenced by that look, which seemed to mean so much more than the words meant, which is not the usual way; but yet he did not know what they meant. He went away a little awestricken; yet he was full of hope.

And it was, I think, the same day that Lucy also sought the stranger with her story. She was more timid than her cousin. She had no confession of wrongdoing to make, in Arthur's way, but yet it was dreadful to the girl to be in opposition to her mother, and to be appealing to a person she knew so little. She said to him prettily, with downcast eyes, that she did not know how it was that it seemed more natural to speak to him than to any of her old friends whom she had known all her life.

"Perhaps it is because I am a stranger," said the prince.

"Oh," cried Lucy, "perhaps it is that! The others would either take sides with mamma or blame her,—and she is not to be blamed, she is right; but oh, prince, you who know everything, I can't help thinking I am right too."

"I am afraid I don't know everything. I am only an inquirer among you little young people on the earth; but you will teach me to know "

"I—teach you! "cried Lucy, clapping her hands; "but if you don't know everything, you understand, and that is better. Oh, prince, I am so full of trouble and difficulty! One thinks naturally that anything one wishes for, very, very much, must be wrong, you know. But this I am quite, quite sure is not wrong."

"Tell me what it is," he said, with a smile.

She gave him a quick glance, and then drooped her head again. "You will know," she said, very softly, "even though I didn't tell you, that it must be something about—about my marriage, prince."

The last words came out with a little rush, as if Lucy were glad to get them said. "Oh!" he said, "is that so?"

"What else could it be?" said Lucy, with a sigh. "Of course on no other subject would I oppose mamma. I know that she understands most things far better than I do; and she is very, very good. She is my best friend; she loves me more than anybody in the world. Oh, prince! you must not think I don't know that."

The prince smiled, looking down upon her benignantly, but said no word.

"But when you think that it is I who must pass my life with him, not she—and that there is one whom—whom I while the other, though I know he is a good man, and that mamma is right about him, and—and all that—yet I could not, I could not bear him, oh, prince, how could I? when there is another—another!"

Lucy put up her hands to her face with a little sound of tears.

"Tell me about this other," the stranger said; "sit down and be composed and tell me—everything you can tell—"

"I can tell you—all!" cried the girl. "I couldn't to anybody else; but I am sure you must have loved—someone, very, very much, and you understand."

He smiled over her downcast head, and in answer to the sudden upward glance of her wet eyes; but the smile was mysterious, reticent, opening no confidences on his own part. He did not assent to the assertion she made, nor yet contradict it. His attention was given solely to the suppliant, not disturbed by any reflection from experiences of his own.

"This gentleman," said Lucy, plunging into the middle of her subject, "whom mamma thinks so much of, is old—at least older a great deal. I seem to have always known him. He is very nice, and he has always been very good to me. I might have done—what mamma and he wanted, and never known anything better, and just lived dull and half alive all my days. But one day last summer I went over quite by accident to see—some other girls at Horndean. I had not been invited. It was only because it was a fine day, and Uncle Hillesborough had given me my pretty little pony-cart, and I thought I should like to go: just a fancy—and quite by accident."

"Quite by accident," the prince echoed, in a tone which

made Lucy look up at him once more; but she did not under-stand either his look or his mysterious spectator-smile.

"And there was—someone, who came in for tennis quite by accident too; they had not asked him; they did not even know he was at home. And we drew each other for partners in the game, and we played all the afternoon; and afterwards he walked by the side of the pony-cart half the way home. He walks so quickly and so light, he went as fast as the pony. Oh, prince, do not you think that when we met like this, without a thought, knowing nothing about it, that it must have been Providence—Providence? heaven itself that brought us together when we never knew!"

"And this was the man?" the prince asked.

"Oh yes! "cried Lucy with fervour, clasping her hands, too earnest even to blush, "this was the man! the only man—the only, only one that I could ever——And it is all so different. I might have married the other gentleman whom I was always meant to marry, and never known what it was at all——But the first moment I saw Harry I knew. I was ready to put my hand in his and go with him anywhere; and I don't mind if he is poor or rich, we could always, always get on together. We don't need even to speak to understand each other. We know what we mean—he me, and I him. And to think that we should have met like that!"

"Quite by accident," the prince repeated, in his musing tone.

"I prefer to say," said Lucy, with great gravity and solemnity, "by Providence, prince! It seems accident to us, but God,"—the girl lowered her voice with tender reverence and enthusiasm,—"God must have put us down for each other long before, and brought it about so, that we might always see His hand in it. He thinks so too. We are quite, quite sure that it has all been brought about by heaven. They say, you know, that marriages are made in heaven," she added, flashing a wistful smile at him out of her shining wet eyes.

"And is it a proof for that that earth opposes?" the prince

asked.

"Mamma opposes," said Lucy; "this is my great trial. He is not rich, and the other gentleman of course is; and she still wants me to marry him, as if our love was a mere fancy and meant nothing: when it means everything—our whole lives! Oh, prince! you can help us; everybody listens to you."

"But," he said, "do you not think that your mother knows best? that this gentleman, whom I do not know, whom she has chosen and selected for you, who has thought of you for years, is very likely a better mate for you than one whom you have met without any choice, inadvertently, quite, as you say, by accident."

"Love doesn't choose," cried Lucy, "it comes! it doesn't think of being suitable or not, it just is, and there is no more to be said. Oh, prince! I shall think you do not know so much as I supposed, have not had so much experience as I thought, if you don't know that. It is the only thing in all the world that is quite, quite true."

"It seems a beautiful thing—through your eyes," he said; "but if I talked with your mother "

"Mamma," cried Lucy, "would not deny that—nobody would deny it; they may try to get over it, but they would not deny it: for everybody at least, though they may go against their knowledge—which is blasphemy—knows what love is."

"They know what love is?"

"Oh yes, yes, prince! and that it comes like the wind in the Bible where it listeth—bloweth where it listeth—comes when no one is thinking of it, without any invitation, without any arrangement."

"Quite by accident!" the prince repeated, with a smile.

Chapter 4

The party at Hillesborough being, as has been said, a party composed of very distinguished persons, with aims and pursuits much above the common, was greatly occupied at this particular moment by discussions concerning the best means of reforming society, and especially concerning the condition of the poor, which takes up so much thought and so many anxious plans in this generation. There were some very active advocates of that which calls itself the Service of Man, and which considers itself an immense improvement upon the Service of God, though that has been for many hundred years the rule by which loving your neighbour as yourself was given forth as the half of law and religion. And there were also many who went in the ways of that older faith.

Much discussion, not only between these different methods, but upon—to their credit be it said—the best way in which each man could try his own method without assailing his neighbour's—was naturally rife, and many schemes were debated in the hearing of the stranger, who listened so courteously to every speaker, but never put in any suggestion or advice of his own. This was his general attitude—hearing everybody speak, without either criticism or judgment, collecting all opinions, and listening with grave respect to what the very humblest had to say. But naturally his imposing presence and all the prestige that surrounded him, the sense of superior intelligence and understanding which everybody felt who approached him, made this silence on his part unnatural, and he soon was referred to on all sides for his opinion. "One who has seen so much as you have," it was said, "with so many varied experiences—so great a student of human nature—"

These words came from different speakers, all pressing upon him to know what he thought.

"A student of human nature, am I?" he said. "Yes, it is perhaps the distinction which I am most willing to adopt. My studies have not been of long duration nor so profound as I should like them to be. But still—human nature is the most interesting thing in the world,—a thing which above all, as the Scriptures say, the——other races desire to look into."

"It is flattering to the Scriptures to be quoted by you—if a little unexpected and old fashioned," someone said.

"Ah, you think so? I am old-fashioned. I have heard even

from some of your clever people that I do not exist," said the prince, with a smile.

There was a little chorus of half laughter. "Berkeley, you mean," with little liftings of the eyebrows, however, between some of the hearers and a murmur of "Old-fashioned indeed!"

The prince replied to this murmur as if it had been the voice of the company in general, distinguishing the whisperer, who had been only heard in the shape of an inarticulate murmur by the rest. "Very old-fashioned, as I told you, keeping many primary ideas; and I have always found very great interest in the human race. To us who are bound by other rules, the mere existence of this delightful vagrant in the universe—a creature always choosing, always changing, acting according to a will which is not the same for two days together—is the miracle of miracles: a being so strange! that can lift up its reasonings, its little round of fantastic argument, against the Lord of heaven and earth; that can defy Him, and yet is not consumed; whose laws of living are so unlike everything else; with whom nothing is settled, nothing certain; the plaything, not of chance, as you say, or of fate, as your predecessors said, but of something far more fantastic and wayward still, his own will. Sometimes I have noticed that a woman, that a child, as being a still more marked embodiment of the law of your being, is an object of the same tender amused observation to you as the universe in general gives to your race."

The circle gathered closer around the prince, with looks, some of aroused curiosity, others of offended surprise. "Our race—which I suppose, whatever difference there may be in nationality, is yours also. You philosophers of the East take much upon you, but scarcely to be above humanity," one speaker said.

"The prince is from Thibet. I knew it," said another, with a laugh.

But the attitude of Lord Hillesborough was the most curious of all. He stood with an expression of the deepest anxiety, and also of an almost agonised entreaty, upon his face, addressing that speechlessly with look and gesture to his friend. The prince gave him a smile, waving his hand as if gently putting the remonstrance away. He made no reply to the comments of the other spectators.

"Your schemes," he said, "are good: there is much in them of that divine charity which some of you acknowledge (as if you were paying a compliment to your God) and some of you do not. You will do something by them, all of you, in proportion to the heart you put into them: yet you will never do anything. For why? It is impossible that you should ever succeed."

"And why should we not ever succeed?" asked one. The circle laughed: it was angry,—there was quite a tumult of feeling round the speaker.

"Because you have to do with a race which learns nothing, which makes no progress, which begins again afresh in every generation——"

His voice was lost in a chorus of laughter and exclamations. "This is too much, in the very age and birthday of the Science of Evolution. We allow all that the Mystic can demand as a matter of argument; but no progress?——Prince, this is too much!"

"You did not think, I suppose, that I spoke of your machinery?—the great paraphernalia of life-convenience that you build about yourselves. That does not make you true or pure, or to walk humbly with your God. What is it this earth of yours wants to make it happy and free of those evils you contend with?"

"Ah, tell us that!" someone cried.

"I will tell you that; it is simple. It is like what you say to a child: it is to be good. It is that it should get once more into harmony with the will of God. It is that it should eschew evil, learn to do well. It is that it should become natural to be pure, to be temperate, to be true. It is that no man should hurt his neighbour, or tempt his neighbour, or vex his neighbour any more; that there should be no excess, no breach of the rules of nature, no rebellion against the institutions of God—"

"Ah that, *par exemple!* long sermons and daily prayers and so forth!"

The prince took no notice. He went on with his calm voice,

as of one who knew no argument, who stated only the most evident unassailable fact—"Whereas," he said, "every human dwelling is full of rebellion and refusal. It is the first thing in the outset of a child upon life. That which is ordained is resisted; the principle of all things is to contradict. It seemed to us others a wonderful possession to have this will, this power of choice—a virtue which none of us could reach who were bound by other laws—the very flower of being: not to follow our Father's guidance only by necessity of nature, but to do it by choice, selecting His noble will by the glory of its own manifestation as the best, the only way. Who to be so much envied, so much thought of, as Men? Even afterwards there was still a charm. It is more wonderful than any evolution—I take your word," he said, looking round him with a smile—"to see a creature of God, standing, choosing, amid all the powers of heaven and earth—everything in love and subordination save he—he alone, by his nature free to do what he will.

"Think of it! We did so and sang for joy. The triumph and the height of all seemed to us to be so made that you could choose. Those who choose not but obey,—who know not hatred nor falsehood nor disturbance, but only the law of love,—applauded, acclaimed to the farthest depths of the infinite. To us, I tell you, it is a charm still to see every new man come into the world, to see him hesitate which turn he will take, to see everything placed before him and his own soul confirm the lesson, and experience point out and conscience protest. Ah, you know that process, every one of you. It is another evolution than your science dreams of. The father has learned the lesson, but that does not teach the son. Over and over, over and over, your own children show it forth before you. To each new generation the world begins over again: each new man makes his choice like the first man—untaught by what has gone before him, undaunted by the misery of the past."

The group which had gathered round the prince was silent. Some of them looked at each other askance, as if saying he has heard of So-and-so or So-and-so: for there were those there who had learned that lesson bitterly in the ruin of their children or their friends. Those who felt in themselves that this stranger was perhaps playing upon the secrets of their lives, confronted him with a pale defiance not to betray their consciousness of that truth; but all were still overawed by his bearing, and the wonder of his attitude, and what he said.

His face suddenly melted as he looked round after that address. A tender smile came upon it. His eyes grew luminous and soft as if with tears. He broke forth in a voice that was slightly broken with a sound of half weeping and half laughter. "But all by accident!" he said. "The new man pauses; he thinks; he chooses in his heart: it is solemn to him as the movement of the spheres—when, lo! a little breeze rises; a little cloud floats over him: a bird sings: a comrade calls: and he turns—into the other way. Not with intention—he has no mind to go wrong: it is only for once—for a moment—and all will be well again. And as it begins so it goes on. His life, that was to be so lofty and so great, becomes an accident—the accident of accidents. He does not know when he wakes in the morning how far he may have gone ere night.

"He goes out heedless and smiling, and meets ruin round the first corner. He makes a thousand plans, and then foils them all in a moment by the lifting of his hand. He cannot tell from hour to hour where his steps are to carry him. He remembers, and ponders, and knows—— yet next time does the same. We who look on are moved by I cannot tell you what wonder, what interest, what pity! We would shout aloud to warn him, but our voices are not as his: and who can warn him who knows all that we could tell him, and the penalties, better than we—yet makes no difference? The wisest cannot tell what he will do next— where his steps may stray. We watch him as you might watch a child upon the edge of a precipice. He totters; he stumbles; he turns aside; the butterfly leads him now to the edge of destruction, now away laughing to the flowery fields: then, while you rejoice, back again like the flight of a bird—over, into the darkness! Ah!" cried the stranger, with a voice that burst forth like a great organ, "that last alone is what appals you. You think then that all is over—whereas it is the great escape."

He paused a little, nobody saying a word, then resumed in a calmer tone: "How are you to set right this round of accident? You cannot make any man begin where his father left off, or profit by his experience. But I have learned one great thing by coming here, and it has been a consolation to me unspeakable, almost making up for everything. It is that he very rarely means any harm when he begins. What he intends is to do well. Take this to your heart, you that are truly troubled. Very, very rarely do they mean any harm. There is one here who meant to be a noble man like those he belonged to—but one heedless step after another has brought him face to face with despair. Ah!" said the prince, with a little start of pleasure, looking round him, "this law works also in things which are not evil but good. I see another who went forth one day like a child to her play, and met—another who is to be her companion through earth and heaven.

"They did not plot it or plan. An hour before they had never heard each other's names. An hour after and the link that is never to be broken was welded between them. They met—by accident. Can I tell you how this was done? Not I: nor can they. Love is: it is not known how it comes; it is an accident like all the rest." Here he turned towards his host and called him by that name which no one understood, or could ever catch distinctly. "Brother," he said, with a tone of mild authority, "you will look to these two, for they are yours. See to it." He paused again, then turned to the little anxious crowd which was full of eager curiosity. "The strange thing is," he said, "that this free soul, this being all will and independence, has never yet, amid all his vagaries, chosen fully and always to be good. This was what we looked for, hoped for, fully expected—that out of so many there would be one here and there who in the fullness of his will would choose.

"There was One as you all know; but He was the only one in heaven or the universe who could do whatever He would,

346

whose existence was His own to use as He pleased. There might have been some among us who would gladly have tried, but each of us belongs to his own sphere, and has his own duty to render; and who could tell that with man's will we might not have failed as he does. There was but One bound by no law; and He, you know, has done it. He took your nature and your will, and exposed Himself to all your accidents, and chose the perfect life, and fulfilled it. You all know. And in the face of the Son the Father sees you all.

"Nay, a greater wonder still than that, if greater wonder can be. When I look at you," the prince said, touching lightly his bosom, bowing slightly his head, "it goes to my heart. You are a little like Him! a little— a little! for He is a man in the fullness of your manhood. You remind us all, like little brothers, like far-off relations, always of Him. Think whether those, whose image our Lord wears, are dear to us or not! There is something in all of you—a look, a movement. You wear His features, and flout Him as if He had never been. The wonder of it! But you are a little like Him all the same—all of you, even in what you call the slums. I, who have been there, have been caught by a glance— just a movement of the eyes, perhaps, a lifting of a hand, something, I cannot tell what, that reminded me of my Lord!" He paused with a long breath of emotion, and there came from the bosom of that little crowd, all gathered round him, a sigh, which was unspeakable, which meant they knew not what,—a strange thrill, an indescribable feeling. The stranger made a slight movement, as if shaking off an impression too deep for the moment, And then he resumed—

"In the meantime, it is very good, very good that you should help your brothers, as that they should help you; and goodwill come—accidentally, as all your actions are swayed. But you will make no fundamental change. If by giving bread and coals, and education and comfort, you could make them good!—but that is the only thing: and as for these thousands of years they have not chosen it, it is not likely they will today. And no one can force them to be good. God may not. His pledge is against it.

They are to be free: it is the law of their being, as it is ours to obey. The consolation is that though all do evil, scarcely one—I have never seen one—meant to do it from the beginning; perhaps not one!—they are swept along by accident after accident. And thus your earth sways undestroyed in the great space and breath of God, which is common to us all. And the years go on towards their accomplishment. And your countenance, the face of man, shines over us in heaven."

"What is all this talk," said one of the spectators, impatient, who had long been trying to get utterance, "of us and you?—as if you had some superiority over our race, or were not subject to all our penalties. You speak well, prince, and your traditions may be so different from ours as to give you this feeling. Still I suppose you are a man like the rest of us. I like that you said about no one meaning harm, and about each starting afresh—I have myself felt that. But—"

The speaker paused confused. He uttered a strange sound as of wonder, remonstrance, bewilderment. Someone said after that there had been a noise in the other part of the room, and that everybody had looked round. I don't know what explanation of the incident there might be in that, or indeed if it really was so at all. But this is certain, that the gentleman who had begun to reply to the stranger suddenly paused, making that wonderful sound in his throat.

And it immediately became apparent to everybody around that the foreign prince, Lord Hillesborough's guest and friend, was no longer there. It happened in a moment, in the twinkling of an eye. Even had the attention of the other guests been called momentarily. away, there was no second door by which he could have left the room, and nobody saw him leave the room. But he was not there, He had been the centre of the group, closely surrounded, and that living circle had not opened that anybody was aware of to let him go forth.

But he was not there. There was, as was natural, a great outcry and hubbub. Some of the women fell a-crying; the man who had been speaking stood with his lips apart, as if still in his consciousness giving forth that strange muffled cry. One man cried in mockery, "I told you he was a *Mahatma* from Thibet!" But perhaps the strangest thing of all was the aspect of old Lord Hillesborough, who was perceived to be standing quite outside the group, with his hands clasped, and the most wonderful expression of tenderness and trouble in his face. Whoever was surprised it was very evident he was not surprised, which to some seemed the most curious of all.

Arthur, the young heir of the house, rushed out of the room as if with the intention of following and finding the visitor who had disappeared. He returned in a few minutes with Jerningham in a state of great excitement, sobbing, with gasps of utterance, and holding an open paper in his hand, "Which I don't deserve it, my lord, I don't deserve it!" he cried. "I've done perhaps no worse than others would have done in my place, and I didn't mean no harm: if he didn't use 'em himself it seemed—it seemed a kind of a pity not to use 'em: and here he says I'm to have all—but I don't deserve it, my lord."

Half-a-dozen people precipitated themselves upon the paper in Jerningham's hand, hoping to discover some mystery: but it was no more than a few simple words, requesting that Jerningham should have all that was in his hands. "He will do better another time," the paper bore, and it was signed by a curious cipher in a language to which no one there had any clue. Jerningham interposed, with convulsive exclamations. "He have put the big diamond into his 'at again," he said; "I thought as something must be up. He didn't leave that—no, my lord, oh no! nor I wouldn't have touched it if he had, seeing how once it took and grabbed me—me that was doing no harm: oh Lord! no, that's not true. But oh, gentlemen, he's took it, and he's gone—and the best of masters, and I'll never see his like again—"

The commotion that ensued in the house, and the way in which many of the gentlemen present endeavoured to trace the mysterious visitor, walking all over the park, going to all the railway stations, and making a hundred inquiries, need scarcely be told. Some of them thought they had accounted for his disappearance more or less satisfactorily. As for Lord Hillesborough, who made no inquiries, he was fully satisfied a few days after by the arrival of a letter from the north of Scotland, written in the scratchy and tremulous handwriting of a woman, and one that did not appear to be an educated woman or belonging to his own class. It ran as follows:—

> Dear Sir and Brother,—One that you will know of has just come in byc to me, and bid me to write and tell you his visit was over, but stepped out of his road to give me a word, as a poor person that has had great privileges and been admitted to things she does not attempt to understand. Dear sir, he bids you to know that he is well satisfied, and glad that he was permitted to come, and has now gone to his own place, the which you will understand better than me; and that if you will take his advice about things you are acquainted with, he is free to say it will be well. He sends you his greetings but no farewell, seeing that he awaits your arrival soon, and also that of me, an unworthy sister, scarce daring to put down, though he gives me the permission, dear sir and brother, my new name, ———

What followed was in the same cipher as that of the prince. The old earl had seen it before, but did not know who was the bearer on earth of that name.

He took the advice of his mysterious counsellor, and abounded more than ever, if that were possible, in good deeds and kindness to all. And one day he was found smiling in his chair, where he had sat in a great peace all the night, having departed many hours before anyone knew. The last thing he had done was to trace on the paper before him a word in the same cipher as the above, which no doubt was also his name there whither he had gone.

And the prince, so far as I am aware, has not been seen or heard of more.

Earthbound

There was but a small party for Christmas at Daintrey. The family were in mourning, which meant more than it usually means, and the whole life of the place was subdued. Nevertheless, the brothers and sisters were young, and were beginning to rise above the impression of the grief which had come upon them. The gloom had lightened a little; they began to forget the details of death, and regard the image of their brother in an aspect more familiar. It was not long since the news had come, and yet already this change had taken place, as was inevitable. The father and mother were less easily cheered; but life must go on even though death interrupts. The girls and boys could not be made to sit like mutes around a grave. They had to rise up again, and go on with their individual existence.

Lady Beresford, who was a wise mother, felt and acknowledged this, though her heart was still bleeding. Christmas was coming; and though there could be no Christmas festivities in the ordinary sense of the word, one or two old friends and connections were invited. Sir Robert, for his part, was opposed to the appearance of strangers. He was never very fond of visitors. 'What do you want with people here?' he said, with a kind of growl, in which he disguised his grief. 'Surely once in a way the girls might get through Christmas without visitors. Christmas! the very idea of these horrible merry Christmases that we shall have to go through makes me ill!

'I should do without them only too gladly, Robert: but the

351

girls and the boys are too young to be cooped up. Grief is so monotonous, and they are so young. It is not that they love *him* the less; but they must live—for that matter, we must all go on living,' she said, keeping with an effort the tears in her eyes. A mother who cannot give herself over to her sorrow, who must work through all her little daily round of duties all the same, and think of the girls' bonnets, and the boots and flannels of the boys at school, and only now and then in a spare moment can shut her door or turn her face to the wall and weep a little over her dead, the tears that have been gathering slowly while she has smiled and talked and kept everything going through the long day—has a hard task when her troubles come; but Lady Beresford bore her burden as sweetly as a woman could, holding up as long as was possible, then stopping to have her cry out, and rising and going on again.

Sir Robert became morose with his grief; but she had no time for self-indulgence. And naturally she had her way, and the few were invited whom it had seemed to her good to invite. One of them was Edmund Coventry, who had been a ward of Sir Robert, and now in his manhood calculated upon being a member of the Daintrey party at all those periods which are specially dedicated to home. He was a young man of excellent character and very fair fortune; and, if the truth must be told, the heads of the house at Daintrey had concluded that he would be a very convenient match for Maud, who was the second girl. Perhaps it would be better to say that one of the heads of the house had already perceived and accepted this view.

A matchmaking mother is a thing that is supposed on English soil to be extremely objectionable; and yet if she does not think of the welfare of her girls, who is to do it? The French mother considers it her first duty. Lady Beresford was a high-minded Englishwoman, and not a scheming mamma; but she could not shut her eyes to the fact that Edmund Coventry was exactly suited to Maud. And so, among the few who came to spend a very quiet Christmas at Daintrey, and 'cheer a sad house,' which was what she said in her invitations, Edmund was one of the first of whom she thought.

'Poor boy!' she said, 'he has always come here. He has no other place where he will care to go. Of course he will know that it will not be lively. But he is a good boy. I do not think he will mind.'

'I am sure, mamma, he will not mind,' said Susan, who was the eldest. Susan was going to make a by no means brilliant marriage. She was to marry a young man who was in the diplomatic service, but had no money, and was scarcely the sort of man to be a diplomat; so that the prizes of that profession seemed improbable to him. And she thought it very desirable that Maud and Edmund Coventry should see a good deal of each other. 'He will be glad to be with us in our trouble,' she said; 'he was always fond of Willie.' Thus the invitation was given half in love and tender certainty of sympathy, yet half with a certain calculation too.

The other guests were of a very quiet kind—a brother of Sir Robert's, a lonely bachelor; a widowed sister of Lady Beresford's with her little boy and girl; the former clergyman of the parish, who had been Willie's tutor once upon a time; a nephew who was an orphan, and had no home to spend his Christmas in; and Edmund. 'He will be the only little bit of liveliness. He will help to cheer us up,' Susan said. Her *attaché* was to come too, but only for a few days. He was one of those to whom social duties were important, and he had a great many visits to pay. But for this mourning they would have been married before now.

Edmund Coventry was a young man who was very well off, and very greatly esteemed. He was twenty-seven—no longer a boy. He had a very nice estate, and a house in town, and no relations to speak of. He was very well-looking, without being handsome, which is perhaps the sort of compromise with nature which is most approved in England. There are a great many people who do not care for unusually handsome men. Beauty is an extravagance, they feel, in the male portion of the world. But Edmund's good looks did not go the length of beauty. He was not a tall, muscular, well-developed hero, but slight, and not more than of middle stature. With all he was an ingratiating, lovable young man, very gentle in manners, very tender in his friendships; no doubt he would make an excellent husband. There was no need to explain to him the position of affairs in the house. He knew all about it, and he sympathised with them in every point.

'Mamma hesitated to ask you,' said Maud, 'because we were to be so quiet.'

'Could I wish to be anything but quiet?' he said, with a tender half-reproach. 'Do you think, after all the happy times here, that I have no feeling.' But, indeed, no one had thought that, as Maud made haste to say.

The carols were sung, but with tears in them. The house was dressed as usual with holly and all the decorations of the time; and there was at least a great deal of conversation which lengthened the gloom and silence of the previous period. Even Sir Robert was glad to talk to Mr. Lightfoot, who had been the rector in former times. On Christmas night the attempt at games was somewhat doleful as it will be, alas! this Christmas in many a sorrowing and many an anxious house; but the talk and the little bustle of renewed movement did everybody good.

The commonplace ghost-stories which are among the ordinary foolishnesses of Christmas did not suit with the more serious tone in which their thoughts flowed; but there was some talk among the older people about those sensations and presentiments that seem sometimes to convey a kind of prophecy, only understood after the event, of sorrow on the way; and the young ones amused themselves after a sort with discussions of those new-fangled fancies which have replaced that old favourite lore. They talked about what is called spiritualism, and of many things, both in that fantastic faith and in the older ghostly traditions, which we are all half glad to think cannot be explained. The older people, indeed, unhesitatingly rejected all mediums and supernatural operators of every kind as impostors; but even on this point various members of the party had things to tell which they did not know how to explain. 'Is not there some

tradition of a ghost about Daintrey?' Mr. Lightfoot, the old rector, said, as they all sat in a wide circle round the great glowing
fire just before the moment should arrive for bed-candles and
general goodnights. There was not very much light in the room,
but, large as it was, it was all ruddy and brilliant with the blaze
of the great cheerful fire.

'Nothing of the sort,' said Sir Robert emphatically. It was he
who was most strong as to the whole thing being an imposition,
and who 'did not believe a word' of the stories he was told.

'I believe there is something—very vague,' said Lady Beresford. But there was a meaning look exchanged between them,
and the talk suddenly came to an end.

And by and by the ladies went all flocking out of the room,
carrying their lights, like a procession of the wise virgins in the
parable. But their black dresses made that procession a sad one,
though the soft bloom of the young faces came out with even
more effect when the light found nothing else to dwell upon.
The young men found a little relief from the gravity of the conversation in the smoking-room, where Mr. Beresford the elder,
the uncle of the party, discoursed upon town and its charms, and
congratulated himself that he was not like his brother Robert,
the head of the family, and compelled to pass his winters in
the middle of those damp acres of park. 'It would kill me in a
year,' Mr. Beresford said. On the whole they were all glad that
the worst was over, and Christmas got safely done with for that
year.

CHAPTER 2

Edmund showed no inclination to cut his visit short; he stayed
on after Uncle Reginald had returned to his dear club and his
rooms in St. James's Street, and the *attaché* had gone on upon his
round of visits, and young Beresford, the cousin, had returned
to his work. The eldest of the sons at home was over twenty; the
other two were boys at school. And Susan and Maud and little
Edie were the girls. It could not be a very sad house, after all,
with all that youth in it; and on the whole Daintrey began to

turn round as it were, like the earth when a new day is breaking, turning itself to meet the light. Edmund was very much at home and very comfortable, and he was pleased to think that he was doing them good, as Lady Beresford told him with a smile of tender gratitude. It had not yet occurred to him that of all people in the world Maud was the one who would suit him most exactly for a wife. But he was in a very promising way for making that discovery, which had already faintly gleamed upon the consciousness of Maud herself as neither unlikely nor unpleasant. They saw a great deal of each other, though not a bit too much. They were like brother and sister, Lady Beresford said; which was quite true: and yet there was always a possibility of something more.

Daintrey was a handsome house of no particular period, built almost due east and west like a church. The front entrance was by a square court shut in by a screen-wall built between the two wings. At the back the wings were very shallow projecting but slightly from the *corps de logis.* On the south side of the house was a green terrace, as high as the windows of the sitting-rooms, ascended by handsome marble steps ornamented with vases as in an Italian garden and separated by the brilliant *parterres* of the flower-garden from the house. Running along the upper end of the garden and connecting it with the west end of the house was the lime-tree walk, a noble bit of avenue at right angles with the terrace. Both of these were beautiful—but the little square corner which connected them was not beautiful.

Here, for no apparent reason at all, a wall had been built, of the date of some hundred years back, a high brick wall, quite out of place, screening in a square and rather gloomy angle of grass, in the midst of which stood a high pedestal surmounted by a large stone vase. Whether this was meant to commemorate anything, or whether it was merely supposed to be ornamental, in the days of George III. nobody could tell; but that it was very funereal and ugly was certain.

In the side of this wall farthest from the house was a door which opened into the byway through the park. Perhaps the wall had been built to stop some right of way; perhaps—but there is little use in multiplying peradventures. There stood the wall built to shut out no one knew what; there loomed aloft the funeral urn upon its pedestal raised to commemorate no one knew what. Sometimes the door would be locked by a sulky gardener, and the key had to be hunted for in the house and out of it, high and low. At such moments Sir Robert, especially if he had himself to wait, would vow that he would throw down the wall and abolish both urn and door. But Sir Robert was an absolute Tory in action, though something of a Liberal in politics; and threatened walls live long, especially when there is no reason why they should live.

Edmund had gone out with the intention of walking to the village one of these wintry afternoons. There had been talk of skating, but the ice was not quite solid enough for skating, and his errands to the village were manifold. He were going to see about Maud's skates, which wanted something done to them. He was going to the rectory to tell the new rector, who was young and a great athlete, to join the party at the pond tomorrow if the frost 'held'; and he had other little commissions to do. When there is nothing better to be done it is something for a man to have commissions in the village—it gives him a reason for his walk; it makes him feel that he is not absolutely without an occupation.

The boys were all about the pond, helping it to freeze, as the keeper said—watching, at least, with the most anxious eyes, how this process went on. Edmund came out at the western door of the house facing a low red sun, which shone into his eyes, casting long level gleams of light across the grass and dying it orange. He was very light-hearted today, with a feeling that poor Willie Beresford had died long ago, and that life had begun again, and that the prospects of existence were opening out. Perhaps it was Maud, whose sweetness and pleasant society had suggested to him long stretches, of happy life to come. He went out, glad even of the sharpness of the air, pleased to hear the crackling under his feet which betokened the frost, and admiring the fairy whiteness in which the great trees had robed themselves. All lit up with those red rays, with warm and gorgeous belts of colour upon the sky, and every prospect of cold and fine weather, the things most desirable when there is a frost and it is Christmas, the prospect round him was of itself exhilarating.

How foolish, he thought, of the girls not to come out, to get the benefit of the smart walk through the park, and the keen fresh air which made his countenance glow. Talk of summer! The park at Daintrey was lovely always, but it never was more beautiful than it was now, with that red sunshine lighting up all those stately white giants in their robes of rime. He started lightly, closing the door after him with a cheerful bang, and turning his steps towards the lime-tree walk, through which one great beam of sunshine like red gold had pierced in the opening between the two greatest trees. This looked like a golden bridge cutting the little avenue in two; beyond it there was the shadow of the wall already described which thrust itself straight in front of the low sun.

While Edmund admired this great broad blaze of light he was startled by seeing something move beyond it in the darker part—something white, which he could not make out so long as he was himself in the sun. But when he had crossed that bridge of light he was still more surprised to see in front of him, at the end of the avenue, a woman, a lady, walking along with the most composed and gentle tread. The road was not exactly a private road—all the people from the village, almost everybody who came to Daintrey on foot, used it. But Edmund thought he knew all the people about, and he certainly did not know anyone whose appearance was at all like that of the lady who preceded him to the door in the wall—unless it were one of the girls masquerading; but he had just left the girls with their mother round the fire, and he could not entertain this idea.

The dress, too, struck him with great surprise. It was a white dress, with a black mantle round the shoulders, and a large hat: not unlike the kind of costume which people in aesthetic circles begin to affect, but far more real and natural, it seemed to him—

though how he could judge at this distance and with only the lady's back visible it would be difficult to tell.

The curious thing was that the moment Edmund saw this pretty figure in front of him his heart began to beat. He had the same feeling which a man sometimes has when he suddenly meets a lovely face and says to himself that, please God, this woman is the one woman for him. But such a thing would be absurd when you consider that it was only her back he saw. Yet it made his heart beat; he was seized with a great desire to follow, to 'get a good look' at her, to know what she could be doing here and who she was. What had she been doing there? Surely a creature of so much grace, moving like that, dressed like that, could not possibly have been visiting the servants' hall; and that she had not been in the drawing-room he was sure.

If she only would turn round at the sound of his step:—but she did not turn round. She moved on as if she heard nothing— across the curious little square, straight to the door in the wall. Come, Edmund said to himself, if she is going to the village I must overtake her. And he did not hurry, feeling sure she could not escape him. He was pleased by the little mystery—Who could it be? But he must find out before he returned, for un- known ladies do not walk about in a park in the country, or go to and fro between the village and the great house, without be- ing easily traceable.

What a pretty walk she had! so light that her step was not au- dible—no creaking and crunching upon fallen twigs and stones and frost-bound sod as with him. He was charmed with the pretty graceful figure—certainly a little like Maud, slimmer and not quite so straight, with a pretty droop in it of fragility and dependence, but yet certainly like—younger perhaps, though Maud was but nineteen. He followed her softly, promising to himself to quicken his steps as soon as she should have passed the door in the wall to which she was leading the way. Presently, about two minutes before him, she reached the door; he was so near that he could see her half turn round as if to look who was behind: but, though she must have perceived him, she closed the door upon him as she passed through—not very civil, he thought; but perhaps she was *espiègle*, and could not resist a little merry affront to him, innocently provocative, as is the fashion of girls. He hurried along the few intervening steps of the way, and opened the door. Perhaps after all she knew him; perhaps it *was* Maud, who was very fond of fun in the old days. The smile was almost a laugh on his mouth when he stepped out of the park and let the door swing carelessly behind him—not shutting it elaborately, as she had taken the trouble to do.

Strange, very strange! There was nobody to be seen on the other side of the door; certainly it must be Maud or one of the girls. She had slipped behind a bush, no doubt, to bewilder him. There were several byways running in different directions— one towards the deserted cricket-ground, another towards the keeper's cottage, beside the straight road which led to the village. Probably she had tucked up her dress and made a dart among the brushwood out of sight. He stood for a moment looking after her, now one way, now another, but he could see no one. 'I know you,' he cried, 'I know you; where are you, Maud?' But there was no answer from among the brushwood.

Finally, he had to make up his mind that her trick had been successful, that she had got away, and that if he was to execute his commissions in the village he must not lose any time. But he went along with only half the spirit with which he had started, his mind quite absorbed in this adventure. As he resumed his way he met one of the keepers coming in the opposite direc-tion, whom he stopped to ask if he had met a lady on his way. The man looked at him as if he thought him mad, but answered No, he had met no one. 'A lady in a white dress and a black mantle,' said Edmund.

'Lord bless you, sir,' said the keeper, 'a white dress!'—and then it occurred to Edmund for the first time how entirely inappro-priate such a garb was to the season. It must have been one of the girls who had 'dressed up' as they used to be so fond of doing in the old days, to give him a fright. And yet in his heart he did not in the least believe this explanation he had given to himself.

Even Maud, though he liked her so much, had never excited that sudden and causeless emotion in his heart. It was someone new—someone who had never crossed his path before, and who was destined to work he knew not what commotion in it. But then, who could it be?

'Did you go out after I went out?' he asked when he went back to Daintrey. 'Tell me, did you or anyone take a run into the park?'

'Oh, no; mother would not let us go. She said we could not go to skate tomorrow if we went out so late today.'

'Or has anyone been here? Did you have any visitors?' Edmund asked, though he knew very well that this could not explain the presence of the lady who must have left the house before he did. Maud looked up at him with her soft blue eyes.

'We have had no one,' she said. 'We did not stir all the afternoon. Mother had a headache, and we did not wish to leave her. After you went out we sat and talked till the dressing-bell rang. That was all; but why do you suppose we must have had visitors?' Edmund felt—he could scarcely tell why—a little shyness and unwillingness to explain himself.

'Because I met a lady in the park,' he said, 'and could not make out who she was. Have you any new neighbours since I have been gone?'

Maud shook her head. 'Nobody,' she said. Nobody had been calling. Nobody had intruded into the neighbourhood. She looked earnestly at the young man, who, for his part, was a little excited by his own questions, but not at all unpleasantly excited.

'I thought for a moment you were playing me a trick. She looked a little like you—that is, her figure looked like you. I did not see her face.'

'Like me?' Maud was half pleased, but more surprised. '*I* play you a trick? I don't think,' she said, with a sad look, 'that I shall ever do that again.'

'But I hope you will a hundred times,' said the young man; and this pleased her, though she could not have told why. 'But help me to find out who it is,' he went on. 'I feel annoyed that I don't know everybody, as I used to do. She was dressed in white with a—'

'In white! You must have been dreaming,' said Maud, in amazement.

He stopped short again. 'That's why I thought it must be you,' he said, yet with a little conscious jesuitry, for he had not thought so—indeed, had assured himself that the little stir of his being which he had experienced could only mean that this was someone of a different kind from any he had met before: a new woman, a creature born to influence him. 'But it is quite true, and I was not dreaming. She had on a white gown. Something black over her shoulders like, the thing ladies have been wearing lately: I forget how you call it—not a cloak nor a scarf—something put round and knotted behind like this,' said Edmund, doing his best to show how, upon himself with his hands.

'A *fichu*, you mean,' said Maud, suffering herself to be betrayed into a smile.

'A *fichu*, that's the thing; and a large broad hat. But she did not look like art-needlework—she looked quite natural.'

'What an interest you must have taken in this lady! When did you meet her? It could not have been anyone coming here, for no one has been here all day.'

'I met her—but I did not meet her—I followed her along the lime-tree walk and out by the little corner door.'

'How very strange! I cannot think who it can have been. And where did she go after?'

'That is the strangest of all,' said Edmund. 'She disappeared somewhere. That was another reason why I thought it must have been you. I cannot tell where she went. Down by the keeper's cottage, I suppose; but I saw her no more.'

'I'll tell you who it was,' said Maud, just a little piqued—'it must have been the keeper's niece, who has come for a little change. She is in a dressmaker's in London. Of course she will dress nicely—though to wear *white* on a winter afternoon, trailing across the damp grass—' She laughed again but not so sweetly as before. 'This must have been your lady, Edmund, I fear.'

'I do not believe it. I cannot believe it,' he said, much vexed; but after a good deal of resistance he was brought to allow that as he had only seen her back, and that at a little distance, he could not have any such certainty as he had supposed that she was a lady.

'Besides,' said Maud, with a little gentle triumph, 'a girl like that may walk like a lady and dress like a lady. She has got to be among ladies most of her time, and to see the best people. Unless you talked to her and found she dropped her h's, or had vulgar ideas, how could you tell? Indeed, sometimes they talk even just as nicely as we do,' said the young lady, more just than many of her kind. This seemed to make an end of the question. At least Edmund could find no more to say; and Lady Beresford, who had observed the long and interesting conversation in which he had been engaged with Maud, gave him a still kinder smile than usual when she bade him goodnight.

CHAPTER 3

Next day the frost held; the pond was bearing, and the whole house turned out to skate—even Sir Robert. Lady Beresford looked on with that indulgent wonder with which a woman regards a man's delight in outdoor amusements, and the charm they exercise over him. She was unfeignedly glad that her husband should be roused from that growling seclusion in the library, which looked like temper and meant grief—glad to the bottom of her heart; and yet there was a wondering in her mind, a sensation of half-grieved, half-smiling surprise. She was glad to get them all out of the house, and said 'Thank God!' fervently, that here was something which would take off the strain, which would bring in a little amusement, and help the convalescence of grief which was working itself so quickly in these young people; and then she went up to her own room and shut her door, feeling as if she, who had the best right to it, had got that faithful sorrow all to herself, and uncovered his picture, and read his last letter, and wept out all the tears that had been gathering and gathering.

Meanwhile, the rest had got out of the shadow for the moment, and the pond was a merry scene. Sir Robert skated about very solemnly at first, taking long turns round the island that lay at one end of the long piece of water; but by and by he began to help little Edie and give directions to Tom. This diversion filled up the whole day and the next. Edmund had been half vexed, half irritated by the supposed discovery that his white lady was the keeper's niece, especially as Maud had already given him several little playful reminders and he determined, accordingly, that he would not allow himself to think any more of the little figure which had so charmed him. Of course it was mere imagination, nothing else—a girl's back, in a black *fichu* and white gown. What could anyone make of that? There was in his mind a lurking purpose of coming home from the ice some evening by the keeper's cottage, just to see; but even that he did not carry out for those two days.

On the third afternoon, however, by some chance, he was left to come home alone. The others had set out before he was ready. He heard their voices sounding cheerily through the frosty night air, a good way on, upon the path before him, when he completed his last long whirl round the island, during which Sir Robert had got impatient, and summoned all his flock about him. They had all lingered to the last moment possible, as there were signs of the frost breaking. It was dark, so dark that Edmund could scarcely see to take his skates off, and all the hollows of the park were frill of mist, and the sky overspread and blurred, and covered with clouds. It was clearer in the east, however, and there an early pale-eyed young moon, with a certain eagerness about her, as though full of impatience to see what was going on in the earth, had got up hastily in a bit of blue. She touched the mists, and made them poetical, gradually lightening over the milky expanse of the park, in which the trees stood up like bands of shadows.

Suddenly it came into Edmund's head that this was the very moment to carry out his intention. He took up his skates hastily, and walked round by the other end of the pond towards the cottage of Ferney the keeper. The moon, getting brighter every moment, threw the whole little settlement of this small habitation in the midst of the park and woods, into brilliant relief. There was a sound of dogs and human voices populating the stillness, and the cluster of low red roofs, the smoke from the chimneys, the cheerful blaze of firelight out of the uncovered windows, seemed to cheer and warm the whole landscape.

Half ashamed of his own artifice, Edmund stopped at the door to give some message to the keeper. In the room beyond he saw a young woman seated at a table sewing, the light of a candle throwing a full light upon her. She was dressed in black, with the usual white collar and little locket—a handsome, pale girl; and as Edmund stared in, forgetful of politeness in his curiosity, she got up, with a reserve that was in itself *coquettish*, and walked to the other end of the room. When he saw this movement he had almost laughed aloud. That the lady of the lime-walk! They might as well have told him that good Mrs, Ferney, with her stout, matronly bulk, and white apron, was the lady he had met. He went off, pleased with his own discrimination, pleased that he had not been mistaken, wondering if he should ever meet her again anywhere. He felt sure that he would know her, wherever he might see her, by her figure and by her walk.

He asked the keeper some trivial question to justify his pause at the house, then walked on, whistling, with cheerful speed, till he came to the little corner door, as it was called; but he had scarcely got within, when he checked himself abruptly. The moon was shining full across the green terrace and the empty beds of the flower-garden, streaming upon this little forlorn angle and its big ugly urn. Full in its light, softly crossing in front of the big pedestal, her pretty figure relieved against it, within half a dozen paces of him, coming towards him, was the lady he had seen before. Her dress was the same, dead white, with the black *fichu*, all frills and fringe, tied behind; a broad hat, thrown back a little from her face. His heart gave a great jump when he saw that in a moment he must pass close, and that she could not in any way conceal herself from him. He almost stopped short, but she came on softly without embarrassment, without alarm. Certainly she was like Maud: a tender little pensive face, with soft, very large eyes—which must be blue, Edmund felt—a pensive half-smile about the mouth.

She was neither startled by the sight of him nor did she take a single step out of his way, but went on at the same composed pace. She had almost passed him, when he bethought himself to pull off his hat. This seemed to give her a little movement of surprise. She half turned her head to look at him, and the half-smile on her delicate lips brightened a little. It was too slight, too evanescent, to be called pleasure; and yet it was something like pleasure that lighted up the gentle face. Then she passed on, and in another moment had gone out by the door. He had not opened it for her, as politeness required. He had been too much taken by surprise—bewildered by the sudden appearance. Even now he stood still, dazed, not knowing what to do, puzzled how to address a lady whom he did not know, to intrude into an acquaintance whether she wished it or not, but yet feeling it impossible to let her go like this. He stood—was it for a moment, or longer?—hesitating, wondering: then rushed after her, meaning to say that she could not possibly cross the park at this hour alone, that she must permit him to accompany her.

In his haste he made a dash at the door, threw it open, plunged out into the wide white desert where she had gone. The moon shone full upon all the breadth of the park. The ground was higher here, and there was less mist; the pathway wound along for a hundred yards or so fully visible; but no one was there. 'Again!' he cried, speaking the word aloud in his confusion and annoyance. The bushes indeed clustered thick upon the way to the keeper's cottage. Could this be a second niece, a daughter, another young woman living there? He was so vexed, so disappointed, so tantalised, that he did not know what to do or say.

'Has Ferney a daughter as well as a niece?' he said to Maud, singling her out again, her mother remarked, from all the rest.

'A daughter? Oh, no; nobody but Jane. They brought her up;

but that is all. Why do you take so much interest in the Ferneys, Edmund? You have always known them, ever since you first came here.'

Then Edmund told his story. How once more he had seen the strange lady: how she had passed through the door, and once more gone down the keeper's way; or, at least, so he supposed. Had she gone to the village he must have seen her. This time Maud became excited, too. She took her mother into council. 'Mother, do you know anyone who has lately come to the village, or to any of the houses about? I should think she must be a crazy person. Edmund has met her twice in the Lime-tree Walk, in a white dress—'

'Edmund must have been dreaming,' Lady Beresford said.

'Not any more than I am now. I saw her quite plain to-night. There is something in her air, generally, that reminds me of Maud. I thought it was Maud herself playing me a trick the first time I saw her.'

'And dressed in white. Such an extraordinary thing!' said Maud. 'Who can it be?'

This incident of the dress moved the ladies more than it did the man. He had to explain to them exactly what kind of a dress it was that she wore. 'Though I daresay he has not a notion,' said Lady Beresford. 'Probably it is only some light colour. Men never know—'

A slight look of uneasiness got into her face. She listened as the dress was described with reluctance, trying to change the subject; but the others were very much interested. 'A dress not like anything you ladies wear now,' Edmund said.

'A dress, I should say, very like what the art people wear. It must be some artistic person who has taken lodgings in the village,' said Mrs. Cole, who was Lady Beresford's sister. 'Depend upon it that is what she is, an art-student, not rich, living in some little rooms, studying the effects of a winter landscape, or something of that sort. Perhaps Ferney has let her his parlour. Hasn't he got a parlour? That is what this strange visitor must be.'

This was not quite so objectionable to Edmund's feelings as the other guess, and the talk got quite animated about his lady. Only Lady Beresford did not quite like it. 'Please not to say anything about her to Sir Robert,' she said; 'he is not fond of strangers about.' And she was visibly uneasy. But no one could tell why.

As for Edmund himself, his mind was very much occupied with this pretty vision. He thought, with a thrill all through him, of the soft look of surprised pleasure that had come over her face as he took off his hat. Why should she be surprised? It was a thing any gentleman ought to have done, meeting her there, all alone, a stranger in the place, where he was himself at home. The thing he regretted was that he had not been a little quicker, that he had not followed her out, and asked her to let him see her safely across the park. Perhaps she would not have liked that. Perhaps the suggestion that it was not safe to walk about alone might have offended her. But she did not look at all like one of those women who assert a right to walk alone, and to do whatever pleases them. Anyhow, he would not let her escape him so another time; and no doubt he would meet her again.

After this he was continually haunting the Lime-tree Walk. The last day of the skating he made an excuse to return early, but she was not there; and, indeed, he did not see her again till his heart had been sick with disappointment on two or three occasions. The frost broke up; then came a day or two of rain, and all the bondage of the ice melted, and the paths ran in little torrents, and a few feeble spikes of snowdrops began to come up in the empty flower-beds. The weather grew mild all of a sudden. And one day the hounds met near Daintrey, and all the party went out. They came back in the afternoon, tired, and damp, and soiled with the mud; but when the others went in to be warmed and dried, and made comfortable, having had enough of air and exercise for the day, Edmund lingered outside, as he now always did, as long as he could get any excuse for doing so. And this time he was rewarded. In the middle of the Lime-tree Walk he saw her suddenly coming towards him.

One moment there had seemed to be nobody about He turned his head to see what was meant by some little stir behind him; and when he turned again she was there, walking towards him, with her soft, gentle, composed tread. Her hands were clasped before her. Her white dress trailed a little behind her, but seemed to have no stain upon it, or mark of the wet. Her head was a little thrown back. Ah, yes! surely they were blue, those eyes; they could not have been anything but blue. And she had very little colour in her face, just enough to make it lifelike, and give an appearance of health and perfection; no sickliness, no incompleteness, was in the hue. The soft little half-smile was still upon the lips—lips that were like rose-coral, not very red, but warm and soft. She came on without paying any attention to Edmund, as if, indeed, she did not see him. And this piqued him a little. But his heart leaped so at the sight of her that he was not capable of cool judgment or criticism.

This time his mind was made up. If it was rude, he was very sorry, but he must speak to her, whatever happened. He stopped suddenly when they met, and once more took off his hat. And then, in a moment, like the sun rising, that expression of pleasure came to her face. The smile grew brighter. She stopped, too, and looked at him with such satisfaction, such a tender interest in her eyes, that he was utterly confounded, and stood gazing at her, the words that he had meant to say failing him. Rude! no, evidently she did not think him rude. A gentle delight seemed to spread over her—affectionate pleasure, as if of a happiness she had vainly expected, and for which she was thankful beyond words. After all, it was she who spoke first. She said, in the softest little musical voice, a little thin, but sweet, like the cooing of a dove; and what she said was as remarkable in its simplicity as the fact that she was the first to begin the acquaintance. 'So you see me!' was, in tones of gentle pleasure, what she said.

'See you!—indeed this is now the third time that I have the pleasure of seeing you,' said Edmund eagerly. 'The last night I could not forgive myself for not asking if I might walk home with you. It was very late for you to walk alone across the park.'

To this she answered nothing, but looked at him with the softest, caressing looks, as if it were a pleasure to her to hear his voice; and yet the perfect modesty, simplicity, and innocence of the virginal countenance uplifted to him, made every thought but those of respect and even reverence impossible to Edmund. At the same time he was slightly abashed by this steadfast look, which might have made a vain man complacent, but for something in it of unapproachable purity and isolation which gave the beholder a sense of awe. Edmund did not know how to go on. It was more difficult than could be told to proceed in the conversation. Phrases about the happiness of making her acquaintance—about the desire of the ladies at Daintrey to know if, they could be of service to the stranger, which he had (though totally without authority) conned and prepared, no longer seemed within his power of utterance. He stammered forth something about 'Lady Beresford—would be glad to see you—to be of use.' To which she shook her head half sadly, half with a kind of shadowy amusement. 'You have come to the neighbourhood lately?' he said at last.

'No; oh, no; I have been here—about Daintrey—a long, long time.' These strange words were interrupted by a little faint laugh like an echo, like a laugh in music, the most spiritual liquid roll of soft words. 'I have been a long time here.'

Edmund grew more and more confused. 'If that was so I must have seen you,' he said; 'but perhaps you think a little time long. It would be natural, you are so young.'

'Nineteen,' she said; 'I never was any more than nineteen; but it is a long, long time ago.'

Then it began to dawn upon Edmund, though it was an idea he received with the greatest reluctance, that this tender, beautiful creature must be, not mad—that was too harsh a word—but like Ophelia, distraught. 'Do you come out alone?' he said, gently. 'Is there no one with you in these winter nights? it is dreary and cold in the park, I don't think you ought to be alone.'

She smiled upon him, again not saying anything for a moment. Then she said suddenly and very low, 'I am always about here.'

'You mean you are fond of this walk,' Edmund said.

Again she smiled. 'I go all about,' she said, very softly, 'sometimes into the house; but no one sees me. That is what made me so glad when you spoke. I have seen you often, but you are confused with the other ones. So many, so many I have seen. Now that you have spoken to me I will always remember which is you.'

Certainly she must be distraught, he was very sorry for her, very much touched by her, but also, though why he could not tell, a little alarmed, his heart beating very unsteadily and plunging in his breast.

'I hope,' he said, 'not out of any intrusive or impertinent feeling, but for safety, I hope you will let me see you home.'

Again he heard the little roll of the laugh, so utterly soft and distant; but she made no reply. 'I have seen a great many, a great many,' she said; 'they all come and go, but they do not see me. That is the punishment I have. The house is altere, but I take a great interest in it: I was always fond of it.' Then the innocent little laugh was succeeded by a gentle, scarcely audible sigh.

All this time the evening had been darkening, the sun had set, the mists were creeping up once more in all the hollows. Edmund felt a chill run through him. 'It is getting late,' he said, 'and cold. If you are going to the village it is a long walk. Forgive me, but I think you should let me take you home.'

She looked at him almost mocking, but with such a tender version of mockery; then turned and went towards the door in the wall. Her movements were so gentle and light that Edmund felt himself noisy, stumbling, awkward in every step he took. Her little feet seemed scarcely to touch the earth. He walked on beside her confused, trembling, afraid, yet full of a strange happiness; and the moon, which had been rising all the time, came shining upon them through the lofty, slender lime branches. It seemed to him, in his bewildered condition, that it was like some poem he had read, or some dream he had dreamt, to walk thus in this measured soft cadence, with the moon upon their heads all broken and chequered by the anatomy of the great trees, like dark lines traced upon the sky. Then they came into the full moonlight, in the corner where the urn stood upon its pedestal. It seemed to Edward that she went more slowly, as if lingering. 'This is a gloomy corner,' he said, forcing himself to speak. For the charm of the silence had come over him, and words seemed hard things to disturb those soft moments as they flowed away.

'Not gloomy to me. I was always fond of it. When it was put up we were all pleased. That was what was wrong in me. You know,' she said, with her little soft laugh, 'I was so fond of the house and the trees, and everything that was our own. I thought there was nothing better, nothing so good. I was all for the earth, and nothing more. That is why I am here so much.' She paused, and gave a little sigh: but then added, brightening, 'It is not hard: when you are used to it, when now and then you meet with someone who sees you, it is not so hard. I am a little sad some-times, but very happy now.'

And again she looked at him with that look of tender pleas-ure—enough to turn any man's head. Edmund's went round and round—he could say nothing more, but stammer, repeating himself, 'It is a long walk; you must let me see you safely home across the park.'

She answered him only by that low laugh, but even softer, sweeter, than before. Then he opened the door for her. As she passed through she smiled upon him with a little wave of her hand. For his part he had put his foot on a soft piece of turf sod-den with the rain, and it took him a minute to extricate the heel of his boot which had sunk into it. A minute, scarcely so much as a minute, but when he stepped out eagerly after her, his head full of that walk across the park, she was nowhere to be seen. One minute, not so much. Where was she? How had she managed to elude him? He was wild with disappointment and anger. Once more he made a hurried search behind all the bushes, in every little clump of brushwood.

There was not a trace of her; though he thought once he

heard her low melodious laugh. Was it a trick she was playing him? What was the meaning of it? But when he had walked about for nearly an hour, Edmund had to go back to the house disappointed. Once more she had escaped him; his head was giddy, his heart beating loud, his whole being full of agitation and excitement. What did it mean? and who was she, this mysterious girl?

Edmund felt like a man in a dream as he came downstairs, and sat among the party at table, where the meal went on amid cheerful conversation. For himself he seemed quite incapable of taking any share in it. It flowed round him like something in which he had no voice. Afterwards the ladies asked him in the drawing-room, their voices coming to him faintly as out of a cloud, whether he had seen the white lady again. But it was impossible to him to speak of her tonight. He answered briefly, saying no, though it was not true; and pretended to have letters to write, that universal excuse for pre-occupation. But when he escaped from the circle on this pretence, he did not write any letters.

He sat in his room, opening his window, though the night was not so balmy as to make this desirable; and with his head supported by his hands, gazed out upon the great darkness round. The moon set early, and the skies were veiled with clouds, and nothing was discernible but the dark outlines of the trees, and a great dimness of space and air. Now and then he almost thought he saw her below, a flicker of white moving about, as if it might have been her dress; and it was only by strenuous resolution that he kept himself from rushing wildly into the night, with a kind of mad hope of meeting her. Then he gathered together in his mind all that she had said, which was so sweet, so tender, and yet, God help him, so wild. 'When you meet with someone who sees you'—'I was nineteen—but it is long, long ago.' What could it mean? Was it, indeed, the sweet bells jangled out of tune, of some lovely nature? Edmund's eyes filled with tears. He said to himself that if it was so, he would take more care of her than anyone; he would be her tender protector, her keeper to preserve her from everything that could hurt her innocence. What a strange fatal charm was it that had fallen upon him thus unawares?

He could think of nothing else. Ophelia—but far more sweet in her madness—pure as a vision, with that dear look of happiness in her face. Could anything be more sweet than that she should be happy when he spoke to her, her face full of pleasure at the sound of his voice? Edmund's heart melted altogether at this thought. But those sweet fairy-tricks should not suffice her another day. He would find her, whatever might happen; he would secure her beyond all possibility of escape. Her reason, what did it matter about her reason. Love would supply the place. And thus he spent the evening in a kind of soft delirium, able to think of nothing, to see and hear nothing, but his new-born yet all-absorbing love.

CHAPTER 4

Edmund did not sleep all night. He rose excited and restless, in the dim cold dawn of the winter morning; he was silent as a ghost at the cheerful breakfast table; he excused himself from all the occupations of the day. He had 'things to do,' he said; and in fact he was impatient and unhappy until he found an opportunity to steal out unseen by anyone. He went hastily through the Lime-tree Walk, following exactly the course he had taken the previous evening with her. There he contemplated the park in the clear daylight with wondering and anxious scrutiny. The little road down by the back of the green terrace, which led to the keeper's cottage, was the only one by which she could possibly have gone. A little plantation of young trees was at the corner, and as it wound downwards, though the declivity was slight, there were various scattered bushes, furze and broom, and a few old knotted hawthorn thickets, darned out and in with pendants of brambles, showing here and there a red leaf still. There any mischievous girl could have played hide-and-seek with a petulant lover for hours together.

Edmund felt a little lightening of the anxiety which possessed him as he saw these interruptions of the way. But if it was indeed by this way she had gone, she could not have afterwards emerged into the park without passing at least by Ferney's cottage. Perhaps, as someone had suggested, she was a lodger there after all. He went slowly towards it, examining every corner of the way, and every bit of cover. His search was so slow and minute that it took him a long time. He emerged upon Ferney's little enclosure almost before he was aware.

When his step was heard on the gravel, someone came to the window to see who it was, and Edmund heard a little exclamation.

'Aunt! here's that gentleman again.' Was he, then, coming to some real elucidation of all his wonderings? Mrs. Ferney came to the half-open door in answer to his summons. He thought she looked a little disturbed. He spoke peremptorily, to leave her no room for thought, or settling beforehand what she was to say. 'I want to know if you have a lodger—a lady living in your house?'

Mrs. Ferney's countenance grew more disturbed than ever.

'Well, sir——, no, Mr. Edmund, I've got no lodger. There's Ferney's niece staying on a visit.'

'Is that your niece sitting in the room on the right hand?' When Edmund said this, a chair was hastily drawn back out of his range of vision, and a voice said, '*La!*'

'I mean a totally different person,' he cried, with a little impatience; 'a lady; very young; very slight; with blue eyes; in a white dress, and something black round her shoulders.'

Mrs. Ferney was gazing at him with wide open eyes, but a visible air of relief. 'No, indeed, sir; nothing of the sort. Not a soul lives here but Ferney and me, and, for the present, Ada Jane.

'Where, then, can she live?' he said half to himself. Mrs. Ferney thought he had taken leave of his senses. She stood and gazed at him with bewildered looks, making a curtsey, and much relieved to see that he was not 'after' Ada Jane. Edmund walked away without so much as a glance at the window where Ada

Jane was lurking expectant. He went to the village, where he walked about not knowing what to do, looking in at every window. He could not stop everybody he met there to ask them did they know where he could find a lady with blue eyes and in a white gown? He did the only other thing that was practicable in the circumstances.

He went to see the rector, whom he asked that question, and to whom he told his little story. The rector was a young man, and he was sympathetic. He thought of all the ladies within twenty miles, and described them, without finding anyone who at all resembled the lady whom Edmund sought. 'Besides,' the young enquirer had still so much reason left in him as to say, 'what would it advantage me if Miss Ingestre, who lives fifteen miles off, were like her? Miss Ingestre would not come here and wander about the Lime-tree Walk.' So that nothing was to be made of it in any direction. When he left the rectory the short afternoon was beginning to wane. He saw nobody along all the length of the way, and when he came to the door in the wall found it locked; evidently she had not passed that way today.

It was again a misty afternoon; the sun veiled in clouds. Edmund went down by the path that led towards Ferney's, and got across the brook and round by the corner of the house, which was a way practicable to one who had been a boy there, and knew all about the surroundings and by-ways of the place. What he meant was to hurry round to the conservatories, in which he was likely to find the head gardener, and get the key from him. What if she should come to her favourite walk and find it closed against her? He was breathless with haste scrambling up the bank, rushing along at his most rapid pace, lest this foolish obstacle should prevent their meeting: when suddenly, in the midst of his excitement, all at once his heart stood still.

In spite of the locked door, she was standing there. It was earlier than he had ever seen her before. His heart stopped short,, then leapt into wilder beating than ever. He did not ask himself how she got through. Why should he think of any such trivial obstacle? She was there, that was all he thought of; and this time it was evident that she was looking for him. She waved her hand to him with the prettiest gesture. She was standing against the pedestal, her white dress standing out from that background. He noticed for the first time how white and pure was the fullness of the flounce where it fell upon the grass, without a mark on it of the wetness around. This seemed to him quite natural, an exquisite quality, somehow, in herself, which kept everything about her white and pure.

'I was going,' he said, flushed and eager, 'to get the key. I thought you would wonder to find it shut. But you came through before it was shut, I suppose.'

She smiled. It seemed to be a rule with her to answer none of his questions. She looked at him with a sort of innocent admiration, mixed with the pleasure in her face. 'It is so long since I have spoken to anyone—since I have seen anyone run to meet me,' she said. 'I wonder how it is that you, out of them all—'

'Yes,' he said, taking up her words, 'that is what I cannot understand, how I, of all the people in Daintrey, should have been so happy as to meet you. We are like old friends now, are we not? we have seen each other so often. I am Edmund Coventry, once Sir Robert's ward, and free of the house. Might I ask your name?'

There was no embarrassment in her face. From first to last she was never embarrassed, but always full of sweet composure: and her smile seemed to express a hundred different feelings. There was amusement in it, and a little regret, and always that affectionate pleasure. 'I was Maud,' she said, quite simply. Edmund could not understand why she should put her name in the past tense, and it gave him a subtle, little thrill of pain, he could scarcely tell why.

'Maud—it is the very sweetest name,' he said, with a half-adoring passion; 'but what else? You will not let me say Maud. Tell me your other name.'

What a strange smile it was! It seemed to go on like an accompaniment in music, confusing the listener who was so anxious to gather every word that came from her lips. He did not seem to know that she had not said anything, so full was the air of that sweet influence. A little while after he began again to speak himself.

'These meetings have made a change in my life,' he said. 'I was taking the future quite easily, not thinking what it was to bring forth; but now I see that one ought to select one's path, to settle, to take up the more serious part of life. All this I have learned since I have known you; since I have loved you,' he added, very low, looking earnestly in her face.

She took the confession quite calmly; not a tinge of additional colour, not the slightest shyness or confusion appeared in her. She kept her quiet, sweet, ease of manner undisturbed. And what was Edmund to say more? He felt somehow baffled, helpless, before this invulnerable calm.

'Won't you say anything to me?' he cried; 'I don't know who you are, or where you are living, but I love you, Maud. Do not be angry.'

'Oh, no! Not angry,' she said, in her soft voice; 'only you cannot understand. I am not here to make friends, though I have always wished that someone might see me and speak. And before you spoke I had noticed you; I thought to myself, This one surely—this one surely! There was something about you; but there had been so many, so many before,' she said, with an innocent, wistful look, like the unconscious protest against neglect, yet acquiescence of a child.

'But you will give me an answer, Maud? I love you, sweet. I do not know,' said Edmund, with passion, 'what has happened to you; what it is that makes you wander like this; but I will not mind, whatever it is. I will take care of you; I will watch over you; it will make no difference to me. Do you not understand me, dear?' He put out his hand to take hers, to secure her attention, to show her how serious he was. And then Edmund felt as if the whole misty heaven and earth were going round about him. He could not find the hand he sought. It was as if some spell prevented him from touching her. He felt again more baffled, more confounded, and hopelessly kept back, than words could say.

'You must not ask me questions,' she made answer, softly, after a pause. 'It is not permitted to answer questions. I am here—for a time. I have been here no one could tell how long. We do not count as you do. If I told you more than this you would not understand.'

'I will understand if it is about you. But, Maud, Maud, answer me first. Give me your hand. Won't you give me your hand?'

A look of trouble came into her face; yet so soft, so shadowy, that it did not seem pain. The smile did not go out of her eyes. She shook her head gently, standing so near him, her hands crossed, clasping each other. He had only to put out his arms and take her into them, but he could not. She was close, close to him, and yet—what was it that stood between? Not the mild refusal with which she shook her head; something that chilled his blood in its ardour, and made his heart contract with awe. He put out his hands beseeching, but seemed to come no nearer; and yet she did not draw back, nor move away from him. Edmund did not seem to himself to know what he was saying, what was happening, and yet he heard and meant every word that rushed to his lips. 'Sweet! I will understand anything; I know there must be something strange. Whatever it is I accept it, I accept it! Say you will love me, Maud! Say you will—marry me!'

What happened? One of the Beresford boys, as Edmund dimly perceived, had been approaching, rushing along towards the door; but somehow the intruder had made no difference to him, and had not stopped him in his impassioned suit. At this moment, however, the boy rushed headlong past, dashing against her, touching Edmund's coat as he plunged along. The lovely, gentle figure was straight in his way. Edmund caught him by the throat with a fury beyond words.

'The lady!' he stammered out; 'you brute, do you not see the lady?' and flung him wildly to a distance upon the wet ground.

Fred Beresford was altogether taken by surprise. He was not a boy of a patient temper, and he was in a hurry; but the wildness of the other bewildered him. He picked himself up, and came forward wondering, to where Edmund stood, pale as death, and gazing wildly about him. Fred's wrath was entirely quailed at this sight. 'What is it?' he asked, quite timidly and softly laying his hand on Edmund's arm.

The young man was trembling in every limb; he did not seem able to move. His eyes were staring wildly here and there. There was no softening dusk as yet to conceal anything; all was white daylight, cold and pale and clear. When he felt Fred's touch he turned upon him for one second, furious, violently thrusting him away.

'You have killed her!' he said; and then clutching the boy again, 'Where is she? where is she? where is she?' Edmund cried. Fred felt the whole trembling weight of his companion upon him. His boyish strength swayed under the burden.

'Are you ill, old fellow?' he said, alarmed. 'What is the matter? I thought you were saying poetry. I don't know what you mean about a lady.'

'You have killed her,' he said, wildly clutching the boy's throat; then, all in a moment, he softened, and burst into a transport of cries. 'Where is she? where is she? Maud! Maud! come back to me,' cried the young man, with a voice of despair. There was nothing to be seen, Fred swore afterwards, nothing, except the big stone pedestal with the urn upon it, and behind, the mossy old wall.

'I say—you are ill,' said the boy. 'Come in, that's the best thing to do; come in to mother. Maud's there with her, if it's Maud you want. Edmund, come along.'

Edmund broke from him, pushing him away. He went all round the pedestal, wandering about it, feeling it with his hands. Then he held out those hands piteously, appealing, into the empty air. 'Maud! Maud!' he cried. 'Don't laugh at me; don't play with me,' as if he were talking to somebody, the astonished boy described. Fred at last ran in alarmed to the library where Sir Robert was sitting. 'I wish you'd come out, father, into the Lime-tree Walk to Edmund—he's gone mad,' the boy cried.

When Sir Robert went out, Edmund was standing leaning

against one of the lime trees, gazing at the green space which contained the pedestal and the urn. When he was entreated to come in, he answered quite gently, that if he only waited patiently she would be sure to come back. 'This is where she always comes. She is fond of this place,' he said. 'There are things I don't understand about her, but she will come. I am sure she will come if you will only let me wait.'

'Tell me, my good fellow, all about it,' Sir Robert said. He was a kind man when his attention was fully roused, and now he remembered that his wife had told him something of a strange lady whom Edmund had seen in the park. Edmund told him the whole story, standing there with his back against the tree. He asked Sir Robert first to stand close to him, almost behind him, that nothing might interfere with his clear vision round. And then he told him all. ft She always tricks me,' he said, with an attempt at a laugh. 'She is so innocent ——like a child. How she got away this time I cannot tell. There seems nothing to hide behind here. But she always does it. I confess, sir,' he added, with great candour and gravity, 'there are many things about her I do not understand; but whatever they are, I am ready to accept them all.'

'Have you ever seen her more than once in the same day?' asked Sir Robert.

'No?'

'Then come with me, Edmund, it is of no use waiting. I think I can tell you something about her.' Sir Robert put his arm into that of the young man. He scarcely knew himself what he meant; but it was clear that something must be done. And Edmund yielded to the mingled reason and temptation. No, he had never seen her twice the same day; and to know about her, was not that what he wanted most in the world? He suffered himself, after one long glance around, to be led away.

Sir Robert took him upstairs to an old gallery which he remembered very well as a child, which had been given up to the children's romps on wet days, a place full of pictures, the accumulations of an old house—all kinds of grim portraits of early Beresfords. There were some good pictures among them, he had always remembered to have heard said, and so long as Edmund could recollect there had been an intention expressed of disinterring these treasures. 'I don't know where it is exactly; I don't know if it is still here. It was by a pupil of Sir Joshua's, and with something of his feeling. I have always intended to bring it downstairs,' Sir Robert said, rummaging as he spoke among old dusty canvasses. Edmund stood by listless, in the lull of reaction after his great excitement. It was not here, he thought, that anything would be told him about *her*. He did not understand what his companion meant. He was only waiting, feeling hazily that he had some further trial of patience to go through, not very anxious now for anything but the end of the day, and that another might dawn, on which, perhaps, he might see her again.

'Was she like this,' said Sir Robert, at last. Edmund went after him slowly, languidly, to the square of light in front of the great window whither he was dragging a picture in an old-fashioned black frame. Then the young man gave a great cry.

There she stood looking out of the old canvas with the smile he knew so well—her blue eyes looking upwards, the soft curves about her mouth, her hands clasped before her, and every detail exactly as he had seen her an hour ago; the white dress with its flounce, the black scarf with all its little frills. Then he fell down on his knees before the beautiful little figure, with a cry which was half alarm and half joy.

Sir Robert drew his breath quick; in fact, he had not been prepared for such success to his experiment. He was confounded by the explanation he had himself suggested. 'Do you mean that this is—the person,' he said, in a husky voice, and glanced round him with a certain shrinking. His ruddy countenance paled. 'I should prefer,' he said, with a little difficulty, 'to tell you the story in my own room. But turn first to the back of the picture and look at the date. Now come along. I don't like this vacant old place.

Edward looked at the date; it did not convey any particular idea to his mind.

'Seven, seven, seven,' he said to himself; seven is one of the numbers of perfection. It must be that the painter had meant. Otherwise it made no impression upon him. He went down to the library, having first placed the picture carefully in the light where he could come and worship it again. Sir Robert sat down in his usual chair, looking pale. 'Sit down, Edmund,' he said, 'my poor boy. I am afraid you are not in your usual health. You must see the doctor; you must try change of scene.'

'What has that to do with it?' said Edmund, astonished. 'You were to tell me who she is—that is of far more importance to me than my health, which is excellent, all the same. Who is she? You gave me your promise—'

'Is——?' said Sir Robert. 'Edmund, my dear fellow, you must have heard the story, though you don't remember it. It must have excited your imagination. Did you notice the date on the picture? I told you to look at it.'

'The date! What has that to do with it? Seven, seven, I forget what it was.'

'Seventeen hundred and seventy-seven,' said Sir Robert, solemnly. 'Seventeen hundred and seventy-seven—nearly a hundred years ago.'

There was no intelligence in Edmund's eyes. 'I knew there must be something strange about her,' he said; 'it would be vain to conceal that from one's self. There are many things I don't understand—but I am willing to accept—anything, Sir Robert—'

'Edward!' cried Sir Robert, almost wildly, 'command yourself. You don't seem to see. My dear fellow, this is all a delusion. You have seen no lady. It has been your imagination working. How in the name of all that is reasonable could you see a woman who has been dead for a hundred years?'

The young man looked up startled. Confusion seemed to envelop everything round him. 'A hundred years,' he said to himself, wondering; then laughed, and repeated, 'I saw no lady? I am going to marry her, Sir Robert.'

'God bless us all! ' said Sir Robert, with a voice of terror. 'Edmund, my dear fellow—Edmund, see a doctor, see a clergyman.

I'll send for old Parkins and for the rector. You can't, you can't go on like this, you know.'

Edmund's brain was still too much confused to take in any impression from what was said. 'A hundred years,' he repeated to himself, with a smile. 'It is strange; but I always felt there was something strange. I told you there were many things I did not understand. But what may be the meaning—this hundred years? Is this all you have to tell me, sir?' he continued, trying to wake up from the confused sense of mystery, yet almost of pleasure, which the picture brought him. He did not understand it—but then in the whole matter there was so little that he could understand.

'All,' Sir Robert said. He was in great excitement and distress. 'I don't want the ladies to know if we can help it. Don't say anything to them, I entreat of you. And, my dear boy, if you would go and lie down, I will send for Parkins to come directly. I'll have the rector up in half an hour. It will yield to remedies—it will yield to remedies,' Sir Robert said.

'I am quite well,' said Edmund. To him it seemed that Sir Robert was going out of his senses. ' But I will not keep you longer, and I will say nothing to the ladies. In the meantime,' he added, in his confusion, I have got—some letters to write.'

'The very best thing you can do; occupy yourself—occupy yourself, my dear fellow,' said Sir Robert, patting him on the shoulder. Edmund felt that his guardian was glad to be rid of him. Perhaps it was not wonderful that Sir Robert did not understand him; he did not understand himself. His head was confused as if the fog had got into it. To some things he seemed to attach no importance at all, while others were quite clear to him, and had all their natural weight. 'Seventeen, seven, seven.' He repeated this over to himself with a smile, but whether it was a charm, or a fact, or what it was, he could not tell; on the other hand, he thought the precaution about the ladies was quite right. And he could not appear without betraying that something had happened to him. He sent word downstairs by his servant that he had caught a cold and was going to keep his room; and there he received the visit of old Dr. Parkins with much conscious amusement, but would not say a word to him of what had befallen him, and utterly confounded the old doctor, who could say nothing but that his pulse was excited, and that it would be necessary for him to keep quiet for a day or two.

Then the rector came, much abashed, as a man called upon to minister to a mind diseased, and knowing nothing about it, was likely to be. When they were gone Edmund spent the night alone. He wrote a long letter to—he did not know whom—giving an account of the whole, so little as there was of it, and so much. 'I know there is something strange,' he wrote, 'but nothing to prevent me taking the charge of her, taking care of her. An hour a day of her will be more to me than twenty-four of any other. I know there are things which I can't understand.' When he had done this it was late, and all the family had gone to bed. He heard them going one by one—a sound of steps in the long passages, mounting the stairs, a little gleam of the passing lights under his door. By and by silence fell upon everything.

There was no sound or stir anywhere—all silent, all dark, the doors shut fast, soft waves of quiet breathing going through the house. He came out with his light in his hand and stood for a moment on the threshold of his door—an adventurer bound upon a last voyage, a sailor setting out into unknown seas. Then he went up, up to the upper part of the house, past all the closed doors, moving quietly through lines of unseen sleepers on every side. The great house was as silent as the grave.

The moon was shining full from the west, just about to set, as she had risen, early. There was a large west window in the gallery, and this was full of silvery light pouring in, making all white and dazzling. The portrait, which had been drawn towards this window to get the evening light, stood there still, receiving the white illumination of the moonlight. Edmund walked up—holding in his hand a candle, which flamed yellow and earthly in that radiance from heaven—through the whiteness, a sort of milky way, with the annals of the past on every side of him. He came to the picture of his love, and threw himself down beside it on the floor. There she stood before him, shadowed in the moonlight—the same, and yet not the same. Something disappointing, narrower, smaller, was in the pictured countenance.

As he gazed at it the confusion grew in his mind; all that was real seemed to die away from him. In the vehemence of this sense of loss, he began to speak to her, tears filling his eyes, and her face shining more and more like life through that tremulous medium. 'Maud! Maud! I do not understand you; I do not know you; but I love you,' he said in a rapture, not knowing that he said it. Then he came to himself with a gasp. There, close to the frame of the picture, her shoulder touching it, stood the original. He held up his candle, like a yellow flaming torch. For the moment, in the silent moonlight, with all the world asleep around, alone with these two—were they two?—his reason went from him. He raised himself to his knees, and knelt like a devotee before a shrine—his arms widely opened, his face raised, wild with worship: were they two, standing side by side, comparing themselves each to each, or were they one?

'You have come to me at last—you have come to me—Maud!'

She looked at him as before with her soft smile. There was no reply in her to his passion. 'I did wrong to speak to you,' she said; 'you do not understand. I was so pleased that you saw me. No one sees me. I come and go, sometimes out, sometimes in. I go to their rooms and they do not see me. Then when I find one that will speak—that will smile, I am glad.' There came from her, mingled together, the soft laugh and the sigh, that made his heart stand still. 'But no more—but no more,' she said.

And there seemed to creep about him a chill. He had never felt it before. When he had seen her first all had been soft as her looks, delightful as the bloom on her face. The bloom was still on her face, but shaded as by a mist. Nor could he see as he did before. The moonlight confused the soft features—or perhaps it was his yellow flaming human candle, not everlasting like the other light, ready to burn out and extinguish itself. His strength and his senses seemed to fail.

'I do not understand,' he cried; 'I do not understand! but whatever it is, I accept—I accept. Dead or living, Maud, Maud, come with me—let us be together! Come!' he said, stretching his arms wildly.

She did not draw back nor move, but neither did he touch her with his longing arms. Did fear seize them halfway extended? He could not tell. They dropped down by his side, and his heart dropped, sinking within him. She stood before him unmoved—always the same calm, the half smile on her lips, her blue eyes pleased and tender. Then she shook her head slowly, gently.

'It is not permitted. I told you I had loved the earth and all that was on it: and now I am earthbound. I could not go if I would, and I would not if I could. What we have to do, that is what we love best. But I never thought that you would mistake so much—that you would not understand. Now I know why there are so few that see us. It is to keep them from harm,' she said with a soft sigh. 'Ah me! when the only thing we long for, it is sometimes to speak—but I will never wish for it more—'

'Maud!' He threw himself at her feet again with a great cry. 'Touch me—mark me, that I may be yours always. If not in life, yet in death. Say we shall meet when I die.'

Once more she shook her head. 'How can I tell? I do not know you in the soul. You will do what is appointed; but do not be sorry, you will like to do it,[1]' she said, with her sweet look of tender pleasure. 'Goodbye, brother—goodbye'

'I will not let you go!' he cried: 'I will not let you go!' and seized her in his arms.

Then in Edmund's head was a roaring of echoes, a clanging of noises, a blast as of great trumpets and music; and he knew no more.

'Edmund is not in his room; his bed has not been slept in,' said Lady Beresford, coming hastily upstairs next morning immediately after she had gone down. Sir Robert had not yet left his dressing-room. She was pale and full of alarm. 'His door was

---

1. Prima *vuol ben; ma non lascia il t lento Che divina giustizia contra voglia, Come fu al peccar, pone al tormento. Purgatorio, Cant.* xxi.

open; there is no trace of him. I have sent out over all the park. He most have left the house last night. And Fred tells me the strangest story. What is it, Robert?' Sir Robert was very much disturbed himself, but he would make no certain reply.

'I daresay he will be found wandering about somewhere. He has got some nonsense in his head.' Then he hurried down to the Lime-tree Walk, and out to the park, looking under the bushes and trees. If he had found Edmund there lying white and stark, Sir Robert would not have been surprised. They searched for him all the morning, but found no trace anywhere. Later in the day, Sir Robert suddenly bethought himself of another possibility. He hurried up to the old gallery, calling his eldest son to go with him. And there, indeed, they found Edmund—lying on the floor. But not dead, nor raving; pale enough, pale as a ghost, but asleep; his candle long ago burnt out to the socket, and the soft little face he had loved, placidly watching over him from the picture, as un-moved, though not so sweet, as the vision he had seen.

It cannot be said that Edmund Coventry was well enough to leave Daintrey that day, nor for several days. But he went away as soon as it was possible, going off from the great door, and by the drive, not approaching the Lime-tree Walk. He had no brain-fever, nor any other kind of fever. Various changes were percep-tible, the Beresfords thought, in his life; but other people were unconscious of them. He had always been a gentle soul, friendly, and charitable, and true. More than a year after, when he met his former guardian and family in town, the old intercourse was re-newed, and that came to pass which Lady Beresford had always thought would be so very suitable. He married Maud, and made her a very good husband. But he would never go to Daintrey again. And though there have been a great many versions of the story scattered abroad, and the Beresfords, once so silent on the subject, have become in their hearts a little proud of it—though it is supposed against their will that it should be known—no one else, so far as we have ever heard, has been again accosted by the gentle little lady who was earthbound. Perhaps her time of willing punishment is over, and she is earthbound no more.

LEONAUR

ALSO FROM LEONAUR
AVAILABLE IN SOFTCOVER OR HARDCOVER WITH DUST JACKET

MR MUKERJI'S GHOSTS *by S. Mukerji*—Supernatural tales from the British Raj period by India's Ghost story collector.

KIPLINGS GHOSTS *by Rudyard Kipling*—Twelve stories of Ghosts, Hauntings, Curses, Werewolves & Magic.

THE COLLECTED SUPERNATURAL AND WEIRD FICTION OF WASHINGTON IRVING: VOLUME 1 *by Washington Irving*—Including one novel 'A History of New York', and nine short stories of the Strange and Unusual.

THE COLLECTED SUPERNATURAL AND WEIRD FICTION OF WASHINGTON IRVING: VOLUME 2 *by Washington Irving*—Including three novelettes 'The Legend of the Sleepy Hollow', 'Dolph Heyliger', 'The Adventure of the Black Fisherman' and thirty-two short stories of the Strange and Unusual.

THE COLLECTED SUPERNATURAL AND WEIRD FICTION OF JOHN KENDRICK BANGS: VOLUME 1 *by John Kendrick Bangs*—Including one novel 'Toppleton's Client or A Spirit in Exile', and ten short stories of the Strange and Unusual.

THE COLLECTED SUPERNATURAL AND WEIRD FICTION OF JOHN KENDRICK BANGS: VOLUME 2 *by John Kendrick Bangs*—Including four novellas 'A House-Boat on the Styx', 'The Pursuit of the House-Boat', 'The Enchanted Typewriter' and 'Mr. Munchausen' of the Strange and Unusual.

THE COLLECTED SUPERNATURAL AND WEIRD FICTION OF JOHN KENDRICK BANGS: VOLUME 3 *by John Kendrick Bangs*—Including twor novellas 'Olympian Nights', 'Roger Camerden: A Strange Story', and ten short stories of the Strange and Unusual.

THE COLLECTED SUPERNATURAL AND WEIRD FICTION OF MARY SHELLEY: VOLUME 1 *by Mary Shelley*—Including one novel 'Frankenstein or the Modern Prometheus', and fourteen short stories of the Strange and Unusual.

THE COLLECTED SUPERNATURAL AND WEIRD FICTION OF MARY SHELLEY: VOLUME 2 *by Mary Shelley*—Including one novel 'The Last Man', and three short stories of the Strange and Unusual.

THE COLLECTED SUPERNATURAL AND WEIRD FICTION OF AMELIA B. EDWARDS *by Amelia B. Edwards*—Contains two novelettes 'Monsieur Maurice', and 'The Discovery of the Treasure Isles', one ballad 'A Legend of Boisguilbert' and seventeen short stories to cill the blood.